ALL

ALSO BY DAVID SZALAY

London and the South-East
The Innocent
Spring

DAVID SZALAY

All That Man Is

JONATHAN CAPE
LONDON

1 3 5 7 9 10 8 6 4 2

Jonathan Cape, an imprint of Vintage Publishing,
20 Vauxhall Bridge Road,
London SW1V 2SA

Jonathan Cape is part of the Penguin Random House group of
companies whose addresses can be found at
global.penguinrandomhouse.com

Copyright © David Szalay 2016

David Szalay has asserted his right to be identified
as the author of this Work in accordance with the Copyright,
Designs and Patents Act 1988

First published by Jonathan Cape in 2016

www.vintage-books.co.uk

A CIP catalogue record for this book is
available from the British Library

ISBN 9780224099776

Thomson Digital Pvt Ltd, Noida, Delhi

To every thing there is a season,
and a time to every purpose under the heaven.

1

Seventeen, I fell in love . . .

1

Berlin-Hauptbahnhof.

It is where the trains from Poland get in and the two young Englishmen are newly arrived from Kraków. They look terrible, these two teenagers, exhausted by the ordeal of the train, and thin and filthy from ten days of Inter Railing. One of them, Simon, stares listlessly at nothing. He is a handsome boy, high-cheekboned, with a solemn, inexpressive, nervous face. The station pub is noisy and smoky at seven in the morning, and he is listening, with disapproval, to the men at the next table – one of them American, it seems, the other German and older, who says, smiling, 'You only lost four hundred thousand soldiers. We lost six *million*.'

The American says something which is lost in the din.

'The Russians lost *twelve* million – we *killed* six million.'

Simon lights a Polish cigarette, sees the word '*Spiegelei*' on a laminated menu, the money on the table, waiting for the waiter to take it – euros, nice-looking, modern-looking money. He likes the fonts the designers have used, plain, unornamented.

'A million died just in Leningrad. A *million!*'

People are drinking beer.

Outside, drizzle is starting to dampen the grey environs of the station.

There was an altercation with the waiter – whether it would be possible to have two cups with a single *Kaffeekännchen*. It was not possible.

They had to share one, Simon and his friend, who is now at the pay-phone – their mobiles don't work here – half-hidden under its smoked plastic hood, trying to speak to Otto.

The waiter, in his stained scarlet waistcoat, had been insolent with them, Simon thought. Obsequious to others, though – Simon's wary eyes follow him as he moves around, moves through the smoke and noise – to men in suits with newspapers, like that one, looking up with a sudden tight smile, looking at his watch as the waiter unloads the tray.

A voice starts to spew information about trains. A hard-edged voice penetrating from somewhere outside where the wind invades the spaces of the station. The voice is like a tap of sound – turned on, turned off.

Simon is familiar now with the facile snatch of tune that precedes each irruption of this voice

of this voice, and its echo.

And the facile snatch of tune, when it sounds, has started to seem like an extension of his exhaustion, like something inside him, something subjective.

The waiter literally bows to the suited man.

The life of the station plunges and swirls like a dirty stream. People. People moving through the station like a dirty stream.

And that question again –

What am I doing here?

He sees his friend Ferdinand hang up the payphone.

They have been trying to speak to Otto for days – he is someone Ferdinand met in London a few weeks ago, a young German who said, probably drunk, probably without expecting it ever to happen, that if he was ever in Berlin he was welcome to stay.

Ferdinand returns to the table with a worried expression.

'Still no answer,' he says.

Simon, smoking, says nothing. He secretly hopes that Otto will never answer. He has never been keen on the idea of staying with him. He did not meet him in London, and what he has heard about him he does not like.

He says, 'What are we going to do then?'

'I don't know,' his friend says. 'Just go to the flat?' He has Otto's address – Otto *is* expecting them at some point this April, that much was arranged from London, sketchily, with messages on Facebook.

They travel two stops on the S-Bahn, and spend a long time looking for the flat, and when eventually they find it – unexpectedly, it is in a dirty little side street – there is no one there except a green-uniformed policeman. He waits on a landing where the stairs turn, one flight down from the door of the flat, in the murky light of a window.

Unsure why the policeman is there

Has Otto been murdered?

they hesitate.

'*Tag*,' the man says. From his voice it is obvious: no one has been murdered.

They say they are looking for Otto, and the policeman, who evidently knows who Otto is, tells them he is not there. No one is there, he says.

They wait.

They wait for over an hour, Ferdinand making a few trips to a payphone in the street to try people who might know where Otto is, while Simon sits on the tiled floor in the huge space of the downstairs hall, and tries to make progress with *The Ambassadors*, a dog-eared Penguin Classics edition that lives in one of the zip-up side pockets of his backpack. His tired eyes find these words –

5

Live all you can; it's a mistake not to. It doesn't so much matter what you do in particular so long as you have your life. If you haven't had that what have you had? I'm too old—too old at any rate for what I see. What one loses one loses; make no mistake about that. Still, we have the illusion of freedom; therefore don't, like me to-day, be without the memory of that illusion. I was either, at the right time, too stupid or too intelligent to have it, and now I'm a case of reaction against the mistake. Do what you like so long as you don't make it. For it was a mistake. Live, live!

He takes a pen from the same pocket of his pack where the novel was and with it makes a vertical line next to those words. Next to the vertical line, in the margin, he writes, *MAIN THEME*.

Ferdinand returns, damp with playful rain, from the street.

'What should we do?' he asks.

The S-Bahn again.

The rain has stopped. From the windows of the train they see things. A memorial stretch of the Wall, thick with psychedelic graffiti. They don't remember that world. They are too young. Sunlight out there on the empty land, shining through the spaces where the Wall used to be. Sunlight. Through the windows of the S-Bahn train, through their lace of impurities, it touches Simon's shrinking eyes.

What am I doing here?

What am I doing here?

The train whacks over points.

What am I

The train slows

       doing here?

into a station, open to the air – Warschauer Straße. Windy platforms, a waste land all around.

A waste land.

April is the . . .

They are in love with Eliot, with his melodious pessimism. They are in awe of Joyce. He is what they want to be, a monument like him. These are the writers whose works made them friends. And Shakespeare's tragedies. And *L'Étranger*. And the plight of Vladimir and Estragon, which they like to think of as their own. Waiting for Otto.

Warschauer Straße. Trains move among the lusty weeds. Spring showers strafe the peeling hoardings, the overpasses spilling the sound of unseen traffic.

In Kreuzberg they sit down exhaustedly to lunch.

Kreuzberg is a disappointment. It was supposed to be the hipster district, the *Alternativ* quarter. Ferdinand, in particular, is disappointed. Simon puts food into his shapely mouth. He had not expected anything from Kreuzberg. He had no interest in it, and finds his friend naïve – though he does not say so – for thinking it would be interesting.

There is some discussion, as they eat, of how much more expensive everything is than in Poland (they did Warsaw, Kraków, Auschwitz) though the higher prices are justified, is their feeling, by the superior quality of everything in Berlin. The food, for instance. They eat hungrily.

Somehow they start talking about people at school. They are in their final year, are taking their A levels this summer, hoping to start at Oxford in the autumn. (Which is why Simon is ploughing joylessly through the works of Henry James, on the lookout for material pertaining to the 'International Theme'.)

So they talk about various people – what twats they are, mostly – and then Ferdinand mentions Karen Fielding.

He has no idea, throwing the name out like some mundane object, that his friend frequently dreams about Karen Fielding – dreams in which they might speak, or exchange looks, or in which their hands might momentarily touch, and from which he wakes, still seeming to feel the touch of her hand, to a single moment of overwhelming joy. He transcribes these dreams to his diary, very earnestly, along with pages and pages on what they might mean, and on the nature of the dreaming process itself.

In the waking world, he and Karen Fielding have hardly spoken to each other, and she is unaware of how he feels – unless she has noticed the way his eyes follow her as she moves with her tray around the dining hall, or tramps back from lacrosse in her muddy kit. Practically the only thing he knows about her is that her family live in Didcot – he overheard her telling someone else – and from that moment the word 'Didcot' started to live in his mind with a special, mysterious promise. Like her name, it seems almost too potent to put down in writing, but in a youth hostel in Warsaw, one evening, while Ferdinand was showering, he wrote, and it made his heart quicken: *It seems pointless to travel Europe when the only where I want to be is humble, suburban, English*

His pen hovered.

Then he did it, he wrote the word.

Didcot.

Her name, more potent still, he has never summoned the nerve to form.

Now, when Ferdinand says it Simon just nods and pours more sugar into his coffee.

He longs to talk about her.

He would like nothing more than to spend the whole afternoon talking about her, or just hearing her name spoken aloud again and again, those four syllables that seem to hold within them everything worth living for in the whole world. Instead, he starts to talk, not for the first time, about the impossibility of achieving any sort of satisfaction as a tourist.

8

Ferdinand lowers his eyes and, stirring his coffee, listens while his friend holds forth ill-temperedly on this subject.

What was the tourist trying to do? See things? See more of life? Life is everywhere – you don't need to traipse around Europe looking for it . . .

the only where I want to be

Withdrawing from even the pretence of listening, Ferdinand starts to write a postcard. The picture: Kraków Cathedral, black and jagged. The postcard is to a girl in England with whom he is involved in a vague flirtation, who he quite likes sometimes – who he thinks, anyway, he ought to keep in play. He smiles and feels the bristle of his strong chin as he writes, *We're both growing beards* – it sounds pleasingly manly. When he has finished, he reads out what he has written for his friend's approval. Then he stands up to look for the loo.

He is away for some time and sitting in the sun-filled restaurant Simon watches the smoke climb from the tip of his cigarette.

It is the tiredness, maybe, that makes him feel like crying.

What am I doing here?

The feeling of loneliness is immense as a storm front. His friend, after ten days of travel, he finds irritating most of the time. He struggled to muster a smile when he read out that postcard, and showed him the little sketch he had done in green ink of a bearded man. And the way he had sprayed himself with his Joop! before putting his pack in the locker at the station. The way he had ostentatiously lifted his T-shirt to spray the Joop!, to show the world the whorl of hair on his chest . . . At that moment . . . And this is supposed to be his *friend* he is with. As immense as a storm front is the feeling of loneliness that overcomes him.

As he watches the smoke climb from the tip of his cigarette.

In the sun-filled restaurant.

*

9

In the evening, they present themselves at the flat again and find Otto's sister there with two male friends in leathers, one small with a faceful of piercings – Lutz – the other much taller with a walrus moustache – Willi. Otto's sister has no idea who Simon and Ferdinand are, but when they explain she suggests they make themselves at home and wait for Otto – he is sure to turn up eventually. She and her friends, she says, are just leaving.

Left alone, Simon and Ferdinand do make themselves at home. The flat is surprisingly large and they wander through it taking minor liberties, helping themselves to some expensive-looking whisky, and opening drawers. In one drawer Simon finds an odd pack of cards. They must be tarot cards, he thinks. Idly, he turns one over – a picture of a hand holding some sort of stick. *As der Stäbe*, it says. Ace of Staves? A phallic symbol, obviously. Not exactly subtle. Whatever. Nonsense. He shuts the drawer.

*

It is about two o'clock in the morning when Otto storms in and finds them in their sleeping bags on the living-room floor.

He switches on the light and screams.

Then he notices Ferdinand, who has just lifted his head and is squinting up at him, and shouts, 'Fuck, man, you *made* it!'

'Otto . . .'

'Fuck!'

'I hope you don't mind . . .' Ferdinand starts.

'What the fuck are you talking about?' Otto screams at him.

'I hope you don't mind that we're here . . .'

'Do you think I mind?' Otto shouts.

'I don't know . . .'

'I was waiting for you.' Someone else is standing there, at Otto's shoulder, peering over it.

'Listen, we tried to phone you . . .'

'Yah?'

'You weren't here.'

'I wasn't here!' Otto explains, still shouting.

'And you weren't answering your mobile . . .'

'I lost it!'

'Oh.'

'Yeah, I lost it,' Otto says, suddenly in a quiet, dismal voice. 'I lost it.'

Having sat down on one of the sofas, he starts to make a spliff, disappointing Simon who had hoped he would immediately turn off the light and leave.

Otto is wearing a silly hat and his jacket sleeves stop well short of his wrists. His Adam's apple goes up and down as he works on the spliff. It turns out that he and his friend have jobs all week serving drinks at an event somewhere outside Berlin. While he makes the spliff, Ferdinand thanks him again and again for letting them stay.

'Listen, again, thank you *so* much,' Ferdinand says, sitting up in his sleeping bag.

'Hey, fuck, forget about it,' Otto says, with lordly indifference, from the sofa, still wearing his hat.

'What, er, what about the policeman?' Ferdinand asks.

Otto doesn't seem to hear the question. 'What?'

'The policeman. You know.' Ferdinand indicates the spliff that is taking shape in Otto's lap.

Otto is dismissive. 'Oh, fuck that man!' Then he adds, 'He doesn't care.'

'What's he doing there anyway?'

'My father,' Otto says. 'It's bullshit.'

'Your father?'

'Yeah, it sucks.' Putting the finishing touches to the spliff, applying saliva with the tip of his little finger, Otto says, 'He's in the government. You know . . .'

'In the government?' Simon says suspiciously, speaking for the first time.

Otto ignores him and sparks the spliff.

Simon has taken an immediate dislike to Otto. He wishes Ferdinand would stop thanking him. For his part, he says almost nothing and when, after the first spliff has been smoked, Otto encourages him to make another, he takes the materials without a word. Otto keeps telling him to use more 'shit'. He and Ferdinand are talking hysterically about people they know in London. Later, Otto says Simon should make another spliff, and again keeps pressing him to use more shit. They are all quite stoned. Someone has turned on the TV and found something possibly pornographic – some naked women in a wheatfield, it seems to be. Simon ignores it. The others are laughing at it. Otto's friend, Simon suddenly notices, has left. Simon has no memory of him leaving. He has an unpleasant feeling that he imagined him, that no one else was ever there. The others are laughing at the women in the wheatfield, Otto staring eagerly at the screen, his eyes shining, his tongue half-out, transfixed.

Simon himself feels very shaky. Without saying anything he stands up and wanders off to find the bathroom. There, forgetting where he is, he spends a long time staring at some shampoo bottles and a wind-up plastic frog on the tiled edge of the bath. He just stands there for a long time, staring at them. He is staring at the wind-up plastic frog, its innocent green face. The hum of the extractor fan sounds more and more like sobbing.

When he sits down on the living-room floor again, about twenty minutes later, Otto asks him, 'How much shit is left?'

12

'None,' Simon says. The living room – all beige and cream and Oriental art – seems unfamiliar, as if he is seeing it for the first time.

'You *finished* the shit?'

Ferdinand, in spite of himself, starts giggling, and then keeps saying, 'I'm sorry, I'm sorry . . .'

'You finished the shit?' Otto says again, still in the same tone of disbelief.

Ferdinand giggles and says he is sorry.

'Yes,' Simon says. He has also hot-rocked the pale, lustrous carpet but he decides not to mention that now.

'Fuck,' Otto says. And then, as if it might have been a joke, 'Really, you finished it?'

'Really.'

'I'm so sorry,' Ferdinand says, suddenly with an extremely serious expression on his face.

Otto sighs. 'Okay,' he says. He has not quite come to terms with it though. 'Fuck,' he says a few seconds later, 'you finished the shit . . .'

Slowly, Simon inserts himself into his sleeping bag and turns away from them. They are still talking when he falls asleep.

*

The next day he and Ferdinand visit Potsdam. It is the one thing Simon seems to want to do while they are in Berlin – see the Palace of Sanssouci.

From Potsdam station, an ornate green-painted gate. Then an avenue of small trees, and the palace on the summit of a terraced hill. At the foot of the hill a fountain flings high into the air, and white stone statues dot the park – men molesting women, or fighting each other, or frowning nobly at something far away, each frozen in some posture of obscure frenzy, frozen among quiet hedges, or next to the still surfaces of ornamental pools.

Simon wanders through this landscape – the long straight tree-lined walks, the fountains where they intersect, the facades where they end – with a kind of exhilaration.

There is a place to have tea and they sit on metal outdoor furniture and he talks about how the whole landscape, like the music of J. S. Bach, is expressive of the natural order of the human mind.

Ferdinand, eating cake, complains about the acne on his back, that it stains his shirt.

Simon has a similar problem but does not mention it. (He is fastidious, also, about concealing his body from his friend.) Instead, he puts down *The Ambassadors*, and tells Ferdinand about Frederick William, Frederick the Great's father, and his obsession with his guardsmen – how they all had to be extremely tall, and how he fussed over the details of their uniforms, and how he liked to watch them march when he was feeling unwell. The story makes Ferdinand laugh. 'That's brilliant,' he says, using his finger to take the last smear of cream from his plate. Complacently, Simon finishes his tea and picks up his book again. It is late afternoon – they had trouble finding the place. The shadows of the statues stretch out over the smooth lawns.

'What should we do this evening?' Ferdinand says.

Simon, without looking up from his book, gives a minimal shrug.

Otto's sister, who was in the flat when they woke up, had suggested they join her, and her friends Lutz and Willi, for a night on the town. Ferdinand now alludes to this possibility. Simon, once again, is studiedly non-committal. The prospect of spending the evening with Otto's sister and her friends fills him with something not unlike fear, a sort of fluttering panic. 'They're twats, aren't they?' he says, still in his book. He and Ferdinand have spent much of the day laughing at Lutz and Willi – their leathers, their piercings, Lutz's shrill laugh, Willi's morose moustache.

'They seem okay,' Ferdinand says wistfully. For ten days, he has had only Simon for company. 'And Otto's sister's nice.'

'Is she?'

'Isn't she?'

'She's okay,' Simon pronounces, turning a page, 'I suppose.'

'Anyway, what else are we going to do?' Ferdinand asks, with a sort of laugh.

'Don't know.'

'I mean, let's just have a drink with them anyway,' Ferdinand says. 'They can't be that bad.'

'What time is it?'

'Time we were getting back.'

'Really?' Simon says, turning his head to look at the shadow-filled park. 'I like it here.'

In the end, they do spend part of the evening with Otto's sister and Lutz and Willi. Simon seems determined not to enjoy himself. He just sits there with a solemn expression on his face while the others talk until Ferdinand is almost embarrassed by his presence – a detached unhappy figure, sipping home-made wine. They are in a hippyish place in Kreuzberg, sitting outside, under some trees whose blossoms have a spermy smell.

'What's the matter with your friend?' Lutz asks Ferdinand, leaning over to whisper it with a jingle of piercings. 'Is he okay?' Lutz is sandy-haired and ugly.

'I don't know,' Ferdinand says, loud enough for Simon to overhear him, though he pretends not to. 'He's always like that.'

'Then he must be fun to travel with.'

Ferdinand just laughs.

Lutz says, 'He's just shy, no?'

'Maybe.'

'I'm sure he's okay.'

'Of course,' Ferdinand says. 'He's very intelligent.'

'I'm sure.'

'And very funny sometimes.'

'Yah?'

'Really.'

'I can't imagine it,' Lutz says.

His friend Willi, however, is almost as taciturn as Simon, and smiles as little, and for the most part the evening is a matter of Ferdinand, Lutz, and Otto's sister. They talk, inevitably, about the places Ferdinand and Simon have already been to, and what they have done there – the tourist sites they have visited, mostly ecclesiastical. This outrages Lutz. 'You can do all that shit when you're older!' he protests. 'You don't need to do that *now*! What do you want to do in *churches*? That's for when your hairs are grey. How old are you boys?' he asks.

They tell him – seventeen.

'You're so young still,' Lutz says feelingly, though he is at most ten years older. 'Have fun, okay? Okay?'

2

Have fun.

An overnight train to Prague. There is not a single empty seat, and they spend the night lying on the floor outside the toilet, where they are frequently kicked by passing feet.

Some time after dawn they stand up and look for something to eat.

Outside, the undulating landscape skims past in lovely morning light.

Pine forests wrapped in smoky mist.

Simon is still thinking of a dream he had during one particular snatch of sleep on the floor. Something to do with something under a lake, something that was his. Then he was talking to someone from school, talking about Karen Fielding. The person he was talking to had used a strange word, a word that might not even exist. And then he had passed Karen Fielding herself in a narrow doorway, and lowered his eyes, and when he looked up she had smiled at him and he had woken saturated, for a moment, with indescribable joy.

'You look totally fucking miserable, mate,' Ferdinand says, sitting opposite him at a table in the dining car.

'Do I?'

'I mean – are you okay? You don't look well.'

Ferdinand is, he thinks, making an obvious effort to patch things up. There was a falling-out the previous day, over the travel plans.

Simon had wanted to take an early train to Prague. Ferdinand had not wanted to do this. He had wanted to take Otto up on his offer of showing them a fun time in Berlin.

Simon had, as usual, silently insisted on having his own way – and then it turned out he wanted to stop in Leipzig to visit the tomb of J. S. Bach.

He had more or less tricked him into the Leipzig stopover, Ferdinand felt, and it had been an awful experience. Ten hours in the station and the diesel-stained streets that surrounded it – the next train to Prague did not leave until the middle of the night – all for the sake of a few minutes in the frigid Thomaskirche, which Simon himself had described as 'intrinsically unimpressive'.

Finally, at about midnight, no longer speaking, they sat down to wait on the station platform, where some young German Christians were singing songs like 'Let It Be' and 'Blowing in the Wind' as the rain fell past the tall lights and out on the dark tracks.

Simon seems not to have noticed the falling-out, let alone his friend's efforts, in the morning, to patch things up.

He is looking out of the window, the low sun on his handsome profile, his hands shaking slightly after the dreadful night.

'We get to Prague in about an hour,' Ferdinand says.

'Yeah?' From somewhere an image has entered Simon's head, an image of human life as bubbles rising through water. The bubbles rise in streams and clouds, touching and mingling and yet each remaining individually defined as they travel upwards from the depths towards the light, until at the surface they cease to exist as individual entities. In the water they existed physically, individually – in the air they are part of the air, part of an endless whole, inseparable from everything else. Yes, he thinks, squinting in the mist-softened sunlight, tears filling his eyes, that is how it is – life and death.

'Where do you think we should stay?' Ferdinand asks.

'I don't know.'

'Hostel?'

'Okay,' Simon says, still watching the landscape, the lifting mist.

It all happens very fast. Desperate-looking men wait on the platform when the train pulls in. Their upturned faces pass in the windows smoothly as the train sheds the last of its speed. The English teenagers are the subject of a tussle as they are still descending the steep steel steps, and a few minutes later are in a Skoda which is older than they are, whose engine sounds like a wasp and blows prodigious quantities of blueish exhaust. The fumes have a heady, sweetish smell. The flowering trees also. Their driver, other than his native language, speaks only a few words of German. '*Zimmer frei, zimmer frei,*' he had insisted at the station, physically seizing their packs and making a dash for his vehicle.

They drive for twenty minutes or so, mostly uphill (and thus very, very slowly), into a spring-greeny suburb of disintegrating tarmac and faded dwellings in small plots of land, until they pull up, finally, in front of a single-storey house with a tree in front of it, the path underneath littered and plastered with fallen blossoms. This is where their driver lives with his wife, and she speaks some English.

Birdsong meets them as they emerge from the Skoda, and she is there too, opening the squeaky front gate with enthusiasm, even a kind of impatience. She is probably about forty and looks as if she has just got out of bed. Her hair – a sort of aureate beige – is loose and unkempt, and she is wearing a yellow towelling dressing gown and blue plastic sandals. She comes forward over the blossom-thick pavement in her blue sandals, through the shattered shade that leaves flecks of light on her smooth-skinned face, smiling, and sticks a pair of kisses on each of the young visitor's faces. Then she hurries them inside and shows them to what will be their room – a single bed, a stained foam mattress on the floor, a leaf-filled window. She smiles at them as they take in the room tiredly. 'Is okay?' she says.

She tells them to leave their things there and join her for breakfast, so they follow her along a passage with a washing machine in it, past what seems to be a nasty bathroom, and into a kitchen.

Simon is still thinking of the dream he had on the train as he follows her into the kitchen with his friend. It seems more present to him than where he is, than the washing machine he has just walked past, than the sunny kitchen where he is being told to sit down.

the only where I want to be

She is doing something now, at this moment, *she* is doing something as he sits down at a small square table in the sunny kitchen. And the smile she showed him in his dream seems realer than the woman now taking things from the fridge and explaining to them why, in opting to stay with her, they have made the right decision.

The smile she showed him in his dream. It is possible he just inferred it. Her face was not actually smiling. Indeed, it had a serious expression. Pale, framed by her dark hair, it had a serious expression. Yet her doll-blue eyes were dense with tenderness and somehow he knew that she was smiling at him. Then he woke to the first daylight filling out the interior of the train, and the feverish sound of the train's wheels.

She says she isn't interested in money – that isn't why she takes people in. She just likes people, she says, and wants to help them. She will do everything she can to help them. 'I will help you,' she says to them. The house, she admits, is not exactly in the centre of town, but she promises them it isn't difficult to get there. She will show them how, and while they eat she does, spreading a map on the kitchen table and tracing with her finger the way to the Metro station, though most of the route seems to lie just at the point where the map folds and the paper is worn and illegible.

They are drinking *slivovice* from little cups the shape of acorns and the air is grey and stinging with cigarette smoke. She is also, as she leans over the tattered, expansive map of Prague with its districts in different colours, being somewhat negligent with her dressing gown, and it is not clear what – if anything – she is wearing underneath it, something that Ferdinand has noticed, and to which he has just tried to draw his friend's attention with a salacious smile and a movement of his head, when her husband steps in, takes the cigarette out of his small mouth and says something in Czech.

She tries to shoo him away, not even looking up from what she is doing – tracing something on the map, a sinuous street, with her chipped fingertip – and they have what seems to be a short, fierce dispute.

Ferdinand is still smiling salaciously.

She is still leaning over the map.

Her husband stands there for a moment, simmering with displeasure. Then he leaves, and she tells them he is off to work. He is a former professional footballer, she explains, now a PE teacher.

She sits down and lights another cigarette and lays a hand on Simon's knee. (She seems, in spite of his silence, to have taken a particular liking to Simon.) 'My hahs-band,' she says, 'he know *nahthing* but football.' There is a pause. Her hand is still on his knee. 'You understand me?'

'Yes,' he says.

Drinking spirits so early in the morning, and after such a terrible night, has made him very woozy. He is not quite sure what is happening, what she is talking about. Everything seems unusually vivid – the sun-flooded kitchen, the pictures of kittens on the wall, the blue eyes of the footballer's wife, her fine parchment-like skin. She is holding him with a disquieting stare. His eyes fall and he finds himself looking at her narrow, naked knees.

Her eyes again.

'He know *nah-thing* but football,' she says. He is looking at her mouth when she says that. 'You understand me.' It does not seem to be a question this time. It sounds more like an instruction.

'And you young boys,' she says, smiling happily, taking up the brandy bottle, 'you like sport?'

'I do,' Ferdinand tells her.

'Yes?'

'Simon doesn't.'

'That's not true,' Simon mutters irritably.

She doesn't seem to hear that. She says, turning to him, 'Oh, no? What do you like? What do you like? I think I know what you like!' And, putting her hand on his knee again, she starts to laugh.

'Simon likes books,' Ferdinand says.

'Oh, you like books! That's *nice*. I like books! Oh –' she puts her hand on her heart – 'I *love* books. My husband, he don't like books. He is not interested in art. You are interested in art, I think?'

'He's interested in art,' Ferdinand confirms.

'Oh, that's *nice*!' With her eyes on Simon, she sighs. 'Beauty,' she says. 'Beauty, beauty. I live for beauty. Look, I show you.'

Full of excitement, she takes him to a painting hanging in the hall. A flat, lifeless landscape in ugly lurid paint. She tells him she got it in Venice.

'It's nice,' he says.

They stand there for a minute in silence.

He is aware, as he stares at the small terrible picture, of her standing next to him, of her hand warm and heavy on his shoulder.

'Your friend,' she says to Ferdinand, lighting another cigarette, 'he understands.' They are in the kitchen again.

'He's very intelligent,' Ferdinand says.

'He understands beauty.'

'Definitely.'

'He *lives* for beauty. He is like me.' And then she says again, unscrewing the cap of the brandy bottle, 'My husband, he know nothing but football.'

'The beautiful game,' Ferdinand jokes.

She laughs, though it isn't clear whether she understood his joke. 'You like football?' she asks.

'I'm more of a rugby man actually,' Ferdinand says.

He then tries to explain what rugby is, while she smokes and listens, and occasionally asks questions that show she hasn't understood anything.

'So is like football?' she asks, waving away some smoke, after several minutes of detailed explanation.

'Uh. Sort of,' Ferdinand says. 'Yes.'

'And girls?' she asks. 'You like girls?'

The question embarrasses Ferdinand less than it does Simon, and he says, after a short pause, 'Of course we like girls.'

She laughs again. 'Of course!'

She is looking at Simon, who is staring at the table. She says, 'You will find lot of girls in Prague.'

Standing on the Charles bridge with its blackened statues, its pointing tourists, Simon pronounces the whole place to be a soulless Disneyland.

In St Vitus cathedral, wandering around in the quiet light and the faint smell of wood polish, he sees a poster for a performance of

Mozart's Mass in C Minor there later that afternoon which marginally perks him up, and when they have acquired tickets, they sit down on the terrace of a touristy pub opposite the cathedral's flank to wait.

Unusually for him, Ferdinand is smoking a cigarette, one of Simon's Philip Morrises. While his friend tells him how much he hates Prague, Ferdinand notices two young women sitting at a nearby table. They are not, perhaps, the lovelies their landlady had promised – they are okay, though. More than okay, one of them. He tries to hear what they are saying, to hear what language they are speaking. They are not locals, obviously.

'How can you be *happy* as a tourist?' Simon is saying. 'Always wandering around, always at a loose end, searching for things . . .'

'You're in a good mood.'

'I'm not in a *bad* mood – I'm just saying . . .'

The girls seem to be English. 'What about *them*?' Ferdinand says quietly.

'What *about* them?' Simon asks.

'Well?'

Simon makes a face, a sort of pained or impatient expression.

'Oh, come on!' Ferdinand says. 'They're not that bad. They're alright. They're nicer than the ones in Warsaw.'

'Well, that's not hard . . .'

'Well, I *am*, if you know what I mean.' Ferdinand laughs. 'I'm going to ask them to join us.'

Simon sighs impatiently and, his hands shaking slightly, lights another cigarette. He watches as Ferdinand, with enviable ease, slides over to the girls and speaks to them. He points to the table where Simon is sitting, and Simon quickly looks away, looks up at the reassuring blackened Gothic bulk of St Vitus. He is still looking at it, or pretending to, when Ferdinand's voice says, 'This is my friend Simon.'

He turns into the sun, squints. They are standing there, holding their drinks. One of them is wearing a sun hat. Ferdinand gestures for them to sit down, which they do, uncertainly. 'So,' Ferdinand says, taking a seat himself, with a loud scraping noise and a sort of exaggerated friendliness, 'how do you like Prague? How long have you been here? We only arrived this morning – we haven't seen much yet, have we, Simon?'

Simon shakes his head. 'No, not really.'

'We had a look in there,' Ferdinand says. 'Simon likes cathedrals.' The girls give him a quick glance, as if expecting him to confirm or deny this, but he says nothing. 'Have you been in there?' Ferdinand asks, directing his question particularly to the one in the sun hat, who is much more attractive than her friend.

'Yeah, yesterday,' she says.

'Quite impressive, isn't it.'

She laughs. 'It's okay,' she says, as if she thinks Ferdinand might have been joking.

'I mean, they're all the same, I suppose,' he says. 'We've been to pretty much every one in this part of Europe, so I can say that with some authority.'

'Yeah?'

'You know what I mean.'

'So where else have you been then?' she asks.

And so they start talking – where have you been, what have you seen.

Simon is irritated by Ferdinand's manner. He thinks of it as a sort of mask that his friend puts on for encounters with strangers, as if there were somehow an intrinsic hypocrisy to it, and thinks of his own silence as a protest against this hypocrisy. And also against the tediousness of it all – when Sun Hat's plump friend asks him what kind of music he likes, he just shrugs and says he doesn't know.

Ferdinand is telling the story of the Japanese couple they saw – he in linen suit and panama hat, she in turquoise dress with sparkles – dancing in the main square of Kraków. Then he tells the story of how he and Simon were hauled off the train at the Polish–German border to be searched by moustached German officials. 'I think they were particularly suspicious of Simon,' he says, with a smile, successfully provoking mirth in the ladies, and Simon also smiles, palely, without pleasure, accepting the part that has, he feels, been forced on him.

'Full-on strip search,' Ferdinand says.

Sun Hat squeals with shocked laughter. 'What, seriously?'

'No,' Simon says, without looking at her. And then he announces, speaking very specifically to Ferdinand, as if they were alone, 'It's nearly five.'

'Is it?' Ferdinand asks, as if he doesn't understand why Simon is telling him that.

'Yes,' Simon says. There is a short silence. 'You know, the . . .'

'Yeah,' Ferdinand says. He seems to think for a moment, while the others wait. Then he turns to Sun Hat. 'Listen, there's this concert at five. It should be quite amazing. Why don't you come with us?'

She looks at her friend, who shrugs. 'Where is it?'

'It's here!' He points to the stone edifice that looms over them. 'In there. It's Mozart or something. Mozart, isn't it?'

'Yes,' Simon says, without enthusiasm.

'Simon's really into that shit,' Ferdinand explains.

The girls look at each other again – something unspoken passes between them.

Their excuse is they don't have much money.

Ferdinand says, 'Well, why don't we meet afterwards?' He is still smiling. 'It won't be that long, I don't think. How long will it be?' he asks Simon, as if he were his secretary.

'I don't know,' Simon says. 'Not more than an hour, I wouldn't have thought.'

'We could just meet here when it's over,' Ferdinand suggests. 'In an hour or so?'

They agree to this, and Ferdinand and Simon set off.

'She's really quite nice, the one in the hat, isn't she?' Ferdinand says.

'She's okay.'

'She's more than okay – she's hot. What about her friend?'

'What about her?'

Ferdinand laughs delightedly. 'Yeah, I know what you mean,' he says. He is humming happily to himself as they take their seats in a pew. 'So what is this again?' he asks.

'Mozart's Mass,' Simon says without looking at him, 'in C Minor.'

'Yeah, that's it.' And as if wanting to extract everything he can from the experience, Ferdinand folds his hands in his lap and shuts his eyes.

The music starts.

The music.

Later, when they return to the pub terrace, swamped by the cathedral's shadow now, they find that the girls have gone. Simon still seems to be hearing the music while his upset friend asks the waiter whether anyone has left a message for him, still seems to be hearing the voice of the unseen soprano, somewhere far up at the front, filling the high stone space. And while they wait on the terrace in case the girls come back, while his friend stands at the edge of the terrace peering into the tourist-filled dusk, Simon sits there smoking and hearing it still, that voice. Something holy about it.

Ferdinand, turning from the edge of the terrace, looks distraught.

Something holy about it.

'Fuck it,' Ferdinand says.

Summoned holiness into the high stone space, that luminous music.

'They're not coming back.'

That luminous music, the voice of the unseen soprano.

Filling the high stone space.

'No,' Simon says.

His friend sits down and takes, without asking, one of his Philip Morrises. He tries to seem okay. 'What shoul' we do?' he says.

They leave the terrace and look for somewhere to eat.

Lost, they wander through little streets.

Ferdinand stops at a stall selling magazines to ask for directions.

While his friend is trying to make himself understood, Simon notices that some of the magazines are pornographic – his eyes find enormous nipples, naked skin, open mouths. The entire stall in fact is devoted to porn. The stallholder, a tired-looking little man, speaks no English and, indicating that Ferdinand should wait there, disappears into a shop with an empty window display.

He emerges a few moments later with a middle-aged woman in a simple blue dress. Simon feels sorry for her, that she has to put up with a stall of filth in front of her shop. 'Yes?' she says, smiling shyly as she approaches them.

Ferdinand explains that they are lost and looking for somewhere to eat.

She tells him how to find their way back to the places they know, and says, apologetically, that she does not know of anywhere to eat nearby that would be open. 'I'm sorry,' she says.

'No, no, don't be silly,' Ferdinand tells her. 'Thank you so much for your help . . .'

'And you buy magazines?' she asks.

The question seems to be mainly for Simon, who is still standing near the stall, smoking a cigarette. He looks at her as if he does not understand it.

'Sex,' she says, indicating the stall.

She starts to smile and her face, when she does, suddenly seems hideous to him – like some evil little animal's, with tiny yellow teeth.

'No,' he says quickly.

'You have a look,' she says, still smiling, and, freeing one of the magazines from the string that holds it, she offers it to him in its plastic sleeve. 'Have a look.'

'We're not interested, thank you,' Ferdinand says.

'Why not?' she asks with a little laugh.

'We're just not,' Ferdinand says, following his friend who is already halfway down the street. 'Thank you.'

They eat at Pizza Hut, and then take the metro all the way out to its suburban terminus.

*

Spread out on the foam mattress on the floor of the room where they are staying, under an orange-and-khaki floral-pattern sheet, Simon struggles to focus on his diary. Ferdinand is showering. Simon is able to hear the hiss of the shower, and while it goes on he knows that his friend will not return. He is also able to hear the shouts from the kitchen as their landlady and her husband argue. He has time – it would not take long. It has been nearly a week since he last . . . That was in the noisy, swaying train toilet as it made its way from Warsaw to Kraków. His fingers have just taken hold of the thrilling solidity under the sheet when he hears the shower stop with a squeaky jolt of the pipework and, pulling up his shorts, he starts to write again, or seem to, is holding only his pen when Ferdinand enters wrapped in a small towel.

'They still at it?' Ferdinand says, of the shouting.

Something smashes, they hear, in the kitchen.

Simon, holding only his pen, says nothing.

'Not a happy bunny,' Ferdinand says. Standing near a small mirror, he is trying to look over his own shoulder at his seething, scarified back. 'It's worse,' he says. 'Have a look. It's worse, isn't it?'

Simon looks up momentarily from his diary and says, 'I don't know.'

'It's worse,' Ferdinand says.

He sighs and takes his place on the bed with his heavily annotated volume of Yeats. After only a few lines –

The young
In one another's arms

– he sighs again and stares for a minute or more at the whitish ceiling.

The young

In one another's arms

He puts the volume of Yeats on the shiny yellow parquet. He pulls the thin quilt over him, and turns to the wall.

Having written nothing, Simon sets aside his diary and switches off the light, a table lamp on the floor next to the mattress on which he is lying.

3

'My husband,' she says the next morning, taking things from the fridge and putting them on the table where they are sitting, 'is in Brno. Football. He will be in Brno three days.'

'Some sort of tournament?' Ferdinand asks.

'What?'

'Is he in Brno for a tournament?' She doesn't seem to understand. 'A match?'

'Match, yes. Important match. Football.'

There is no *slivovice*. There is coffee and cigarettes. Stale bread if anyone wants it. She is cheerfully hungover. She asks Simon, sitting down next to him in her knee-length yellow dressing gown, 'You find some girls?'

He looks embarrassed, unsure what to say. 'Uh . . .'

'No?' she asks, in a tone of surprise. 'It should be easy for you, I think.'

'Well, we did meet some,' Ferdinand says.

'You *like* girls?'

Though the question was addressed to Simon, it is Ferdinand who answers. 'Yes,' he says, 'very much so.'

She is still looking at Simon, smiling. 'And you?'

He takes a worried pull on his cigarette. 'Yes,' he says.

She studies him, his long frowning profile, as he in turn seems to study the table, as if trying to memorise all the objects that are on it –

a carton of milk – *mléko* – of very simple design

his Philip Morrises, the health warning in German

her Petras, in a paper packet with a red sash

a Cricket lighter

'You are very handsome boy,' she says.

a glass ashtray, full

a plastic bowl with a few slices of stale bread in it

'When I was young,' she says, 'I would like very much to meet hand-some boy like you.'

a small plate with a piece of whitish butter on it

When I was young . . .

She tells them about her own youth.

And it turns out she is not Czech at all. She is Serbian. She and her husband met in Yugoslavia, as it then was – he was there playing football. She was a tall member of the local sports club that was looking after the arrangements for his team. Fair-haired, blue-eyed, talkative, lively, she would shepherd the team to and from meals, travel on the bus with them to matches.

Her husband was one of the stars of his team, she proudly explains. They first made love in a park, at night. Well, she still lived with her parents. He slept in a dormitory with his teammates. Where else could they go?

'We were young,' she says. 'When you are young . . . Yes.' She lights a cigarette. Sighs. Then says more briskly, 'I was young, but it was not first time for me.'

'No?' Ferdinand seems interested.

She starts to tell them about how she lost her virginity with a swimming coach, in a hostel in Italy, when she was fifteen.

'He was older than me,' she says. 'That was nice, you know.'

34

Simon sits with hunched shoulders, not seeming to hear, smoking.

'It is nice, first time, with someone older,' she says to him.

And Ferdinand tells her how he, at the same age, was seduced by his sister's nanny, who was ten years older than he was, and how nice that was.

'Yes,' she says, with a serious look in her deep-set eyes, 'is *nice*.'

'It *was* nice,' Ferdinand says, looking pleased with himself.

'Is always the best way,' she says, 'with someone who is older, more experienced. Someone who is nice.'

Simon sits with hunched shoulders, not seeming to hear, smoking.

'You understand me?'

The question is for him. She wants to know whether he has understood her.

They are waiting for him to say something, to indicate that he has understood, that he has heard what has been said.

And then the telephone rings, somewhere else, in some other room. The telephone rings and she stands up and hurries out through the eddying smoke in her knee-length yellow dressing gown, and they hear her answer it and start talking to somebody.

They spend the morning looking for Sun Hat. Looking for Sun Hat in the sun. Ferdinand puts some thought into where she is likely to be, into which tourist spots to loiter at, primed to seem surprised if she should make a sudden appearance. It soon seems hopeless. The city is huge, sprawling – even the tourist parts are all jumbled up into cobbled alleys and little hidden squares. He tries to think the way she would think, tries to put himself in the position of a young woman, his own age or a year or two older, not particularly intelligent, frequently lusted after, with turquoise-painted toenails, about to start secretarial school . . . An Australian pub? They spend two hours there, sinking lagers, hardly speaking.

Simon, too, seems preoccupied.

Sitting there in the Australian pub, he pictures to himself human interactions as the pouring together of liquids. Violent explosions, he thinks, pleased with the way he is elaborating his initial idea, or instant freezing were the worst forms of reaction. A simple failure to mix perhaps the most normal. And love?

Karen Fielding

Well, love, he thinks, would be something like this – a flicker in the middle of the liquids, which mingle so that they seem to be only one transparent liquid

Karen Fielding

the flicker steadying to a point, which strengthens slowly until the whole mixture emits a soft, steady light.

Karen Fielding

Yes, he thinks, that is love.

And the day slips away.

Soon it is late afternoon.

Ferdinand stands on the Charles bridge, in the hard wind, looking at the wide sweep of the banks, the roofs and spires stacking up away from the water. Sun Hat, somewhere, somewhere . . . Unless she has left the city already. And then how foolishly he has wasted the day, he thinks, while Simon waits for him, facing away from the view.

Simon takes up the subject of tourism's pointlessness again in the next pub, a subterranean variation, vaulted, with lots of Gothic script.

'Why did you want to do this then?' Ferdinand asks, irritably, after a few minutes.

'Do what?'

'This trip.'

'I thought it would be good,' Simon says.

'You don't think it's good?'

'It's okay.'

'What were you hoping for?'

Simon thinks for a moment. 'I don't know,' he says.

Still, he was hoping for something. He set out on the train from St Pancras station two weeks ago with some sort of obscure hope.

Prostitutes everywhere in the shadows of the avenue as they walk to the metro station, through the early night.

There is something almost nice about being in her kitchen again, under the neon light. It feels almost like home. She laughs through waves of smoke as Ferdinand tells her about the search for Sun Hat, tells the whole story starting with the meeting yesterday under the walls of St Vitus.

'So you find a girl?' she says, smiling at him.

'And lost her again.'

'And she was Czech?'

'No, English.'

'English! You should find Czech girl – she will not run away from you.'

'Wouldn't she?'

'No. She think you are rich.'

'I'm not rich.'

'She think you are. And she was beautiful, this English girl?'

'Well . . . She wasn't bad.'

37

'You will find beautiful Czech girl. And you.' She turns to Simon, her expression somehow more serious. 'You find girl?'

Simon looks down. 'No,' he says, and immediately lifts his cigarette to his lips. He looks up again, to find her eyes still on him.

She is looking at him intently, and with a sort of sadness. 'And you are such handsome boy,' she says.

Simon shrugs.

There is a silence.

Her eyes are still on him; he feels them even though he is looking at his own knees.

And then Ferdinand stands up and says he is off to bed.

'Ah, you are tired,' she says with approval. 'Okay. You sleep.'

When Simon also stands, which he does a second later, with a sort of panicky swiftness, she takes hold of his wrist.

She frees it immediately when, with an involuntary movement, he tugs it away.

'I'm tired too,' he says.

'You leave me alone?' she laughs. 'You leave a lady alone?'

'I'm tired.'

'But you are young – you should be wake all night.'

'Stay and finish your beer,' Ferdinand says unhelpfully.

'Yes,' she says, 'stay.'

'I don't want it. Really, I'm tired.'

Simon has started to edge round the table to where the door is when she takes his hand. She does it in a way that is tender, not forceful. Tenderly she takes his hand. 'Stay and talk to me,' she says, looking up at him from her seat.

'Tomorrow.' He extricates his hand from the warm hold of her fingers. 'Okay? We'll talk tomorrow.'

'Today is today,' she says enigmatically, as if it were a proverb. Her hand is on his leg, on the denim somewhere near his hip.

'I'm tired,' he pleads.

Ferdinand is already leaving.

'Stay with me,' she says quietly, her face serious now, her hand moving round to the front of his thigh.

'Please,' he says, seeming nearly tearful. 'I'm sorry. I'm tired.'

And then he just leaves, and follows his friend into the dark, past the washing machine.

*

'She wants you, mate,' Ferdinand says. They are sitting at a wrought-iron table in a park where peacocks occasionally shriek and he is talking, of course, about their landlady.

Simon smokes worriedly.

'Do it,' Ferdinand says. 'Fuck her.'

The idea that he might actually do this has never even occurred to Simon and instead of answering he just frowns at his friend.

'Why not?' Ferdinand asks.

Simon's frown intensifies. He says dismissively, 'She must be forty.'

'So what?' Ferdinand says. He turns for a moment to inspect the terrace where they are sitting. 'She definitely knows a thing or two,' he says. 'And you know, she's really not too bad. Very nice legs. Have you noticed?'

Simon says nothing.

'She's quite *sexy*,' Ferdinand says. 'I mean, when she was young, she was probably quite hot.'

'Maybe, when she was *young*,' Simon mutters.

'What did she say she was?'

Simon waits for a few moments, then says, 'She said she was almost a champion swimmer . . .'

'Except she was the wrong shape, that's it. That was quite funny.' Ferdinand smiles. 'Well, those swimmers are all totally flat-chested. Why don't you fuck her?' he asks.

'You wouldn't.'

'She doesn't *want* me,' Ferdinand points out. 'It's you she wants.'

'She was drunk.'

'She's always drunk.'

'What do you want to do this afternoon?' Simon starts to ask.

'I think you should fuck her,' Ferdinand says.

'Seriously . . .'

'I am being serious . . .'

'No, I mean what should we do this afternoon?'

'Don't you find her attractive? At all?'

'No,' Simon says. 'Not really.'

'Not really?'

'No.'

'I think she's okay,' Ferdinand says. 'Seriously, I think you should do her.'

Simon lights another cigarette. He has been smoking heavily, even more heavily than usual, all morning.

'You know,' Ferdinand says, 'you can tell from a woman's eyebrows exactly what her pubes are like.'

Simon laughs – a single embarrassed exhalation. He is about to ask, again, what they should do that afternoon, when his friend says, 'Don't you want to get laid?'

Simon shrugs and puts the cigarette to his lips. He stares at the paint-thick wrought iron of the tabletop.

'It's not a big deal,' Ferdinand says. 'I just think you should do her. You might enjoy it, that's all.'

They sit in silence for a minute, Simon still staring at the metal lattice of the table, Ferdinand turning his head to look around at the other people there. Then he says, 'So, what are we going to do this afternoon?'

Simon, having found his voice again, suggests something about Kafka, an exhibition.

'Yeah, okay,' Ferdinand says.

In the end, though, despite hours of searching, they do not succeed in finding it, the Kafka exhibition, and spend another afternoon rattling around the tram- and tourist-filled centre of an old European capital.

'Do you really not want her?' Ferdinand says later.

They are sitting opposite each other on the benches of a beer hall, in a clatter of voices, each with a litre jug of Prague lager, half-drunk.

'She's not an unattractive woman,' Ferdinand says. 'I wonder what she looks like naked. I mean, don't you just want to see her naked?'

Simon does not seem to hear. He is looking away. A pinkness, however, suffuses his face.

Finally he turns to Ferdinand. 'I think we should leave tomorrow,' he says. 'I mean, leave Prague.'

'Really?' Ferdinand seems surprised.

'Do you want to stay?'

'Not particularly.'

'I don't,' Simon says.

'Okay.'

'So we'll leave tomorrow?'

'If you want.'

They stop at the station to look at timetables. Vienna, they have decided, will be their next destination – Simon, it seems, is interested in some *Kunst* they have there. There is a train at about ten in the morning.

Then they make their way out to the suburbs again.

They make their way to the smoky kitchen, where she is waiting for them in her yellow dressing gown.

Simon has been hoping all day that her husband will have returned from Brno – that by that simple development the whole situation will be defused.

Her husband has not returned from Brno.

She is waiting for them alone and they take their seats in the kitchen. Simon is hardly able to look at her. It was the same in the morning – he seemed frightened when he finally appeared, still moist from his interminable shower. She does not pay so much attention to him this evening, however. She talks more to Ferdinand, who seems keen to save his friend embarrassment and makes an effort to engage her, to draw her attention away from Simon, who does not speak at all until Ferdinand says, after only half an hour or so, 'Well, we're quite tired, I think – aren't we, mate?'

Then Simon says, 'Yes,' and immediately stands up.

'So we'll be off to bed, I suppose,' Ferdinand says, also standing.

She makes them have another *slivovice*, standing there, and then lets them leave.

*

Simon wakes the next morning to find Ferdinand not there. This is unusual. Usually it is Simon who wakes first. He listens, trying to hear voices from the kitchen, or the sound of the shower perhaps. There is nothing. Shadows from the tree outside the window move shiveringly on the wall. He pulls on his jeans, his T-shirt. He visits the fetid toilet – a flimsy door, ventilated at ankle level, in the windowless passage where the washing machine is.

Then he finds Ferdinand in the kitchen, sitting at the table, eating the sour yoghurt-like stuff she serves, which Simon does not like even with jam in it. Ferdinand is alone. 'Morning,' he says.

'Where is she?' Simon asks.

'She's around somewhere,' Ferdinand says between spoonfuls of yoghurt.

'You've seen her?'

Ferdinand just nods. Something strange about the way he does that.

'You're up early, aren't you?' Simon asks him.

'Not really.'

'How long have you been up?'

'Uh.' With the little spoon, not looking at his friend, Ferdinand scrapes the last out of the yoghurt pot. 'Half an hour?'

'Is there any coffee?'

'She made some. It's probably on the hob, isn't it?'

Simon, at the hob, pours himself some. As he turns to take his seat again he sees something on the floor. Though it seems familiar, he is not sure what it is. Only as he sits down again does it strike him – it is her yellow dressing gown. Her dressing gown, there on the kitchen floor.

'How'd you sleep?' Ferdinand asks.

'Okay.'

Ferdinand says, 'You still want to leave today?'

'Yes,' Simon says.

Her dressing gown, there on the kitchen floor.

And then the train to Vienna. Ferdinand falls asleep immediately, as it leaves Prague, is snoring in his seat as it flows ker-thunking over points, and suburbs pass in the windows. Simon, awake, stands in the corridor and watches the landmarks of the city dwindle.

There is a strange sense of loss, a sense of loss without an obvious object.

He takes his seat.

He looks at his friend, sleeping opposite him, and for the first time he feels a sort of envy. That he . . . With her . . . If Ferdinand was willing to . . . And saw her . . .

Her dressing gown, there on the kitchen floor.

The Ambassadors makes him sleepy.

He puts it down.

He looks out the window, and the suburbs evaporate in front of his eyes.

2

1

The office, showroom and warehouse occupy adjoining units of an industrial estate in the suburbs of Lille, within earshot of the E42 motorway. It is here that Bérnard has been spending his days this spring, working for his uncle Clovis, who sells windows. The office is as dull a space as it is possible to imagine – laminate floor, air-freshener smell, lightly soiled furniture.

Five fifteen on Wednesday afternoon.

From the large windows, listless spring light, and the sounds of the industrial estate. Bérnard is waiting for his uncle to lock up. He is already wearing his jacket, and sits there staring at the objects on the desk – next to a depressed-looking plant, the figurine of the little fairy maiden, winged and sitting under a drooping flower head with a melancholy smile on her heart-shaped face.

Clovis arrives and makes sure that all the drawers are locked.

'Cheer up,' he says unhelpfully.

Bérnard follows him down the spare, Clorox-smelling stairs.

Outside they take their places in the BMW, parked as always in the space nearest the door.

There is no way that Clovis would have taken Bérnard on if he wasn't his sister's son. Clovis thinks his nephew is a bit thick. Slow, like his father, the train driver. Easily pleased. Able to stare for hours at something like rain running down a window. It is typical of him,

Clovis thinks, that he should have *dropped out* of university. Clovis's own attitude to university is ambivalent. He suspects that it is mostly just a way for well-to-do kids to avoid working for a few more years. Still, they must learn *something* there. Some of them, after all, end up as surgeons, as lawyers. So to spend two whole years at university and then *drop out*, as Bérnard did, with nothing to show for it, seems like the worst of all worlds. A pathetic waste of time.

They leave the estate and feed onto the E42.

The kid smokes pot. That's not even a secret any more. He smokes it in his room at home – he still lives with his parents, in their narrow brick house in a quiet working-class residential district. He shows no sign of wanting to leave. His meals are made for him, his washing is done. And how old is he now? Twenty-one? Twenty-two? Unmanly, is the word.

He once tried to have a talk with him, Clovis did, for his sister's sake. (The boy's father was obviously not going to do it.) He sat him down in a bar with a beer and said, in so many words, 'You've got to grow up.'

And the boy just stared at him out of his vague blueish eyes, his blonde hair falling into them, and said, in so many words, 'What d'you mean?'

And, in so many words, Clovis said, 'You're a loser, mate.'

And the boy – if that was the word, his chin was thick with orange stubble – drank his beer and seemed to have nothing more to say for himself.

So Clovis left it at that.

And then Mathilde said to him, when he was trying to tell her, post their drink together, what he thought of her son, 'Well, if you want to help so much, Clovis, why don't you give him a job?'

So he had to make a place for him – first in the warehouse, and then, where there was less scope for him to do any damage (they sent the wrong windows to a site once, which Bérnard had loaded onto the truck), in the office. Though he is totally forbidden to answer the phone. And not allowed anywhere near anything to do with money. Which means there isn't much, in the office, for him to do. He tidies up. And for that, for a bit of ineffectual tidying, he is paid two hundred and fifty euros a week.

Clovis sighs, audibly, as they wait at a traffic light on their way into town. His fingers tap the steering wheel.

They stop at a petrol station to fill up, the Shell station which Clovis favours on Avenue de Dunkerque.

Bérnard, in the passenger seat, is staring out of the window.

Clovis pays for the petrol, V-Power Nitro+, and some summer windscreen-wiper fluid, which he sees they have on sale, and takes his seat in the BMW again.

He is just strapping himself in when his nephew says, speaking for the first time since they left the office, 'Is it okay if I go on holiday?'

The presumptuous directness of the question, the total lack of supplicatory preamble, are shocking.

'Holiday?' Clovis says, almost sarcastically.

'Yes.'

'You've only just started.'

To that, Bérnard says nothing, and Clovis has to focus, for a few moments, on leaving the petrol station. Then he says, again, 'You've only just started.'

'I get holidays though, don't I?' Bérnard says.

Clovis laughs.

'I worry about your attitude,' he says.

Bérnard meets that statement with silence.

Holding the steering wheel, Clovis absorbs waves of outrage.

The silly thing is, he would be more than happy to have his nephew out of the way for a week or two. Or – who knows? – for ever.

'You planning to go somewhere?' he asks.

'Cyprus,' Bérnard says.

'Ah, Cyprus. And how long,' Clovis asks, 'do you plan to spend in Cyprus?'

'A week.'

'I see.'

They travel about a kilometre. Then Clovis says, 'I'll think about it, okay?'

Bérnard says nothing.

Clovis half-turns to him and says again, 'Okay?'

Bérnard, for the first time, seems slightly embarrassed. 'Well. I've already paid for it. That's the thing. The holiday.'

A further, stronger wave of outrage, and Clovis says, 'Well, that was a bit silly.'

'So I need to go,' Bérnard explains.

'When is it, this holiday?' Clovis asks, no longer trying to hide his irritation – if anything, playing it up, enjoying it.

'It's next week.'

'Next week?' Said with a theatrical expression of surprise.

'Yeah.'

'Well, you need to give at least a month's notice.'

'Do I? You didn't tell me that.'

'It's in your contract.'

'Well . . . I didn't know.'

'You should read documents,' Clovis says, 'before you sign them.'

'I didn't think you'd try to take advantage of me . . .'

'Is *that* what I'm doing?'

'Look,' Bérnard says, 'I've already paid for it.'

Clovis says nothing.

'You're not really going to try and stop me?'

'I worry about your attitude, Bérnard.'

They have arrived in Bérnard's parents' street, the featureless street of narrow brick houses.

The BMW stops in front of one of them and first Bérnard, and then, more slowly, Clovis, emerges from it.

Unusually, Clovis comes into the house.

Bérnard's parents are both there. His father, in a vest, is drinking a beer. He has, within the last half-hour, returned from work. He is short, blonde, with a moustache – Asterix, basically. He is sitting at the table in the front room, the room into which the front door directly opens, with a single window onto the street, in the light of which he is studying *La Voix du Nord*. Bérnard's mother, further back in the same space, where the kitchen is, is doing the washing-up.

On Bérnard's entrance, neither of them looks up from what they are doing.

'*Salut*,' he says.

They both murmur something. His father has a swig from the brown bottle in his hand.

'André,' Clovis says to him.

At that, André looks up from the paper. Mathilde, too, looks across from the neon puddle of the kitchen. She smiles to see her brother.

André does not smile.

If happiness is having one euro more than your brother-in-law, then Clovis is happy a million times over.

And André – André is fucked.

Clovis steps forward into the room.

'To what do we owe the honour?' André says.

Mathilde asks her brother if he'd like something.

'No, thank you,' Clovis says.

Having left the harsh light of the kitchen, she kisses him on the face.

'I find myself in a difficult position,' Clovis says.

His sister indicates that he should sit. Again, he declines.

'I wanted to help,' he says. 'I tried to help. But Bérnard has made it clear that he does not want the sort of help that I am able to offer him.'

At the sound of his name, Bérnard, who has been peering into the fridge, looks at his uncle.

'I'm afraid so,' Clovis says sadly.

'What do you mean?' André asks.

Clovis looks at him and says, 'I'm sacking your son.'

He half-turns his head in the direction of the kitchen and says, 'Yes, that's right, Bérnard – you can go where you like now.'

Bérnard, still illuminated by the open fridge, just stares at his uncle.

Mathilde is already pleading with him.

He is shaking his head. 'No, no,' he is saying. 'No, I've made up my mind.'

'I knew this would happen,' André murmurs furiously.

'What?' Clovis asks him. 'What did you know?'

Through a friend at the Chambre de Commerce et d'Industrie, he had, a few years ago, found André a job as a Eurostar driver; the interview would have been a formality. André, saying something about the long hours, had turned the opportunity down, and still spends his days trundling back and forth between Lille and Dunkerque, Lille and Amiens. The stopping service. Local routes. Not even the Paris gig.

'What did you know?' Clovis asks him, looming over the table where André is sitting with his paper.

André says, clinging to his beer, 'You didn't really want to help, did you?'

'Oh, I did,' Clovis tells him. 'I did indeed. Your son is lazy.' He throws his voice towards the kitchen. 'Yes, Bérnard. I'm sorry to say it, but you are. You have no ambition. No desire to improve yourself, to move up in the world . . .'

'Please, Clovis, please,' Mathilde is still saying.

He silences her with a lightly placed hand – her shoulder. 'I'm sorry. I am sorry,' he says. 'Despite what your husband says, I did want to help. And I tried. I did what I could. And I will pay him,' he says, drawing himself up like a monarch in his suede jacket, 'a month's wages in lieu of notice.'

'Clovis . . .'

'There is only so much I can do,' he tells her. 'What can I do? What do you want me to do?'

'Give him one more chance.'

'If I thought it would help *him*, I would.'

André mutters something.

'What?'

'Bollocks,' André says more distinctly.

'No. No, André, it is not *bollocks*,' Clovis says, speaking quietly, in a voice trembling with anger. 'How have I benefited in any way from taking Bérnard on? Tell me how I have benefited.'

There is a tense silence.

Then Clovis, in a sad voice, says, 'I'm sorry, Bérnard.'

Bérnard, now eating a yoghurt, just nods. He is not as upset as either of his parents seem to be.

He is not actually upset at all. The main facts, as he sees them, are: 1) he does not have to go to work tomorrow, or ever again, and 2) he is getting a thousand euros for nothing.

His mother's near-tearfulness, his father's smouldering fury, are just familiar parts of the family scenery.

He is aware that there exists between his father and his uncle some terrible issue, some fundamental unfriendliness – it is not something, however, that he understands. It has always been there. It is just part of life.

Like the way his parents argue.

They are arguing now.

From his room on the top floor of the house he hears them, far below.

When they argue it is either about money – which is always tight – or about Bérnard.

They worry about him, that he understands. They are arguing now out of their worry, shouting at each other.

He does not worry about himself. *Their* worry, however, sets off a sort of unwelcome humming in his psyche; like the high-pitched pulse of an alarm somewhere far off down the street, leaking anxiety into the night. Their voices now, travelling up through two floors, are like that. They are arguing about him, about what he is going 'to do with his life'.

To him, the question seems entirely abstract.

He is playing a first-person shooter, listlessly massacring thousands of monstrous enemies.

After an hour or so he tires of it, and decides to visit Baudouin.

Baudouin is also playing a first-person shooter, albeit on a much larger and more expensive display – a vast display, flanked by muscular speakers. His father, also Baudouin, is a dentist, and the younger Baudouin is himself studying dentistry at the university. He is the only university friend with whom Bérnard is still in touch.

In keeping with his impeccably provisioned life, Baudouin always has a substantial stash of super-skunk – imported from Holland, and oozing crystals of THC – and Bérnard skins up while his friend finishes the level.

He says, 'I've been sacked.'

Baudouin, the future dentist, takes out half a dozen zombies. 'I thought you worked for your uncle,' he says.

'Yeah. He sacked me.'

'What a twat.'

'He is a twat.'

Baudouin stretches out a white hand for the spliff.

Bérnard obliges him. 'I don't give a shit,' he says, as if worried that his friend might think he did.

Baudouin, blasting, grunts.

'I get a month's pay. Severance or whatever.' Bérnard says that with some pride.

Baudouin, however, seems unimpressed: 'Yeah?'

'And now I can come to Cyprus for sure.'

Passing him the spliff again, and without looking at him, Baudouin says, 'Oh, I need to talk to you about that.'

'What?'

'I can't go.'

'What d'you mean?'

'I didn't pass Biochemistry Two,' Baudouin says. 'I need to take it again.'

'When's the exam?' Bérnard asks.

'In two weeks.'

'So why can't you go?'

'My dad won't let me.'

'Fuck that.'

Baudouin laughs, as if in agreement. Then he says, 'No, he says it's important I don't fail again.'

Bérnard, sitting somewhat behind him on one of the tatami mats that litter the floor, has a pull on the spliff. He feels deeply let down. 'You seriously not coming then?' he asks, unable to help sounding hurt.

What makes it worse, the whole thing was Baudouin's idea.

It had been he who found, somewhere online, the shockingly inexpensive package that included flights from Charleroi airport and seven nights at the Hotel Poseidon in Protaras. It had been he who persuaded Bérnard – admittedly, he needed little persuading – that Protaras was a hedonistic paradise, that the weather in Cyprus would be well hot enough in mid-May, and that it was an excellent time for a holiday. He had stoked up Bérnard's enthusiasm for the idea until it was the only thing on which he fixed his mind as he tried to survive the interminable afternoons on the greyish-brown industrial estate.

And now he says, still mostly focused on the screen in front of him, 'No. Seriously. I can't.'

His hand, stretched out, is waiting for the spliff.

Bérnard passes it to him, silently.

'What am I supposed to do?' he asks after a while.

'Go!' Baudouin says, over the manic whamming of the speakers. 'Obviously, go. Why wouldn't you? I would.'

'On my own?'

'Why wouldn't you?'

'Only saddoes,' Bérnard says, 'go on holiday on their own.'

'Don't be stupid . . .'

'It's true.'

'It's not.'

Bérnard has the spliff again, what's left of it, an acrid stub. 'It so is.' He says, 'I'll feel like a fucking loser.'

'Don't be stupid,' Baudouin says, finishing the level finally and saving his position. He turns to Bérnard. 'Think Steve McQueen,' he says. Baudouin is a fan of the late American actor. He has a large poster of him – squinting magisterially astride a vintage motorbike – on the wall of the room in which they sit. 'Think Belmondo.'

'Whatever.'

'Do you think I'm pleased I can't go?' Baudouin asks. A Windows Desktop, weirdly vast and static, now fills the towering screen.

'Whatever,' Bérnard says again.

While he moodily sets to work on the next spliff, massaging the tobacco from one of his friend's Marlboro Lights, Baudouin starts an MP4 of *Iron Man 3* – a film which has yet to arrive in the Lille cinemas.

'You seen this?' he asks, after drinking at length from a bottle of Evian.

'What is it?'

'*Iron Man Three*.'

'No.'

'It's got Gwyneth Paltrow in it,' Baudouin says.

'Yeah, I know.'

They watch it in English, which they both speak well enough for the dialogue to present no major problems.

Whenever Gwyneth Paltrow is on screen Baudouin stops talking and starts devotedly ogling. He has, as they say, a 'thing' about her. It is not a 'thing' his friend understands, particularly – not the full hormonal, worshipping intensity of it.

'She's alright,' Bérnard says.

'You, my friend, are working class.'

'She's got no tits,' Bérnard says.

'That you should say that,' Baudouin tells him, 'does sort of prove my point.'

Then he says, in a scholarly tone, 'In *Shakespeare in Love* you see her tits. They're not as small as you might think.'

Willing to be proven wrong, Bérnard makes a mental note to torrent the film when he gets home.

Which he does, and discovers that his friend has a point – there is indeed something there, something appreciable. And, hunched over himself, a hand-picked frame on the screen, he does appreciate it.

2

At four o'clock on Monday morning, on the bus to Charleroi airport, he feels sad, loserish, very lonely. Dawn arrives on the empty motorway. The sun, smacking him in the face. Shadows everywhere. He stares, through smarting eyes, at the landscape as it passes – its flatness, its shimmer. There is an exhilarating whisper of freedom, then, that lasts until he sees a plane hanging low in the sky, and again finds himself facing the affront to his ego of having to holiday alone.

3

From Larnaca airport – newer and shinier than Charleroi – a minibus operated by the holiday firm takes him, and about twelve other people, to Protaras. A dusty, unpleasant landscape. No sign of the sea. He is, on that air-conditioned bus, with little blue curtains that can be closed against the midday sun, the only person travelling on his own.

The drop-offs start.

He is the last to be dropped off.

Most of the others are set down at newish white hotels next to the sea, which did eventually appear, hotels that look like the top halves of cruise ships.

Then, when he is alone on the bus, it leaves the shore and starts inland, taking him first through some semi-pedestrianised streets full of lurid impermanent-looking pubs and then, the townscape thinning out, past a sizeable Lidl and into an arid half-made hinterland, without much happening, where the Hotel Poseidon is.

The Hotel Poseidon.

Three storeys of white-painted concrete, studded with identical small balconies. Broken concrete steps leading up to a brown glass door.

It is now the heat of the day – the streets around the hotel are empty and shadowless as the sun drops straight down on them. In the lobby the air is hot and humid. At first he thinks there is no one there. Then he sees the two women lurking in the warm semi-darkness behind the desk.

He explains, in English, who he is.

They listen, unimpressed.

Having taken his passport, one of them then leads him up some dim stairs to the floor above, and into a narrow space with a single window at one end and two low single beds placed end to end against one wall.

A sinister door is pointed to. 'The bathroom,' she says.

And then he is alone again.

He is able to hear, indistinctly, voices, from several directions. From somewhere above him, footsteps. From somewhere else, a well-defined sneeze.

He stands at the window: there are some trees, some scrubby derelict land, some walls.

Far away, a horizontal blue line hints at the presence of the sea.

He is standing there feeling sorry for himself when there is a knock on the door.

It is a short man in an ill-fitting suit. Unlike the two women in the lobby, he is smiling. 'Hello, sir,' he says, still smiling.

'Hello,' Bérnard says.

'I hope you are enjoying your stay,' the man says. 'I just wanted to have a word with you please about the shower.'

'Yes?'

'Please don't use the shower.'

After a short pause, Bérnard says, 'Okay.' And then, feeling obscurely that he should ask, 'Why not?'

The man is still smiling. 'It leaks, you see,' he says. 'It leaks into the lobby. So please don't use it. I hope you understand.'

Bérnard nods and says, 'Sure. Okay.'

'Thank you, sir,' the man says.

When he has left, Bérnard has a look at the bathroom. It is a windowless shaft with a toilet, a sink, a metal nozzle in the wall over the toilet and what seems to be an associated tap – which is presumably the unusable shower – a flaky drain in the middle of the floor, and a sign in Greek, and also in Russian, Bérnard thinks, of which the only thing he can understand are the numerous exclamation marks. He switches off the light.

Sitting on one of the single beds, he starts to feel that it is probably unacceptable for him not to have access to a shower, and decides to speak to someone about it.

There is no one in the lobby, though, so after waiting for ten minutes, he leaves the hotel and starts to walk in what he thinks is the direction of the sea.

In addition to the shower, there is something else he feels might be unsatisfactory: he was sure the hotel was supposed to have a pool. Baudouin had talked about afternoons spent 'vegging next to the pool', had even sent him a link to a picture of it – the picture had shown what appeared to be some sort of aqua park, with a number of different pools and water slides, populated by smiling people. The whole thing had seemed, from the picture, to be more or less next to the sea.

And that was another thing.

The hotel was advertised as five minutes' walk from the sea, yet he has been trudging for at least double that through the desolate heat and is only just passing the Lidl.

In fact, to walk to the sea takes half an hour.

Once there he hangs about for a while – stands at the landward margin of a brown beach, thick with sun umbrellas down to the listless flop of the surf.

He has a pint in a pub hung with Union Jacks and England flags, and advertising English football matches, and then walks slowly back to his hotel. The Lidl is easy to find: there are signs for it throughout the town. And from the Lidl he is able, with only one or two wrong turnings, to find the Hotel Poseidon.

In the hot lobby he walks up to the desk, where there is now someone on duty, intending to talk about the shower situation and the lack of a swimming pool on the premises.

It is the smiling man, who says, 'Good afternoon, sir. There is a message for you.'

'For me?'

'For you, sir.' The smiling man – middle-aged, with a lean, tanned face – pushes a slip of paper across the desk.

It is a handwritten note:

Dropped by – you weren't in. I'll be in Waves from 5 if you wanna meet up and talk things through. Leif

Bérnard looks up at the smiling man's kind, avuncular face.

'Are you sure this is for me?' he asks.

Still smiling kindly, the man nods.

Looking at the note again, Bérnard asks him if he knows where Waves is.

It is near the sea, the man tells him, and explains how to get there. 'It's a popular place with *young* people,' he says.

Bérnard thanks him. It is already five, and he is about to set off again when he remembers the shower, and turns back. He does not know exactly how to put it, how to express his dissatisfaction. He says, uncertainly, 'Listen, um. The shower . . .'

Immediately, as soon as the word *shower* has been spoken, the smiling man says, 'The problem will be sorted out tomorrow.' For the first time, he is not smiling. He looks very serious. His eyes are full of apology. 'I'm very sorry, sir.'

'Okay,' Bérnard says. 'Thank you.'

'I'm sorry, sir,' the man says again, this time with a small deferential smile.

'There is one other thing,' Bérnard says, emboldened.

'Yes, sir?'

'There is a swimming pool?'

The man's expression turns sad, almost mournful. 'At the moment, no, sir, there is not,' he says. He starts to explain the situation – something about a legal dispute with the apartments next door – until Bérnard interrupts him, protesting mildly that the hotel had been sold to him as having a pool, so it seems wrong that there isn't one.

The smiling man says, 'We have an arrangement with the Hotel Vangelis, sir.'

There is a moment of silence in the oppressive damp heat of the lobby.

'An arrangement?'

'Yes, sir.'

'What sort of arrangement?'

The arrangement turns out to be that for ten euros a day inmates of the Poseidon can use the pool facilities of the Hotel Vangelis, which are extensive – the aqua park pictured on the Poseidon's website, and also in the leaflet which the smiling man is now pressing into Bérnard's hand.

The smiling man has a moustache, Bérnard notices at that point. 'Okay,' he says. 'Thank you. What time is supper?'

'Seven o'clock, sir.'

'And where?'

'In the dining room.' The smiling man points to a glass door on the other side of the lobby. Dirty yellow curtains hang on either side of the door. Next to the door there is an empty lectern. The room on the other side of the door is dark.

'You wanna party, yeah?' Leif asks, smiling lazily, as Bérnard, with a perspiring Keo, the local industrial lager, takes a seat opposite him.

Bérnard nods. 'Of course,' he says, fairly seriously.

A tall, tanned Icelander, only a few years older than Bérnard, Leif turned out to be the company rep.

Now he is telling Bérnard about the night life of Protaras. He is talking about some nightclub – Jesters – and the details of a happy-hour offer there. 'And then three cocktails for the price of two from seven till eight,' he says. 'Take advantage of it. Like I told the others, it's one of the best offers in the resort.'

'Okay,' Bérnard says.

Leif is drinking a huge smoothie. He keeps talking about 'the others', and Bérnard wonders whether he missed some prearranged meeting that no one told him about.

Who were these 'others'?

'Kebabs,' Leif says, as if it were a section heading. 'The best place is Porkies, okay? It's just over there.' He takes his large splayed hand from the back of his shaved head and points up the street. Bérnard looks and sees an orange sign: *Porkies*.

'Okay,' he says.

They are sitting on the terrace of Waves, he and Leif. Inside, music thumps. Although it is only just six, there are already plenty of drunk people about. A drinking game is in progress somewhere, with lots of excitable shouting.

'It's open twenty-four hours,' Leif says, still talking about Porkies.

'Okay.'

'And be careful – the hot sauce *is* hot.'

He says this so seriously that Bérnard thinks he must be joking and laughs.

Just as seriously, though, Leif says, 'It is a really fucking hot sauce.' He tips the last of his smoothie into his mouth. There is a sort of very faint disdain in the way he speaks to Bérnard. His attention always seems vaguely elsewhere; he keeps slowly turning his head to look up and down the street, which is just starting to acquire its evening hum, though the sun is still shining, long-shadowedly.

'So that's about it,' he says. He has the air of a man who gets laid effortlessly and often. Indeed, there is something post-coital about his exaggeratedly laid-back manner. Bérnard is intimidated by him. He nods and has a sip of his beer.

'You here with some mates?' Leif asks him.

'No, uh . . .'

'On your own?'

Bérnard tries to explain. 'I was supposed to be with a friend . . .' He stops. Leif, obviously, is not interested.

'Okay,' Leif says, looking in the direction of Porkies as if he is expecting someone.

Then he turns to Bérnard again and says, 'I'll leave you to it. You have any questions just let me know, yeah.'

He is already standing up.

Bérnard says, 'Okay. Thanks.'

'See you round,' Leif says.

He doesn't seem to hear Bérnard saying, 'Yeah, see you.'

As he walks away the golden hair on his arms and legs glows in the low sun.

Bérnard finishes his drink quickly. Then he leaves Waves – where the music is now at full nightclub volume – and starts to walk, again, towards the Hotel Poseidon.

He feels slightly worse, slightly more isolated, after the meeting with Leif. He had somehow assumed, when he first sat down, that Leif would show him an evening of hedonism, or at least provide *some* sort of entrée into the native depravity of the place. That he did not, that he just left him on the terrace of Waves to finish his drink alone, leaves Bérnard feeling that he has failed a test – perhaps a fundamental one.

This feeling widening slowly into something like depression, he walks into the dead hinterland where the Hotel Poseidon is.

It is just after seven when he arrives at the hotel. The lobby is sultry and unlit. The dining room, on the other hand, is lit like a hospital A&E department. It doesn't seem to have any windows, the dining room. The walls are hung with dirty drapes. He sits down at a table. He seems to be the last to arrive – most of the other tables are occupied, people lowering their faces towards the grey soup, spooning it into their mouths. It is eerily quiet. Someone is speaking in Russian. Other than that the only sound, from all around, is the tinking of spoon on plate. And a strange humming, quite loud, that lasts for twenty or thirty seconds, then stops, then starts again. A waiter puts a plate of soup in front of him. Bérnard picks up his spoon, and notices the encrustations on its cloudy metal surface, the hard deposits of earlier meals. With a napkin – which itself shows evidence of previous use – he tries to scrub them off. The voice is still speaking in Russian, monotonously. Having cleaned his spoon, he turns his attention to the soup. It is a strange grey colour. And it is cold. He looks around, as if expecting someone to explain. No one explains. What he does notice, however, is the microwave on the other side of the room – the source of the strange intermittent humming – and the queue of people waiting to use it, each with a plate of soup. He picks up his own soup and joins them.

He is preceded in the queue by a woman in her mid-forties, probably, who is quite short and very fat. She has blonde hair, and an orange face – red under her eyes and along the top of her nose. He noticed her sitting at a table near him when he sat down – she is the sort of fat person it is hard to miss. What makes her harder to miss is that she is with another woman, younger than her and even fatter. This younger

66

woman – her daughter perhaps – is actually fascinatingly huge. Bérnard tried not to stare.

After they have been standing in the microwave queue for a few minutes, listening to the whirr of the machine and taking a step forward every time it stops, the older woman says to him, in English, 'It's a disgrace, really, isn't it?'

'Mm,' Bérnard agrees, surprised at being spoken to.

The woman is sweating freely – the dining room is very warm. 'Every night the same,' she says.

'Really?'

'Really,' she says, and then it is her turn and she shoves her plate into the microwave.

4

Iveta. Ah, Iveta.

He first sees her the next morning, in Porkies.

He has had almost no sleep, is tipsy with fatigue. It was a *nuit blanche*, nearly. He wasn't out late, it wasn't that – he had a few lonely drinks on the lurid stretch, tried unsuccessfully to talk to some people, was humiliatingly stung in a hostess bar, and then, feeling quite depressed, made his way back to the Poseidon. At that point he was just looking forward to getting some sleep. And that's when the problems started. Though the hotel seemed totally isolated, there was at least one place in the immediate vicinity which thudded with dance music till the grey of dawn. Within the hotel itself, doors slammed all night, and voices shouted and sang, and people fucked noisily on all sides.

Finally, just as natural light started to filter through the ineffectual curtains, everything went quiet.

Bérnard, sitting up, looked at his watch. It was nearly five, and he had not slept at all.

And then, from the vacant lot next door, where people would ill-egally park, they started towing the cars.

He must have fallen asleep somehow while they were still doing that, while the alarms were still being triggered, one after another – when he next sat up and looked at his watch it was ten past ten.

Which meant he had missed the hotel breakfast.

So he went out into the morning, which was already hot, to find something to eat, and ended up in Porkies.

Porkies, even at ten thirty a.m., is doing a steady trade. Many of the people there, queuing for their kebabs, are obviously on the final stop of a night out. Hoarsely, they talk to each other or, still damp from the foam disco, stare in the fresh sunlight near the front of the shop, where a machine is loudly extracting the juice from orange halves.

With his heavy kebab Bérnard finds a seat at the end of the counter, the last of the stools that are there.

Next to him, facing the brown-tinted mirror tiles and still in their party kit with plenty of flesh on show, is a line of young women, laughing noisily as they eat their kebabs, and speaking a language he is unable to place.

He gets talking to the one sitting next to him when he asks her to pass him the squeezable thing of sauce and then, taking it from her, says, 'It was a nice night?'

'Where are you from?' he asks her next – the inevitable Protaras question.

She is Latvian, she says, she and her friends. Bérnard isn't sure where Latvia is. One of those obscure Eastern European places, he supposes.

He informs her that he is French.

She is on the small side, with a slightly too-prominent forehead, and spongy blonde hair – a cheap chemical blonde, displaced by something mousier near the roots. Still, he likes her. He likes her little arms and shoulders, her childish hands holding the kebab. The tired points of glitter on her nose.

He introduces himself. 'Bérnard,' he says.

Iveta, she tells him her name is.

'I like that name,' he says. He smiles, and she smiles too, and he notes her nice straight white teeth.

'You have very nice teeth,' he says.

And then learns that her father is a dentist.

He says, mildly bragging, 'I know a guy, his father is a dentist.'

She seems interested. 'Yes?'

There is something effortless about this, as they sit there eating their kebabs. Effortlessly, almost inadvertently, he has detached her from the others. She has turned away from them, towards him.

'You like Cyprus?' he asks.

Eating, she nods.

This is her second time in Protaras, he discovers. 'Maybe you can show me around,' he suggests easily. 'I don't know it. It's my first time here.'

And she just says, with a simplicity which makes him feel sure he is onto something here, 'Okay.'

'Where are you staying?' he asks.

She mentions some youth hostel, and he feels proud of the fact that he is staying in a proper hotel – proud enough to say, as if it were a totally natural question, 'What are you doing today?'

Her friends are starting to leave.

'Sleeping!'

She says that with a laugh that unsettles him, makes him feel that maybe their whole interaction has been, for her, a sort of joke, something with no significance, something that will lead nowhere. And he wants her now. He wants her. She is wearing denim hot pants, he sees for the first time, and sandals with a slight heel.

'What about later?' he says, trying not to sound desperate. The sense of effortlessness has evaporated. It evaporated the moment she seemed happy to leave without any prospect of seeing him again.

Now, however, she lingers.

Her friends are leaving, and yet she is still there, lingering.

'You want to meet later?' she says, with some seriousness.

70

'I want to see you again.'

She looks at him for a few moments. 'We'll be in Jesters tonight,' she says. 'You know Jesters?'

'I heard of it,' Bérnard says. 'I never been there.'

'Okay,' she says, still with this serious look on her face. And she tells him, in unnecessary detail, and making sure he understands, how to find it.

'Okay,' he says, smiling easily again. 'I'll see you there. Okay?'

She nods, and hurries to join her friends, who are waiting near the door.

He watches them leave and then, squirting more sauce onto it, unhurriedly finishes his kebab.

His mood, of course, is totally transformed. He fucking loves this place now, Protaras. Walking down the street in the sun, everything looks different, everything pleases his eye. He wonders whether he's in love, and then stops at the pharmacy next to McDonald's for a ten-pack of Durex.

'Hello, my friend,' he says to the smiling man, who is on duty in the humid lobby of the Hotel Poseidon.

'Good morning, sir. You slept well, sir?'

'Very well,' Bérnard says, without thinking. 'Yesterday you said something, about another hotel, the swimming pool . . . ?'

'The Hotel Vangelis, yes, sir.'

'Where is that?'

Bérnard, eventually finding the Hotel Vangelis, says he is staying at the Hotel Poseidon, pays ten euros, gets stamped on the hand with a smudged logo, and then follows a pointed finger down a passage smelling of pool chemicals to a locker room, and the sudden noise and dazzle of the aqua park.

In knee-length trunks, he swims. His skin is milky from the Lille winter. He does a few sedate laps of the serious swimmers' pool, then queues with kids for a spin on the water slide. Next he tries the wave-machine pool, lifting and sinking in the water, in the chlorine sparkle, one wet head among many, all the time thinking of Iveta.

And still thinking of her afterwards, drying on a sunlounger. His eyes are shut. His hair looks orangeish when it is wet. There is a tuft of it in the middle of his flat, white chest. His arms and legs are long and smooth. The trunks hang wetly on his loins and thighs, sticking to them heavily.

Slowly, the sun swings round.

One of the pools features a bar – a circular, straw-roofed structure in the shallow end, the seats of the stools that surround it set just above the surface of the water. Where it touches the side of the pool, there is a gate that allows the barman to enter the dry interior, where the drinks are kept in a stainless-steel fridge.

Some time in the afternoon, Bérnard is wallowing in this shallow pool, thinking of Iveta, when, on a whim, he paddles over and takes a seat on one of the stools. His legs, still in the water, look white as marble. He orders a Keo. He is impatient for evening, for Iveta. The day has started to be tiresome.

He is sitting there, under the thatch, holding his plastic pot of lager and looking mostly at his blue-veined feet, when a voice quite near him says, 'Hello again.'

A woman's voice.

He looks up.

It is the woman from the Hotel Poseidon, the fat one he spoke to in the microwave queue last night. She and her even fatter daughter are wading towards him through the shallow turquoise water of the pool – and weirdly, though they are in the pool, they are both wearing dresses, simple ones that hang from stringy shoulder straps, sticking wetly to their immense midriffs, and floating soggily on the waterline.

'Hello again,' the mother says, reaching the stool next to Bérnard's, her face and shoulders and her colossal cleavage sunburnt, her great barrel of a body filling the thin wet dress.

'Hello,' Bérnard says.

The daughter, moving slowly in the water, has arrived at the next stool along. She, it seems, is more careful in the sun than her mother – her skin everywhere has a lardy pallor. Only her face has a very slight tan.

'Hello,' Bérnard says to her, politely.

He wonders – with a mixture of amusement and pity – whether she will be able to sit on the stool. Surely not.

Somehow, though, she manages it.

Her mother is already in place. She says, 'Not bad, this, is it?'

Bérnard is still looking at the daughter. 'Yeah, it's good,' he says.

'Better than we expected, I have to say.'

'It's good,' Bérnard says again.

When the two of them have their sweating plastic tankards of Magners, the older woman says, 'So what do you think of the Hotel Poseidon then?' The tone in which she asks the question suggests that she doesn't think much of it herself.

'It's okay,' Bérnard answers.

'You think so?'

'Yeah. Okay,' he admits, 'maybe there are some problems . . .'

The woman laughs. 'You can say that again.'

'Yeah, okay,' Bérnard says. 'Like my shower, you can say.'

'Your shower? What about your shower?'

Bérnard explains the situation with his shower – which the smiling man this morning again warned him against using. It would, he promised Bérnard, be sorted out by tomorrow.

73

The older woman turns to her daughter. 'Well, that's just typical,' she says, 'isn't it? Isn't it?' she says again, and the younger woman, who is drinking her Magners through a straw, nods.

'We've had no end of things like that,' the mother says to Bérnard. 'Like what happened with the towels.'

'The towels?'

'One morning the towels go missing,' she tells him. 'While we're downstairs. They just disappear. Don't they?' she asks her daughter, who nods again.

'And then,' the mother says, 'when we ask for some more, they tell us we must have stolen them. They say we've got to pay forty euros for new ones, or we won't get our passports back.'

Bérnard murmurs sympathetically.

He has a swig of his drink. He is still fascinated by the daughter's body – by the pillow-sized folds of fat on her sitting midriff, the way her elbows show only as dimples in the distended shapes of her arms. How small her head seems . . .

Her mother is talking about something else now, about some Bulgarians in the next room. 'Keep us up half the night, shouting and God knows what,' she says. 'The walls are like paper. We can hear everything – and I do mean everything. We call them the *vulgar Bulgars*, don't we?' she says to her daughter. 'You know what we saw them doing? We saw them stealing food from the dining room.'

Bérnard laughs.

'Why they would want to steal that food I don't know. It's awful. Well, you experienced it last night. You ask if they've any fish – I mean we are next to the sea, aren't we – they bring you a tin of tuna. It's unbelievable. And the flies, especially at lunchtime. I've never seen anything like it. It's not fit for human consumption. We were both down with the squits for a few days last week,' she says, and Bérnard, unwilling to dwell on that idea, lets his thoughts drift again to Iveta – her thin tanned thighs, her pretty feet in the jewelly sandals – while the fat Englishwoman keeps talking.

They are English, these two, he has worked that out now.

'One day we thought, enough's enough, we're going to eat somewhere else,' the older woman says. 'So we asked our rep about good places to eat and he suggested this place the Aphrodite . . . Do you know it?'

Bérnard shakes his head.

'Well, we went there on Saturday,' she says, 'and after spending over fifty euros on drinks and dinner, I went to the toilet and was told I had to pay a euro to use it. Well, I wasn't happy and I told the woman I was a customer. And she said that doesn't matter, you still have to pay. And I said well, I'm not paying, and when I tried to go into the toilet anyway, she pushed me away. She physically pushed me away. Wouldn't let me use it. So I asked to speak to the manager, and after about fifteen minutes this man appears – Nick, he says his name is – and when I explain to him what happened, he just laughs, laughs in my face. And when that happened . . . Well, I got so angry. He just laughed in my face. Can you imagine. The Aphrodite,' she says. 'Stay away from it.'

'I will,' Bérnard tells her.

'We love Cyprus,' she says, moving on her stool. 'Every year we come here. Don't we? I'm Sandra, by the way. And this is Charmian.'

'Bérnard,' says Bérnard.

They stay there drinking for two hours, until the hotel's shadow starts to move over them. They get quite drunk. And then Bérnard, whose thoughts have never been far from Iveta and what will happen that evening, notices the time and says he has to leave.

The two women have just ordered another pair of Magners – their fourth or fifth – and Sandra says, 'We'll see you at supper then.'

Bérnard is wading away. 'Okay,' he says.

Showering in the locker room a few minutes later, he has already forgotten about them.

*

When he wakes up it is dark. He is in his room in the Hotel Poseidon. The narrow room is very hot and music thuds from the place nearby.

It was about six when he got back from the Hotel Vangelis, and having a slight headache, he thought he would lie down for a while before supper. He must have fallen into a deep sleep. Sitting up suddenly, he looks at his watch, fearful that it might be too late to find Iveta at Jesters. It is only ten, though, and he lies down again. He is sweating in the close heat of the room. Last night he tried the air conditioning, and it didn't work.

He washes, as best he can, at the sink.

The light in the bathroom is so dim he can barely see his face in the mirror.

Then he tidies up a bit. It is his assumption that Iveta will be in this room later, and he does not want it littered with his dirty stuff.

He spends quite a lot of time deciding what to wear, finally opting for the dressier look of the plain white shirt, and leaving the horizontally striped polo for another night. He leaves the top three buttons of the shirt undone, so that it is open down to the tuft of hair on his sternum, and digs in his suitcase for the tiny sample of Ermenegildo Zegna Uomo that was once stuck to a magazine in his uncle's office. He squirts about half of it on himself, and then, after inquisitively sniffing his wrists, squirts the other half on as well.

Satisfied, he turns his attention to his hair, combing back the habitual mop to the line of his skull – thereby disclosing, unusually, his low forehead – and holding the combed hair in place with a generous scoop of scented gel.

In the buzzing light of the bathroom he inspects himself.

He buttons the third button of his shirt.

Then he unbuttons it again.

Then he buttons it again.

His forehead, paler than the rest of his face, looks weird, he thinks.

Working with the comb he tries to hide it, but that just makes it look even weirder.

Finally, impatient with himself, he tries to put the hair back the way it was before.

There is still something weird about it, and he worries as he hurries down the stairs to the lobby and, in a travelling zone of Uomo, out into the warm night.

It is nearly eleven now, and he has not eaten anything. It's not that he is hungry – far from it – it's just that he feels he ought to 'line' his stomach.

He stops at Porkies and eats part of a kebab, forcing a few mouthfuls down. He is almost shaking with excitement, with anticipation. He tries to still his nerves with a vodka-Red Bull, and with the memories of how easily they talked in the morning, of how eagerly she had told him how to find Jesters – she practically drew him a map. The memories help.

He abandons the kebab and starts for Jesters, through the heaving streets.

He finds it easily, following a pack of shirtless singing youths to its shed-like facade, outlined in hellish neon tubes. The looming neon cap-and-bells, the drunken queue.

Five euros, he hands over.

Inside, he looks for her.

Moving through strobe light, through a wall of throbbing sound, he looks for her.

The place is solid flesh. Limbs flickering in darkness. He could search all night, he thinks, and not find her.

Holding his expensive Beck's, he scans the place with increasing desperation. For the first time it occurs to him that she might not actually be there.

He has a nervous pull of the lager and pushes his way through a hedge of partying anonymity.

Some girls, on heat, are flaunting on a platform.

At their feet, a pool of staring lads in sweat-wet T-shirts. He watches for a moment, up-skirting with the other males, and then, with a shock of adrenalin, he sees someone, a face he sort of knows – one of her friends from this morning, he thinks it is, moving away from him.

He follows her. His eyes stuck to the skin of her exposed back, its dull shine of perspiration, he tears a path through interlacing limbs.

And she leads him to Iveta. She leads him to Iveta. He sees her in a pop of light as the music winds up. She does not see him. Her eyes are shut. She is in a man's hands, mouths melting together.

And then the hit crashes into its chorus.

5

The Hotel Vangelis, the next afternoon. Waist deep in water he is at the in-pool bar, drinking Cypriot lager and absorbing sunburn. He still smells of Ermenegildo Zegna Uomo. He had welcomed the arrival, about an hour before, of Sandra and Charmian. They are stationed next to him now, huge on their submerged stools, and Sandra is talking. She is telling him how the man she always refers to as 'Charmian's father' died horrifically after falling into a vat of molten zinc – he worked in an industrial installation of some sort – and how heartbroken she was after that. Tasting his Keo, Bérnard appreciates the parity she seems to accord that event and his finding a girl he had only just met snogging someone else in a nightclub.

Already quite drunk, and exhausted by a night spent wandering the litter-strewn streets of Protaras, he had told them about that. He found he wanted to talk about it. And when he had finished his story, Sandra sighed and said she knew how he felt, and told him the story of her husband's death.

It was awful enough to be on the news – she is telling him how upsetting it was to see strangers talking about it on the local TV news.

'And the worst thing,' she says, 'is they think he was *alive* for up to twenty seconds after he fell in.'

'When did it happen?' Bérnard asks her morosely.

'Nine years ago,' Sandra says, sighing again. 'And I miss him every single day.'

Bérnard finishes his Keo and hands the empty plastic pot to the barman.

'What do you do, Bernard?' Sandra asks him, pronouncing his name the English way.

He tells her he was working for his uncle, until he was sacked.

'Why'd he sack you then?' she asks.

'He sounds like a tosser,' she says, when he has told her what happened.

'I don't know,' he says. 'What is it, a tosser?'

'A tosser?' Sandra laughs, and looks at Charmian. 'How would you explain?'

'Sort of like an idiot?' Charmian suggests.

'But what's it mean literally?'

'Literally?'

'Yes.'

'Well, it's like wanker, isn't it?'

Sandra laughs again. 'How do we explain that to Bernard?'

'I don't know.'

Sandra says, turning to Bérnard, 'Literally, it means someone who plays with himself.'

'Okay.'

'You know what I mean?' Sandra is smirking.

Charmian seems embarrassed – her face has turned all pink, and she is urgently sucking up cider and looking the other way.

'I think so,' Bérnard says, smiling slightly embarrassedly himself.

'But really it just means an idiot, someone we don't like.'

'Then he is a tosser, my uncle.'

'He sounds like it.' She turns to Charmian again. 'Imagine sacking your own nephew, just because he wants to go on holiday!'

Charmian nods. She looks quickly at Bérnard.

Warming to the subject, Bérnard starts to tell them more about his uncle – how he lives in Belgium to pay less tax, how he . . .

'Where you from then, Bernard?' Sandra asks him.

'Lille.'

'Where's that then?'

'It's sort of near Belgium, isn't it?' Charmian ventures shyly.

Bérnard nods.

'How'd you know that then?' Sandra asks her, impressed.

Charmian says, 'The Eurostar goes through there sometimes, doesn't it?' The question is addressed, somewhat awkwardly, to Bérnard.

Who just says, 'Yeah,' and turns his head towards the sparkle of the pool.

'We're from Northampton,' Sandra tells him. 'It's famous for shoes.'

They swim together, later. The ladies, still in their billowing dresses, letting the water lift them, and Bérnard moving more vigorously, doing little displays of front crawl, and then lolling on his back in the water, letting the sun dazzle his chlorine-stung eyes. Sandra encourages him to do a handstand in the shallow end. Not totally sober, he obliges her. He surfaces to ask how it was, and she shouts at him to keep his legs straight next time, while Charmian, still bobbing about nearby, staying where she can find the cool blue tiles with her toes, looks on. He does another handstand, unsteady in his long wet trunks. The ladies applaud. Triumphant, he dives again, into watery silence, blue world, losing all vertical aplomb as his big hands strive for the tiles. His legs thrash to drive him down. His lungs keep lifting his splayed hands from the tiles. His face feels full of blood. Streams of bubbles pass over him, upwards from his nostrils. And then he is in air again, squatting shoulder deep in the tepid water, the water sharp and bright with chemicals streaming from orange slicks of hair that hang over his eyes. He feels queasy for a moment. All those Keo lagers . . . He fears, just for a moment, that he is going to throw up.

Then he notices a lifeguard looming over them, his shadow on the water. He is talking to Sandra. He has just finished saying something, and he moves away, and takes his seat again, up a sloping ladder, like a tennis umpire.

'We've been told off,' Sandra says, hanging languidly in the water, only her sunburnt head, with its mannish jawline and feathery blonde pudding-bowl, above the surface.

Bérnard isn't sure what's going on. He still feels light-headed, vaguely unwell. 'What?'

'We've been told off,' Sandra says again.

Bérnard, from his crouch in the water, which feels chilly now that he has stopped moving, just stares at her. His body is bony. Individual vertebrae show on his white back. Sandra is still saying something to him. Her voice sounds muffled. '. . . told to stop being so immature . . .' he hears it say.

She has started to swim away from him – her head moving away on a very slow, lazy breaststroke.

The surface of the pool, which had been all discomposed by his antics, is smoothing itself out again, is slapping the sides with diminishing vigour.

After the horseplay they lie on the side, on sunloungers. Sandra just about fits onto one. Charmian, however, needs to push two together. Bérnard helps her. Then, without saying anything, he takes his place on his own lounger and shuts his eyes. It is late afternoon. The sun has a dull heat. In their dripping dresses, Sandra and Charmian are smoking cigarettes and talking about food. Bérnard isn't really listening.

Then Sandra's voice says, 'Bernard,' and he opens his eyes.

They are both looking at him.

Charmian, however, quickly looks away.

'We're going out for a meal tonight,' Sandra says. 'Want to come?'

*

They meet in the lobby of the hotel. Bérnard is talking to the smiling man – who is telling him that his shower will definitely be fixed tomorrow – when the ladies appear. There *is* an awkwardness. Unlike the previous night, Bérnard has made absolutely no effort at all with his preparations. The ladies, on the other hand, have to some extent dressed up. He sees that immediately. They have make-up on – quite a lot of make-up – and though Sandra is wearing a dress similar to the one she swims in, hanging from flimsy shoulder straps, its green-and-white floral pattern straining to hold the enormities of her figure, Charmian, extraordinarily, is in a pair of jeans and a blouse with delicate lacy details.

'All set then?' Sandra says, as Bérnard turns to them.

The smiling man watches tactfully as they leave.

They proceed in silence, initially, through the plain half-made streets near the hotel. The evening is no more than pleasantly warm – the nights are still mild sometimes, this early in the season. Even so, and in spite of the fact that they are walking downhill, Charmian, in particular, is soon shedding sheets of watery sweat.

'It's not far,' Sandra says, panting.

'What . . . what sort of place is it?' Bérnard asks.

'Typical Greek,' Sandra tells him.

It turns out to be a long single-storey construction on an arid stretch of road, painted deep red, and covered with signage.

In the huge air-conditioned interior they are shown to a table. Music is playing, the latest international hits, and on screens attached to the walls men are playing golf in America. It is still too early for the place to be very full. The waitress brings big laminated menus, which they study in silence. There are pictures of each item – unappealingly documentary images like police evidence photos.

Things loosen up once the wine starts to take effect – a large jug of it that Sandra orders, which tastes faintly of pine trees.

'I love this stuff,' she says.

A stainless-steel plate of stuffed vine leaves also appears, leaking olive oil, and dishes of taramasalata and hummus, and a plate of warm pitta bread.

Bérnard pours himself some more of the weird wine, and then tops the others up as well. He is telling them about his experience in the hostess bar, his first night there, when he was intimidated into emptying his wallet on overpriced drinks for a pair of haughty, painted ladies. Sandra had told him how the taxi driver had tried to overcharge them on the way home from the Hotel Vangelis that afternoon, and he is offering his own tale of unscrupulous piracy. Mopping up the last of the tarama with the last piece of pitta, Sandra says, 'You don't need to take that, Bernard.'

'It's okay,' Bérnard says mellowly. 'Shit happens.' He drinks some more wine.

'You *shouldn't* take it,' she says. 'A hundred euros?'

'Yes.'

'I tell you what we're going to do,' she says, looking around for the waiter. 'When we've finished here, we're going to go over there and get your money back.'

Bérnard laughs quietly.

'I'm not joking,' Sandra says. 'We're going to go over there and get your money back. You can't let them get away with that, Bernard.'

Bérnard sighs. 'They won't give it back,' he says.

'Yes,' Sandra says, 'they will. When we tell them we're going to the police they'll give it back. Remember what happened to us that time in Turkey?' she asks Charmian, who nods. Charmian has hardly said a word all evening, has only eaten half-heartedly four or five stuffed vine leaves. She seems out of sorts. Turning to Bérnard again, Sandra starts on the Turkish story. 'This man tried to rip us off changing money in the street. Well, he shouldn't have picked on us, should he . . .'

Then the main course arrives.

There is enough food, Bérnard thinks, for eight or ten people.

Platters of grilled lamb, chicken, fish. A huge dish of rice. Portions of fries for everyone and a heap of Greek salad which would on its own have fed a whole family. Also another jug of the wine, even though the first one is still half-full.

With some help from Bérnard the ladies obliterate the spread in under half an hour.

Sandra pours out the last of the wine.

Bérnard is drunk. Quite how drunk, he didn't understand until he went to the toilet – his shiny face in the mirror stared back at him with eerie impassivity, then suddenly put out its tongue.

The others, however, seem unaffected, except that Sandra looks even redder than usual.

The place has filled up a bit and a band has started playing.

Sandra and the waiter have some sort of dispute over the bill – the manager is summoned – and when that is finally sorted out, she pays and they leave.

Bérnard had tried to offer some money, and on the pavement out-side, he tries again. He says, with his wallet once more in his hand, 'So . . . ?'

'I think I'm just going to use the lav,' Sandra says, apparently not having heard him, and leaves him there with Charmian.

He pockets his wallet.

Charmian isn't looking at him. She is facing the other way, as if she does not want to be associated with him. He wonders whether he has offended her somehow.

He stands there, drunk, looking at her, the slabs of her arms protruding from the frilly sleeves of her blouse, the grotesque inflations of her jeans.

When Sandra rejoins them, he is still just standing there, and Charmian is still staring off down the street.

In the end, he is unable to find the hostess bar. They spend about half an hour looking for it, on the fringes of Protaras's nightlife, in the streets where the neon stops. They drop into a snack bar for pizza slices, sit eating them in a plastic booth. Then a place with live music – some zithering 'traditional' band and older couples swaying under a turning glitter ball. Bérnard, badly drunk now, gives Sandra a spin on the dance floor, treading on her feet, feeling the immense swell of her side hot and damp under his hand. He offers to do the same for Charmian but she just shakes her head.

'Oh, go on!' Sandra says to her, sweating dangerously, her vast red cleavage shining as if with varnish.

Charmian shakes her head again.

'You are sure?' Bérnard asks, out of breath.

When Charmian just ignores him, Sandra says, 'Don't be so rude!'

She gives Bérnard an apologetic, exasperated look.

Then they sit down to finish the red wine.

Their final stop of the evening is Porkies, for a kebab. Bérnard does not have one. He just watches the others eat. In his state of extreme drunkenness, Charmian has taken on a strange, fascinating quality. Sitting opposite her, he watches her eating the kebab with what seem to be modest flickers of desire. They surprise him. Her face, admittedly, is nice enough and there is nothing wrong with the pale blue of her long-lashed eyes . . .

He looks away, wondering what to make of this. What, if anything, to *do* about it.

He is still wondering in the taxi that takes them back to the Hotel Poseidon. He is sitting in the front, next to the driver. The surprising question presses itself on him: Should he make some sort of move?

Awkward, with her mother there.

The taxi stops at the crumbling concrete steps of the Poseidon.

With difficulty, with Bérnard helping, heaving heavy flesh, the ladies extract themselves from its low seats.

And then they are in the lobby.

And he almost says to Charmian something about whether she wants to see his room.

And then it is too late.

Sandra has kissed him goodnight.

He is alone in his room, which starts to turn if he shuts his eyes.

He tries a wank, but he is too drunk.

6

In the morning he lies there on the single bed, imprisoned in his hangover, trying to piece together the fragments of the evening and feeling that he nearly did something very, very silly.

He opens his eyes.

The heat of the sun throbs from the closed curtains and the sounds of the street intrude into the painful stillness of the dim, narrow room. He lies there for most of the morning, instantly feeling sick if he moves at all.

At some point he falls asleep again, and when he wakes up he feels okay.

He is able to move.

To sit.

To stand.

To peel back the edge of the curtain and squint at the white, fiery day – the glare of the vacant lot next door.

The sky's merciless scream of blue.

It is eleven fifty, nearly time for lunch, and he is hungry now.

He feels strange, as if in a dream, as he descends the cool stairs.

Descending the cool stairs, he really feels as if he is still in bed, and dreaming this.

The dining room.

Murmur of voices – Russian, Bulgarian.

The buffet of congealed brown food.

The microwave queue.

And there they are, Sandra and Charmian, at their usual table, which is where he sits now too.

As he approaches – feeling weightless, as if he is floating over the filthy carpet – Sandra says, 'We didn't see you at breakfast, Bernard.'

She seems more or less unaffected by the night's drinking – her ruddiness only slightly attenuated, her voice only marginally hoarser than normal.

Charmian, sitting next to her, looks quite pale.

'No, I, er . . .' Bérnard mumbles, taking a seat. 'I was sleeping.'

'Last night too much for you, was it?'

Bérnard laughs weakly. Then there is a short pause. The thought of eating has lost most of its appeal. 'It was good,' he says finally.

'It was, wasn't it,' Sandra says.

She has already eaten – the emptied plate is on the table in front of her. Charmian too is just finishing up.

Bérnard opens his can of Fanta and pours most of it into a greasy glass.

'You not having anything?' Sandra asks him, moving her faint blonde eyebrows in the direction of the buffet.

'Later, maybe,' Bérnard says. He is starting to think that this was a mistake, making an appearance here. He feels less normal than he thought he did. The taste of the Fanta – a tiny sip, the first thing to have passed his lips today – makes him feel slightly more grounded.

Charmian stands abruptly.

He finds it hard to believe, now, that he considered making some sort of move on her last night.

He is pretty sure he didn't actually say anything, or do anything. Still, even just having had the idea embarrasses him.

She is off to the buffet for seconds. He watches, briefly, her cumbersome waddle as she passes among the tables. Others are watching her too, he sees.

Somewhere near him, Sandra's voice says, 'I don't know if you've noticed, but Charmian really likes you.'

Bérnard feels, again, that he is still in bed upstairs and just dreaming this.

'I don't know if you've noticed,' Sandra says, when he turns to her, with a look of pale incomprehension on his face.

'Have you?' she asks.

He shakes his head.

Sandra looks away and a few seconds pass. Some Russians laugh at something.

Then Sandra says, 'Do you like sex, Bernard?'

Bérnard tries to steady himself with another sip of Fanta. 'Sex?' he says. 'Yes.'

'Of course . . .'

Sandra chuckles. 'Spoken like a true Frenchman.'

He is not sure what she means by this, or even if he heard her properly. 'I'm sorry . . . ?' he asks.

'Why don't you ask Charmian up to your room after lunch?' Sandra says. 'I think she'd like that.'

Puzzled, Bérnard says, 'To my room?'

'Yes. I think she'd like that.'

He does not have time to ask any more questions – Charmian is there again, has taken her place at the table without a word, without looking at Bérnard, and is tucking into her next plate of microwaved lunch.

They are in the lobby afterwards when he says to her, 'You would like to see my room?'

90

The words, flat and matter-of-fact, just seem to escape him. He had not planned to say them, or to say anything.

She looks at her mother.

Sandra says, 'I'm going to have a little lie-down.'

She starts up the stairs on her own.

After a few moments, without saying anything else, they follow her. They follow her as far as the first floor. She is taking a breather where the stairs turn and just nods at them as they leave her there in the stairwell window's soiled light and enter, with Bérnard one pace ahead, the shadows of the passageway.

They stop, in semi-darkness, at Bérnard's door. He operates the key, and lets Charmian precede him into the room.

He is aware, following her into it, that the narrow room smells quite strongly. The curtains are drawn and his dirty clothes are all over the floor.

'I am sorry about the mess,' he says, shutting the door.

'Our room's just the same,' she tells him.

'Yes?'

They stand there, in the soupy air. He has that feeling, again, that he's dreaming this. She is huge. Her hugeness makes the whole situation seem more dreamlike.

'What do you want to do then?' she asks, still taking the place in – looking at the open suitcase still half-full of stuff on the neatly made bed, the one he doesn't sleep in, nearer the door.

He shrugs, as if he hasn't any idea what he wants to do, as if he hasn't even thought about it.

'Do you want to have a shower?' she asks without obvious enthusiasm, looking at him now.

'The shower doesn't work.'

'Oh, yeah – you said.'

'Yes.'

They stand there for a while longer, and then she says, 'Do you want to see my tits?'

After hesitating for a second, he says, 'Okay.'

In the dim light she takes her top off – a frilly-edged shirt like the one she was wearing last night – and extricates herself from the colossal bra. The tits hang down. Doughy, blue-veined, they sit on the shelf of the next tier of her, each one equivalent, more or less, to Bérnard's head. The nipples are pale pink, very pale, and the size of saucers – they occupy meaningful territory.

It is a strange moment – him just standing there, looking, while she waits.

He notices, eventually, that he has an erection.

She notices too, and with slow movements, she kneels in front of him and slides down the zip of his jeans.

Her mouth is soft and warm.

'You have done this before,' he says after a while, sincerely impressed.

She just shrugs. She wipes her mouth and moves back a bit. With a fair amount of shoving and tugging she gets herself out of her jeans.

Her legs do not quite have the overwhelmingly vertical quality of a normal leg – they have a definite and assertive horizontal dimension too. And not much in the way of knees. When she drags down her lace-edged pants, he sees, for a moment, somewhere among all the whitish flesh, a soft tuft of hair the colour of peanut butter.

She takes his hand and pulls him towards the bed where he sleeps, its sweaty mess of sheets.

While she stands there waiting, he sits on the edge of the bed and pulls his own jeans over his feet, his horizontally striped polo shirt over his head.

They are both naked now, and his hard-on is almost embarrassingly fervent. It almost hurts. She tries to lie back on the bed and open her legs. She needs to open her legs as wide as they will go or the flesh, pouring in from every direction, will obstruct him. The single bed, however, in its position flush to the wall, is simply too narrow for her to do that. She hardly fits onto it with her legs held parallel. After a few moments of frustration, Bérnard says, 'I know. We put the mattress on the floor, okay?'

They stand up and start to move the mattress onto the floor.

Bérnard's aching erection knocks against his stomach as he struggles with his end of the mattress.

They put it down on the brown tiles.

For a moment she stands there, in the veiled light, naked, looking like a huge melted candle, all drips and slumps of round-shaped waxy flesh. Pendulous surrenders. Those pale pink nipples the size of his face. There is just so much of her, it seems to him, standing at his end, stunned by how much he wants her now, so much of her, a quantity of woman nearly equal, if that were possible, to his need to possess it, physically, in every way imaginable. Though in fact at this moment that need seems infinite. His member nodding, his lungs pulling at the air, it seems that there is nothing else to him, that that is all he is.

She takes her place on the mattress.

And then it starts.

*

It lasts all afternoon, and into the evening. The light softens in the folds of the curtains. Finally they sleep for a while, and when he opens his eyes, she is dressing herself. Though she is wearing her shirt, she seems to be naked from the waist down.

'What time is it?' he asks.

'Seven,' she says. 'You coming to supper?'

She pulls one of the curtains open and admits a wedge of light in which she immediately finds her enormous knickers. Sitting heavily on the second bed, she manoeuvres them on.

'I don't think so,' Bérnard says. He is lying naked on the mattress on the floor, supine. Worn out by orgasms – at least five of them, he isn't sure exactly how many – he feels sleepy and immobile. The idea of dressing, of dragging himself down to the dining room, seems impossible.

'Fair enough,' Charmian says, working her jeans on now.

'I'll see you later then?' she says, when she is dressed, and standing at the door.

'Yes, see you,' Bérnard says.

When she has left, he lies there still, the air warm on his skin, his eyes fixed on the soiled paintwork of the ceiling as darkness slowly hides it.

Sounds arrive at the window
      a moped's noisy whirr
            a snatch of music
                  very distant shouts

7

At lunch the next day he is shy and embarrassed. The women are normal, the same as always. Charmian, focusing on the food, hardly says anything, hardly looks at him. Sandra talks. She says, 'You weren't at the pool this morning, Bernard.'

He says he went to the beach.

'Was that nice?' Sandra asks.

He says it was.

'We don't really like the sea, do we?'

Charmian says, trying to force some last strings of meat from a scrawny, bleeding chicken leg, 'It's okay.'

'I'm scared of sharks,' Sandra says.

'That is not a problem here, I think,' Bérnard tells her.

Sandra is adamant – 'Oh, there are sharks here. And anyway I always end up with my knickers full of sand. Sand everywhere. You know what I mean? Still finding it when we get home. Still finding it *weeks* later.'

'Okay,' Bérnard says.

'They sorted out your shower yet?' she asks him.

'No.'

'*No?* It's just disgraceful. You need to be more assertive, Bernard.'

'Yes,' he agrees, 'I think so . . .'

'You've been here nearly a week now and they still haven't sorted it out. It's just not acceptable.'

'No.'

Bérnard looks shyly at Charmian again. She seems to be avoiding his eye.

'We're going horse-riding this afternoon,' Sandra announces, improbably.

'Horse-riding?'

'Yes. Our rep sorted it out for us.'

'There is horse-riding?' Bérnard asks.

'Apparently.'

After lunch, while they wait in the lobby, Bérnard says to Charmian, 'I will see you later? You will come to my room?'

Despite the exhaustiveness of yesterday's session he finds, slightly to his own surprise, that he wants more.

She is eating a pack of toffee popcorn, the sort of thing she always has on her, in her handbag. She looks at him for a moment as if she doesn't know what he's talking about. Then she says, 'Yeah, okay.'

'Okay,' Bérnard says, feeling pleased with himself. 'I will see you later.'

He looks quickly at Sandra – it was awkward, somehow, to speak out with her there. She doesn't seem to have heard, though. She is just fanning herself with a brochure, and looking towards the brown glass door.

The afternoon passes slowly. Bérnard sprawls on the pummelled, stained mattress on the floor of his room. He looks out the window. Nothing interests him. The only thing he is able to think about is what will happen later, when Charmian shows up.

Finally, at about five there is a knock on the door.

He opens it, wearing only his pants.

It is not Charmian.

It is her mother – feathery blonde pudding-bowl, red face, even redder cleavage.

'Hello, Bernard,' she says.

He swings the door mostly shut, leaving only his shocked face visible to her. He doesn't know what to say. He doesn't even manage hello.

'Can I come in then?' Sandra asks.

'I need . . . I need to get dressed.'

'Don't bother about that,' Sandra says authoritatively. 'Come on – let me in.'

He opens the door and stands aside and Sandra advances, with obvious interest, into the narrow stale-smelling room.

The thin sundress drapes her distended physique.

Her face is papery, parched, especially around the eyes.

'Our room's just like this,' she says.

Bérnard is standing there in his pants.

'You look worried, Bernard,' she says. She looks at the mattress in its odd position on the floor. 'You've got nothing to worry about.' Her eyes stay on the mattress for a few seconds, as if inspecting it, and then she says, 'I've heard good things about you, Bernard.'

He looks puzzled.

'Oh, yes, very good things.'

'What things?' he asks worriedly.

She laughs at the expression on his face. 'Well, what d'you think? You know why I'm here, don't you?' she says, looking him in the eye.

It takes him a few seconds.

Then he understands.

'That's more like it,' she says, immediately noticing. She smiles, showing her small yellow teeth. 'She said you were insatiable, and you are as well.' She puts her hand on his smooth chest and says, 'Charmian'll be back tomorrow, don't worry. She's a bit sore today. Didn't think she was up to it. So I asked her if it was alright if I had a go. I've never had a Frenchman before,' she says, almost tremulously. 'I want you to show me what all the fuss is about – alright?' She is looking up at him, her hand on his face now. 'Will you do that for me, Bernard?' Her sea-green eyes are full of imploration. 'Will you?'

*

She leaves after dark – she was more eager, more humble than the younger woman – and he sleeps until eight in the morning, without waking once.

When he does wake, still lying on the mattress on the floor, the room is full of sunlight.

He walks to Porkies and has an egg roll, a Greek coffee.

And then, already in his trunks, and equipped with one of the Poseidon's small, scratchy towels, he makes his way to the sea.

As he had the previous day, he woke with a desire to swim in the sea.

It is still too early for the beach to be full. The Russians are there, of course, with their pungent cigarettes, their Thermoses of peat-coloured tea.

He walks down to the low surf – it is quite far from the road, the tide is out – and takes off his shirt and shoes. He puts his wallet in one of the shoes, and puts his shirt on top of them, weighing it down with an empty bottle he finds. The sand feels cold between his toes. The wind is quite strong and also feels cold when it blows. The waves, flopping onto the shore, are greenish. He lets the foaming surf wash the powdery sand from his white feet.

He wades out into the waves until they wet his long trunks, lifting his arms as the cloudy water rises around him, and lowering them as it sinks away. His skin puckers in the water, the windy air. An oncoming wave pours over him. For a moment, pouring over him, it obliterates everything in noise and push of water.

He feels its strength, feels it move away, and then he is in the smoother water on the far side of the falling waves. He is lying on the shining surface, the sea holding him, sun on his face and whispering salt water filling his ears. With his eyes shut, it seems to him that he can hear every grain of sand moving on the sea floor.

The tumbling surf feels warm now. It slides up the shore, stretching as far as its energy will take it, laying a lace of popping foam on the smoothed, shining sand.

Further up the sand is hot.

Tingling, he lies on it, lungs filling and emptying.

Arm over eyes, mouth open. Heart working.

Mind empty.

He is aware of nothing except the heat of the sun. The heat of the sun. Life.

3

1

It is ten o'clock in the morning and the kitchen is full of standing smoke and the smell of stuffed cabbages. 'So you're off to London?' Emma's mother says. Though she is not an old woman, probably not even fifty, she has the sour demeanour of someone disappointedly older. She looks older too as she moves ponderously around the kitchen in a shapeless tracksuit, or leans heavily on the grim, antiquated gas cooker.

Gábor says, 'We'll bring you something back. What do you want?'

'You don't need to bring me anything,' she says. Her hair is dyed a maximal black. White roots show. Outside the window, its sill crammed with dusty cacti, an arterial road growls. She lights a cigarette. 'I don't need anything,' she says.

'It's not about needing,' Gábor tells her. 'What do you *want*?' he asks.

She shrugs and lifts the cigarette to her seamed mouth, to rudimentary dentures. 'What have they got in London?'

Gábor laughs. 'What *haven't* they got?'

She puts a plate with two slices of bread on it on the small, square table next to Balázs's Michaelangelesque elbow. (His mouth working, he acknowledges it with a nod of his head.)

Gábor says, 'We'll find you something. Whatever.'

'You've got business there, have you?' the woman says.

'That's right.'

'And your friend?' she asks. (Balázs keeps on eating.) 'Has he got business there too?'

'He's helping me.'

'Is he?' She is staring straight at him, at 'Gábor's friend' – a sun-toughened lump of muscle in a tight T-shirt, skin tattooed, face lightly pockmarked.

'Security,' Gábor specifies.

'How's the cabbage?' she asks, still staring at Balázs. 'Okay?'

He looks up. 'Yeah,' he says. 'Thanks.'

She turns back to Gábor. 'And what's Emma going to do while you two take care of your business?'

'What do you think?' Gábor says. 'Shopping.'

They aren't actually friends. They know each other from the gym. Balázs is Gábor's personal trainer, though Gábor's attendance is uneven – he might turn up four or five times one week, then not for a whole month, thus undoing all the work they put in together on the machines and treadmills. He also eats and drinks too much of too many of the wrong things. When he does show up, Emma is sometimes with him, and sometimes she is there on her own. These days she is there more often than he is – Monday, Wednesday, Friday, every week. All the men who work at the gym want to fuck her, Balázs isn't alone in that. He wants it more than the others though – or he wants something more than they do, something more from her. It's starting to be an unhealthy, obsessive thing.

She doesn't even acknowledge him when she comes into the kitchen. Without seeming to (he is lighting a Park Lane) he notices that she is wearing the cork-soled platform shoes that make him think of porn-ography. In fact, he has an idea that Gábor – like not a few of the members of the gym, with their BMWs parked outside – is somehow involved in the production of pornography. One of the BMW drivers even offered him a part in a film, offered him a month's wages for one day's 'work' – Balázs had the well-muscled, tattoo-festooned look the producer favoured. His lightly pockmarked face was apparently not a problem, though the man had intimated that his size might be. Balázs had turned him down; partly to leave no hint that he was worried he might be too small, he had told him, or implied, that his girlfriend wouldn't let him do it. That wasn't true. He has no girlfriend.

Nor was it that he didn't need the money. He did. He needs whatever bits and pieces of extra work he can find. He has been employed by Gábor as a minder several times already – usually when he visits people at their offices, often in smart villas in the leafier parts of Budapest – though what Gábor does exactly, and what his business is in London, Balázs does not know.

The easyJet flight to Luton is four hours delayed. Gábor does not take this well. He seems especially concerned about Zoli, who for a while he is unable to reach on the phone. Zoli is evidently some associate of his in London, who will be meeting them at the airport, and Gábor is frantic at the idea that he might have to wait for them there for hours. When Gábor finally speaks to him, Zoli already knows about the delay.

They are by then installed at a table in the sun-dappled interior of the terminal. Gábor finishes apologising to Zoli and puts down his phone. 'It's alright,' he says.

Balázs nods and takes a mouthful of lager. The two men each have a half-litre of Heineken.

Balázs wonders how it will be in London. He imagines meetings in soporific offices, himself standing near the door, or waiting outside. For Emma, though, this is a sort of holiday so she and Gábor will probably want to have some time to themselves.

It is extremely stressful, he finds, to be in her presence outside the safely purposeful space of the gym. It was the same in the car, in

Gábor's Audi Q3, when she was there. Sometimes Gábor would go in somewhere and leave them in the car together – she in the front, Balázs in the back – and he would be so intensely aware of her presence, of the minuscule squeaks when she moved on the leather seat, or flipped down the sun visor to tweak an eyebrow in the vanity mirror, that, just to hold himself together, he had to fix his eyes on some object outside the darkened window and keep them there, unable to think about anything except how he had masturbated to her, twice, the previous night, which did not seem like a promising starting point for conversation. They never spoke. Sometimes they would be alone in the car for twenty minutes – Gábor was always away for at least twice as long as he said he would be – and they never spoke.

What she is like 'as a person' he has no idea. There is something princessy about her. She seems to look down on the staff in the gym – she isn't friendly with them anyway. The women who work there hate her, and it is assumed that she is with Gábor, who is slightly shorter than her, for his money. She always listens to music while she works out, possibly to stop people trying to talk to her. Balázs has never seen her smile.

He was surprised to see what her mother was like, where she lived. He had expected something smarter, something in Buda maybe, a house with roses in front and a well-preserved fifty-year old offering them coffee, not that wreck of a woman living in that smoky hole of a flat. The time-browned tower block, the odours and voices of the stairwell, the neglected pot plants by the yellow window where the stairs turned – those things were all familiar to him. Most of the people he knew emanated from places like that, himself included. That she did, however, was a surprise.

He finishes the Heineken and says something about stepping outside for a cigarette. Gábor, waggling his fingers at the screen of his phone, says, 'Yeah, okay. We'll just be here.' She does not even look up from her magazine.

He smokes on the observation terrace, from where, through a barrier of hardened glass, you can watch the planes taxiing to the end of the runway and taking off at intervals of a few minutes. Standing there and watching them through the feeble heat haze, the sound of the engines coming to him across several hundred metres of warm air, makes him think of the days he spent at Balad Air Base, with the rest of the Hungarian unit, waiting for the flight home. He now looks back on that year with something like nostalgia. He should have stayed in the army – it was safe there, and there were things to do. Since then he has just been treading water, waiting for something to happen . . . What was going to happen, though?

Gábor is standing there.

He lights a cigarette, a more expensive one than the Park Lanes Balázs smokes. 'Sorry about the delay,' he says.

In moulded plastic wrap-around shades, Balázs nods tolerantly.

Gábor seems nervous. It is as if he has something to say but isn't sure how to say it.

Balázs has started to think that maybe he doesn't have anything to say after all, when Gábor says, 'I should tell you what we'll be doing in London.'

There follow a few seconds during which they stare together at the scene in front of them – the open space of the airport in the sun, the smooth-skinned planes waiting in the shade near the terminal.

'Emma,' Gábor says, as if she were there and he were addressing her.

Balázs half-turns his head.

She isn't there.

Gábor says, 'Emma's going to be doing some work in London.'

They watch as a narrow-bodied Lufthansa turboprop starts its take-off. After a few hundred metres it leaps into the air with a steepness of ascent that is quite startling, as if it were being jerked into the sky on a string. They watch it dwindle to a point in the sky's hazy dazzle, and then, at some indefinite moment, disappear.

Gábor says, 'And your job . . .' He finds a more satisfactory pronoun. '*Our* job is to look after her. Okay?'

Balázs simply nods.

'Okay,' Gábor says, with finality, having performed what was obviously an embarrassing task. 'Just thought I'd tell you.' He drops his cigarette and extinguishes it under the toe of his trainer. 'See you inside.'

Mimicking his employer, Balázs toes out his own cigarette. Then he lights another, and squints out at the shimmer standing on the tarmac.

The flight is uneventful. The plane is full, but Gábor has paid for priority boarding and they have seats together – Balázs squashed into the window seat, Gábor stretching his legs in the aisle, and Emma in the middle, listening to music and staring at the plastic seat-back a few inches from the tip of her nose.

Balázs concentrates on the window. There is nothing to see, except a section of wing and fierce light on the endless expanse of white fluffiness far below. You would fall straight through it, he thinks, solid as it looks. He isn't sure, now, that he understood what Gábor meant when he said that Emma would be 'doing some work' in London. Had he even heard him properly? The light hurts his eyes and he half-lowers the plastic shutter. He folds his swollen hands in his lap and sits there, listening to the serrated whisper of her headphones, only just perceptible over the massive white noise of the labouring engines.

*

Zoli meets them at Luton airport in a long silver Mercedes.

Zoli is tall, and not unhandsome, and manages a moustache without looking silly. He has an air of slightly savage intelligence about him – he is in fact a doctor, a gynaecologist, though not currently practising. It is true that there is an unhealthy puffiness to his face, a swollenness, his eyes protruding more than is ideal, but Balázs does not notice these things until he sees them, intermittently, in the rear-view mirror – he is sitting in the back of the Mercedes with Emma, the lowered leather armrest emphatically separating them – as they make their way towards London.

They do so with single-minded speed, Zoli pushing the powerful car through holes in the traffic on the motorway. Holding onto the spring-hinged handle over the window, Balázs sees fleeting past a landscape somehow more thoroughly filled than any in his own country. It seems more orderly. It is very obviously more monied. It is early June and everything looks plump and fresh.

Gábor lights a cigarette. He is sitting in the front with Zoli, who immediately tells him to put it out.

Gábor apologises and presses it into the ashtray.

Still forcing the Mercedes forward, Zoli explains that he has borrowed it from a friend of his who has a luxury limousine hire service. He promised he wouldn't smoke in it.

'Sorry,' Gábor says again. Then he says, 'This is the new S-Class, yeah? Very nice.'

Zoli agrees vaguely.

He is in his early thirties, only a few years older than the others. Even so, Gábor is having trouble relating to him as an equal, something he normally manages quite easily with older and more important-seeming men. They *had* made some small talk as they drove out of the airport – though even that came to an abrupt end (Gábor was in the middle of saying something) when Zoli had to pay for the parking – and, as they head into London, Gábor's usual effortless friendliness seems to have faltered. Whether that is because he is simply intimidated by Zoli, or for some other reason, Balázs does not know. Seeing them shake hands in the arrivals lounge the situation had seemed to him to be this – they had met before but did not know each other well. Zoli and Emma, on the other hand, seemed never to have met. Gábor introduced them, with a strange sort of formality, and Zoli was very friendly to her – a wide smile, a pair of kisses. To Balázs – obviously the minder, with his shit clothes and his muscles – he had offered only a peremptory hand-shake. Then he had hurried them to short-term parking. They were in a hurry because, as Zoli said, 'There's one tonight' and what with the delay they were pressed for time, as they had first to go to the flat. Zoli, it seemed, had sorted out a flat for them to stay in while they were in London.

They spend some time stuck in traffic, the flow of the motorway silting up as it enters the metropolis. They are slowed by traffic lights. (The air conditioning is on – outside the tinted windows London, what they are able to see of it, swelters.) Then there are smaller thorough-fares, a more local look to things. There are neighbourhoods, parks, high streets, overflowing pubs. Smudged impressions of urban life on an early summer evening. All that goes on for much longer than Balázs imagined it would.

Finally they arrive. The flat is on a quiet street with a few trees in it. Small two-storey houses, all exactly the same. They wait with their luggage and Duty Free while Zoli opens the front door of one of them, swearing to himself as he struggles with the unfamiliar keys. They walk up some narrow stairs to the upper floor, where there is another strug-gle with the keys, and then they go in. One bedroom, white and sparse-ly furnished. For Balázs, the sofa in the living room, which overlooks the quiet road. On the other side of the landing, lurking mustily, is a windowless bathroom, into which Emma disappears with her washbag as soon as they arrive.

The men wait in the living room, Gábor on the sofa, Zoli pacing slowly and taking in the view from the uncurtained window, and Balázs just standing there staring at the old lion-coloured carpet and its mass of cigarette burns and other blemishes. Gábor wonders out loud where they might get something to eat. Zoli offers only an uninterested shrug. He says he doesn't know the area well – he lives in another part of London. Turning to the window again, he says the high street is nearby – there will be something there.

'D'you mind popping out,' Gábor says to Balázs, 'and getting some kebabs or something?'

Balázs looks up from the carpet. 'Okay.'

'Do you want something?' Gábor says.

The question is addressed to Zoli. He is still staring out the window and doesn't answer.

'Zoli?' Gábor says, tentatively. 'D'you want something?'

'No,' he says, without turning.

'Okay. So, yeah, just get some kebabs,' Gábor says.

Balázs nods. Then he asks, 'How many should I get?'

'I don't know. I'll have one. Do you want one?'

'Uh . . . Yeah.'

'And Emma might want one. Four?' Gábor suggests.

The stairs are almost too narrow for his shoulders, he almost has to make his way down sideways. The downstairs hall is dark, despite the frosted square pane in the front door, which opens as he nears the foot of the stairs and admits a youngish woman in a charcoal trouser suit. She leaves the door open for him. Otherwise they ignore each other.

It is very warm and light out in the street, a nice soft evening light that flatters the parked Merc. He lights a Park Lane, and then sets off through the little mazy streets of pinched, identical houses in the direction Zoli had indicated. It takes him twenty minutes to find the high street, and when he does there seems to be nowhere selling specifically kebabs. He walks up and down, sweating now in the summer evening, his orange T-shirt stuck to his skin. He notices a Polish supermarket, and the number of non-white people in the street. Then he phones Gábor. 'Is chicken okay?' he says.

Gábor doesn't seem to understand the question. 'What?'

'Chicken,' Balázs says emphatically. 'Is it okay?'

'Chicken?'

'Yeah.' He is standing outside a fried chicken place. The street lights have just flickered on, greenish. There is a faint smell of putrefaction. 'There's this fried chicken place . . .' he says.

'Yeah, that's fine,' Gábor tells him. Then, 'I mean – does it look okay?'

Balázs looks at the place. 'Yeah, it looks okay.'

'Yeah, fine,' Gábor says. 'And don't be too long. We've got to leave at ten.'

Balázs slips his phone into the hip pocket of his jeans and steps into the pitiless light. There is a small queue. While he waits he studies the menu – some backlit plastic panels – and when it is his turn, orders without mishap. (His English is quite fluent; he learned it in Iraq – it was the only way they could communicate with the Polish soldiers they were stationed with, and of course with whatever Americans they happened to meet.) He has trouble, though, finding his way back to the flat and has to phone Gábor again for help. Then they sit in the living room, he and Gábor, on the low sofa, eating with their hands from the flimsy grease-stained boxes. The overhead light is on in its torn paper shade and the stagnant air is full of loitering smoke and the smell of their meal, in the hurried eating of which Balázs is so involved that he does not notice Emma's presence until Zoli speaks.

Then he lifts his head.

His mouth is full and his fingers are shiny with the grease of the chicken pieces. She is standing in the doorway.

'Wow,' Zoli had said.

And now, as if speaking Balázs's thoughts, he says it again.

'*Wow.*'

Later, sitting in the pearly Merc, he finds an after-image of how she had looked, standing in the doorway, still singed into his vision as he stares out of the window at other things. The London night is as glossy as the page of a magazine. Nobody speaks now as the smoothly moving Merc takes them into the heart of the city, where the money is.

2

It is awkward, especially that first night. In the driver's seat, Gábor seems morose – he spends a lot of time with his head lolling on the leather headrest, staring out through the windscreen at the plutocratic side street in which they are parked, or studying the Tibetan inscription tattooed on the inside of his left forearm. Unusually for him, he hardly says a word for hours at a time. The hotel is a few minutes' walk away, on the avenue known as Park Lane – after which Balázs's inexpensive cigarettes, he has now learned, are named.

When they arrived, Zoli made a phone call. A few minutes later they were joined by a young woman, also Hungarian, who was introduced as Juli and who, it seemed, worked at the hotel. Then she, Zoli and Emma set off, and Gábor told Balázs that the two of them would be waiting there, in the parked Merc, until Emma returned.

It is a pretty miserable night they spend there, mostly in a silence exacerbated by the tepid stillness of the weather.

There are instances of listless conversation, such as when Gábor asks Balázs whether this is his first time in London. Balázs says it is, and Gábor suggests that he might like to do some sightseeing. When Balázs, showing polite interest, asks what he should see, Gábor seems at a loss for a few moments, then mentions Madame Tussauds. 'They have waxworks of famous people,' he says. 'You know.' He tries to think of one, a famous person. 'Messi,' he says finally. 'Whatever. Emma wants to see it. Anyway, it's something for you to do, if you want.'

'Okay, yeah,' Balázs says, nodding thoughtfully.

They then lapse into a long silence, except for Gábor's index finger tapping the upholstered steering wheel, a sound like slow dripping, slowly filling a dark sink of preoccupation from which Balázs's next question, asked some time later, seems mysteriously to flow.

He asks Gábor how he knows Zoli.

'Zoli?' Gábor seems surprised that it is something Balázs would have any interest in. 'Uh,' he says, as if he has actually forgotten. 'Friend of a friend. You know.' There is another longish pause and then, perhaps finding that it is something he wants to talk about after all, Gábor goes on. 'I met him last time I was here, in London. He suggested we set something up.'

*

She taps on the misted window just after five in the morning. It is light and quite cold. Not much is said as Gábor, waking, unlocks the door and she gets in. Nor while he fiddles with the satnav. Then he switches on the engine, sets the de-mister noisily to work on the windows, and they pull out into the empty street.

She looks tired, more than anything, still in her skimpy dress and heels – though now she has shed the shoes and drawn her legs up under her on the seat. The two men managed a few hours' sleep while they waited; it is hard to say whether she has. Her brown-ringed eyes suggest not. Her residual alertness seems chemically assisted.

'Everything was okay?' Gábor says eventually, while they wait at a traffic light.

'M-hm.'

'Are you hungry?' is his next question, a minute or so later.

'I don't know,' she says. 'Maybe.'

'You should eat something,' he advises.

'Okay.'

They stop at a McDonald's and Balázs is sent in. He is aware, in her presence, of his own obvious stink – he has been wearing the same T-shirt for twenty-four hours. She wants a Big Mac and large fries, and a Diet Coke.

'Thanks,' she says, when he gets back to the car and, turning in the passenger seat, passes her the brown bag.

It is the first word she has ever spoken to him.

To her, he says, 'No problem,' though she might not have heard, as at that moment Gábor starts the engine.

She pushes the plastic straw into the cup's lid and starts to drink.

Zoli shows up in the middle of the afternoon, while they are all still asleep.

Gábor emerges vague and tousled in a singlet and boxer shorts to hand over Zoli's share of the money, which he does in the recessed corner of the living room that has been turned into a derisory pine kitchenette. Zoli then hands out strongly chilled lagers and, as they open them, asks after Emma. She has not been seen since the morning – not by Balázs anyway – when she disappeared into the bedroom as soon as they got back to the flat.

Gábor had joined her soon after, leaving Balázs to press his face into the odorous sofa as he tried to escape the light that flooded in through the windows and ignore the sounds from the street, intermittent but easily audible from the first floor, and fall asleep. At about ten o'clock, still unable to sleep, he had masturbated under a weak shower to a torrent of images of Emma in a vaguely delineated hotel room, images of the sort that had filled his head all night. A shocking quantity of seed turned down the plughole. Some time after that, with a T-shirt tied over his eyes, he did finally fall asleep.

'So everything went okay?' Zoli says, and swigs.

'Yeah, I think so,' Gábor says, with a sort of sleepy snuffle. They are standing at the pine breakfast bar.

'I know him, that guy,' Zoli says. 'He's okay. He's a nice guy. I put him in first because I knew he wouldn't cause any hassle.'

Gábor just nods.

'Some of the others I don't know,' Zoli says. And then, 'I'm not expecting any hassle, though.'

'No,' Gábor says.

'These aren't people who want to talk to the police, to journalists, you know what I mean. They've got too much to lose. Some of them are famous, I think.'

'Yeah?' Gábor says. He doesn't seem interested.

'I think so,' Zoli says, with a nod and a swig. 'She still asleep?' he asks.

'Yeah,' Gábor says.

Zoli doesn't stay long, and after he leaves Gábor goes back to bed. If he had had a bed, Balázs might have done the same. Instead he goes out into the blinding day and gets another box of chicken pieces from the same place as the night before. Then he lies on the sofa with the window open, smoking and trying to read a book – *Harry Potter és a Titkok Kamrája*. He is working his way slowly through the series.

He finds it difficult to focus on the story.

Then he finds it difficult to focus on the words.

When he wakes up she is standing in the doorway, in a dressing gown. He has no idea what time it is. It is still daylight.

'Hi,' she says in a neutral voice.

'Hi.' He sits up. 'What, uh, what time is it?'

'I don't know,' she says. 'Gábor wants to go shopping.'

Balázs is not sure what to say.

She tilts her head as if looking at something upside down – *Harry Potter és a Titkok Kamrája*. 'Is that any good?' she asks.

'Uh.' He picks it up and looks at the front, as if the answer might be there. 'It's alright,' he says. He tries to think of something else to say about it.

She stays there for a few moments more, in the mote-filled afternoon light.

Then she yawns, and leaves.

*

Later, when they are sitting in the parked Merc, Gábor tells him about the shopping trip – two and a half hours in the scrum of Oxford Street, followed by a meal in the red velvet interior of an Angus Steakhouse. They have been talking more than they did the first night, the two men. It is drizzling. Maybe that helps, the way the surrounding hubbub softens the silence. The fact is, they do not know each other well. Even in the context of the gym they are not particularly friendly.

At about midnight, Balázs leaves the Merc and walks through the drizzle to the nearby KFC to get their 'lunch' – two 'Fully Loaded' meals.

Taking his seat again, he finds Gábor in a pensive mood. 'Sometimes I worry about my attitude to women,' Gábor says. Water trickles down the window against which his head is silhouetted. 'D'you worry about that?'

Balázs has just bitten into his chicken fillet burger and cannot immediately answer. When he has swallowed what is in his mouth, he says, 'What d'you mean?'

'Just my attitude to women,' Gábor says miserably. 'Maybe it isn't healthy.' He turns to Balázs, still wet in the passenger seat, and says, 'What do you think?'

Balázs just stares at him.

'What would you do in my position?' Gábor asks.

'What would *I* do?'

'Yeah, if you were in my position.'

'What d'you mean?'

'If you and Emma were ... whatever,' Gábor says impatiently. 'Would you let her do this?'

'Would I *let* her?'

'Yeah.'

Balázs is having trouble imagining, with any emotional specificity, the situation Gábor wants him to – a situation in which he and Emma were ... whatever. Sex, is all he is able to imagine, and that of an impossibly lubricious kind. 'Don' know,' he says. And then, trying to be more helpful, 'Maybe.'

'You would?'

'Well ...' Balázs attempts to think about it honestly. 'Maybe not,' he says. 'It depends.'

'On what?'

'On what ... You know ... What sort of relationship ...?'

'*That's* it,' Gábor says. 'That's my point. That's what I'm talking about.' He turns his attention, finally, to the food in his lap.

'You're worried this won't be, uh ... this won't be positive for your relationship?' Balázs asks.

'Yeah,' Gábor says simply, and pushes a sheaf of French fries into his mouth.

'Well ... D'you talk to her about it?'

Gábor shakes his head, and speaks with his mouth full. 'Not really, to be honest. I mean, I try sometimes. She doesn't want to. Whatever.'

They eat.

'It's her birthday next week.' Gábor sounds slightly wistful now.

'Yeah?'

'Yeah. I'm taking her to a kind of wellness spa place.'

'Yeah?' Balázs says again.

'In Slovakia. They've got this luxury hotel up in the mountains. We've been there before. Kempinski hotel. You know those hotels?'

Balázs frowns, as if trying to remember, then shakes his head.

'Fucking nice,' Gábor tells him. 'There's this lake, surrounded by mountain peaks – she loves that shit. They've got every kind of treatment,' he says. 'Literally. You know. Mud baths, whatever.'

*

The days pass, and every day is the same, from Zoli's visit in the mid-afternoon, through the long night, to the stop at McDonald's in the smeary sun and the spasm in the mildewed shower, which smoothes the way to sleep.

Still, his sleep is poor. He feels stretched thin with fatigue, feels as insubstantial sometimes as the sails of smoke that sag in the windless air of the warm living room. Sometimes he feels transparent, at other times insufferably solid, but all the time there is the small furtive thrill of inhabiting the same space as her. Of using, for instance, the same bathroom. The small, water-stained bathroom is full of her stuff. He examines it with intense interest.

If her proximity thrills him, however, it tortures him as well in the long pallid hours of each afternoon, as he lies on the sofa knowing that she is there, on the other side of the flimsy wall, at which he stares as if trying to see through it, while the fantasies unspool in his smooth skull.

As for her, he marvels at how fresh she seems. If on Monday, which was the fourth day, she looked a little haggard and hungover when she appeared at four o'clock in the afternoon in her old towelling dressing gown, it was nothing she was not able to magic away with twenty minutes in front of the bathroom mirror.

Monday was the night they had the problem, the night of the incident. It was still early, not even eleven, when Gábor got the text. 'Shit,' he said.

'What is it?'

'It's from Emma.'

'What's it say?' Balázs asked.

'Nothing.'

'Isn't that the signal?'

'Maybe it's a mistake,' Gábor said.

'Isn't it the signal?' Balázs asked again.

'Yeah,' Gábor sighed. 'Okay,' he said heavily, 'let's go.' He was scared, Balázs thought. That's why he was taking the hammer – he had a hammer with him, he kept it under the driver's seat. Now it was up his sleeve.

They started to walk towards the hotel. Gábor was shaking his head, his face full of sorrowful intensity and fear. As they walked, he phoned Juli, who was working nights all week. She said she would meet them at the staff entrance.

She was waiting there, smoking nervously, when they arrived.

They followed her along a passageway with a green plastic floor, to the service stairs. 'It's the fourth floor,' she told them, handing Gábor the key card. Gábor nodded, and he and Balázs started solemnly up the stairs.

Scuffed walls, a neon tube over each landing.

'You ready?' Gábor asked.

Balázs shrugged.

Gábor said, 'This is where you earn your money.'

'Okay.'

'I'll make sure she's okay, you deal with him. I mean, if there's any trouble.'

'Okay.'

'And the minimum of necessary force, yeah? I know I don't need to tell you that. We don't want . . . You know what I mean.'

He was worrying about the police, obviously. It was something that was on Balázs's mind too. 'Why don't you leave the hammer here?' he said, stopping.

'What?'

'Leave the hammer here. You can get it later.'

'Why?'

Balázs wondered how to put it. 'Look,' he said, 'if . . .' He started again. 'Let's say the police get involved, and you've got a hammer . . . A *weapon*. D'you see what I'm saying? We won't need it anyway.'

Gábor was doubtful. 'We won't need it?'

'No.'

'Are you sure?' After a further hesitation, Gábor said, 'Okay.' He put the hammer down quietly and they passed through a fire door into the heavy, monied hush of the hallway on the other side. It was unlike anywhere Balázs had ever been, the sort of place he had only seen in American films – that was how it felt, like he was in an American film.

They were standing outside 425, the lacquered woodwork of the door. Listening, they heard nothing. Then Gábor swiped the sensor, the lock whirred and disengaged, and they went in.

'What's this?' Gábor said. He sounded surprised, almost disappointed.

There were three people in the room, which was large and well lit – Emma and two Indian men, all sitting down, and all seemingly waiting patiently, in polite silence.

'Okay, listen,' one of the Indians said immediately, standing. 'We want to talk to you.' He was much the older of the two of them and had been sitting on an upholstered chair between the tall, draped windows.

Gábor ignored him and said to Emma, in Hungarian, 'What's going on?'

She shrugged. 'There are two of them.'

'I can see that. What's been happening?'

'Nothing.'

The older man was wearing a tweed jacket and seemed to be waiting for Gábor to finish speaking to Emma.

Gábor turned to him and said, in English, 'Only one of you can be here.'

'Yes, this is what we want to talk to you about,' the man said.

'Only one of you,' Gábor told him again.

'I understand, I understand . . .'

'Okay, you understand. So one of you go. Please.'

The Indians – the older with his nice jacket and manners, his elegant cologne; the younger, scrawny in a Lacoste polo shirt, and still in his seat – were profoundly unintimidating. There was a fairly obvious sense that Balázs, standing with his arms folded near the door, displacing a lot of air, would be able to deal with them simultaneously if necessary. The older man's exaggerated politeness, with its weird edge of suppressed hysteria, may just have been an acknowledgement of that.

'I understand,' he was saying yet again. 'The young lady told us that only one of us could, uh . . . you know,' he said. 'I understand. That's okay. That's okay. My, uh, my young friend will be . . . will be doing that.'

Moving only his eyes, Balázs looked at the younger man. He was about twenty perhaps, or even younger, and, slumped in his seat, staring at his loafers, seemed not even to be following what was happening.

Gábor said to Emma, again in Hungarian, 'Do you have the money?'

She nodded.

'Who paid you?'

She pointed to the older Indian, who said, 'I just want to watch.'

Gábor turned to him. 'You want to watch?'

'Yes.'

'*Baszd meg.*'

'Is it a problem?'

'Yes, it's a problem,' Gábor said in a louder voice.

'Why?'

'Why? *Why?*' With what seemed to be a sudden loss of temper, Gábor seized the man by the scruff of his jacket and first swung and then started shoving him towards the door, until Balázs, packed into his lurid turquoise shirt, intervened and separated them.

There was a moment of tense quiet while Gábor, evidently struggling to maintain a professional demeanour, focused on his shoes.

Then he looked up and said, tautly, 'It's a problem, okay. A problem. Please?' With stiff politeness, an extended hand, he showed the man the door.

The Indian was starting to sweat somewhat. Nevertheless he seemed determined to negotiate it out. Panting slightly, he said, 'No, just a minute. Please. I also say please. Just a minute.'

'Let's go,' Gábor said.

'Please,' the man went on. 'Let's just talk for a minute. Let's just talk. Your friend said the money was for a whole night with the, the young lady. Your friend said that.'

'Yes,' Gábor said, with strained patience.

'Now, listen,' the Indian said, his pate starting to shine, 'what I want to suggest is, uh, that we only take an hour or two of her time – *but* that I'm allowed to watch. Just watch! Is that fair? Doesn't that seem fair?'

'Look,' Gábor said. 'She doesn't do stuff like that, okay? She's a nice girl.'

'Oh, she's a nice girl – of course she's a nice girl . . .'

'Yeah, she's a nice girl. Let's go.'

'Okay, you want more money,' the Indian said, as if surrendering, as Gábor took hold of his arm. 'How much? How much? A thousand pounds,' he offered.

Gábor, transparently surprised by the size of the offer, did not say anything. He swallowed cautiously and looked at Emma.

'Okay? A thousand pounds?'

'Uh,' Gábor said, frowning as if trying to work something out. He seemed unable to do so, however, and finally said, 'It's up to her.'

'Of course!' The man turned smartly to Emma. She was sitting, with some dignity, in a tub chair. The man said, 'A thousand pounds, madam, simply to sit in the corner. I'll be as quiet as a mouse. What say you?'

Even the young Indian lifted his overlarge head, with its cockatooish plume of blow-dried hair, and looked at her now as they all waited to hear what she would answer.

'Just say no,' Gábor said to her, in their own language. 'Just say no, and we'll get rid of him.'

'Why?' she said finally. 'What difference does it make?'

Gábor's face underwent a very slight distortion.

'What difference does it make?' she said again.

'You'll do it then?'

She shrugged, and Gábor turned to the waiting Indian, who had not understood the exchange, and said, 'Okay. Where's the money?'

'I, uh, I have it here.' He took from the inside pocket of his jacket a tan leather wallet.

As he counted out the money, Gábor said, 'You just watch.'

125

'Of course, of course,' the man said distractedly.

'You don't touch.'

A shake of the shining head. 'No.'

'Any trouble, we'll be here.'

The man held out the money. 'I promise you, there won't be any trouble.'

'Give the money to her,' Gábor said.

'Oh, excuse me. *Madame?*'

Emma stood up – even without her shoes she was taller than the dapper man – and took the money and put it in the small handbag which was on one of the tables next to the brocaded expanse of the bed.

'Okay,' Gábor said to Balázs, while she was doing that. 'Let's go.'

Gábor hardly spoke for the rest of the night, his face swallowed by shadow in the parked Merc. He had speculated bitterly, as they walked back, on the nature of the Indian's perversion, but once they had taken their seats on the anthracite leather, he seemed to have nothing more to say.

The previous night had also challenged his composure, though not nearly to the same extent. Zoli had told them, when he came as usual to collect his money, that the client for that night did not want to go to the hotel, so they should go instead to his house. It turned out to be in a grand square of stucco terraces. The two men had watched through the windscreen as Emma, in the familiar little flesh-coloured sheath of a dress, went up the steps to the porticoed entrance, with its big hanging lantern, and pushed the doorbell. A minute later the house swallowed her.

'Whatever,' Gábor said.

The house spat her out at four in the morning, just as the birds were starting to sing in the railinged gardens.

She was drunk. As they drove through the empty streets, she apologised for hiccupping, and then, when she couldn't stop, seemed to get the giggles.

'You're in a good mood,' Gábor said, fixing her momentarily in the rear-view mirror. 'D'you have fun then?'

'Don't be stupid,' she said softly.

'You're drunk.'

'Yes, I'm drunk. I've had about two bottles of champagne.'

'Champagne?' Gábor said. 'Nice.'

She ignored the sarcasm. 'Not really.'

'No? Did he make you drink it?'

She turned to the window, to the blue streets, dawn seeping into them. Monday morning. 'It helps,' she said.

*

Tuesday night, the one after the incident with the Indians, is her night off. When she appears as usual at four p.m., Gábor says that Zoli has invited them out. He seems surprised and hurt when she tells him she is tired and wants to stay in. Later he tries again to persuade her – Balázs hears this through the wall – and when he meets with no success, emerges himself in a sharply pressed indigo shirt and extends the invitation half-heartedly to Balázs, who says that he, too, is tired and wants to stay in. Without making any effort to persuade *him*, Gábor phones Zoli and apologetically passes on the news that Emma won't be joining them.

'Nah,' he says, standing in the middle of the living room with his phone to his ear, 'nah, she wants to stay in. She says she wants to stay in.' Zoli says something. 'I did tell her that,' Gábor says. Zoli makes some other point, and Gábor says, with feeling, 'I know, I know.' Finally Zoli desists and Gábor mixes a JD and Coke in the pine kitchenette, and having hurriedly swallowed it, heads out into the evening.

When the slam of the door has dissipated, a very pure silence settles on the small flat.

Balázs, pretending to read *Harry Potter és a Titkok Kamrája*, listens hard for any sound, any sign of life from the other room.

After about twenty minutes he hears what sounds like the squeak of a bedspring.

Some time after that – quite a long time, during which his hopeful theory that she turned down the night out specifically so that she would find herself alone in the flat with him is severely tested by the uninterrupted silence – he puts down the novel, with which he is making little progress and, passing quietly through the hall, goes out to get himself some supper.

Her light was on when he left – he saw it under the door.

When he gets back he sees, with a squeeze of disappointment, that it is off. He should have tapped on her door before he went out and asked if she wanted anything. That would have been the obvious thing to do. Now it is too late. Without enthusiasm, he eats his food and, when he has finished, lights the first of a long sequence of Park Lanes.

When he finally falls asleep, it is after two o'clock and the ashtray on the floor next to the sofa is full.

3

'Is there any coffee?' she asks, hearing him stir.

She is in the kitchenette, in her dressing gown, opening pine cupboards.

'No,' he says, squinting. The room is full of clean sunlight. 'I don't think so.'

'I only drink coffee in the morning,' she explains. It is ten o'clock in the morning, a time when they are normally asleep.

Naked in his sleeping bag but for a pair of black nylon briefs, Balázs does not move from where he is. 'Did . . . Did Gábor get back?' he asks.

'He's sleeping,' she says.

She has stopped searching the cupboards and is just staring at the kitchenette.

'Where can I get some coffee?' she wonders.

And as if it were the simplest thing in the world, he makes his suggestion.

'If you like,' he says, 'I know a place.'

She looks at him, sitting there, up to his waist in the sleeping bag, his tattooed biceps and toaster-like pecs, his small pale eyes obscurely imploring.

They are in the habit of speaking to each other now, up to a point. Still, it feels extremely intimate to pass through the downstairs hall together, to leave the house, and walk down the street.

Balázs knows the way to the high street well by now and has seen some coffee places there, some with a few metal tables outside on the narrow, stained pavement. They sit on aluminium chairs, under a restless awning. He is wearing his sunglasses, the soldierly plastic wraparounds with their iridescent wing-shaped lenses, and his orange T-shirt is tucked into his jeans. He sucks at the lid of his coffee cup and looks at the sunny, trading street. 'Nice day,' he says.

Also wearing sunglasses, she just smiles, not unsympathetically.

'Did you sleep okay?' he asks.

She says she did.

As if aware of some possible impropriety in the situation, she is, it seems, pointedly unforthcoming.

There is a silence.

Wondering what to say next, Balázs has another go at his coffee cup.

Unable to think of anything, he offers her a Park Lane, which she takes. He lights it for her. There is a simple glass ashtray on the aluminium tabletop.

Then he says, 'I thought I might have a look round today. See some sights or whatever.' He had hoped she would show some immediate enthusiasm for this idea but she doesn't. Sitting on the other side of the little round table in a sleeveless top that shows the tattooed sprig of barbed wire encircling her slender upper arm, she just takes a pull of the Park Lane and says nothing. 'There must be loads to see here,' he says. When she still doesn't play along, he opts for a more direct approach, and asks, 'There anything you want to see? While we're here.'

She sort of laughs. 'I don't know.'

The laugh is very discouraging, and he is about to drop the whole subject, when she says, without seeming interested, 'What is there?'

'Well, uh.' He tries to sound spontaneous. 'There's some waxworks place, isn't there?'

'Oh, that.' She seems a lot less into it than Gábor had suggested.

'What about that?' he suggests.

She says she doesn't know where it is.

He says it wouldn't be a problem to find out.

She seems amused now. She is smiling at him as if he amuses her. 'Are you really interested?'

He shrugs. 'Yeah,' he says. 'Why not?'

'I don't know,' she says. 'You don't seem like that sort of person.'

'What sort of person?'

Still evasively smiling, she says, 'You know what I mean.'

'The sort who's interested in waxworks?'

'Yes.'

'I'm interested in waxworks,' he says, implausibly. And then, seeing an opening, 'What sort of person *do* I seem like?'

She ignores the question. 'What time is it?'

He looks at his watch, its muddle of intersecting dials, most of which seem to have no function, and tells her.

'You're really interested?' she asks.

And with a totally straight face, he says, 'Yeah.'

They have to take the underground, and he enjoys, standing in the noisy train, the envy of the other men, the way they watch her in her tall shoes and torn denim. She seems not to notice that she is being looked at, or to notice anything, as she sways with the movements of the train, her sunglasses fixed on some advertisement for a dating service or hair-loss product, or the diagram of the line.

She had said to Balázs, while they were waiting on the platform at Finsbury Park, that she was impressed by his English. Where had he learned it? 'Iraq,' he said, surprisingly, and he told her, while they waited, about his time there. He didn't try to pretend that it had been

131

exciting, or even very interesting. He had spent more or less the entire time in various town-sized bases, playing computer games in plain, air-conditioned rooms and eating American food. He had spoken to not a single Iraqi – except one interpreter who had tried to sell him drugs – and had never fired his weapon. He *had* done some patrols, though even that only involved travelling around in an armoured vehicle, peering through a tiny window at the flat, beige land. Nothing had ever happened. His most abiding memory, he tells her, was of the heat, the way it took you the moment you stepped out of the air conditioning, the instant watery profuseness of the sweat.

Standing on the up escalator at Baker Street Station, he asks her which famous person she is most looking forward to seeing in the museum. Her answer does not please him. He fucking hates Johnny Depp and those pirate films he is in. More than that, it seems possible that in selecting Depp, she was sending a deliberate message that he, Balázs, was 'not her type', that he shouldn't get any ideas. (Why hadn't she said Bruce Willis?) He wishes he hadn't asked her the question, and doesn't speak again as they leave the station.

Out in the sunlight at street level, they look for the museum. When they find it, the queue of people waiting 'to meet the stars' is shocking. Where it starts, far up a side street, there is a sort of diffuse, subsidiary queue of people wondering whether to join the main queue, which is marked, every twenty metres or so, with signs indicating how long the wait will be from that point – *Approx. 2½ hrs* is the first, though that itself is quite far from where the queue is now being supplied with new material. Further ahead – in the vicinity of *Approx. 1 hr* – mime artists and a man on stilts attempt to entertain distraught and exhausted children.

Balázs, absorbing the situation with weary stoicism, takes his place in the queue. He is docile and long-suffering when it comes to queuing – he takes a sort of joyless pride in waiting his turn, and in not being deterred by having to do so.

'We're not really going to wait, are we?' she says, standing beside him.

'Well . . .'

She laughs. 'I mean, we'll be here for hours.'

'Yeah,' Balázs agrees.

'Do we really want to do that?'

'I dunno.'

She folds her arms and they stand there for a minute or two in the fresh shade of the early-summer morning, a minute or two during which the queue does not move at all, and Balázs senses a souring of her mood – she has started to frown at her own feet. 'Shou' we do something else then?' he ventures, lighting a Park Lane.

'Like what?' she asks.

He shrugs, looks uninspired.

'We could just walk a bit,' she suggests.

There is a glimmer of green at the end of the side street and they start to walk towards it, initially in silence.

Just as the silence is threatening to turn awkward, she says, 'When did you get back from Iraq?'

'Uh.' He has to think for a moment. 'Eight years ago.'

It seems amazing – awful – that eight *years* have passed since then.

In fact it is more – it was December 2004, that winter day, the windy airfield. Home. 'Eight and a half,' he says, making the amendment. He was twenty then, had been in the army since he was eighteen. He tells her that he stayed in the army for a year or two after that.

'And what have you been doing since then?' she asks. 'Working at the gym?'

'Yeah,' he says, 'working at the gym, and some other things.'

'What sort of things?'

'I was a security guard for a bit.' He asks her if she knows a particular Tesco in Budapest. She says she does. 'There,' he says.

The subject seems likely to peter out at this point, and then she says, 'What was that like?'

What was that like? Well, there was the humid nylon pseudo-law-enforcement uniform, the hours of loitering near the entrance, the dull CCTV screens of the security station. 'It was okay,' he says.

They have arrived at a perpendicular street. On the other side is a stunning cliff face of pristine cream houses, through a wide opening in which the green trees of a park are visible. The street they are walking down goes through the opening, where it acquires a red tarmac cycle lane, and on into the park. They wait at the lights while the traffic streams past. This place, he thinks, staring at the high houses while they wait, is *made* of money. He says, 'I got sacked in the end. From Tesco.'

'Why was that?'

'Suspected collusion with shoplifters,' he says.

'Suspected?'

'Yeah, suspected. I didn't collude with anybody.'

'Why did they suspect you then?'

'Well, they were losing a lot of stuff. So I wasn't much good at the job anyway.' It was true that he had had a tendency to fall for what turned out to be diversionary tactics. The staged scuffle, the fake heart attack, the swarthy old woman selling violets, the old man with the never-ending story. He was probably a soft touch that way. That might have been what the manager thought too. Still, it's easier to sack someone for being dishonest.

'Isn't it?' he says.

They have entered the park and are walking along an asphalt path that follows the edge of a thin, green lake. There aren't many people around.

'Did you contest it?' she asks.

'Nah. They said if I went quietly they'd give me a decent reference, so . . .' He shrugs.

'And did they?'

'Yeah,' he admits.

'And then you got the job at the gym?'

'Well, yeah, eventually.'

At its narrowest point, there is a small wooden bridge over the lake and they walk out onto it.

'But that's not really enough,' he says. 'In itself. It's only part-time really. So I've got to do other stuff as well.'

'Stuff like this,' she suggests.

'Well, yeah,' he says. They have stopped on the bridge, and looking out at the murky green water he lights a cigarette. He seems uneasy, even embarrassed, that she has touched on why they are in London – or had he touched on it first? He hadn't meant to, he doesn't think. Indeed, he shies away from the subject, and says, 'When I was a kid, I wanted to be a water-polo player.'

'Did you?'

'Yeah. I was alright,' he tells her. 'I thought I might do it professionally.'

'And?'

'I don't know,' he says. 'It didn't happen somehow. Maybe I wasn't aggressive enough. There were other guys, more aggressive.' He is squinting at the water. 'Anyway, it didn't happen.'

'That's a shame.'

'Yeah.' He had thought it was something he had entirely come to terms with. Just for a moment, though, he feels the pain of it again – feels it, in fact, more nearly, more immediately than he ever has before. It's as though he understands, for the first time, exactly what was at stake – his whole life, everything.

135

'What did you want to do,' he asks, 'when you were a kid?'

The question sounds odd somehow.

She seems to think, for a few seconds, about whether to answer it at all.

'I don't know,' she says. 'Escape.'

She puts her hands on the sun-pocked paint of the wooden bridge and looks down into the water. Green water, feathers floating on it. 'It's a shame we don't have some bread for those ducks. There's something so restful about feeding ducks, isn't there?'

Balázs joins her at the handrail.

'Don't you find?'

'Uh . . .'

'It's probably not something you do much, is it?' she says, smiling at him. 'A big tough man like you.'

'Well, no, not much.'

'I was joking,' she says.

'Okay.'

'When I was little,' she says, 'we used to go and stay with my grand-parents. They lived in a village somewhere. I used to feed the chickens. I didn't like that, actually. They were so smelly.'

'Yeah, chickens stink,' Balázs says, like someone who knows.

She laughs. 'Don't they? They really do.'

They start to walk again, under trees now, on the other side of the lake, its wind-wrinkled surface visible through stirring leaves – the bloodstain-coloured leaves of a copper beech.

'It's nice this park, isn't it?' she says.

He looks around, as if he had not noticed until now that they were *in* a park. 'Yeah,' he says.

'It's so well *kept*. Look at those flower beds. Are you in a relationship at the moment?' she asks matter-of-factly.

Startled by the question, he says, 'Uh, no, not at the moment.'

They walk on, and seconds pass without him saying anything more on the subject. He feels he should, somehow. What is there to say, though? The answer is no. 'Not at the moment,' he says again.

Without meaning to they seem to have walked in a circle and are back at the place where they entered the park, the road with the red tarmac cycle lane.

He says, 'Uh, d'you wanna get a drink or something?'

In the muted red interior of a pub called the Globe, with Hogarth reproductions on the striped wallpaper, while the traffic tumbles past outside, they sit with pints, and a few other tourists.

'So how long have you and Gábor been . . . ?' he asks, not knowing quite how to put it. Gábor is in fact the last thing he wants to talk about, but he can't think of anything else to say.

'About a year,' she says.

'How'd you meet?' Balázs asks, stuck with the subject now.

'Through work,' she says. 'He was involved with a film I made. We met that way.'

'He was *involved*?'

'Yes.'

'How?' And then, almost apologetically, 'I've just never been sure what he . . . ?'

'The technical side,' she says smoothly. 'Post-production. Distribution. More distribution. He knows about computers. Or he knows people who do. You know – it's mostly online.'

'Okay.' Balázs lifts his pint.

'That was my last film, actually,' she tells him a few moments later, as if it is something that might interest him.

'Oh, yeah?'

137

'Gábor wanted me to stop,' she explains. 'He was fine with it at first. I mean, he was more than fine with it.' She laughs. 'I'm pretty sure he liked it, actually. But then, when we'd been together for a few months, it started to bother him. That's when he said he wanted me to stop.'

Balázs says, 'But he's okay with you doing . . . I mean . . .'

'This?' she says.

'Yeah.'

'Well, it wasn't his idea, if that's what you mean.'

'No?'

'No.' Then, as if something has occurred to her, she says, 'Did he tell you it was?'

Balázs thinks for a second. 'No.'

'It was Zoli's idea,' she says. 'You know Zoli.'

'Zoli, yeah.'

'It was his idea.'

'He's a friend of Gábor's, yeah?'

'Not really. I mean, they're not really *friends*. They know each other somehow.'

'It was his idea then,' Balázs says, unwilling now to leave it there, though trying not to show quite how interested he is.

'Well, he told me how much money I could make here, and said he'd sort it out. I said I'd think about it. Gábor didn't like the idea. He didn't want me to do it.'

'Well . . . I don't know,' Balázs says thoughtfully.

The open doors of the pub admit the passing wail of a police siren.

'I wouldn't be able to live with it, if I was him.'

She smiles. 'That's a nice thing to say. Can we smoke in here?'

'Uh.' He looks for ashtrays, sees *No Smoking* signs. 'I don't think so.'

'Do you want to go outside then?'

They stand on the pavement in the steady traffic noise. 'Zoli wants me to move here,' she shouts.

'Does he?'

'He *suggested* it. The first night, when we were in the hotel, and Gábor wasn't there. He said I should move here. He said he'd set me up somewhere nice. My own place. I'd only have to work once or twice a month or something.'

'What did you say?'

'I didn't say anything – I laughed. He said he was serious, I shouldn't laugh.'

'Do you want to move here?'

'What, and deal with Zoli all the time? I don't think so. He's a total shit, that's obvious. Isn't it?'

'Yeah, I s'pose,' Balázs says, as if the idea had never occurred to him.

He still seems to be thinking about it when she says, 'Do you know why I like you?'

He just stares at her.

'You don't judge people,' she says.

'Don't I?' he asks.

'No,' she says. 'Not even Zoli. Definitely not me. *Definitely* not me. And I know when I'm being judged.'

When they have finished their pints he asks her if she wants another. After asking him what time it is, she says no. 'I don't think I'd better.' Then she excuses herself and goes to look for the ladies. Some elderly Americans, sitting at a nearby table with a map and soft drinks, seem to inspect her as she passes them. When she has moved on, one of them says something and there is a murmur of laughter. Yeah, they're judging her, Balázs thinks, leaning forward on the tabletop over his folded arms in an attempt to see her as she walks away on the cork-soled shoes. It is nearly one o'clock. Despite her not wanting another pint, he assumes that they will spend the whole afternoon together – what else is there to do? – and he is shocked when she sits down again and says, 'Should we head back to the flat then?'

He feels as though he has been slapped.

'Yeah?' he says. And then, when that doesn't seem to express enough disapproval of the suggestion, 'Really?'

'What do *you* want to do?' It's as if she is negotiating.

'I dunno.' He scratches his head.

In fact, he does know – the knowledge is painfully present to him.

When maybe ten seconds have passed without him saying anything else, she says, 'I think we should head back.'

He shrugs sadly. 'Yeah, okay.'

They walk to the underground in silence, and hardly speak on the train.

4

The parked Merc, its familiar shadows. Gábor says, 'So I hear you and Emma did some sightseeing today.' He was still sleeping when they got back from their excursion, and Balázs doesn't know what Emma has told him about it. That she has told him about it at all is somehow disappointing. Warily, he says, 'Yeah, uh . . .'

'You went to the wax museum,' Gábor says.

'Well, yeah. We didn't go in, though.' Still unsure what Gábor thinks about it, Balázs's tone is defensive.

'No, that's what she said,' Gábor says. 'She said you'd've had to queue for two hours or something.'

'More,' Balázs says.

'You can get priority tickets,' Gábor tells him.

'Yeah?'

'Yeah.' With his index fingers on the steering wheel, Gábor is staring straight ahead, through the wide windscreen at the long dark Mayfair street. 'That's what I did, when I went.'

'I didn't know that,' Balázs admits.

'So what'd you do then?' Gábor asks. There is something strange about the question – if she has told him about the museum and the queue, then surely Gábor has asked her, and she has told him, what they did next. So why, Balázs wonders uneasily, is he asking *him*? Is he suspicious? Is he feeling for discrepancies with Emma's story?

'Nothing really,' Balázs says. 'Went for a walk. How was . . . How was last night?'

Gábor doesn't seem to mind changing the subject. 'It was excellent,' he says. 'You should've come.'

'I was tired,' Balázs says apologetically.

'Yeah?' It's as if Gábor doesn't quite believe him.

'Yeah.'

'I thought maybe you wanted to make a move on Emma.' Gábor is smiling when he says this – it might be a joke. 'Especially when you went off together like that today.'

'What d'you mean?' Balázs says.

'No?' Gábor is still smiling.

'No,' Balázs says. He feels the heat in his face, the way it seems to implicate him.

'It's just that most guys around Emma,' Gábor says, looking at him slyly, 'they've got their fucking tongues hanging out, you know what I mean? You don't seem that into her.'

'No,' Balázs says.

That doesn't seem enough, though.

The way Gábor had said it – 'You don't seem that into her' – it sounded like something that needed explaining.

'You're not gay, are you?' Gábor says, as if it is something he has been meaning to ask for some time.

Balázs is, for a moment, too surprised to speak. Then he says, 'No.'

'It's not a problem if you are,' Gábor tells him.

'No,' Balázs says. 'No, I'm not. I, uh. No.'

'She's just not your type, or what?'

With an almost pained expression, Balázs says, 'Look . . . I dunno . . .'

'Hey, whatever, man. I didn' mean to get personal.'

'It's okay.'

'She's not your type, she's not your type,' Gábor says. 'Whatever.'
They don't talk much after that.

A sort of depression, Balázs finds, seems to have engulfed him. It's like a storm that has threatened all afternoon – in the terrible stillness of the smoky living room – and has now fallen on him in a silent maelstrom of despair. Sitting there in the shadows, he thinks with shame and sadness of his own life, his own things, his own pathetic pleasures.

Gábor's phone.

It is her, and there is obviously some problem. 'Okay, just stay there,' Gábor says. 'Just stay where you are. We'll be there in a minute.'

When he has hung up, he says, 'We've got to go up there again. She had to lock herself in the bathroom.'

The anonymous opulence of room 425. The TV is on loud. Sitting on the bed, its linen an energetic mess like stiffly whipped egg white, is a man. He is about forty, thinnish, the length of his face exaggerated by the way he is losing his hair. Emma is not there, though her dress, which is all she wears on these occasions, is on the floor. The man's clothes are on the floor too – he is naked. He stands up with a strange lack of urgency when he hears them come in. 'Who are you?' he says.

'Where is she?' Gábor asks.

'There.' The man indicates a door. Then he says, more fiercely, 'Who the fuck are you?'

'Watch him,' Gábor says to Balázs, and knocks on the door. 'Hey, it's me,' he shouts, and a moment later is let in.

In the well-lit room, Balázs is left standing face to face with the naked man, no more than a metre from him. The man seems unembarrassed by his nakedness. He sniffs loudly and says, 'I'm not finished with her, okay?'

Balázs says nothing, and probably looks as if he didn't understand, because the man says, 'You speak English, you fucking gorilla?

I'm not finished. So why don't you and your friend just get out of here?'

When Balázs still says nothing, the man says, 'You think I hurt her? I didn't hurt her,' he tells Balázs's impassive face. 'I just told her she's a slut, which she is. That's what I told her, and that's what she is. Hey, gorilla, you fucking ape! I'm talking to

Whoosh

There is a noise like a dog enjoying a knuckle of gristle as the nose breaks and fills with blood.

The man staggers back against the bed, looking confused. There is suddenly a huge amount of blood, all over his mouth.

'She's okay . . .' Gábor says from the open bathroom door. 'What the fuck . . .'

The man is on his knees, with his blood-smeared hands at his face and blood dripping quickly into the deep pile of the carpet.

Balázs is already leaving. Outside in the corridor it is as if he has never been there before. Blinded by adrenalin he is unable to find the service stairs and descends instead in a jewel-box of a lift. The doors open on the lobby, its dull dazzle. The shimmering cloud of a chandelier. The blood on his hand, slippery a minute ago, is now sticky, and his hand is starting to throb. With a single smooth turn, the revolving door exchanges the silent lobby for the noises of the night – the intermittent hiss of traffic from the avenue, the more immediate thrum of a taxi pulling up to the hotel entrance.

Balázs walks. He is in the avenue's trench of triple-shadowed light. Every few seconds some vehicle overtakes him. He isn't thinking anything, just feeling the night air on the skin of his face.

Slowly he becomes aware of things – the trees, their leaves a lurid green in the towering lamplight. The darkness on the other side of the avenue that must be some sort of park. Some people waiting at a bus stop.

He stops in front of a ghostly BMW showroom. He wonders what he is going to do. Tremblingly, the situation starting unpleasantly to impinge, he lights a Park Lane. He isn't even sure what happened. He hit the man – at least once – he knows that. Judging by the throb and soreness in his own hand he hit him hard. Probably he broke his nose. Staring without seeing them at the waxed and frowning BMWs, Balázs tells himself that the man will not want to involve the police. He was wearing a wedding ring, for one thing – Balázs had noticed that. He would have to tell his wife some lie to explain the damage to his face, but he would have had to tell her some lie anyway.

Balázs starts to walk again. He remembers now the way that Gábor had shouted at him when he emerged from the bathroom to find the man bleeding onto the carpet, had shouted after him as he left the room. It isn't what Gábor would have wanted. And Emma . . . Just as he was leaving he had been aware of her emerging from the bathroom too, in one of the hotel's towelling robes, and releasing a short scream . . .

Balázs wonders, for a moment, whether he should just flee the whole situation – just head home on his own, hurry to the airport *now*. He doesn't have his passport on him, is one problem. Everything is at the house. No, he will walk a bit more while the adrenalin works its way out of his system. Then he will face whatever it is he has to face.

When, some time later, he finds the side street where they were parked, however, the Mercedes is not there.

He doesn't know how to get home from the hotel, except on the underground, so he has to wait for the trains to start. Four o'clock finds him in Knightsbridge, pressing his nose to the windows of Harrods. Half an hour later he is wandering through Eaton Square. At five, watched by suspicious policemen, he passes in front of Buckingham Palace. It is fully light now, the sun is up, and he waits in Green Park for the station to open.

An hour later he finds Gábor in the smoke-filled living room of the flat, on the phone. He is obviously talking to Zoli.

While he talks he does not acknowledge Balázs's presence, standing there waiting for him to finish, until he says to Zoli, in a quiet voice, 'Yeah, he's here. He just got back.'

A minute later he puts down his phone and says, 'Zoli is fucking livid.'

'I'm sorry,' Balázs says.

'Do you know who that is whose nose you broke?'

Balázs shakes his head.

'What the fuck were you doing?' Gábor shouts at him.

'I'm sorry,' Balázs says again, lowering his eyes.

'I mean, are you out of your fucking mind?'

'I thought . . . I thought he hurt her,' Balázs says.

'No, he did *not* hurt her. I told you she was okay.'

'She's okay? So what happened, why did she . . . ?'

'Do you have any idea,' Gábor says, ignoring him, 'what I have had to deal with?'

Balázs, after a long silence, is about to say sorry again, when Gábor goes on. He speaks in a ferocious semi-whisper, perhaps because Emma is trying to sleep in the other room. 'First I've got to deal with the guy with the broken nose,' Gábor says, 'this guy on the floor. Give him towels to soak up the blood, find his teeth and give them to him – I mean, it was *disgusting*, man! Then he starts saying he's going to call the police. I mean, he gets really fucking angry suddenly. So I have to try and calm him down, tell him he probably doesn't want to call the police, that he probably doesn't want to involve them. And he tells me to go fuck myself, he doesn't give a shit, he's going to call them, and we're all going to get arrested. And I'm worried he *is* going to call them – that he isn't thinking straight, he's full of cocaine, he's probably concussed or something. I mean, he might do something stupid, something *he* regrets later as well. So I tell him I'm going to call Zoli and talk to him, and he shouldn't do anything till I've done that. And anyway he's still dizzy and can't even stand up, and doesn't know where his phone is – his clothes and stuff's all over the place. I mean, he's still fucking naked at this point, and when he tries to stand up he just falls over again. So I call Zoli, yeah, and of course he's asleep, because it's the middle of the fucking night, and at first he doesn't answer, but I keep trying and eventually he picks up, and obviously he knows there's a problem otherwise I wouldn't be calling him in the middle of the night, but then I've got to tell him what happened, I've got to tell him that you broke the guy's fucking nose. And he says, "What did the guy do?" And I've got to tell him that the guy did nothing, basically, you just broke his nose. I mean, Zoli can hardly fucking *believe* it when I tell him that,' Gabor says, suddenly flaring up himself, and taking a moment to light a cigarette. 'And he immediately starts having a go at *me* for bringing you into this whole thing – I mean, like it was *my* fault what happened. And then he starts saying he's going to break your legs and stuff. I mean, he says it like he really means it, and maybe he knows people who can do that, I don't know. Anyway, I tell him the guy's threatening to call the police. And he says I can't let him do that. And I say, "What the fuck do you want me to do – kill him?" And Zoli says, "Let me talk to him." So I tell the guy Zoli wants to talk to him, and give him the phone. And the guy looks fucking terrible – I mean, his face is swollen like a fucking balloon and all purple, and his nose is just a fucking grotesque mess. Anyway, he takes the phone and talks to Zoli, and he's still really fucking angry – he's shouting about how he's going to call the police and how it might be embarrassing for him but we're the ones who are going to go to jail and stuff. Fuck, it takes Zoli about half an hour to calm him down, and then he gives the phone back to me and says Zoli wants to talk to me again, and Zoli tells me he's agreed with the guy that he won't call the police if we give him his money back, and at that point I'm just fucking relieved to have this sorted out so he's not going to call the police, so I tell Emma to get the money and she does, and I give it back to the guy. That felt really shit.' Gábor stubs out his cigarette.

Balázs is still standing there, near the door.

Gábor says, 'I tell him to get dressed and clean himself up, and I'll be back in ten minutes. Then I take Emma back to the car, and leave her there and go back up to the room, where the guy's got his clothes on and has washed most of the blood off his face. Anyway, he leaves and then I've got to try and clean the fucking room up. I mean, there's blood everywhere.' Gábor sighs, weary with telling the story now. 'So I call Juli and we find some kind of carpet-cleaning machine in a cupboard somewhere, some kind of steam cleaner, and she shows me how to use it, and I've got to try and clean the carpet with it.' Almost tearfully he shouts at Balázs, 'I mean, this fucking unwieldy machine! I didn't even know how to work it properly!' He lights yet another cigarette. Still standing there, Balázs lights one too. 'I mean, I fucking hated you while I was doing that,' Gábor says. 'I wanted to fucking kill you.'

'I'm really sorry,' Balázs says.

'Where the fuck did you go?'

'I dunno. Nowhere.'

Gábor looks at him for a few moments, as if he doesn't understand. Then he says, 'I can't pay you, man. I mean, what I was going to pay you for this week. I mean, we had to give the guy his money back – which is much more than I was going to pay you, okay. I mean, we lost that money because of what you did, so . . .'

Though it had not occurred to him that this might happen, Balázs just shrugs.

'I mean, Zoli wants you to pay us the difference,' Gábor says, with some vehemence. 'He wants you to pay us the fucking difference, and that's like a million forints. I told him you can't do that, you just don't have the money, and he said maybe you'd prefer to have your legs broken. I mean, he is *fucking* angry, man. And so is Emma,' Gábor says more moodily, looking away.

'Is she?' Balázs says quietly, surprised.

'Well, yeah! She had to fuck that guy,' Gábor says, spelling it out, 'and she didn't even get paid.'

'Yeah.'

'So yeah, she's angry.'

'But she's okay?'

Gábor ignores the question. 'Listen,' he says, 'there's two more nights. I think you should just stay here, whatever. I'll take care of things.'

'What do you mean?'

'I think you should just be out of this from now on. I mean, we're not paying you now, so . . . Look, just forget it. Leave it to me. Your work is done. Okay?'

Zoli does not come round that day, of course, since there is no money to collect, and by the time he appears the next day, he seems to have calmed down and merely ignores Balázs. Balázs, lying on the sofa with *Harry Potter és a Titkok Kamrája*, ignores him back. There is no talk of leg-breaking – only the coldness normally accorded to someone who has seriously fucked up.

And this coldness extended, Balázs found, to Emma. She had seemed to avoid him the previous afternoon. She had stayed out of the living room, and it was only when they met accidentally at the bathroom door that they spoke.

Without looking him in the eye, she said, 'Oh, sorry.'

And Balázs, emerging, said, 'No, it's okay, I've finished.'

149

Still filling the door, he was in her way.

'Look, I'm sorry,' he said.

Still without looking at him, she nodded. 'Okay.'

And that was it – he stood aside and she went past into the damp reek of the bathroom.

A few hours later she and Gábor left for the hotel.

Gábor put his head round the living-room door. 'Okay, we're going,' he said.

'Yeah,' Balázs said, 'okay.'

When they had left he sat there for a while. Meditatively, he smoked two Park Lanes, then he put on his jacket and went out into the street. The sky was a super-intense evening blue, and subdivided by jet trails in various states of dispersal, some plain white, some, perhaps those higher up, a fanciful pink. Down where he walked, dusk was deep in the small street, silvering the windscreens of the parked cars. Everything was quiet, and there was a pleasant emptiness inside him too – something like the unlit windows of the houses he walked past, a peaceful vacancy. Silent interiors. No one home.

It was less than a week since he had first done this walk, from the flat to the high street, and already it felt like something totally familiar – something that, no matter how hard he looked, would show him nothing new.

And then there was the girl at the chicken place. She was always there, serving the customers, but he hadn't really noticed her until tonight. The little smile she gave him when she took his order, it occurred to him, as he sat down to wait for his food, was not the first. Part of the lace edge of her bra showed in the V-shaped neckline of her T-shirt, where a little gold cross lay on the skin. He watched her dealing with the next customer, her earnest manner, her hand tightly gripping the pen with which she wrote the orders down. He wondered what she thought about things. Though she was not smiling now, she had a nice face.

4

1

It is light when he leaves the hotel. Light. Primordial sunlight disclosing empty streets, disclosing form with shadow, the stucco facades. And silence. Here in the middle of London, silence. Not quite silence, of course. Never true silence here. The sublimated rumble of a plane. The burble of pigeons courting on a cornice. A taxi's busy rattle along Sussex Gardens, past the terraced hotel fronts, from one of which he now emerges.

He feels that he is leaving London unseen, slipping out while everyone else is still asleep, as he walks, with his single small holdall, to the square where he left the car. The square is hotel-fringed, shabby. A few benches and plants in the middle. Sticky pavements. The car is still there, surrounded by empty parking spaces. It is not his. It is someone else's. He is simply delivering it. Slinging his holdall onto the passenger seat, he takes his place at the wheel.

He sits there for a few seconds, enjoying a feeling of inviolable solitude. Solitude, freedom. They seem like nearly the same thing as he sits there.

Then he starts the engine, which sounds loud in the silence of the square.

He is aware now that he does not know exactly which way to go. He looked yesterday and it all seemed simple enough, the way out of London, south-east, towards Dover. Now even finding his way to the river seems problematic. He tries to picture it, the streets he will need to take. When he has formed some sort of mental picture of where he is going, and only then, he pulls out.

He waits at a light on Park Lane, some posh hotel on one side, the park on the other, staring sleepily straight ahead.

When he gets to the river there might be a problem. He hopes there will be signs for Dover. The possibility of getting lost makes him mildly nervous, even though he would not be in any serious danger of missing the ferry. He has plenty of time. It is his habit, when travelling, always to allow more time than he needs.

He went to sleep very early last night. The previous night, Friday, he had been out late, with Macintyre, the Germanic philology specialist at UCL. And then he had had to get up early on Saturday to take the train to Nottingham and pick up the car from its previous 'keeper', a Pakistani doctor. (Dr N. Khan was the name on the documents.) He had done the whole thing on a hangover, which had made the day pass over him like a dream – made it seem even now like something he had dreamed, the time he spent in Dr Khan's front room, looking through the service history, while the doctor's cat watched him.

He swings around Hyde Park Corner, the sun pouring down Piccadilly like something out of Turner, the palaces opposite the park half-dissolving in a flood of light.

He squints, tries to push it away with his hand.

Macintyre had not been very helpful. He was supposed to have looked at the manuscript, the section on Dutch and German analogues in particular. They had talked about it for a while, in The Lowlander. Macintyre, with a suggestion of subtle mockery that was entirely typical of him, always insisted on meeting there. The early modern shifts in German pronunciation, for instance. The way some dialects . . .

He has to focus, as he flows through them, on the layout of the streets around Victoria station.

154

The way some dialects were still impervious to those shifts, after more than five hundred years.

The traffic system pulls him one way, then another, past empty office towers. He looks for the lane that will throw him left eventually, onto Vauxhall Bridge Road.

There.

No, Macintyre had not been as helpful as he might have been. Obviously, he was holding back. Professional jealousies were operative. He did not want to give too much away about what he was working on now. That was why he had wanted to talk about other things. Kept steering the talk away from shop. Wanted to know, when he had had a few Duvels, about his 'sex life'. 'How's your sex life, then?' he had said.

Well, he had mentioned Waleria. Said something about her. Something non-committal.

The lights halfway down Vauxhall Bridge Road start to turn as he approaches them and after a moment's hesitation he stops.

Macintyre was married, wasn't he? Kids.

The lights go green. Unhurriedly he moves off. A minute later – the Thames. That exhilarating momentary sense of space. The water, sun-white.

Then streets again.

In south London he feels even freer. These are streets he does not know, that may be why. Strange to him, these sleeping estates. These hulks, slowly mouldering. He has a vague idea that he needs to find the Old Kent Road. Old Kent Road. That insane game of Monopoly that happened in the SCR once. He thinks of that for a moment, and imagines the Old Kent Road to be liveried in a drab brown.

Signs for Dover draw him deeper into the maze of south-east London. The maze marvellously unpeopled – the low high streets with their tattered shops. The sun shining on their grubby brick faces. Dirty windows hung with curtains. Only at the petrol stations are there signs of life. Someone filling up.

Someone walking away.

He has so much time, he thinks he might make the earlier ferry. His own 'sails', as they still say, just after eight. So yes, he may well make the previous one – it is not yet five thirty and already he is in the vicinity of Blackheath, already he is merging onto an empty motorway, its surface shining like water. Speed. There is a tangle of motorways here. He must keep an eye out for signs.

Yes, Macintyre has several kids. No wonder he seemed so threadbare and fed up. So tetchy. Some little house somewhere in outer London, full of stuff. Full of noise. He and his wife at each other's throats. Too worn out to fuck. Who wants it?

Canterbury, says the sign.

And he thinks, with a little frisson of excitement, *This is the way Chaucer's pilgrims went. Trotting horses. Stories. Muddy lanes. And when it started to rain – a hood. Wet hands.*

His dry hands hold the leather-trimmed wheel. Through sunglasses he eyes the wide oncoming lanes. He has the motorway to himself.

Wonderful to imagine it, though. The whole appeal of medieval studies – the languages, the literature, the history, the art and architecture – to immerse oneself in that world. That other world. Safely other. Other in almost every way, except that it was *here*. Look at those fields on either side of the motorway. Those low hills. It was here. *They* were here, as we are here now. And this too shall pass. We don't actually believe that, though, do we? We are unable to believe that our own world *will* pass. So it will go on for ever? No. It will turn into something else. Slowly – too slowly to be perceived by the people living in it. Which is already happening, is always happening. We just can't see it. Like sound changes, spoken language.

'Some Remarks on the Representation of Spoken Dialect in "The Reeve's Tale"'.

The kick-ass title of his first published work. Published in *Medium Ævum LXXIV*. Originally written for Hamer's *Festschrift* – Hamer who had supervised his doctoral work when he first turned up at Oxford, that first year. A tall, bald man with spacious elegant rooms in Christ Church. Would literally offer you a sherry when you arrived – *that* old school, that English. The author of works such as *Old English Sound Changes for Beginners* (1967). Professor Hamer lived, it had seemed, in a fortress of abstrusity. Asleep at night, he must have dreamed, so his young foreign pupil had thought, sipping his sherry, of palatal diphthongisation, of loss of *h* and compensatory lengthening.

And he had envied him those harmless dreams. Something so profoundly peaceful about them.

Something so profoundly peaceful about them.

Everything so settled, you see. It all happened a thousand years ago. And the medievalist sits in his study, in a shaft of sunlight, lost in a reverie of life on the far side of that immense lapse of time. The whole exercise is, in its way, a memento mori. A meditation on the effacing nature of time.

He likes the little world of the university. Some people, he knows, hate it. They long for London.

He likes it. The fairy-tale topography of the town. A make-believe world of walled gardens. The quietness of summer. The stone-floored lodge, and the deferential porter. Yes, a make-believe world, like something imagined by a shy child.

Somewhere to hide.

Dreaming spires.

Sun sparkles on wide motorway.

It is just after six and he will be at Dover, he estimates, in an hour.

Yes, he likes the little world of the university. He *likes* its claustral narrowness. Sometimes he wishes it were narrower still. That the world of the present was even more absent. He would have quite enjoyed, he thinks, the way of life of a medieval monastery – as a scholarly brother, largely exempt from manual labour. He would have enjoyed that.

With, naturally, the one obvious proviso.

Without noticing, he has pushed the car well into the nineties. It manages the speed without effort. He eases off the accelerator and the needle immediately starts to sink and for the first time this morning he feels sleepy – a mesmeric sleepiness induced by the level hum of the engine and the monotonous, empty perspective in front of him. It seems, for long moments, like something on a screen, something spewing from a CPU. Just pictures. Without consequences. He shakes his head, moves his hands on the wheel.

Yes. The one obvious proviso.

Last year, during the Hilary term, he had done the thing he had long wanted to, and had an affair with an undergraduate. It had been something he had had in view since his arrival in Oxford to finish his doctorate. It had taken years to achieve – and the affair itself, when it finally happened, was in many ways unsatisfactory. Just two weeks it had lasted. And yet the memories of it, of her youth . . .

He was sad in an abstracted way, for a day or two, when she ended it with that letter in her schoolgirl's handwriting, that letter which so pathetically overestimated his own emotional engagement in the situation. And he understood that he had also overestimated her emotional engagement in it. As he had been intent on enacting his own long-standing fantasy, so she had been enacting a fantasy of *her* own, in no way less selfish. Except that she was nineteen or twenty, and still entitled to selfishness – not having learned yet, perhaps, how easily and lastingly people are hurt – and he was more than ten years older and ought to have understood that by now.

Only when he saw her, soon after, in the arms of someone her own age – some kid – did he experience anything like a moment's actual pain, something Nabokovian and poisonous, seeing them there in the spring sunlight of the quad.

And by then he was already mixed up with Erica, the medieval Latin scholar from Oriel. That didn't last long either.

The days he has just spent in London have exhausted him. Not only the meeting with Macintyre. He also had a meeting with his publisher. And a symposium on Old English sound changes at UCL, for which he was one of the speakers. Various social things. He had seen Emmanuele, the short, snobbish, scholarly Italian who had finished his DPhil a few summers ago and was now a lawyer in London. Emmanuele had asked after Waleria, what was happening there? It was at a party of Mani's, last September, that he had met her. 'I don't know,' he had said. 'Something. Maybe. We're seeing each other. I don't know.'

*

Solitude, freedom. There is that feeling, still, on the ferry. This in spite of the other people; they are transient strangers, they do not fix him in place. They know nothing about him. He has no obligations to them. Sea wind disperses summer's heat on the open deck, hung with lifeboats. The floor see-saws. Is sucked down, then pushes at his feet. England dwindles. The wind booms, pulls his hair. Inside, in the sealed warmth, people eat and shop. He wanders among them, nameless and invisible. Sits at a table on his own. His solitude, for the hour it takes to travel to France, is inviolable. He stands at a window, golden with salt in the sunlight. He watches the playful waves. He feels as free as the gulls hanging on the wind. Solitude, freedom.

*

As soon as he has driven off the ship he puts on the A/C and Vivaldi's *Gloria* – pours into the French motorway system with that ecstatic music filling his ears.

Dum-dee

Dum-dum-dum-dee

Dum-dum-dum

The asphalt glitters. It is Sunday morning. Farms lie in the flat bright land on either side of the motorway.

And he knows this motorway well. It follows the so-called Côte d'Opale, towards Ostend. To the left as he drives are the windy dunes.

Welkom in West-Vlaanderen says the sign.

And now it is like he is driving through his own past, through a landscape full of living nerves, of names that are almost painfully evocative. Koksijde, where he went once with Delphine and her mother's dog – the small dog digging in the sand among tufts of wind-flattened grass. Nieuwpoort – where they spent that summer, he and his parents. The smell of the sea finding its way inland, up little streets – and at the ends of the streets, when you walked down them to meet the sea with your plastic spade in your hand, a milky horizon. Roeselare, where they would visit his father's parents – the suburban house, with hop fields at the end of the neat garden. Though the memories possess a jewel-like sharpness they seem surprisingly small and far away, as if seen through the wrong end of a telescope. It has been years since he was here, on this flat tract of land next to the ship-strewn sea, and that his own life has been going on long enough now for things like that windy day at Koksijde to lie more than ten, more than fifteen years in the past is somehow a shock

160

to him. He was already an adult then, more or less, and yet he still thinks of his adulthood as something that is just getting under way.

Feeling a little shaken, he stops for petrol.

Holding the nozzle into the tank he stares at the motorway, the thin Sunday traffic.

That desire for everything to just stay the same. That day at Koksijde, stretched out over a whole lifetime. Why is the idea of that so appealing? Or today, this very moment, the hum of the flowing petrol, its heady sickening smell. The motorway, the thin Sunday traffic. Here and now. The pallid heaven of these hours. Solitude and freedom. Stretched out over a whole lifetime. That desire for everything to just stay the same.

The tank is full.

Walking back from the till – where it felt strange, somehow, to speak his own language with the woman there – he finds himself enjoying the sight of the luxury SUV in which he is travelling. He feels pleased and proud to take his place in it, to start the engine with the touch of a button. Stańko is trusting him to hand it over, to sign the papers that will transfer the ownership. And though he does not know him very well – has only met him once, in fact – Stańko has every reason to think that he *will* hand it over.

Stańko is, after all, a policeman. The senior policeman of Skawina, a town in southern Poland, nowadays a suburb of Kraków – tractors farting in fields of potatoes next to a multiplex showing the latest films.

You don't fuck with Stańko. Not in Skawina or the neighbouring townships, in Libertów or Wołowice.

It is easy to picture him in this car, moving through the banal landscape of his beat, his wallet abulge.

How that brooding ogre and his ugly little wife produced something as lovely as Waleria . . .

Well, maybe she wouldn't age well. It was worth thinking about, though he feels no inclination to long-term thoughts. He still doesn't see things that way. It still feels new, this situation, even somehow provisional. There was a sense, for some time, that they had no obligation to each other, that they were free to see other people. He didn't. (Unless you include Erica the Latinist, who was still, last September, just about extant.) Whether Waleria did or not he doesn't know.

He has turned inland, passed Bruges.

Later, Ghent, where he did his undergraduate degree. English and German. *Sir Gawain and the Green Knight. Parzifal.*

After Christmas last year he spent a few days in her parents' dayglo orange house. A scalloped balcony over the white front door. Snow disfiguring all the garden ornaments. Waleria met him at Kraków airport, and drove him to the house, which was near a petrol station on the edge of Skawina.

Every day while he was there, they went skiing at Zakopane. ('Do you ski?' she had asked him, making small talk, when they first met, at Mani's party. 'Do I ski? I'm Belgian,' he had deadpanned. It made her smile.) She was an excellent skier. Warily, he had followed her down the stiffest slopes Zakopane had to offer.

As he approaches Brussels, clouds close over him in the sky. Wind moves the trees at the side of the motorway. There will be rain. Shafts of hard light pick out the distant prominences of the city as he passes. He knows the way without having to think about it – the leaky underpasses, the glimpse of Uccle (those tree-lined avenues, where he was once a bookish schoolboy who lived in a big flat), and then out on the E40 towards Liège, as the rain starts to fall. He feels for the lever that sets the wipers swinging.

Since then, since Christmas, they have seen each other every few weeks. A sense evolved that they were in some way together, a sense of mutual obligation. He wouldn't put it more strongly than that. Sometimes she visits him in Oxford, or they spend a weekend in London, or somewhere else. They meet, for the most part, in the neutral spaces of hotels. There was Florence in February. There was, at Easter, a week in the Dodecanese, island-hopping, the windy deck of the hydrofoil in its world of vivid blues.

Slowly, they are finding each other out. 'You,' she said, 'are a typical only child.'

'Which means?'

'Selfish,' she told him. 'Spoilt. It never occurs to you,' she said, 'that you might not be the centre of the universe. Which is what gives you this personal magnetism you have . . .'

'Now you're flattering me . . .'

'It's nerdy,' she said. 'Still, it's there.'

She was shuffling her cards, her tarot pack. That was a surprise. It seemed she had this New Agey side to her – it wasn't, he told himself, fundamental to who she was.

'Okay. You're going to take three cards,' she said. 'Past, present, future.'

They were lying on his bed. Oxford. It was Saturday morning. Last month.

'So.' She offered him the pack, fanning it out. 'Take one.'

Humouring her, he prised out a card.

'Ace of Wands,' she said. 'Past. Take another.'

'The Tower.' She made a face of mock alarm. 'Fuck. Present. Last one,' she instructed him. And said, when he had taken it and turned it over, 'The Emperor. Future.'

'That sounds good,' he suggested, looking pleased with himself.

She was studying the three cards, now lined up crookedly on the sheet. 'Okay,' she said, provisionally. 'I *think* I understand.'

'Tell me.'

'It's time to grow up. That's the headline.'

He laughed. 'What does *that* mean?'

'Well, look at this.' She was pointing to the Ace of Wands. She said, 'It's obviously, you know . . . it's a phallic symbol.'

It did seem to be. The picture was of a hand holding a long wand, which thickened towards the top into a fleshy knob, a divided hemisphere.

'Yes,' he said. 'So it seems.'

'Well, that's the *past*.'

'What – so I might as well kill myself now?'

'Don't be silly.' It was difficult to say how seriously she took this. She looked quite solemn. 'The present,' she said. 'The Tower. Some kind of unexpected crisis. Everything turned upside down.'

'I'm not aware of anything like that.'

'That's the point. You won't be, until it hits you.'

'Unless it's you.'

She ignored that. 'Now let's look at the future. The Emperor – worldly power . . .'

And he made some silly remark about how that sounded like him and started to fondle her nipple, to tease it into life. They were naked.

She said, 'I think these cards are suggesting that you should maybe stop thinking about your . . . *thing* all the time.'

He laughed. 'My thing?'

'This.'

She put her finger on it.

'What it means,' she said, looking him in the eye, 'is that your skirt-chasing days are over.'

'But I don't chase skirt. I'm not that type.'

'Oh, yes, you are.'

'I promise you,' he told her, 'I'm not.'

*

164

It is ideal, he thinks, the set-up they have. He is unable to imagine anything more perfect. He is unable to imagine living more happily in the present.

The huge sheds of the Stella Artois plant at Leuven, its steaming stacks, are half-obscured by the drenching weather.

How well he knows this stretch of motorway, its different surfaces, the sound of the tyres shifting suddenly, dropping in pitch, as you pass from Flanders to Wallonia. How often, in the years he was studying in Ghent, did he drive it, and how insignificant a distance it seems now, as part of his longer journey – he is already halfway to Liège and it feels as though he has only just left Brussels.

And now here it is, Liège – the place where the road plunges down into the valley.

Pines start to appear in the woods as he mounts the heights on the other side, overtaking trucks in the slow lane.

Suddenly fresh, everything.

He needs to finish the piece for the *Journal of English and Germanic Philology*; he was hoping to have it done by now. The question of whether, in the pre-West Saxon period, *æ* sometimes reverted to *a* – or whether in fact the initial change from *a* to *æ*, postulated for the West Germanic period, that is to say prior to the Anglo-Saxon settlement of Britain, never in fact took place at all. The principle evidence for the former hypothesis was always the form '*slēan*' – if *that* form could be shown to be anomalous, then the whole venerable thesis would start to look very questionable. Hence the importance of his proposed paper, already accepted in principle by the journal, 'Anomalous Factors in the Form "*Slēan*" – Some Suggestions'.

He had used some of the material, teasingly, in his talk to the UCL symposium last week. Quite a stir. (The look on Macintyre's face!)

Yes, this might be it – the thing he has been looking for, the thing that makes him, in the world of Germanic philology, a household name. Something everyone in the field simply *has* to have read. Worldly power. So he must take time over it – seclude himself with it for the rest of the summer. Stop thinking about his *thing* all the time.

He is eating a chorizo sandwich, drinking Spa water.

Sitting in a huge Shell services with a Formula 1 theme. Francorchamps is nearby, somewhere in these forests.

There are not many people about. Even though it is high summer – the second week of July – the weather is foul, and there is little to do up here in the woods when the rain is just steadily falling, seeming to hang whitely against the dark slopes of pines.

With cold hands, he puts more petrol in the car. He has an idea that it is cheaper here than in Germany. He isn't sure. Stańko is paying for the petrol anyway. He tucks the receipt into his wallet with the others as he walks out again into the rain.

This is where he leaves the road he knows – the motorway running east towards Cologne. He looks, sitting in the car while the rain falls, at the printed Google map. An indistinct line drops diagonally down from where he is into Germany, just missing Luxembourg. The E42. It ought to be easy. He folds the map and sits there, in the rain-pelted car, finishing his coffee. Luxembourg. Never been there. Like Surrey was a country. Silly. *Anomalous.* Like '*slēan*'. A household name. He just needs to devote himself to his work. Stop thinking about his thing. Time to grow up. That's the headline. He had liked the way she said that.

The windscreen is a mass of trickles. Summer. Still, there is something romantic about the rain. There are not many people about. It was her idea to meet at Frankfurt airport. Not *the* Frankfurt airport – Frankfurt-Hahn, a no-frills-type place deep in the countryside, and nowhere near Frankfurt; Frankfurt doesn't even appear on his Google map, even though the little pin indicating the airport is almost in the middle of it. They are used to airports like that, these lovers. Sleepy places next to a village with twenty flights a day at most. They have been in and out of them a dozen times so far this year. In and out. In and out. It was her idea to meet there, and finish the journey to Skawina together, taking their time, spending a night or two on the road.

2

The airport is harder to find than he thought it would be. There is more driving, when he leaves the straightforwardness of the E42, on narrow twisting lanes, more following tractors. A hilly landscape. The day is grey and humid. There is insufficient signage. He passes through a village, starting to worry that he might be late after all, and then quite suddenly it is there. Soon he is moving among parked vehicles, looking for a space, in a hurry now.

He finds a space.

And then it happens.

There is a loud ugly metallic noise that for a moment he does not understand.

Then he does and his heart stops.

When it starts again he is sweating heavily.

She looks up from her magazine, smiles.

'Sorry I'm late,' he says.

'You're not late. The plane was early.'

'Everything was okay?'

She is putting her magazine in her bag. 'Yes. Fine. You must be tired,' she says, looking up at him. He appears pale and shaken. 'You've had a long drive.'

'I'm okay, actually,' he says. 'Probably it will hit me later.'

'Do you want something to eat?'

'Uh.' He thinks about it. He was hungry, half an hour ago. He has had nothing to eat all day except a *pain au chocolat* on the ferry and that chorizo sandwich, up in the rainy Ardennes. Now, however, he isn't hungry. In fact, he feels slightly sick on account of what has happened to Staṅko's luxury SUV. 'Maybe I should,' he says. 'Have *you* eaten?'

'I had something.'

'Maybe I should,' he says again.

'Okay. Are you okay?' she asks, suddenly sounding worried.

'Yes. Yes,' he says. 'Fine.'

They speak English to each other. His English is more or less native-speaker standard. Hers is only slightly less perfect.

He queues at some sort of food place, one of only a few in the airport. The airport is shabby and unexciting. Modest improvement works are taking place behind plastic sheets and warning signs. He orders, in flawless German, a ham sandwich, a double latte.

'Look,' he says, sitting down next to her. 'There's something I need to tell you.'

To his surprise, her face instantly tightens. She looks frightened. 'Yes?' she says.

'I had an accident,' he says, taking the plastic lid off his latte. 'With the car. In the car park. Here. There's some damage. To the paintwork.'

She doesn't say anything.

'I hope your father won't be too pissed off.'

'I don't know,' she says.

'Do you want any of this?' he asks, offering her the sandwich. 'I'm not really hungry.' When she shakes her head, he says, 'How was the flight? Okay?'

'Yes, it was fine.'

'From Katowice?' he asks.

'Yes.'

'We're staying tonight in a place called Trennfeld,' he says, soldiering on with the sandwich. 'It's a couple of hours' drive from here. According to Google maps anyway.'

'Okay.'

'Gasthaus Sonne,' he says.

Though she smiles at him, something seems to be wrong.

'Okay?' he says.

She smiles at him again, and he wonders if it's just him – is he just imagining it, or does she seem nervous about something?

'Let's go?' she says.

He takes her little suitcase and they leave and walk to the car park, where she inspects, without passion, the huge scuff on the side of her father's new car.

He sighs theatrically.

'See?'

'M-hm.'

'I hope your father won't be too pissed off,' he says again.

It starts to rain as he walks to the machine by the chain-link fence and pushes euros into it to pay for his stay.

When he comes back, she is sitting in the passenger seat, staring straight ahead.

There is some trouble about getting back to the E42 towards Frankfurt. They spend some time lost in dung-strewn lanes, the dull farm country.

When they are finally on the motorway, they travel at first in silence, as though hypnotised by the movement of the wipers, which are struggling to keep up with a downpour.

He is still thinking about the damage.

About how easily it might *not* have happened. If he had only arrived a few minutes earlier or later, for instance, he would surely have found a different place to park. There was one slightly tricky space near the entrance that he had almost taken – then he kept on looking, though the space he ended up in, after a few minutes of irritable prowling, was even tighter.

He had needed a piss. That might also have played its part – the way it made him still more impatient and unfocused on what he was doing. And he was tired and hungry and in a hurry and had been stuck behind a tractor for ten minutes while he tried to find the airport. And all of these factors, all of these individually unlikely or indecisive factors had united in the fateful moment, had placed him exactly *then* and *there*, and the damage was done.

And what will happen about it?

He will have to pay to have the fucking . . .

'There's something I need to tell *you*, Karel,' she says.

He doesn't quite understand the emphasis, has forgotten that he used the same phrase himself, half an hour earlier, in the airport.

'What?'

A long silence.

He is still thinking about how much the paint job will be, and whether Stańko knows someone who can do it for less than the usual price, when he notices that the silence is still going on.

'There's something I need to tell you,' she had said.

And the number of things she might have to tell him shrinks, as the silence extends, until there are only one or two left.

One part of his mind takes that in; the other part is still energetically fretting over the scraped wing.

She is either about to end their little affair, their succession of tousled hotel-rooms, or

'You're pregnant,' he says, throwing the indicator lever, moving out to overtake in a tunnel of spray.

He hopes that she will immediately negative this.

Instead the silence just prolongs further.

Outside, a wet, grey world unfurls around them, wind-whacked trees huddling at its edges, pouring into peripheral vision.

Part of him is still doggedly preoccupied with the prang. That is starting to drift away, though, as if into infinite space.

'Are you?' he asks.

Those moments when everything changes. How many in a life? Not more than a few.

Here, now, the moment. On this rainswept German motorway. Here and now.

'That's shit,' he says, still searching the road ahead with agitated eyes.

Finally she had spoken. 'I think so,' she said. And then, 'Yes.'

'That's shit,' he says again.

The prang is far off now, though he is still just about aware of it, like some object far out in the darkness.

His whole life seems to be out there, divested.

What is left? What is he to wrap himself in, now that everything has floated off into space?

It hangs out there, in the darkness, like debris.

She is, he notices, shaking with sobs.

It takes him by surprise.

And then she starts, still sobbing, to hit her own forehead with a small white-knuckled fist.

'Please,' he says. 'Stop that.'

'Stop the car,' she says through tears.

And then screams at him, 'STOP THE CAR!'

'Why?' His voice is shrill and frightened. 'Why? I can't . . . What the fuck are you doing?'

She had started to open the passenger door. Wind noise roared at her. Cold air and water were sucked momentarily into the civilised leather interior.

'Are you fucking crazy?'

Her tears redouble and she says, piteously now, 'Stop the car, stop the car . . .'

He stares more frazzledly at the oncoming world. Suddenly it seems unrecognisable. 'Why?' he says. 'Why?'

She has started to hit her forehead again, her fist knocking on the taut pale skin with a sound that inordinately upsets him.

And then an Aral station's lit pylon looms out of the rain – the blue word *ARAL* high above everything – and, indicating, he slows into the lake of the exit lane.

As soon as the car stops moving, or even a moment before, she is out of it.

He sees her, through the still-working wipers, walk away, hugging herself, and wonders numbly what to do.

He had just stopped on the apron of tarmac short of the petrol station. Now he lifts his foot from the brake and the car moves on at walking pace, under the huge canopy that protects the pumps from the rain.

He has lost sight of her.

One of the parking spaces in front of the shop is empty and he slides straight into it. With his thumb he shoves the button that kills the engine and then just sits there for a few minutes. That is, for a fairly long time. The life of the service station swirls around him, as if in time lapse. He is staring at the stitching of the steering wheel, the elegant leather. There is a temptation just to drive away – drive back to his own life, which feels as if it is somewhere else.

There is no question of actually doing that, however.

Instead he discovers he has tears in his eyes.

Tears just sort of sitting there.

Tears of shock.

Inside the shop, he peers about, looking for her. He hangs around outside the ladies for a minute or two, as if she might emerge. He tries her phone.

He starts to worry that she might have done something silly. That she might have taken a lift from a stranger or something.

He is in the car again, moving slowly through the acres of parked trucks along the side of the motorway, when he finds her. She is still walking. Walking with purpose. She must have been walking, all this time.

'What are you doing?' he shouts through the open window, keeping pace with her.

She ignores him.

He overtakes her and pulls into a space among the trucks some way ahead. He sits there for a few seconds, fighting a furious urge to just drive away. Instead, getting out of the car and hunching his shoulders against the rain, he takes his umbrella from the back seat. It bangs into place above him, and immediately fills with sound.

As soon as she notices it – it is very large and has 'University of Oxford' written on it – she turns and starts to walk the other way.

Only for show – he is able, with no more than a slight quickening of his pace, to draw level with her, and take hold of her arm.

A truck lumbers past and he drags her out of the way of its spray, into the puddled alley formed by two other, stationary trucks.

'What are you doing?' he says. 'Where are you going?'

Her face is twisted into an unfamiliar tear-drenched ugliness.

This whole situation, this awful scene among the trucks, has taken him totally by surprise.

He waits for her to say something.

Finally she says, 'I don't know. Anywhere. Away from you.'

'Why?' he asks. 'Why?'

It has been his assumption, from the first moment, that there will be an abortion, that that is what she wants as well.

Now he starts to see, as if it is something still far away, that that may not be so. It is initially just something that his mind, working through every possible permutation in its machine-like effort to understand, throws up as a potential explanation for what she is doing. She does not want to have an abortion. She is not willing to have an abortion.

In a sense this is the true moment of shock.

He fights off a splurge of panic.

She has not said anything, is still just sobbing in the noisy tent of the umbrella.

He asks, trying to sound loving or sympathetic or something, 'What do *you* want to do?'

'You can't make me have an abortion,' she says.

He wonders, *Is she a Catholic? A proper Catholic?* She is Polish, after all. They have never talked about it.

'I don't want to make you do anything,' he says.

'Yes, you do. You want me to have an abortion.'

This he does not deny. It is not, after all, the same thing.

He says again, 'What do you want?'

And then when she says nothing, 'It's true. I don't think you should keep . . . Fuck, *stop!*'

She has tried to pull away from him, to leave the shelter of the umbrella. He is holding her arm now, tightly, and saying to her, '*Think about it!* Think about what it would mean. It might fuck up your whole life . . .'

She shouts into his face, 'You already have fucked up my whole life.'

'What?'

'You have fucked up my whole life,' she says.

'How?' He asks again, '*How?*'

'By saying that.'

'What?'

'What you said.'

'What did I say?'

'"That's shit,"' she says.

His face is a mad mask of incomprehension.

'You said that!'

Yes, he did say that.

She is sobbing again, violently, next to the towering snout of a truck. Droplets hang on the truck's snout. He sees them, hanging there, white. They shake, and some of them fall, as a moment of fierce wind hits everything. Some of them fall. Some of them don't. They hold on, shaking. He says, loosening his hold on her shaking arm, just wanting to end this awful episode among the trucks, 'I'm sorry. I'm sorry I said that.'

*

It seems so smooth, the way it moves on the endless tarmac. Whispering wheels. It is quiet. No one seems to have anything to say. Not even the weather now. For some kilometres a light mist comes off the motorway, and then it is just blandly dry.

Pearl-grey afternoon.

At Mainz, they cross the Rhine.

He knows Mainz as the city where Gutenberg invented printing, and thus ended the Middle Ages; that was what they decided, anyway, at a seminar he attended at Bologna University some years ago, *The Middle Ages: Approaching the Question of a Terminal Date.* He

176

was asked, afterwards, to write an introduction to their transcripted proceedings.

He finds himself thinking about that, about the terminal date of the Middle Ages, as they pass across the Weisenauer Rheinbrücke, the water on either side a sluggish khaki.

Modernity was what happened next.

Modernity, which has never much interested him. Modernity, what's happening now.

It started here in Mainz.

And the Roman Empire ended here – from here the legions tried to outstare the tribes on the other side of the demarcating waterway, where now there is the Opel factory at Rüsselsheim, and a little further on Frankfurt airport, the actual airport, an enormity flanking the motorway for five whole minutes.

And the weather darkens again as they leave the airport behind.

What has been said in the last hour?

Nothing.

Nothing has been said.

Pine forests on hillsides start to envelop them on the east side of the Main. And fog.

> *Nel mezzo del cammin di nostra vita*
> *Mi ritrovai per una selva oscura*
> *Ché la diritta via era smarrita*

Well, here it is. Dark pine forests, hemming the motorway. Shapes of fog throw themselves at the windscreen.

Finally someone speaks. He says, 'When did you find out?'

'A few days ago,' she says. 'I didn't want to tell you on the phone.'

'No.'

A few more minutes, and then he says, 'And is it mine? Are you sure it's mine? I have to ask.'

She says nothing.

'Well, I just don't know, do I?' he says.

*

Sex happens, surprisingly, at the Gasthaus Sonne in Trennfeld. It's what they always do – hurry to the hired space to undress. It's what they always do, and they do it now out of habit, not knowing what else to do when they are alone in the hotel room. This time, however, he makes no effort to please her. He wants her to dislike him. If she decides she dislikes him, he thinks, she may decide that she does not want this pregnancy. He is hurried, forceful, almost violent. And when she is in tears afterwards, he feels awful and sits on the toilet with his head in his hands.

It took them an hour to find Trennfeld in the fog – a village of tall half-timbered houses on a steep bluff above the Main. Every second house with a sign saying *Zimmer Frei*. A few more formal inns – with parking space in front and paths down to the river at the back – in one of which they have a room.

He had told her, as they picked their way through the fog, that she should not assume, should she decide to keep this child, that it would mean they would stay together. It would not necessarily mean that. Not at all. It was only fair, he said, that he should tell her that.

She said nothing.

She had said little or nothing for the last two hours.

Then she said, 'You don't understand.'

Sliding across a mysterious foggy junction, he said, 'What don't I understand?'

'That I love you,' she said drily.

Well, she would say that, he thought, *wouldn't she.* Still, his hands took a firmer hold on the wheel.

A sign at the roadside told them, then, that they had arrived at Trennfeld.

And there it was, the picturesque street of half-timbered houses. The Gasthaus Sonne. The low-beamed reception area. The narrow stairs with the Internet router flickering on the wall, up which the smiling Frau led them to their room.

She had a shower and found him lying on the bed, on the grape-coloured counterpane, waiting for her.

Later, when he emerges from the bathroom's rose-tiled box, she is still crying, naked except for the coverlet that she has pulled partially over herself. 'I'm sorry,' he says, sitting down on the edge of the bed. It does not sound very sincere so he says it again. 'I'm sorry.'

'It's just,' he says, 'this is such a shock. To me.'

'You don't think it's a shock to me?' There is a pillow over her head. Her voice is muffled, tear-clogged, defiant.

He looks from her pale shoulders to the insipid watercolour on the orange wall.

'Of course it is,' he says. 'That's why we need to think about this. We need to think about it seriously. I mean . . .' He wonders how to put this. 'You need to think about *your* life.'

He knows she is ambitious. She is a TV journalist – pops up on the local Kraków news interviewing farmers about the drought, or the mayor of some nearby town about his new leisure centre and how he managed to snare matching funds from the European Union. She is only twenty-five, and she is sort of famous, in the Kraków area. (She probably makes more money than he does, now he thinks about it.) People say hello to her in the street sometimes, point to her on the shopping-centre escalator. He was there when that happened. 'What was that about?' he said. 'You're famous?'

'No,' she laughed. 'Not really.'

She is though, and she wants more. He knows that.

'Do you see what I'm saying?' he asks.

*

They spend a few hours in the dim, curtained room as the afternoon wears on. Nothing outside the room, on the other side of the crimson curtains, which glow dully with the daylight pressing on them from without, seems to have any significance. The room itself seems pregnant, swollen with futures in the blood-dim light.

And the light persists. It is high summer. The evenings last for ever.

Finally, as if outstared by the sun, they dress and leave.

Outside it is warm and humid. They start to walk up the picturesque half-timbered street. There are some other people around, people strolling in the evening, and on the terraces of the two or three inns, people.

She has said nothing. He feels, however, he feels more and more, that when she thinks about the situation, she will see that it would not be sensible to keep it. It would just not be *sensible*. And she *is* sensible. He knows that about her. She is not sentimental. She takes her own life seriously. Has plans for herself, is successfully putting them in train. It is one of the things he likes about her.

He notices that there are cigarette vending machines, several of them, in the street, out in the open. They look strange among the fairy-tale houses. A village of neurotic smokers. He would like to have a cigarette himself. Sometimes, *in extremis*, he still smokes.

Nothing seems very solid, and in fact there is a mist, nearly imperceptible, hanging in the street as the warm evening sucks the moisture out of the wet earth.

They sit down at a table on one of the terraces.

He wonders what to talk about. Should he just talk about anything? About this pretty place? About the high steep roofs of the houses? About the carved gables? About the long day he has had? About what they might do tomorrow?

None of these subjects seems to have any significance. And on the one subject that does seem to, he feels he has said everything there is to say. He does not want to say it all again. He does not want her to feel that he is pressuring her.

It is very important, he thinks, that the decision should be hers, that she should *feel* it was hers.

They sit in silence for a while, surrounded by soft German voices. Older people, mostly, in this place. Older people on their summer holidays.

He says, desperate to know, 'What are you thinking?'

'Why did you choose this place?'

'Why?' He is not prepared for the simple, ordinary question. 'It wasn't too far from the airport,' he says. 'I didn't want to drive too much further today. It was in the direction we were going. The hotel looked okay. That's all. It's okay, isn't it?'

'It's fine,' she says.

He turns his head to take in part of the street and says, 'It's not very interesting, I know.'

'That's why I like it.' They share that too – an interest in uninteresting places.

'I wouldn't like to stay here for a week or something,' he says.

'No,' she agrees.

Though after all, why not? He does find a lot to like in this place. It is tidy. Quietly prosperous. Secluded in its modestly hilly landscape. Evidently, not much ever happens. There aren't even any shops – or perhaps there is one somewhere, one that is open mornings only, on weekdays (except

Wednesday). Hence, presumably, the cigarette machines. Maybe, with a teaching post at the Universität Würzburg, twenty minutes up the motorway, he would be able to find a way of living here . . .

As a train of thought it is absurd.

And escapist, in its own weird way.

A weird escapist fantasy, is what it is.

A fantasy of hiding himself in a place where nothing ever happens.

She has another taste of her peach juice. She is drinking peach juice, though that does not necessarily mean anything – she is not a habitual drinker.

'And now,' she says, 'we'll never forget it.'

The noises around them seem to slide away to the edges of a tight, soundless space. He hears his own voice saying, 'Why will we never forget it?' as if it wasn't obvious what she meant. And when she says nothing, he wonders, fighting down a wave of panic, *Is this her way of telling me?*

He does not want her to feel that he is pressuring her.

Panicking, he says, 'Please don't make a decision now that you'll wish later you hadn't made.'

'I won't,' she says.

They sit there, swifts shrieking in the hot white sky.

'Just,' he says. 'Please. You know what I think. I won't say it all again.'

And then a minute later, he is saying it all again, everything he said in the hotel.

About how they don't know each other that well.

About the impact it will have on her life. On their life together.

There is a furtive desperation in his eyes.

'Stop this, *please*,' she says, turning away in her sunglasses. 'Stop it.'

'I'm sorry . . .'

She starts to well up again; a solitary tear plummets down her face.

'I'm sorry,' he says again, embarrassed. People are starting to look at them.

He has, he thinks, really fucked this up now. His hand moves to take hers, then stops.

He feels as if his surface has been stripped, like a layer of paint, all the underlying terrors exposed.

'I just need to know,' he says.

'*What* do you need to know?'

It seems obvious. 'What's going to *happen*?'

'What you want to happen,' she says.

'It's not what *I* want . . .'

'Yes, it is.'

'I don't want you to do it just because *I* want it . . .'

'I'm *not* doing it just because *you* want it.'

It is like waking up from a nightmare, to find your life still there, as you left it. The sounds of the world, too, are there again. It is as if his ears have popped. 'Okay,' he says, now taking her hand. 'Okay.' It would not do to seem too happy. And in fact, to his surprise, there is a trace of sadness now, somewhere inside him – a sort of vapour trail of sadness on the otherwise blue sky of his mind.

She sobs for a minute or two, quietly, while he holds her hand and tries to ignore the looks of the pensioners who are watching them now without pretence, as if, in this place where nothing ever happens, they were a piece of street theatre.

Which they aren't.

3

The motorway is taking them north-east, towards Dresden. In the vicinity of each town the traffic thickens. The sun looks down at it all, at the hurrying traffic glittering on the motorways of Germany. It is Monday.

They woke late, to find the sun beating at the curtains, beating to be let in. Heat throbbed from the sun-beaten curtains. They had kicked off the bedding. She had not slept well. She was, in some sense, it seemed to him, in mourning. He had no intention of talking about it, not today.

Last night, after the scene on the terrace, they had walked for an hour, walked to the end of the village and then along the river – little paths led down to it, to wooden jetties where boats were tied in the green water. Steep banks on the other side, where there were more pretty houses. Clouds of gnats floated over the water. It was evening, then, finally. Dusk.

They walked back to the Gasthaus Sonne. They hadn't eaten anything.

In the harshly lit room, she said, 'You always get what you want. I know that.'

'That isn't true,' he murmured. Though even then he thought, *Maybe it is. Maybe I do.*

She was undressing. 'I should get used to that,' she said. 'I know people like you.'

'Meaning?'

'People that just drift through life, always getting what they want.' She was speaking quietly, not looking at him.

'You don't know me,' he told her.

'I know you well enough,' she said.

'Well enough for what?'

She went into the bathroom with her washbag.

He lay down on the soft mattress. He was still trying to think of a single significant instance, in his whole life, when he did not get what he wanted. The fact was, his life was exactly how he wanted it to be.

It had been his plan to visit Bamberg the next morning, and that is what they did. They stuck to his plan, and spent the morning sightseeing, as if nothing had happened. In the Romanesque simplicity of the cathedral, he pored over the tombs of Holy Roman Emperors.

Heinrich II, † 1024

The middle ages. Yesterday's mad scenes next to the motorway, among the trucks, seemed very far away in the limpid atmosphere of the nave. Their feet whispered on the stone floor. They were walking together, looking at statues. He felt safe there, doing that. He did not want to leave, to step out of the hush into the sun, the blinding white square.

She still wasn't saying much. She had hardly spoken to him all morning.

Maybe this *was* the end, he thought, as they walked in the streets of Bamberg, every blue shadow vibrating with detail.

Maybe she had decided – as he had intended, in the madness of yesterday – that she didn't like him.

He had disappointed her, there was no doubt about that.

Lunch, though, was almost normal.

Sunlight fell through leaves into the quiet garden where waiters moved among the tables. *This* was what he had imagined. This was what he had had in mind. Not the scenes next to the motorway. This windless walled garden, the still shadows of these leaves. This was what he wanted.

That she was pregnant, and what would happen about that, was the one thing he did not want to talk about. The decision had been made. There was nothing else to say. They would, at some point, have to discuss practicalities. Doctors. Money. Until then, talking about it might simply open it up again – might somehow unmake the decision – so he stayed away from the subject, or anything like it.

After lunch they drove out of the town to the church of the Vierzehnheiligen. They were standing outside the church, and he was reading from a leaflet they had picked up at one of the tourist stands. "'On 24 September 1445,'" he read, "'Hermann Leicht, the young shepherd of a nearby Franciscan monastery, saw . . .'"

He stopped.

He would not have started if he had known how the story went.

He went on, quickly, "'A crying child in a field that belonged to the nearby Cistercian monastery of Langheim. As he bent down to pick up the child . . .'"

He had already started on the next sentence when he saw that it was even worse.

"'As he bent down to pick up the child, it abruptly disappeared.'"

He wondered whether to stop reading the thing out.

Deciding that that would only make matters worse, he went on. When he had finished, he shoved the leaflet into his pocket. 'Should we go in?' he said.

And then inside, in the mad marble dream of the interior, something similar happened.

They were standing at the altar, inspecting the statuary there – each statue was numbered and there was a key to indentify them. That was what he was doing. Pointing to each of the fourteen saints, and telling her who they were, and what they did. For instance, he pointed to one and said, 'St Agathius, invoked against headache.' Or, 'St Catherine of Alexandria, invoked against sudden death.' Or, 'St Margaret of Antioch, invoked in . . .'

It was too late – he had to say it.

'Childbirth.'

He wished then more than ever that they had not driven out there, in the heat of the day. He didn't like baroque, or whatever this was. And he had a feeling that something was coming unstuck.

The next saint, he told her, was St Vitus, invoked against epilepsy.

'St Vitus's dance. And so on,' he said. Her eyes, he was sure, were still on St Margaret of Antioch. 'Here, I won't read them all.' He handed her the paper and, after standing there for a few seconds, started off at a leisurely pace across the brown marble floor, past pinkish columns, their markings swirling like the clouds of Jupiter.

She was still at the altar.

The place was as full as a station at rush hour.

Full of murmurous voices like the wind in a forest.

He found himself standing in front of the font – another extraordinary accretion of kitsch – staring at its pinks, its golds, its powder blues.

A stone bishop holding in his hands his own gold-hatted head.

As weird, he thought, as anything in any Inca or Hindu house of worship.

A stone bishop holding in his hands his own gold-hatted head.

A martyr. Presumably. And he wondered, with the habit of wanting to know, who this man was. This man, who had invited oblivion on himself, or taken it peaceably – the stone face on the severed head was nothing if not peaceful – when it took him.

Oblivion.

He looked up, looked for her.

She was not at the altar now. She was near the entrance, where the devotional candles were. And she had put a euro in the box and was taking a candle and lighting it from one of the ones already there.

He wondered, again, whether she was in any sense devout. Her personal mores – as far as he had been able to make them out – suggested not. Or at least had not in any way led him to think that she might be. The first time he had set eyes on her, more or less, she had been snorting cocaine, at Mani's party.

Everyone else in that space was moving, it seemed, and she was standing still. She was standing still and watching the little flame that she had lit.

Which meant what?

He wanted to ask her. He did not dare. He was frightened about what she might say.

'I preferred the cathedral in Bamberg,' he said, as they walked down the hill, hoping that she would agree – as if *that* would mean anything. As if it would dispel the worries that had started, since they arrived at this place, to interfere with his tranquillity.

She said she would have expected him to prefer the cathedral. 'You're not interested in anything post about fifteen hundred,' she said, 'are you?'

'Fifteen hundred,' he said, pleased that she was at least being flippant, 'at the very latest.'

'Why is that, do you think?'

'I don't know.'

'You must have some idea. You must have thought about it.'

'It's just an aesthetic preference.'

'Is it?' She was sceptical.

'I think so. I just feel no love,' he said, 'for a place like that.' He meant the Vierzehnheiligen, and he seemed determined to do it down.

When she started to praise the tumbling fecundity of its decoration, he took it almost personally.

'I just don't like it,' he said. 'Okay?'

She laughed. 'Okay.'

'I'm sorry. Whatever. You liked it. I didn't. Fine.'

They drove back to the motorway – a few kilometres through humid fields of yellow rapeseed.

'Why did you light that candle?' he asked, trying to sound no more than vaguely interested.

'I don't know.'

'I didn't know you were religious,' he said.

'I'm not.'

'So?'

'I just felt like it. Is it a problem?'

'Of course not. I was wondering, that's all.'

'I just felt like it,' she said again.

He asked, 'You don't believe in God?'

'I don't know. No. Do you?'

He laughed as if it should be obvious. 'No. Not even slightly.'

And then they were on the motorway again, north-east, towards Dresden.

He said, after a while, 'I'll pay for it, of course. The . . .' He found himself unable to say the word.

He needed to know, however, that the decision still stood.

It seemed it did.

She said, just looking levelly out at the motorway, 'Okay.' And then, 'Thank you.'

He wondered, having started to talk about it, whether to talk about it some more. To ask, for instance, *where* she wanted to have it done. To nail it down with details. Specific places. Times.

The silence, while he wondered this, ended up lasting for over an hour.

And now they are stuck in traffic outside Dresden. It is five in the afternoon. Light screams off windscreens. The air conditioning pours frigid air over them.

Satisfied again that he has no major problem, small ones start to trouble him. It was a fault in his plan for today, he thinks, that they should be passing Dresden at this time. He ought to have known that this would happen. It was foreseeable. (He moves forward another few metres, sick of the sight of the van in front of him.) It was an unforced error.

And the damage to Stańko's paintwork – that is still there, to be talked about, to be apologised for.

To be paid for.

Another thing to be paid for.

4

He is thinking about the piece he needs to write for the *Journal of English and Germanic Philology*. 'Anomalous Factors in the Form *"Slēan"* – Some Suggestions'. He is in the shower, offering his face to the warm streams of water, thinking about it. Thinking about the work that needs to be done. The hours that will need to be spent in libraries – Oxford, London, Paris, Heidelberg. The shower is in a sort of hollow in a stone wall – the whole bathroom is like that. The windows, two of them, are narrow slits. The functional elements, though, are impeccably modern. The tiles on the floor are warm to the soles of his feet when he steps out of the shower and takes a heavy towel. Tastefully done, everything. Once it was a monastery, now it is an upmarket hotel. While he towels himself he leans towards one of the windows, which is set in a deep narrowing slot in the wall, to see out – steep forested hills, quite far away. He likes to imagine the time when this *was* a monastery, when it sat in fields next to the meandering, pristine waters of the Elbe. When the only way to get to Königstein was by walking for an hour. When Dresden was a whole day's walk away. He towels his hair, flattens it with his hand until he is satisfied with how it looks. 'Anomalous Factors in the Form *"Slēan"*'. That must be his focus now. Now that this nightmare is over, and the future is there again.

It is early evening. The sun puts warm shapes on the wall opposite the windows. The decoration is monastic minimalist: fluid lines, unelaborated. Polished stone. White sheets. Everything white.

She is sitting on a pale leather sofa, hugging her knees, looking towards one of the windows, with its view over neat modern houses to the hills farther away. Disappointingly, the hotel is surrounded by suburban normality. Streets of newish single-family houses, and a sort of industrial estate.

Kilted in the white towel he descends the two stone steps from the shower room. He starts to search in his suitcase for his deodorant. 'Are you hungry?' he asks.

She is sitting on the sofa, hugging her knees.

He applies deodorant.

'Are you hungry?' he asks again, not impatiently, just with a different intonation, as if she might not have heard him the first time, though she must have.

'The food's supposed to be excellent,' he tells her, looking forward to the meal himself. 'French. They've got a Michelin star.'

This was to be their treat, this immaculate hotel and its Michelin-starred food – their indulgence, their luxury. Tomorrow night they will be at her place in Kraków. The day after that, she will be at work again, on television, and he will be on a flight to Stansted. She likes her work. Just after they arrived at the hotel, late this afternoon, someone phoned her. It turned out to be her producer. It was interesting to hear her work voice, and it seemed obvious, overhearing her – just from the tone, he understood nothing else – where her priorities were.

He is doing up his linen shirt.

She is sitting on the sofa, hugging her knees.

'I can't do it.'

'Can't do what?' He thinks she might mean the Michelin-starred meal, that she is feeling too depressed or something.

When she doesn't answer him, he starts to see that this is wrong. She does not mean the meal.

'I thought you decided,' he says, quietly, trying to sound unperturbed as he does up his shirt.

'So did I.'

He finishes doing up his shirt. What this means, he thinks, is that he will have to do it all again. He will have to do yesterday evening, again. She is going to make them do that again. He sits down on the pale sofa. She is sitting sideways with her feet on the sofa, facing away from him, and he puts his hands on her shoulders and starts to say, again, all the things he said yesterday.

'I know,' she says.

He is saying the things, softly saying them, with a tired voice, as if he is unpacking them, and putting them out on a table for her to see.

'I know,' she says.

He is whispering them in her ear, his mouth is next to her ear. He is able to smell the light scent of her sweat – fresh sweat and stale sweat. To feel on his face, which sometimes touches hers, the dampness of her tears.

'I know,' she says, 'I know.'

His arms are encircling her, his hands on her stomach.

'It's all true what you're saying,' she says.

'Yes, it is . . .'

'And none of it makes any difference. I just can't.'

She takes his hands in her hands. Other than that, she does not move. Her hands are very warm and very damp.

She says, 'This child has chosen me to be its mother, and . . . and I just can't turn it away. Please understand.'

'Karel,' she says, 'please understand.'

His forehead is heavy on her shoulder.

'Do you understand?' she wants to know, in a whisper.

'No,' he says. It is not quite true. Not quite.

The situation, anyway, is simpler than he thought. It was always very simple. The last two days have been a sort of illusion. There was only ever one possible outcome. He sees that now.

They stay there for a long time, on the pale sofa.

The sun won't stop shining.

'Now what?' he says finally. What he means is: Where does this leave us? Where does this leave our two lives?

'Are you hungry?' she asks.

'No,' he immediately says. He finds it hard to imagine ever feeling hunger again. He finds it hard to imagine anything. The future, again, seems no longer to be there.

'Do you want to go for a walk?' she asks, for the first time shifting her position, turning towards him, so that her shoulder moves, and he has to lift his head. 'Let's go for a walk,' she says.

'Where?' Having lifted his head, he is looking at the elegantly minimalist room as if he does not know where he is.

'I don't know,' she says. 'Wherever. Why don't you put some trousers on?'

Docilely, he does.

*

They leave the hotel and start to walk towards Königstein. The pavement follows the main road. Traffic sometimes whizzes past. Sometimes there is silence. Sometimes there are trees, or from somewhere the smell of cut grass.

It is five kilometres to Königstein, the sign says. They do not stop. It is high summer. The light will last for hours. They have time to walk it, if they want to.

5

Lascia Amor e siegui Marte!

1

Every morning he takes his daughters to school, or in the summer holidays to their tennis lesson. It is usually the only time he sees them during the day, since he arrives home late, long after they are asleep. So he has promised to take them to school in the morning, or to their tennis lesson. It is a promise he has kept so far.

Their school is on his way to work anyway. The Dansk Tennis Klub involves a detour. To drive there takes twenty minutes at least. The traffic is quite heavy at that time in the morning. He talks to them, his daughters, Tine and Vikki, while he drives – about television and pop music and famous people mostly. Tine is eleven. Vikki is eight. They like to talk about television stars. Pop stars. He knows quite a lot about that, even though it is no longer his area of particular expertise, as it once was.

They arrive at the tennis club at about ten to nine, and the girls spill out with their stuff, their water and tennis equipment, and wave perfunctorily as he turns in his seat to see them off. When they are inside he pulls away, and puts the radio on. Usually he does not put the radio on until he has dropped them off, though sometimes they listen to music together as they drive, and sometimes they sing along to songs they know.

On his own, he listens to the news. It is usually the sport at that time, five to nine, as he drives past Søerne, the lakes.

The Audi is quite new – less than a year – and he still enjoys driving it. An A4, silver, with black leather seats. An unobtrusive executive saloon. Anonymous, almost. When he was deciding what sort of car to get he found a website that said of this model that it was 'coldly, rationally competent in just about every department'. He immediately liked the sound of it.

From the tennis club, it takes another ten minutes or so, depending on the traffic, to get to his office in town.

Sometimes he is a few minutes late for the morning meeting, and slips in to take the seat nearest the door while Elin is already talking.

This morning there is a special meeting. Elin phoned him very late last night and said she had just spoken to Jeppe, the news editor. He'd told her about a story he had. It was about the defence minister, Edvard Dahlin, and an affair he was supposedly having with a married woman.

'Has Jeppe spoken to you about this?' Elin asked him.

'No', Kristian said.

Jeppe had told her he was sure the story was true because he had access to phone data that left no doubt – highly suggestive metadata, and also, more significantly, the actual words of text messages. Elin wanted to know how Jeppe had got his hands on that information, whether anything illegal had been done. He told her that if it had, no one on the paper's payroll was directly involved.

After telling all that to Kristian, she asked him what he thought.

He said he would need to see the information first.

This morning they're meeting to discuss it.

When he arrives, Kristian finds Jeppe and his deputy David Jespersen waiting outside the meeting room. Jeppe, obese, is sitting on the only seat, a plastic cup of water in his hand.

'Elin here yet?' Kristian asks.

'She's in there with Morten,' Jeppe says. He must be nearly sixty now. He has been on the paper, has been news editor, since Kristian first started working there as an intern.

'Talking to him about your dodgy phone data?' Kristian asks.

Jeppe shrugs. There is something monstrous about his lack of neck. His white hair is cut in a scruffy pudding-bowl.

'What have you got exactly?' Kristian asks him.

He knows that Jeppe keeps things from him, has a direct line to Elin and tries to go over his head whenever he can. Jeppe wanted the deputy editor position when it opened up two years ago – instead it went to Kristian, who was then editor of the showbiz and television pages, and is twenty years younger than him. There's not been much warmth between them since then.

Jeppe says, looking into his plastic cup, 'I'll tell you in there. I don't want to say it all twice.'

'Fair enough.' Kristian turns to David Jespersen. 'Morning, David.'

'Hello, mate.'

'You joining us too?'

'That's right.'

'Very exciting,' Kristian says.

When they are summoned in, they find Elin with Morten, the in-house lawyer. He doesn't look like a lawyer. He's wearing a tracksuit.

They all say good morning to each other and take seats at the long table. There are bottles of mineral water. There is a view of Peblinge Lake. It is a hot, still August morning.

Elin says to Jeppe, 'Okay, tell us what you have.'

'David,' Jeppe says.

David Jespersen, with some eagerness, sits forward. He is the same age as Kristian – exactly the same age; they were at school together in Sundbyøster. David went to university, entered journalism that way. Kristian didn't, and for some time David was the senior of the two of them. He is lean, handsome, slightly yellow as if he has liver trouble. He sits forward. He says, 'Okay. What have we got. We have hard evidence,' he says, speaking primarily to Elin, 'that Edvard Dahlin is having an affair with a married woman. It's been going on for a few years. We've been working on this for some time now, actually. The woman's called Natasha Ohmsen. She's married to Søren Ohmsen—'

Elin interrupts. 'Dahlin's not married?'

'No. Divorced,' David says. 'Ohmsen's married.'

Elin nods.

'Yeah, it's been going on for a few years,' David says. 'Now it seems like it might be ending. She's ending it. Dahlin's not happy about that.'

'He's heartbroken,' Jeppe puts in.

'And you know all this because you have access to phone data?' Elin asks. 'What actually do you have? Who did you get it from?'

David looks at Jeppe – nervously, Kristian thinks, watching him.

'Someone in the phone company,' Jeppe says. 'Like I told you, they have access to Dahlin's phone records, this person. Who he calls. When. His voicemails. Text messages.'

'And you have that information?'

'Yeah.'

'How?' Elin asks.

'We were approached.'

'I assume some form of payment was involved.'

'Yeah,' Jeppe says again, looking down at the table.

'How much?'

Jeppe looks up. 'Are you sure you want to know?'

Elin looks at Morten, who shakes his head.

'So what do you have, exactly?' she asks.

David hands her a flash memory stick, half-standing to lean across the table. 'All the texts are on there,' he says. 'And a summary of the main points.'

'It's the texts are important,' Jeppe points out.

'Texts from him to her?'

'And from her to him,' David says. 'It's all there.'

She plugs the memory stick into a laptop and opens a file. For a minute or so she looks at it, while the others look at the wall, or at the lake out of the window, the low skyline of Copenhagen – the houses on the other side of the lake look like expensive toys.

'You're sure,' she says suddenly, 'these are kosher? Not some kind of hoax?'

'One hundred per cent sure,' Jeppe says.

'How?'

'We tested the source.'

'Oh?'

'Sent some texts ourselves,' Jeppe says, 'to Dahlin's number. They're in there. Exact times, everything.'

Elin seems satisfied with this, even impressed, and David, in particular, looks pleased with himself.

Elin says, 'Only problem is, we can't print any of this. The messages.'

'No,' Jeppe tells her. 'That would expose our source. And what he's done, it's not strictly speaking legal, is it. I mean, I don't know. He'd be opening himself to prosecution, possibly.'

'Okay.' Elin turns to Morten, who is looking at the messages on the laptop screen, standing at her shoulder. 'So we can't do it?' she asks, twisting in her seat to look up at him.

'No,' Morten says. 'If Dahlin sues, and you can't use this material in court, you've got nothing else. So no.'

'So where does that leave us? Jeppe?'

David Jespersen, looking worried, sets his jaw and directs his eyes to the windows. He models himself, to some extent, on David Beckham. The sharply tailored jacket. The 1930s haircut. The groomed blonde stubble.

Jeppe starts to talk about the national security implications of the story.

Elin interrupts him.

'Yes, okay,' she says impatiently. 'If he sues, we have no defence. That's the point. What do you think?' she asks Kristian, who has said nothing so far.

He too has left his seat and is leaning over the laptop screen, looking through the texts. There are hundreds of them. It's embarrassing, in a way, to see them. The language of them. *I want you. You're breaking my heart.* All that sort of stuff.

He straightens himself up. 'It's a major story,' he says. 'He's a senior minister. It's got to be a major story.'

'So you think we should do it?' Elin asks him.

'I think we've got to.'

'He'll sue and you'll probably lose,' Morten says, taking a seat again in his tracksuit, knees spread. 'It'll be very expensive if you do. I have to tell you that.'

Elin is still looking at Kristian. He has a very serene energy, Kristian. A soft, slightly pudgy face. In his narrow-lapelled suit, his thin blue tie, he might be an unusually elegant accountant, or even a young undertaker. It's easy to imagine him dealing tactfully with the family of the deceased, knowing what to say, and how to say it. 'Sure,' he says to Morten. 'I understand. We just need something more. Another source.'

'Like who?' Elin asks.

'How about Edvard himself? What if he admits it?'

'Why would he do that?' Jeppe says

Kristian ignores him. 'He doesn't know this is all we've got,' he says to Elin. 'He doesn't know *what* we know, or how we know it.' Now he looks at Jeppe. 'Does he?'

Jeppe just stares at him with open hostility until he looks at Elin again.

'We make him think we're going to do the story anyway,' Kristian says, 'and say we're offering him a chance to have his say, to put his side of it . . .'

'What if he just denies it?' Jeppe asks.

'Then he denies it,' Kristian says. 'I don't think he will.' He says, to Elin again now, 'I know him quite well.'

She says quietly, 'You do, don't you.'

He shrugs modestly.

'I mean, that's the other thing,' Elin says. 'We like Dahlin, don't we?'

'We can't ignore the story just because of that,' Jeppe says.

'We can't ignore the story for all sorts of reasons,' Kristian says. 'It does mean we should talk to him first. He'd expect that. We want to handle it as sympathetically as possible. That's what we tell him. If he thinks we're going to do it anyway, it just wouldn't make sense for him to deny it.'

'*You* should talk to him,' Elin says to Kristian.

Jeppe sighs petulantly.

'Has anybody else got this?' Elin asks him.

Jeppe says, 'No. I don't think so.'

'You don't think so?'

'No,' he says. 'They don't.'

'Still, we should move quickly with it,' Kristian suggests. 'We don't want anyone else stumbling on it. And we want to do it before she dumps him, if she does. I'll talk to Edvard today?'

Elin says, 'Okay, talk to him. Let's see what he has to say for himself. And well done, you two,' she says to the others. 'Okay, that's it.'

As they start to leave, she asks Kristian to stay.

Hanging back, Morten says to her, 'If you want to do this, I advise you not to name the woman. She's a private citizen. She'd have some sort of case against you for invasion of privacy, even if your story is a hundred per cent true and not otherwise actionable.'

'Okay,' Elin says. 'I'll think about it. Thanks, Morten.'

When they are alone, she asks Kristian to set up the meeting with Dahlin and he phones Ulrik Larssen, the defence minister's media advisor. Kristian knows Ulrik fairly well. They talk, typically, several times a week.

'Ulrik,' he says. 'Kristian.'

A few pleasantries, then he says, 'Listen, Ulrik, I need a meeting with Edvard. Face to face. Oh.' He looks at Elin. 'He's in Spain, is he?' he says, for her to hear. 'Well, can I meet him down there? I can fly out this morning. It *is* important,' he says. 'It's very important. He'll want to hear what I have to tell him. No, I can't tell him over the phone. Okay, let me know what he says. Thanks, Ulrik.'

He hangs up, and says, 'He's in Spain for a few days.'

'Officially?'

'No, he's on holiday.'

While they wait for Ulrik to call back Elin says to him, 'There's going to be a fairly major shake-up around here, Kristian. Our new proprietor – he wants to take out a lot of costs. He needs to. *We* need to. You know that.'

He nods at her, smiles.

She says, 'We're going to have to lose some people. Quite a few people.'

'I know,' he says.

They have taken adjacent seats at the long table. His phone is on the table in front of them, waiting for Ulrik.

'You're always so smartly dressed,' she says, smiling at him admiringly.

'I try my best.'

'Jeppe's a slob.'

He says nothing, just aligns his phone with the edge of the table.

'What do you think of him?'

'You thinking of losing him?' he asks, his eyes still on his phone.

'He's hanging by a thread,' she admits.

'This might help. If it comes off.'

'I'm sure David did all the work.'

'I'm sure,' he agrees.

'Can you see David doing Jeppe's job?' she asks.

She is looking at him, in that way of hers – as if he is the only thing in the world that interests her. It's very flattering. 'I'm not sure,' he says.

'I can't,' she says. 'If I'm honest.'

'Maybe he'd grow into it,' Kristian suggests.

'We don't have the space to experiment.'

'No,' he agrees.

'You get quite a lot of stories from Dahlin, don't you?' she asks.

'A fair few. He's a decent source. We have a relationship.'

'Won't this damage that?'

Kristian knits his soft white hands and frowns thoughtfully. 'No,' he says finally. 'That's about self-interest, on both sides. That won't change. And if it does,' he says, 'it's worth it. I think.'

'I could send someone else.'

A faint smile acknowledges her thoughtfulness. He shakes his head – his haircut is corporate, mouse-coloured. 'No.'

'Might this cost him his job?' she asks.

'No, I don't think so.' He thinks about it some more. 'No. If he was married, maybe. But he isn't.'

'What about Natasha Ohmsen?' Elin asks.

'Yeah, I was thinking about that,' Kristian says, taking off his glasses. 'We should keep an eye on her. Find out where she lives. We have her number, obviously – we can flip the phone. See what she's up to. If Edvard tells me to fuck off – which he might, he's pig-headed when he wants to be – we might get what we need from her.'

'I'll put someone on it.'

They sit briefly in silence.

Then she says, with a quiet smile, 'How're the girls?'

He is about to answer, to say something vague and positive, when his phone starts. Ulrik.

When they have spoken, he puts the phone in his jacket pocket. He says to Elin, 'Edvard's expecting me at his house in Spain this afternoon.'

2

It is forty degrees in Málaga when he arrives in the middle of the afternoon. The sea, from the plane, looked as dark as denim. The mountains looked prehistoric. From Hertz he picks up a white VW Passat, and with the air con shoved up as high as it will go, he enters Edvard's address into the satnav.

The house is in a village somewhere up the motorway towards Córdoba. About an hour it will take to drive there, apparently.

He and Edvard last met only a week ago. That's what he is thinking of as he drives away from the airport. The newspaper's new owner threw a party. Edvard wasn't the only minister there, but he was the most senior – the deputy leader of the party in power. He turned up as a personal favour to Kristian – Kristian's own house-warming present for the new proprietor – and he stayed for only half an hour or so, sipping champagne on the lawn of the modest Danish-style stately home that had been hired for the occasion. Kristian made the introduction: Newspaper-owning millionaire, defence minister. Defence minister, newspaper-owning millionaire. He stood there watching with a sort of pride as they exchanged small talk. Afterwards he and Edvard spoke together for a while, at the edge of the gathering near an impeccably clipped hedge. Exchanged some tittle-tattle, discussed Edvard's own prospects. Politically, the paper was on the minister's side. He even wrote for them occasionally. Pieces were published under his name, anyway. Kristian sometimes wrote them.

Most recently one about the virtues of less onerous labour-market regulation. Slightly odd, that the *defence* minister should be publishing something on an area of economic policy. He had his eye on the top job, that was an open secret. Which was partly why, as well, he stood on the lawn for half an hour nursing a glass of champagne last week in the pleasant summer weather – somewhat cloudy but no real threat of rain.

The motorway slams through a landscape of dry hills. For long stretches the only vegetation is the olive trees, millions of them, planted in tedious lines.

Near a town called Lucena the satnav instructs him to leave the motorway. The landscape is marginally less arid now. Some trees other than olives, not many, stand in the withering sunlight, shadows at their feet. Thin sheep on a hillside. A village with a white church, bells hanging still in little arches. The streets are empty. Siesta, he supposes. On the edge of the village is a house.

This is it.

The satnav tells him he is there.

A wall around a plot of land, one tree outside the wall, in the limited shade of which he attempts to position the white hire car. Then the gate, squeaking open on its hinges, a frisking from the minister's close protection officers – two of them, expecting him, sweating in the heat – and the path up to the house.

The house is modest. A single-storey, white, with a porch at the front, a few white pillars. Some palmy-type plants of various sizes in pots. Dusty oleander. Some unpretentious furniture on the porch, a table and a few chairs: green-painted metal, with green-and-white striped cushions. On the wall of the house under the porch, some plates hung up for decoration.

The defence minister, in shorts, flip-flops and a short-sleeved shirt, is moving a sprinkler when Kristian arrives. His shirt hangs open to show the whitish hair on his front. He is also wearing a panama hat and sunglasses. He sees his visitor. 'Oh, hello,' he says, putting the sprinkler down. A green hose trails across the dry ground to a standpipe with a tap at the side of the house. A spray of water is visible where the hose is attached to the tap, obviously not very well.

The minister walks over to where Kristian is standing, sweating heavily, on the path.

'Hello, Kristian.'

'Hello, Minister.'

They shake hands. The minister's handshake is exaggeratedly firm.

His face is tanned, handsome, tense.

'Come and sit down,' he says, gesturing towards the furniture on the porch. 'You're not dressed for this weather, are you?' he laughs as they make their way there. Kristian has only been out of the A/C for a minute or two and already his shirt is sticking extravagantly to his back. Where his suit jacket hangs over his arm, his sleeve is sodden. 'I didn't have time to think of that,' he says.

'No,' the minister says. 'Please, have a seat. Would you like a drink?'

'Just some water, please.'

Strings of beads hang in the open door of the house and the minister passes through them to fetch the drinks.

A minute later he emerges with another swish of the beads. He hands Kristian a glass of sparkling water with ice and a piece of lemon in it. He has furnished himself with a San Miguel. Heavily he sits down in the chair opposite and says, 'Cheers.' He is sweating too, though more lightly than his guest.

'Cheers,' Kristian says.

They drink thirstily in the waves of insect noise that assail the hot shade of the porch.

'This is your house?' Kristian asks.

'It's my ex-wife's,' the minister tells him. 'She lets me use it sometimes. She's Spanish,' he adds.

'I didn't know that.'

'Well, now you do.'

Kristian lets his eyes wander nervously over the struggling vegetation.

'Now,' the minister says, impatient with the small talk, 'why are you here, Kristian, and in such a hurry?' He is plainly eager to know. His toes, having freed themselves from a flip-flop, have taken hold of a metal strut under the table.

Kristian has another sip of sparkling water, then he puts the dripping glass down on the table. He makes himself look the defence minister in the eye. He says, 'Natasha Ohmsen. We know about you and Natasha Ohmsen.'

The insects, like the teeth of a comb sawing at something.

Finally the minister says, 'What's that supposed to mean?'

Kristian smiles unhurriedly and takes off his glasses and wipes the sweat from his face with his sleeve. He puts his glasses back on. 'You do know her?' he says.

'Yes, I know Natasha,' Edvard says. 'So?'

'I have sources,' Kristian says. 'People talk.'

'Who? What sources? What do you mean?'

'I think you know what I mean.'

'Well, I don't know what you've heard . . .'

'I have total faith,' Kristian says, 'in the information I have.'

'Which is?'

'Which is that you and Mrs Ohmsen are having an affair.'

'That's nonsense.'

Kristian shakes his head. 'I don't believe it is.'

'Well, I'm telling you now – it's nonsense. We're friends, yes. Natasha—'

'You're more than friends,' Kristian says, interrupting him. 'This story isn't about friendship. This story is about the fact that you and Mrs Ohmsen are, and have been for some time, very much more than friends.'

When Edvard says nothing, Kristian smiles again. It is a friendly smile. 'Listen,' he says. 'I would not have gone to all this trouble today if I didn't *know* this was true.'

He takes a sip of his water.

Then he says, 'I don't have any photographs to show you or anything like that.'

'Then what makes you think it's true?'

'It's my job to know what's true, and this is true. The information I have is from sources I absolutely trust.'

'Who?' Edvard demands.

Kristian sighs tolerantly. He says, 'All I would ask is that you look at what I have done here – I am here, in person, in Spain, to see you, today – and perhaps just admit that the information I have is true.'

The defence minister is picking nervously at the wet San Miguel label. He doesn't say anything. The sunglasses make it difficult to tell what he's thinking. His mouth is a hard horizontal line.

Kristian says, tenderly, 'People know about this affair, Edvard. People are aware of it.'

And when Edvard still does not speak, he says, 'It's my opinion that if *I* don't do this story, at least one of my sources will take this information to another newspaper. The story is out. You have to accept that now.'

'I've done nothing wrong,' Edvard says at last.

'And we have no desire at all,' Kristian tells him, 'to damage you, politically or otherwise. We would not want to see anything published that would damage you.'

'Then why publish it?'

'Edvard,' Kristian says, 'the story is out. It *will* be published. The only question is when and by whom. And as I say, *we* have no desire to damage you politically . . .'

'This *will* damage me politically.'

'Maybe not. It depends how it's presented.'

'Anyway, politics is one thing,' Edvard says, angrier, 'private life is another. I *want* a private life. I'm young enough to want a private life. You must be able to understand that . . .'

'Of course I can.'

'If you don't have a private life, you don't have anything, you have nothing. You *are* nothing. You're not a person, you're just . . .'

'I understand . . .'

'Do you?'

The minister's face is flushed, and shiny with indignant sweat.

Kristian waits for a few moments. Then he says, technocratically, 'My view is that there are some matters, some stories, that have to be dealt with.'

'That's your view, is it?'

'Yes.'

'What stories? Stories like this one?' Edvard asks.

'Like this one, yes . . .'

'Why? This is my *private* life. I'm not married. I've always kept my private life private. I don't tell other people how they should live their lives. You know I don't. I'm entitled to a private life.'

Kristian says, 'In an ideal world, that's perhaps how it should be.'

An incredulous laugh from Edvard. 'In an ideal world? Why? Why not in this world?'

Kristian says, after a few moments, 'You are a senior minister and I don't think you can use arguments about privacy to swat away an accusation that you have had an affair with a married woman.'

'An *accusation*? That's an interesting word.'

'Allegation, then . . .'

'*I'm* not married.'

'I know that . . .'

'I haven't lied to anyone . . .'

'I'm not suggesting that you have.'

'What have I done wrong?'

'Nothing.'

'Then why must I be punished?'

'This isn't about punishment.'

'What is it about?'

'It's about the public's right to know . . .'

'Oh, for fuck's sake,' Edvard mutters.

'With respect, you are an elected public official.'

'Does that mean I have no right to a private life?'

'It means your right to one has to be balanced against other considerations.'

Edvard's thumbnail has shredded part of the San Miguel label.

'Other rights,' Kristian says.

'And Natasha? Is she an elected public official?'

'No.'

'Does she have no right to privacy then?'

Kristian frowns thoughtfully.

'If this is published,' Edvard says, finger jabbing, 'it's going to be open season on my private life *and* hers. You *know* that.'

Kristian wipes the sweat from his face again. He looks at his watch. It is quarter to five. He doesn't have much time, if they're to splash with this in the morning. He says, 'I'll tell you what. We won't name Mrs Ohmsen. Okay? We won't mention her name – if you work with us on this.' He is sitting forward now. He feels his shirt adhering to his back. He says, 'The story is out there, Edvard. It *will* come out. We want to help you on this. We want to do this as sympathetically as possible. So work with us. Okay?'

Edvard stands up. He looks out at the patchy lawn, his hand on one of the white pillars of the porch. 'It's not true that it won't damage me politically,' he says.

'Why? As you say, you're not married . . .'

'And anyway,' he says, 'I think it's over. With Natasha.'

Kristian feigns surprise.

'Yes,' Edvard says. 'She's ending it.'

'I didn't know.'

'How would you know?' A hollow laugh. 'Unless your source is Natasha herself.'

'It isn't.'

'It's not what I want,' Edvard says. 'I mean, to end it.'

'How long has it been going on?' Kristian asks.

'Two years. More or less. I was hoping,' Edvard says, still looking out to where the sprinkler has succeeded in making a muddy patch in the middle of the lawn, 'I was hoping she'd leave her husband. No,' he says. 'She doesn't want to do that.' He sighs, pained. He is in his mid-fifties. Still in decent shape. Only a slight paunch, leathery with sunlight, with Spanish weekends. Long thin legs.

He turns to Kristian and takes off his sunglasses. His eyebrows are thick and fair. His eyes pale blue.

'I feel like a fool, at my age, Kristian, feeling like this,' he says. 'About a woman.'

'You shouldn't.'

'Well, I do.' He has turned from the garden, the dry field of scraping insects, and is looking at Kristian, who is still in his seat, sweating. 'When they said you wanted to see me, I hoped it wouldn't be about this.'

Kristian smiles sadly. '*C'est la guerre,*' he says.

'You know I'll never be prime minister now?'

'No, I don't know that . . .'

'Oh, you do. This isn't France, Kristian.'

'And thank God for that.'

Ignoring the flippancy, the minister says, 'It will make me seem unsound, won't it. Not so much morally as emotionally . . . Unserious . . .'

Kristian says, 'I think you should tell me what happened, from the start, just to make sure we have everything straight.'

'You expect me to tell you everything?'

'Not everything: just the main points. When did it start? How did you meet?'

3

In the parked Passat, with the air conditioning screaming, he phones Elin.

'It's okay,' he says. 'He didn't put up much of a fight. He'll work with us on it. I'll try and knock something out at the airport and send it to you. One thing,' he says, thinking ahead, 'see if you can't find any photos of them together. They've met at social events. Her husband was there too, Søren Ohmsen. Maybe there's a photo of them together. The three of them. That would be perfect.'

He says, 'My plane's at seven something. I should be in the office by elevenish. I'll see you there.'

It is half past five. The sun is starting to leave its seat in the top of the sky, to lose some of its force. The thermometer on the dash says *37°*. The steering wheel, for a few minutes, is too hot for him to hold. He has to keep moving his hands on it as the satnav directs him back through the village and towards the motorway, south to Málaga.

He is thinking about the splash. Something like:

DEFENCE

MINISTER'S

SECRET

LOVE

And then a smaller headline underneath:

WEEKENDS OF PASSION IN SCORCHING SPAIN

Defence Minister Edvard Dahlin has been having a secret love affair with a married woman for more than two years. The 55-year-old father of two . . .

USES EX-WIFE'S HOUSE FOR SECRET LIAISON

The 55-year-old father of two . . .

The fifty-five-year-old father of two had tried, as they parted, to make a deal with him.

Kristian, already standing, holding his jacket, sweating, thought about it for a moment.

Then he said, 'That's nice to know.'

And smiled. And left. Walked down the path. Said, 'Thanks, lads,' to the minister's security detail – two men in sweat-stained polo shirts and wrap-around sunglasses, sitting on white plastic chairs in the shade of a bulge of bougainvillea next to the gate.

It was an offer of sorts, wasn't it, that Edvard had made him.

Not a serious one.

Not one worthy of serious consideration.

Edvard was not, to be honest, in much of a position to be making offers.

The 55-year-old father of two says he is 'heartbroken' that the mystery married woman . . .

That's something to think about. The thing about not naming her. She'll have to be named at some point. Hence his interest in the photos. She'll be named within forty-eight hours, he thinks, staring at the motorway, overtaking yet another Dutch mobile home. Once people know she exists, she'll be found and named within forty-eight hours. Will have to let someone else have the honour. Include some hints in the piece tomorrow. Yeah, mention her age.

The 55-year-old father of two says he is 'heartbroken' that the mystery married woman, 40, . . .

217

Maybe say something about her husband.

How about

The stunning brunette, 40, is refusing to leave her husband, one of Denmark's richest men . . .

That might narrow it down *too* much. Want someone else to name her asap, that's all, so we can tackle the thing properly. Use the pictures. He's sure he's seen a picture of them together, Edvard and Natasha Ohmsen, and maybe Søren Ohmsen too. Would be perfect, a picture of the three of them, with her looking at Edvard. Where was that picture taken that he saw? At some National Gallery event? Does Ohmsen give money to the gallery? Probably.

Does Ohmsen even know about the affair?

What about we just phone him up and say, 'Good evening, Mr Ohmsen. Do you know that your wife's having an affair with the defence minister?' See what he says.

The woman's husband, one of Denmark's richest men, said he was 'shocked' . . .

'Are you shocked, Mr Ohmsen? Are you dismayed?'

The woman's husband, one of Denmark's richest men, said he was 'shocked' and 'dismayed' to hear . . .

Soothed by the billowing cold of the air con, Kristian refocuses on the bright motorway, on the endless caravan of migrating Teutons in the slow lane.

It's an advantage, actually, to hold the name back for a day or two – extends the life of the story. It's a major story, and very timely. The next few days they're doing the monthly audit. That was what Elin was thinking about this morning, more than anything. Her job, it's about those numbers. If they're up, she's winning. If they're down, she's not. It actually is that simple. Nothing else matters, in the end. Everything is fairly simple, in the final analysis, he thinks. Seeing the true simplicity of everything, that was important. That was how someone like him, someone who started out in social housing in Sundbyøster, made their way in this world.

It is six o'clock.

He is not far from Málaga. The first ugly signs of the city are appearing on the hillsides.

The thermometer says *34°*.

He thinks of the shitty school he went to in Sundbyøster, patched with new paint where the latest graffiti had been obliterated. Barbed wire on the perimeter fence. The awful smell of the kitchen. Doorless stalls in the toilets.

It just happened, is how it sometimes feels, that he has this life. Deputy editor of the top-selling tabloid in Scandinavia, laying down terms to senior ministers. It was always just one step after another. He discovered, when he was eighteen years old, that he loved working on a newspaper – a local paper, that he had delivered as a kid, took him on for work experience after he left school. That was the first step. They liked that he was keen, energetic, willing to do anything. And he had this instinctive understanding of what it was all about. Not until the last few years has he looked further than just the next step. When they made him deputy editor. Yeah, that was when he first looked down and saw how high he was, how he was nearer the top now, much nearer, than the place where he'd started – that flat. Fourth floor. Lift out of order. Hear every sound the neighbours make. His father still lives there, on his own. He drove that lorry all over Europe, his father, from Portugal to Poland he drove it. That was what *he* did with his life. Now he hardly ever leaves Sundbyøster. Hardly ever leaves the fucking estate. When was Kristian last there? More than a year ago. In spring, smell of pollen on the estate. And in the flat, cigarette smoke. TV on. Sports newspapers. Sit at the tiny table in the kitchen, talking about

FC Copenhagen, what a shit season they're having. Window open. Smell of pollen. Sound of the Øresundmotorvejen, leaking onto the estate.

Shouts of kids.

There's this feeling he sometimes has that he's a long way from home. That nobody's there for him if it all goes wrong.

*

It is still well over thirty degrees when he returns the car at the airport. The heat still takes him by surprise – it's like opening an oven – when he emerges from the air conditioning and walks across the soft tarmac to the office to hand back the keys and sign the papers. Then he heads for the terminal, where his flight departs in just over an hour.

Departures is a nightmare. Thousands of people are travelling on this evening in August, thousands of sun-scorched northerners on their way home, to Dublin, Manchester, Hamburg, Helsinki. Holiday-makers. He hates holidays, personally. What are you supposed to do on holiday? He doesn't understand. He would never go on holiday if it weren't for the wife and kids. Ten days in Dubai, they did, this spring. And even then he was on his phone so much to people in the office, Laura eventually hid it. His phone. So they had a huge row about that. *Where is my fucking phone?*

Where's my fucking phone?

He is in the security queue, untying his shoes, when it starts to whistle and throb. His phone. He answers it. It's Elin.

'No way,' he says, when he hears what she has to tell him. 'You're joking.'

He indicates to the people behind him in the queue that they should move ahead.

'You're sure?' he says, shuffling out of their way.

And then, putting his shoes back on, 'Okay. Yes, phone him, tell him I'll be there in about an hour. Okay.'

A few minutes later he is at Hertz again. He says, frustrated with how slowly they are dealing with him, 'It doesn't have to, be the same car. Any car.'

It is a different car, a Seat.

And then the same motorway, towards Córdoba, at over 140 kilometres per hour.

It is nearly eight.

29° says the thermometer.

*

He leaves the motorway, again, at Lucena. It is dusk. Exhausted, lurid hues in the west. There are people about now. Strip malls, the shops all still open, and supermarkets on the outskirts of the town, sitting lit up in darkening scrubland. Some sort of stadium. Football, he assumes at first. A match this evening. Floodlights. A traffic jam outside. Then he sees, from signs and posters, that it's not football that happens there. And then he has passed it, is driving away into the dark evening, away from the lights of the town, towards the village where Edvard is.

It seems strange to him, somehow, that bullfighting actually exists. He knows about it, obviously. It's just that to actually see it like that seems strange. That something so savage, to his Nordic sensibility, takes place with all the trappings of modernity – the floodlights, the ticketing systems, the parking facilities. And in the middle of it all, slaughter. Slaughter. Slaughter as a spectator sport, as entertainment.

What is sadder than the furious exhaustion of the bull? Than the bull's failure to understand, even at the very end, that his death is inevitable, and always has been? Is just part of a show.

The village is quiet in the deep dusk. Some sort of bar is open in the square where the church is.

It is still oppressively hot.

*

'What are you doing here again?' Edvard says, standing on the steps of the porch. 'What do you want?' He is still in his shorts, his flip-flops.

'There's something important you didn't tell me, Edvard.'

'What?'

'She's pregnant, isn't she.'

Edvard looks amazed.

'You didn't know?'

'What are you saying?'

'I'm telling you – she's pregnant. Is it yours?'

'For fuck's sake,' Edvard says in a loud voice. He has been drinking. His lips are stained with red wine. 'What are you talking about? I don't know what you're talking about.'

Kristian is at the steps now. Looking up at Edvard, who is a head taller than him even without the advantage of the two steps, he says, more quietly, 'Mrs Ohmsen is pregnant. If you didn't know, I'm sorry it has to be me who tells you that.'

'How the fuck do *you* know?'

Elin had Mrs Ohmsen followed, and Mrs Ohmsen led two journalists to a private antenatal clinic where she spent more than an hour. That was what Elin told him on the phone.

'I just know,' Kristian says. 'You didn't?'

'No,' Edvard says, pathetically.

'Do you think it's yours?' Kristian asks him.

'Will you just fuck off,' Edvard says. 'I don't know what you're doing here. This is *my* life we're talking about.'

'Yes, it is . . .'

'It's *my* life. Not yours.'

'I know . . .'

Edvard says, 'Why don't we talk about your life? Would you like that?'

'I'm not here to talk about my life . . .'

'There are some things I know about your life.'

'I'm sure you do . . .'

'I know about you and Elin Møllgaard,' Edvard says, speaking more quietly, 'your editor.'

After a momentary hesitation, Kristian says, 'I'm not interested in that.'

'You and Elin,' Edvard says, sensing that he has, if only very slightly, unsettled Kristian, and liking it. 'Does your wife know about that?'

'Edvard . . .'

'Does she?'

'Edvard, nobody's interested in that. They're interested in you. They're not interested in me. You are the defence minister of Denmark. You have been having an affair with a married woman, Mrs Ohmsen. Mrs Ohmsen is pregnant. It might be yours. That is a matter of public interest . . .'

'It is not a matter of public interest,' Edvard says from the step, a silhouette against the dim light which is on in the porch. 'There's no public interest there.'

Kristian says, 'It's my opinion that there is.'

'No, there isn't. That's just a pretence. It's just a way for people like you to have power over people like me.'

'People like me?'

'Yes.'

'I'm sorry, I'm not sure what you mean by that.'

From the step, Edvard eyes him furiously, woundedly.

'You're upset, Edvard,' Kristian says. 'I understand that. And I'm truly sorry to have dropped this on you like this. I assumed you knew.

You probably want to phone Mrs Ohmsen, don't you, and find out what's going on. Why don't you do that? Okay? I'll wait here.'

Edvard stands there for a few seconds. Then he turns and enters the dark house, and Kristian waits on the path in the hot twilight. He does not sit down on the porch. There is, he notices, the debris of a solitary meal on the table there. He is hungry, suddenly. He hasn't had anything to eat himself since a sandwich on the plane this morning. He often forgets to eat when things are moving fast.

It is dark when Edvard emerges from the house again, into the shadowy electric light of the porch. Kristian, left waiting for nearly half an hour, has finally sat down.

Now he stands. Edvard, he thinks, has shed a few tears. Something about his discoloured nose, the evident fragility of his self-possession.

'Did you speak to her?' Kristian asks.

'Yes, I did.'

'And?'

'She doesn't know how you could know about it. She hasn't told anybody. She thinks you must have bribed somebody at the clinic where she went.'

'We didn't.'

'You say that.'

'Is it yours?'

'I don't have to answer that.'

'No, you don't. The question will be asked. You will have to address it at some point.'

'Maybe.'

'It would better for you,' Kristian says, 'to put everything out there now, rather than have it trickle out over a longer period of time. It will be less damaging that way, and less painful.'

'Are you my media advisor now?'

'I'm trying to help you, Edvard.'

'No, you're not.'

There is a prolonged silence, only the implacable throbbing of the insects. Then Edvard says, 'It's mine, she says. She isn't keeping it.'

'I'm sorry.'

'Now please leave.'

*

'This,' he says to Elin, travelling south again on the dark motorway, the air conditioning still purring, 'is a sensational story now.'

'It is,' she says. 'Well done.'

'I'm thinking,' he says, 'do the basic story tomorrow, without naming her, without saying she's pregnant. Then hope someone else names her during the day. Then Friday we do the full story, with names, pictures, everything. Don't do the pregnancy, though – save that for Saturday.'

'Sounds fine,' she says. 'Unless someone scoops us on it.'

'They won't.'

'I'll think about it.'

'Should help with the audit,' he suggests.

She laughs. 'That is the furthest thing from my mind at this point.'

He laughs too. 'If you say so.' He says, 'I'm hoping I haven't missed the last flight. I should get to the airport at tenish. So office some time after two.'

'We'll be waiting for you,' she says.

He has missed the last flight. When he phones Elin to tell her, she suggests he stay in a hotel and take the first flight in the morning.

'No,' he says. 'There's an Air France flight to Paris in about half an hour, and then one to Copenhagen at fourish. It gets in at five forty-five.'

'Are you sure you want to do that?' she says. 'It sounds totally exhausting. Everything's okay here.'

'Yeah, I need to do that,' he says.

'Why?'

'Don't worry about it.'

'Okay. If that's what you want. How long do you have to spend at the airport in Paris?' she asks.

'Two or three hours.'

'That sounds fun.'

'I'm going to love every minute of it,' he says.

And indeed the exhilaration he is feeling – the thrill of feeling that he is smack in the middle of things, major news events, things that everybody is talking about – takes him through the flight to Paris and the hours at Charles de Gaulle, the hours from one to four in the morning, when more people start to arrive in the huge lounge where he has been sitting and looking at the stuff Elin sent him. The first edition:

DEFENCE

MINISTER'S

SECRET

LOVE

A picture of the minister looking shocked that they found some-where, archive. Another, on the inside pages, of him looking sad.

The stunning brunette, 40, is refusing to leave her husband, one of Denmark's richest men . . .

He finally falls asleep on the flight to Copenhagen.

It is already light. Paris, familiar, in the little oval window.

He does not see it. He is asleep.

And then, mild Danish air.

He is aware, taking his seat in the Audi, that he stinks. He literally stinks.

4

Every morning he takes his daughters to school, or in the summer holidays to their tennis lesson. It is something he has promised to do. It is a promise he has kept so far.

When he parks in front of the house in Hellerup it is just after seven. He has time to shower and shave, to eat a bowl of Alpen, to drink two Nespressos: a Ristretto and then a Linizio Lungo with some skimmed milk in it.

'You look shit,' his wife says.

'I feel wonderful,' he tells her.

'Have you slept?'

'An hour on the plane from Paris.'

'You were in Spain?'

It seems strange now. 'Yeah,' he says. 'Málaga, place near there.'

Tine and Vikki are looking at the paper's iPad app, the front page:

DEFENCE

MINISTER'S

SECRET

LOVE

And the minister, open-mouthed with shock.

The TV news have picked it up. The TV is on in the kitchen, as usual, and there it is, the same picture, as the newsreader talks about the 'allegations' that have been made.

'Who is she?' Tine, eleven, asks.

Her father, eating Alpen, shrugs. 'It's a secret,' he says.

'Who is she? Tell us! Who is she?'

'I'll tell you tomorrow,' he says, with a jolly wink.

'Tell us now! Tell us!'

'Tomorrow,' he says.

On the Internet, the story is proliferating. Speculation about who the minister's 'secret love' might be is spreading on social media. Among the many names mentioned so far is that of Natasha Ohmsen.

They leave the house at the usual time, he and his daughters with their tennis stuff. Though he looks pale, he feels eerily fine.

Hellerup is serene in the morning sunlight, chestnut trees full and green in quiet streets of detached houses. Tall beech hedges against prying eyes. No shops. He is one of the youngest householders in the area, not yet forty. Most of the neighbours are older than that, well into middle age.

Somewhere, in an even more exclusive part of the suburb, where tennis courts and swimming pools are standard, the Ohmsens have their house.

*

Once, two years ago, when Kristian was still the showbiz and TV editor, he went with David Jespersen, the deputy news editor and his erstwhile schoolmate from Sundbyøster, to a pub in town to watch FC Copenhagen on the telly. It was a Sunday afternoon. They had been in the office, working. David was spending more time in the office than he usually did, especially at weekends. His wife had thrown him out of their flat after one 'indiscretion' too many and David was staying with friends and didn't want to be there all the time at the weekend. Kristian was in the office every Sunday anyway, so they were seeing more of each other than they had done for a while.

They arrived at the pub with about ten minutes until kick-off.

David had a Carlsberg. Kristian a tomato juice – he was going back to work after the match.

They talked a bit about David's situation, about the thrills and spills of his private life – the nannies he'd showered with, the hurried unions in nightclub toilets.

Then David said, 'What about you? You don't play away sometimes?'

'I don't have time, mate,' Kristian said.

'What about Elin? Any truth in that?'

Kristian just trickled some peanuts into his mouth and turned to the TV, up near the ceiling in a corner of the room. The team sheets.

David was smiling. 'I know it's true,' he said. 'Lucky you, mate. She's sexy, Elin.'

'It was nothing,' Kristian admitted, taking a gulp of tomato juice. Then he said, holding his glass out to the barman, 'Oi, Torben – put some vodka in that, will you?'

'I thought you were going back to work after.'

'I am.'

'So it was nothing?'

'It was short and sweet,' Kristian said, taking back his fortified drink. 'And now it's over. That's it.'

'You could make time for *her* then?'

'It happened in the office, mate. That's the point. We didn't have to make time. We were there all the time anyway.'

'Where'd you do it?' David asked through a scurrilous smile. Nicotine-stained teeth. 'Stationary cupboard?'

'In her office mostly.'

'In her orifice.'

Kristian swivelled on his stool more squarely to face the TV. He said, 'It's starting.'

A more serious question – 'Did Laura know about it?'

'No, she didn't,' Kristian said. 'And she won't. And it's not going to happen again.' He took a swig of his drink, winced at the vodka, and said, 'It was a mistake.' And then, his attention already on the starting match, 'We both lost focus for a bit.'

*

'How did he take it?' Elin asks him.

'Not great,' he says.

Elin makes a pained face.

Kristian says, 'There *were* a few tears.'

'I'm sorry you had to do that, Kristian.'

'*C'est la guerre*,' he says. 'I felt sorry for him, though.'

'Well, again,' Elin says, 'I'm sorry you had to do it.'

He smiles – quietly, sadly maybe. Just for a moment. 'So how are we looking?' he asks.

'Oh, she's been named,' Elin says. 'Natasha has.'

'What, already?' He thought it would be quick – not this quick. It's not even ten in the morning.

'It's all over the Internet,' Elin says.

'Are any other papers naming her? We can't be the first . . .'

'Not yet. We're watching.'

He says, 'I think we can give Søren Ohmsen a call at this point, don't you? He might not know yet. I'll get David to call him, okay?'

'What's he going to say to him?'

Kristian says in a sunny voice, '"Good morning, Mr Ohmsen. Did you know your wife is having an affair with the defence minister?"'

She sniggers. 'We are terrible, aren't we.'

'*C'est la guerre*.'

'Is that your catchphrase or something?'

'Seems to be, yeah,' he says. 'Did you get that picture? Of the three of them. I'm sure there is one.'

'Mikkel will be here in a minute,' she says, 'with what he's got.'

They are in the secret office – the one used for sensitive stories. It's not actually secret, just away from the hustle of the newsroom, on another floor.

She says, 'Do you want to take a few hours, go home, get some sleep?'

'Do I look that bad?' he smiles. 'Laura said I looked like shit.'

'How is Laura?' Elin asks.

There's a knock on the door. They expect it to be Mikkel. It's not. It's Elin's PA, Pernille. She says, 'I've got Ulrik Larssen on the phone. From Dahlin's office. He's angry.'

'I'll talk to him,' Kristian says. 'Okay?'

Elin says, 'I don't mind talking to him.'

'I think it's better if I do.'

'Okay,' she says, 'fine.'

To Pernille he says, 'Tell him I'll call him back in a minute. Thanks.'

'What are you going to say to him?' Elin asks, when Pernille has left them alone again.

'That we're going to handle this as sympathetically as possible. That we don't want to damage Edvard, etcetera, etcetera. Same as what I told Edvard. It's even true. Ish. I'll ask him if Edvard wants to do an interview.'

'You're shameless,' Elin says, smiling at him in a way he likes.

'I've got a thick skin,' he tells her. 'You know,' he says, 'Edvard said to me last night if he'd have become prime minister, he'd have offered me Ulrik's job?'

'Yeah, yeah. Do you think he was serious?'

'Who knows. It's a hypothetical situation, isn't it. Now.'

'I suppose we'll have to increase your salary,' she says, still smiling at him. 'Again.'

'You know I'm not in it for the money.'

'I thought you said this wouldn't damage him. Edvard.'

'Well, it depends what you mean by damage. He's safe in his current job, I'd say. I'd better call Ulrik.'

'What,' Ulrik says, 'the *fuck* do you think you're doing?'

'Morning, Ulrik . . .' Kristian is standing on the fire stairs, in a patch of sunlight.

When he has finished with Ulrik, about ten minutes later, and spoken to David Jespersen, he finds Mikkel, the pictures editor, in the secret office with Elin. Mikkel has laid a load of photos out on the table and they are looking at them. Elin looks up. 'What did Ulrik say?'

'He feels we shouldn't be running this story.'

'Did he threaten us?'

'Not with legal action. It's fine,' Kristian says, touching her on the elbow. 'Hi, Mikkel.'

'Alright,' Mikkel says, hardly looking up from the images on the table, whose positions he is minutely, and frequently, and pointlessly, adjusting with trembling fingers. Edvard is in most of the pictures – a wide variety of settings and expressions. Natasha Ohmsen is in a few. There are one or two of Søren Ohmsen. And . . .

'That's the one!' Kristian shouts, stabbing it with his index finger. He hardly ever shouts. It feels strange. 'That's the one,' he says.

The three of them. And yes, she is looking not at her diminutive husband, on whose arm she is – she is looking at the defence minister, tall and handsome and himself looking straight into the lens with a wonderfully sly smile. 'That,' Kristian says, 'is fucking perfect. Tomorrow's front page, yeah?'

'I think so,' Elin says.

Mikkel silently moves it apart from the others.

They are still looking at the pictures, trying to pick one of Natasha on her own, when Jeppe, the news editor, waddles in without knocking and says, 'What's going on here?'

Kristian says, 'We're just having a look at these pictures, mate.'

Ignoring him, Jeppe talks to Elin. 'This is my story,' he says, obviously outraged. 'It's my fucking story. You didn't even want it at first.'

'Yes,' Elin says, turning to him, 'it is, Jeppe, and you should be proud of it.'

'So why you excluding me from it now?'

'What I need from you this morning, Jeppe,' Elin says, sort of taking him aside, 'is to stay on top of all the other news. There is some other news, isn't there?' she laughs.

'Why are you excluding me?' Jeppe still wants to know.

'Did you hear me, Jeppe?' Elin asks, not laughing now. 'I need you to stay on top of everything else this morning. *I'm* dealing with this. Okay?'

'Isn't that the deputy editor's job?' Jeppe says. 'To stay on top of everything else.'

Elin lets a few seconds pass, then says, 'It's what I need you to do. Okay? So go and do it.'

Jeppe doesn't move.

You are so dead, mate, Kristian is thinking, still leaning over the photos.

And then David Jespersen arrives excitedly, saying, 'Just spoke to Ohmsen. The husband.'

'And?' Elin asks him, turning away from Jeppe, who is still standing there.

'He told me to fuck off.'

'That's it?'

'No,' David says. 'He said I was scum.'

'The man knows what he's talking about,' Kristian jokes, turning from the photos. 'Did he already know about the affair?'

'What I reckon happened,' David says. 'I think he did. What I reckon happened is yesterday night Dahlin told Natasha it was all coming out this morning, and she should tell her husband. So she told him.'

'Yeah, maybe,' Kristian says.

'And you know what makes it worse?' David says. 'It's his fucking birthday today. Søren Ohmsen's.'

Kristian laughs. 'You're joking.'

'I was looking at his Wikipedia entry. August fifth, nineteen fifty-eight. It *is* his birthday.'

'No way.'

'Happy birthday, Mr Ohmsen,' David says, enjoying himself.

'Have a look at these,' Kristian says, meaning the photos.

'Ah, the pics, brilliant,' says David, taking a place at the table. 'Alright, Mikkel.'

Mikkel, a man of few words, just nods, and with his quaking middle finger moves one of the pictures a millimetre to the left.

'So nothing we can use from Ohmsen?' Kristian asks. 'No quotable quotes?'

David says, 'Are you shocked, Mr Ohmsen? Eff off. Are you dismayed? You, sir, are scum. Is there anything you would like to say, Mr Ohmsen? Mr Ohmsen? Not there. Hung up on me.' David is looking at one particular picture of Natasha Ohmsen – the one where she looks really tasty. 'Actually,' he says, 'he did say something else.'

'What?'

'How did you get this number?'

'How did we get it?'

'From his wife's phone records.'

'Keep quiet about that,' Elin says, finally joining them. She has been standing apart, in thought, since Jeppe left a few moments earlier. 'So,' she says, 'which ones we going to use then?'

While she and Kristian discuss that question, Mikkel wordlessly shows David some unusable pap shots – he just starts handing them to him, they speak for themselves – of a famous actress sunbathing naked. 'Fuckinell,' David says.

'When you've finished looking at those,' Elin says to him, 'I want you to get on to the antenatal clinic. I want more information about that before we do anything on it. At the moment all we've got is Edvard's word.'

'That's right,' Kristian says. It was something he discussed with Elin earlier, something that had occurred to him in the middle of the night, waiting for his flight at Charles de Gaulle: that Edvard might have been lying to him when he said, 'It's mine, she says. She isn't keeping it.' There was something weird about the way he said that. And if they printed it and it wasn't true – if it wasn't his, or she was keeping it, or she wasn't even pregnant – he would have his opening to sue the shit out of them.

'What, you think he might be lying?' David asks, still taking pictures from Mikkel. 'Fuckin*ell*,' he says again, even more impressed.

'Who knows?'

'That would be pretty devious, wouldn't it?'

'I want something more than just what he said to Kristian.'

'Fair enough. I have been in all night, though,' David points out.

'I'll take care of it,' Kristian tells her.

'Yeah?' she says. 'Okay.'

'I'll get Katrine onto it,' he says, surveying their final selection of photos. 'It's her sort of thing.'

'Does that mean I can go home and get some kip?' David asks.

'I suppose it does,' Elin says kindly. 'Off you go then, fuck off.'

*

235

When he has sent Katrine to the antenatal clinic, with some money, to try and find out exactly why Natasha Ohmsen spent an hour there yesterday, Kristian takes the lift down to Starbucks. There are some franchises at street level, and sometimes he spends ten minutes in the Starbucks, having a small latte and letting his head clear.

He finds David Jespersen in there, eating a sandwich. 'I thought you were going home, mate,' Kristian says, joining him.

'I am, after this,' David says. 'Did you see those shots Mikkel had of what's-her-name?'

'Yeah.'

'Muff on display and everything.'

Kristian, unsmilingly, is taking the lid off his latte.

'We okay to use them?' David asks.

'Maybe one of the topless ones. Next week, when things are quieter. They're with Morten.'

'Was it just me,' David asks, 'or was there some sort of vibe this morning? I mean with Jeppe, when I came in.'

'It wasn't just you.'

'What's up?'

Kristian shrugs. 'I don't know. There's going to be a shake-up soon. Maybe something to do with that.'

'What sort of shake-up?'

'The sort where people get sacked.'

'Seriously?'

'That's what I'm told.'

'We don't have enough people as it is,' David says.

'I know.'

'The work each of us is doing, it used to be done by two, three people.'

'Those days aren't coming back,' Kristian says.

They are sitting on tall stools at the counter in the window. Outside, people pass by. Suits, office workers. The still surface of Peblinge Lake is blackish, full of clouds. It is one of those fresh northern summer days. Leaves moving languidly in mild wind.

'What about me?' David asks.

'What about you?'

'Am I safe?'

Kristian tips latte into his mouth. 'You'll be okay,' he says. 'Don't worry about it.'

'I need this job,' David says. 'Two years' time, I'll be forty.'

'Me too, mate.'

'I've got two kids to pay for.'

'I said don't worry about it. You can still go home now, if that's what you're wondering.'

'Nothing's going to stop me doing that,' David says. 'I'm a fucking zombie. What about you? You alright?'

'I'm fine.'

'You did an all-nighter as well, yeah?'

'Yeah. I suppose.'

'You don't want to go home, get some kip?'

'No.'

'What,' David says, trying to understand, 'you're worried about this shake-up?'

'Not at all.'

'So why don't you take a few hours off?'

Kristian, tired, is staring at the surface of the lake.

Then he says, 'You don't understand, mate. There's nowhere else I want to be. This is where I want to be.'

A moment passes.

David is looking at him, trying to understand.

'This is what I live for,' Kristian says. 'This. What happens here.'

And that's the truth, he thinks, finishing his latte, when David has left.

David Jespersen has left.

Headed home to the flat in Nørrebro he lives in now. The flat with not a lot of furniture in it. Empty fridge – a few lagers, not much else. Monochrome bedroom. Not unlike the place the two of them shared . . .

What?

Nearly twenty years ago.

Went out on the pull together then, sometimes. Saturday afternoon, watched football together. IKEA sofa. Empty fridge – a few lagers, not much else. Weird that that's Dave's life again now. Out on the pull.

He has finished his latte. Is still staring at the unperturbed surface of the lake.

Must be tired, to sit here staring like that.

Out on the pull.

Seems like another world, that.

He thinks for a moment, with something that threatens to turn into pain, of Elin, and the times they had. Two years ago.

Two and a half.

Very professional they were about it.

Lost focus. In the office. Orifice. Office. Office. Is what I live for. And that's the truth. He has left the Starbucks and is in the lobby – modern marble – waiting for the lift. Thinking of Edvard now, Natasha Ohmsen. The story. The dangerous information detonating, tearing through the fabric of public life. He feels the adrenalin start to move in him. The lift doors shut. Yeah, this is what it's about now. This. The guerre.

6

1

He leaves the office two hours earlier than usual. Mid-afternoon, half-empty train to Gatwick. A window seat on the plane. Weak tea, and a square of chocolate with a picture of Alpine pasture on the wrapper. And then it hits him. Floating over the world, the hard earth fathoms down through shrouds of mist and vapour, the thought hits him like a missile. Wham. This is it. This is all there is. There *is* nothing else.

A silent explosion.

He is still staring out the window.

This is all there is.

It's not a joke. Life is not a joke.

She is waiting for him at arrivals, holding up an iPad with his name on it, though she knows what he looks like from his picture on the website and approaches him, smiling, as he stands there facing the wall of drivers with their flimsy signs.

'James?' she says.

The difference in height is significant.

'You must be Paulette.'

She has a scar – is it? – on her lower lip, a pale little lump, somewhat off centre. There is a handshake. 'Welcome to Geneva,' she says.

And then, the motorway – on stilts, through tunnels. France. The low sun on one side of his face. Fresh evening light.

She says, 'So, tomorrow.'

'Yes.' He is watching something outside, something on the move in the green-gold light. Everywhere he looks, he sees money.

'I've arranged for us to meet them at the site,' she says.

'Fine. Thank you.' She is efficient, he knows that. She answers his emails promptly, with everything he needs.

He had started speaking to her in French, as he followed her out of the arrivals lounge. She had answered in English, and for a minute there was a silly situation with each of them speaking the other's language.

An immaculate, turning tunnel – a sound like holding a shell to your ear.

Then the long, late-summer dusk again.

He says, in English, 'What's the weather going to be like? Tomorrow.' It is important, will make a difference.

'Like this,' she says. 'Perfect.'

'That's nice.'

'I arranged it for you.' It sounds slightly awkward, the way she says that.

He smiles tiredly.

Stops smiling.

Shifts his feet in the footwell.

'Well,' he says, after too long a pause, 'thank you.'

The surge of the motorway is making him sleepy.

The lush glow of everything. Outside, green slopes strive skywards, rich with evening sunlight, thickly gold.

Les Chalets du Midi Apartments consists of twelve brand new apartments in one of the most lovely valleys in the French Alps. There is a wide variety of 1, 2, 3 and 4 bedroom apartments available from 252,000 euros ex VAT

located in a central location in the lively and popular village of Samoëns.
The village of Samoëns is a charming French village with many shops,
restaurants and bars . . .

How many years has he been doing this now?

They leave the motorway at Cluses, and she pays a toll.

Cluses is prosaic, a series of small roundabouts. Flower baskets
hanging from street lights. Midget plane trees brutally pollarded in the
French fashion. It is where she lives, she tells him. She leans forward
over the wheel to look up at some window and, pointing with a lifted
index finger, says, 'That's where I live.'

'Okay,' he says, pretending to be interested.

Then they have left the town and are hairpinning up the side of the
valley. On the other side, mountains soak up what is left of the sunlight.

She lowers her window a little. The air smells of manure, wet grass.
'Do you know the area?' she asks.

He says he doesn't. 'Mostly we do stuff a bit further south,' he explains. 'Cham. Val d'Isère.'

She nods.

'Courchevel.'

She works for the developer, Noyer.

'I cover part of Switzerland too,' he tells her.

'I see.'

The hairpins are over. The road passes through villages, under trees,
through massing shadow.

'This is nice,' he says politely.

She nods again. 'Yes, it's nice, up here.'

'Very. Has Monsieur Noyer got other plans?' he asks, trying not to
sound too interested. 'After this.'

'I think so. You can ask him, on Friday.'

'I will.' He wonders what Noyer is like, whether they'll get on. What Noyer will make of his proposal. He isn't even sure what his proposal will be yet. He needs to think about that.

'It's more and more popular, this area,' she says.

'I bet.'

'It's more typical,' she says, 'than the more established areas.'

'Seems like it.'

A village. They slow markedly – severe speed humps. Trees heavy with moss. Ski-hire shops – *Location du ski* – shuttered out of season. Signs advertising honey for sale.

'We're nearly there,' she says, accelerating as they leave the village. 'It's the next one.'

It is evening now, unambiguously. She has turned on the headlights.

There is a long straight stretch with solemn tall pines. Then the road swings left, passes over the noise of hurrying water – he sees it fraying white over stones – and they are there. 'Here we are,' she says.

A mass of signage meets them – signs for hotels, pizzerias, walking trails, ski lifts. Everyone trying to make some sort of living.

And then the deeper gloom of a modest avenue of trees.

On either side of the road, among the apartment buildings, a few old blackened barns still stand in unsold fields.

Quickly, imprecisely, seeing them through the trees, he tries to work out what they might be worth, those fields.

*

He walks for a while, in the last light. It is still there, pink, on the peaks that hang over the village. One in particular hangs there, implacable. Fading pink. A fountain warbles somewhere. Ice-cold water. In the old village, past the petrol station, there are handsome stone houses. He feels sad.

These trips to the Alps, alone. The empty evening hours.

Now a strange blue light stretches itself over the rocky tops of the peaks. It is dark in the street.

There is a decent amount going on after the lifts close in Samoëns with a good number of bars to keep you entertained and restaurants that offer a wide range of local specialties ...

No sign of that tonight.

Instead, a solitary meal in the hotel dining room, peach-pink tablecloths and an inhibiting quiet. Table for one. While he waits for his food, he looks over the shiny brochures, his own prose – he can hear his voice in that stuff, his own voice saying it.

There is a decent amount going on after the lifts close in Samoëns ...

A decent amount ...

Ugh.

Not that he would know what goes on here. This is the first time he's seen the place. Giles was out in the spring, and made the deal with Noyer – exclusive marketing deal. Since then, James, speaking to him on the phone in slick French, has had the sense that Noyer feels neglected. He feels unloved. It is a situation that struck James, not so long ago, waiting on the wet platform of Earlsfield station one morning, as an opportunity, perhaps.

The fact is, for Giles this isn't much. He himself hasn't spoken to Noyer since that visit in the spring. Giles is now in Hong Kong – or Singapore, maybe, today – selling Alpine property to the Chinese. Selling whole developments. (What's five per cent of twelve million euros? A nice day's work.) Giles, Air Miles. 'Air Miles in today?' they say, James and the others, arriving at the office in Esher for another day of phoning and emailing.

How much does Giles make? They talk about that over their Pret sandwiches at lunchtime.

And how much is he worth?

He started the firm in the late eighties. He was in on some of the early deals himself, had a stake in them, is what John says – John who's been there since the start, and somehow doesn't have much to show for it. *He* wasn't in on some of the early deals himself.

You don't want to end up like John.

Alone at a table in the hotel dining room he turns over the shiny brochures. Faint smell of fresh ink. *Les Chalets du Midi Apartments.* Nearly finished now, apparently. Will be done in time for the skiing season. Furnished, everything. Ten to sell in the next few months. Should be okay. Will be out here a few times. Will know *this* place, the Hôtel Savoie. He looks up, looks at the starched, peach-pink space. He already does know it. Yeah, he knows it. He has stayed in how many hotels like this? Half-empty on an early September evening. First week of September – summer season over, more or less.

He wonders, finishing his flute of Alpine lager, what Noyer is like, whether they'll get on.

After eating, he walks over to the apartments. It is a five-minute walk from the hotel, out of the stone centre of the village, into a silent area where there are still some open fields in the moonlight.

As well as mountain biking there are also a number of hiking trails with beautiful scenery. You can visit the vast natural parks in the region and see the extensive natural beauty the Alps have to offer. If you are feeling more adventurous you can go paragliding off the mountainside, rock climbing, or 4x4 driving off-road. Equally if you are feeling less adventurous there are much less strenuous activities to undertake . . .

The new apartments stand in a lumpy wasteland. He stops on the moon-shiny tarmac in front, putting his hands in his pockets. There is a pleasant smell of young timber lingering in the dark air. Pretty low-end

246

stuff, he sees immediately. A standard design with some superficial 'chalet' trim, thrown up in a hurry in one short summer.

'Miri?'

He is lying on the hotel bed, in his underwear. Neon light floods out of the open bathroom door.

'It's me.'

His voice sounds noisy in the staid hush of the hotel room.

'Everything was fine,' he says. 'No, that was fine.'

Pine walls, waxed pine.

'It's, you know – Alpine. No, nice. Perfectly nice.'

'Tomorrow I've got to spend the day with the punters,' he says. '*Do my thing*. Wine them. Dine them. Show them a shop that sells nice cheese. You need a shop that sells nice cheese.'

He laughs at something.

'I'm told there is one, yeah.'

'No,' he says, 'on Friday it's the developer.'

'How are you?' he asks. 'How are things there?'

He says, 'Yeah? Well, we expected that, didn't we?'

'I s'ppose,' he says. 'I don't know. Why don't you ask him?'

'I wouldn't worry about it,' he says.

He yawns and says, 'Well, I wouldn't worry about it.'

'Do I?' he asks.

'I am, I s'ppose.'

'Yeah,' he says.

There is a pause, and then he says, 'Same here.'

'Night,' he says.

'Okay. Night.'

2

She is waiting for him, unexpectedly, at the hotel in the morning. She is there in the large pine lobby, talking to the manager as if she knows him well.

'Hello,' James says, sailing up to them in a well-pressed open-necked shirt. She turns to him and he sees, as if for the first time, the scar on her lower lip. It is texturally distinct from the flesh of her lip – like a small drip of wax, almost. He tries not to look at it. 'Are you here for me?' he asks.

'Of course.'

'That's nice of you.'

She introduces him to the manager, and they talk for a few minutes in French, and with a sort of exaggerated politeness, about the village, how it's developing.

Outside, among the postcards and mountain knick-knacks, she puts on Ray-Ban Wayfarers.

Her little Peugeot is parked in front of a shop selling artisanal *eaux-de-vie*.

They stroll towards it.

How well he knows these Alpine villages. Spick and span. Flowers and flags everywhere. The mountains hanging there decoratively, harmlessly, looking like pictures of themselves. And in the streets, the atmosphere of a posh suburb. Not a leaf out of place. An oppressive tidiness. Still, there is something here – a vestigial sense of a place with a life of its own. A few little streets that are still unspoilt, he thinks. There is still scope, in other words, for some money to be made.

She asks him, as she searches for her keys, hauling up handfuls of stuff from the depths of a large leather handbag, how he slept.

He says, 'Perfectly. Thank you.'

'That's good.'

From his high forehead the hair, greying, hangs back in waves. He is getting craggy with the years – his sunglasses accentuate this. A sort of authority is growing in him too. He waits for her to find her keys.

'And where,' he asks, 'will the new *télécabine* go from?'

'Over there.' She pushes her sunglasses up her nose and points past the petrol station, towards the entrance to the village where they arrived yesterday, the avenue of linden trees.

'And when will it be finished?' The question is important.

'In time for the season,' she says. She has found her keys, and is looking at some message on her phone.

'Promise?'

She looks up.

He is smiling.

'I promise,' she says.

It takes less than a minute to drive to Les Chalets du Midi Apartments. They look smaller in the sunlight than they did last night, and even less inspired. The wasteland around them looks scruffier too, full of weeds and muddy hollows where huge puddles were, after the latest storm to trundle thunderously down the valley.

He stands there, looking at it, while she talks on her phone.

It might be Noyer she is talking to and he tries to hear what she is saying.

When she has finished, he half-turns his head to her and says, 'That was the boss?'

'It was.'

'Everything okay?'

'Everything,' she says, 'is okay.'

'What's he like?'

The question seems to surprise her. 'What's he like?'

'Yeah.'

'He's . . .' She takes a moment to think about it. 'Fine.'

'Does he know what he's doing?'

Again she seems surprised. She says, 'I'm sure he does. Why?'

'Just wondering.'

Not only is her English perfect – she has, when she says some words, some vowels, an actual English accent, a sort of semi-posh London accent.

'You must have lived in London at some point,' he suggests, smiling at her in his sunglasses, not moving from where he is standing.

She says, 'I did.'

'Thought so.'

He is still looking at her. She is petite, a neat little figure. The dress she is wearing stops halfway down her thighs. Quite a stylish dress. He thinks – *La belle plume fait le bel oiseau.* The thought makes him smile again.

'So – what do you think?' she asks seriously, after a few seconds. Her finger finds the scar on her lip. She has a habit of touching it sometimes, of putting a finger to it for a moment.

He turns his attention to the brown development, its dour little windows.

There is nothing interesting about it whatsoever.

'Nice,' he says, finally. 'Shall we?'

For the layout of these spacious apartments, the architect strived to achieve the maximum use of the available space. As a result, these apartments have a very practical layout. The living room with open kitchen provides access to the spacious terrace of 8m². The terrace is south facing and offers impressive views over the valley. Furthermore, these apartments offer a spacious bedroom . . .

His own words, written without ever seeing the place. Off-plan prose.

They stand in the show apartment.

Even after the unpromising exterior, he is disappointed. The whole thing makes a naff impression. The laminate flooring, the sub-IKEA furniture, the shitty pictures on the walls. Expense *has* been spared – that hits him the moment he steps in the door. The spaces are too tight. It isn't 'spacious' at all, not even in the estate-agent definition of the word. It feels pinched. There is definitely no wow factor, except slightly out on the terrace, with the mountains shoving up into the sunlight.

Still, it won't be an easy sell. Not at the list prices.

Who was advising Noyer? he wonders, stepping back inside. All this tatty stuff is just a false economy. Unless he didn't have the money. In which case other investors should have been found. No problem. James knows where to find them, where to find money for things like that. Once Giles took him along to an event at the Gherkin – the money was waiting for them there, suited, smiling, munching nibbles.

Must be that Air Miles just wasn't paying attention here. This *is* pretty small-time stuff. No oligarchs venture up this sleepy valley. Méribel it ain't. Might as well do it properly, though. Squeeze everything you can out of it. Like this you'll end up selling them for fifty thousand less. Why throw that money away? A few showy pieces of furniture, Smeg fridge, a touch of marble in the bathroom. Stuff like that makes the deal happen. These people fly in for a day. First impression is all they have.

He opens and shuts something flimsy in the kitchen.

Has to be *some* kind of wow factor.

The curtains, he thinks, look like something from a youth hostel. Some kind of hideous floral print, for fuck's sake.

She sees he isn't impressed.

'You don't like it?'

'It's fine,' he tells her. 'I mean,' he says, 'it's economy, of course.'

He smiles at her. Sees she knows what he means. Has had the same thought herself. 'Who was advising Monsieur Noyer here?' he asks. And then says, smiling at her again, 'I know you weren't.' From the way she dresses, just that, he knows she wasn't. He wonders whether to say it to her. Something like that.

It's too late, though. She is already saying, 'No, I wasn't. I don't know.'

'Madame Noyer, maybe?' It's a joke, sort of.

She just says again, 'I don't know.'

'*Is* there a Madame Noyer?' he asks.

'There is.'

'Let's have a look at the others then,' he says.

Unfurnished, the other apartments are more appealing. There is, at least, a sense of potential in their emptiness. They will all, though, be the same as the show apartment. Despite what she said, Noyer obviously does *not* know what he's doing. He needs help. He needs someone to hold his hand. Which is exactly what James was hoping to find – someone in need of help.

He wonders whether to even *show* them the show apartment. Might be better to show them these empty ones.

He stands at a window in the 'penthouse' – four hundred and twenty-five thousand euros (excluding VAT) – a duplex at the top of the development, with views up and down the valley. The valley ends in a mass of overlapping peaks. A wall of them. The other way, the horizon is low.

There is no flooring down here yet, just the screed under his feet as he walks around.

'This one sleeps six, yeah?' he asks.

'Eight,' she tells him.

'Eight?' He sounds sceptical, like a journalist interviewing a politician on TV.

She says, 'Including the sofa bed in the living room.'

'Right. Okay.'

He wanders over to one of the windows, larger here than in the other apartments.

'Fireplaces would have been nice,' he mentions.

'There was an issue,' she says. 'About the insurance.'

'Yeah?' He stands at the window, looking out. 'Still.'

His hand is on the cold glass. On the other side, green slopes leap up, the sides of the valley, high pastures and stands of pine. The trees, from here, look like toys. Pointy toy trees. He is looking at them. So still, everything up there.

'Nice, the double aspect here,' he says.

She is waiting near the door, on the other side of the room. 'Yes.'

'Is there a shop in the village that sells nice cheese?' he asks.

Again, the question seems to take her by surprise. She says, 'Nice cheese?'

'A posh cheese shop,' he says, turning from the window. 'Is there one?'

'There's a cheese shop,' she says. 'I don't know what you mean by posh, exactly.'

'I'm sure you do,' he says with an encouraging smile.

'I suppose you could call it posh.'

'Lots of nice cheese?'

'Yes,' she says with a single emphatic nod.

'Fine. We need one of those. We need a shop that sells nice cheese. It's important to the sort of people we're dealing with. Their idea of what buying a property in France involves. *La douceur de vivre*. What time is it?'

She looks at her watch and says, 'Nearly quarter to eleven.'

'Mind giving me a lift up top?' he asks. 'I'd better have a look at the infrastructure up there, I suppose. So I can at least *pretend* I know what I'm talking about.' He smiles. 'Then we'll have lunch.'

They leave the way they arrived yesterday, down the little avenue of linden trees. Immediately after leaving the village, though, they take a small turn-off that zigzags steeply up into the forest. She shifts from second to third to second as they take the steep turns.

Moves into fourth for a kilometre of open pasture. Sun. Farmhouse with deep eaves, time-blackened.

Then some more houses, almost a village.

All this land – what's it worth? Fortunes here.

And more forest, then. And views, sometimes, through the trees, as they turn, and turn, of the valley, now falling away.

Second, third. Third, second, third. Her thin, tanned arm is permanently in action. Her elegantly sandaled foot. (Well-maintained toenails, he notices – hard pink shine like the inside of a shell.)

It takes twenty minutes to drive to the top.

'Ah,' he says, as they emerge from a final stretch of hugging shade and everything seems to open out. There is a lot of tarmac, suddenly, and further up, a major development, not so new – flats, a hotel maybe. Huts, houses. She parks on an empty expanse of tarmac in the shadow of the flats, and switches off.

There is no one around. Standing there in the sunlight he hears the throb of the pastures. And when the wind blows a quiet singing from overhead cables. Otherwise silence.

'So, tell me about this,' he says.

She starts talking about ski lifts and pistes.

Only half-listening to her, he has walked to the edge of the tarmac. Slopes fall away in slow undulations. There is a shuttered crêperie. The hum of insects. The ice-edged wind. And from somewhere, the lazy sound of cowbells, a sound like a spoon stirring something in a glass.

She is talking about ski school, École du Ski Français.

Yes, he knows memories of that. Long ago, that was. Snowploughing in line behind the vermilion uniform. Foggy day. Wet snow.

He feels the sun on his eyelids. The wind on his skin. Hands. Face.

With his eyes shut, he hears the cowbells, fading in and out on the wind.

Life has become so dense, these last years. There is so much happening. Thing after thing. So little space. In the thick of life now. Too near to see it.

The sun on his eyelids.

Cowbells fading in and out on the wind.

Warmth of the sun.

Wind on his skin.

To withdraw, somehow, to just this.

Hopeless.

                                        It's not a joke. Life is not a joke.

He opens his eyes.

Shimmering grass, shivering.

She says, 'Eighty per cent of the slopes are north facing. The spring skiing here is particularly nice.'

This is it. This is his life, these things that are happening.

This is all there is.

She is standing next to him, quite near him.

'Yes?' he says. 'How much is there? Skiing. Kilometres.'

'Including the whole Grand Massif?'

'Whatever.'

'About two hundred and sixty kilometres.'

'Wow.'

She says, 'Including Flaine, Morillon, Les Carroz, Sixt and Samoëns.'

'And they're all interlinked, with lifts?'

'Of course.'

'One pass covers them all?'

'You can get it,' she tells him.

'Okay,' he says. Nice to have some facts.

For a moment he shuts his eyes again but there is nothing there now.

*

Lunch. A few minor confidences over a pizza. She was at art school in London. Then dropped out . . .

'Why?' he asks.

'I fell in love.'

'Love,' he says. 'It messes everything up, doesn't it?'

'You're very cynical.'

'Yes, I probably am,' he admits.

'Isn't love the whole point?'

'The whole point of what?'

'Of life.'

'So I've heard. What did you do then?' he asks. 'After you dropped out.'

She found a job as an estate agent.

So they talk about estate agenting – he did that too, once. And is doing it again now. 'That seems to be my fate,' he says.

'Do you *believe* in fate?' she asks, amused.

'I do now,' he says.

'I don't.'

'Of course you don't,' he says. 'You're too young.'

She laughs at that. 'Young?'

'How old are you?'

She is twenty-nine.

'I would have said twenty-five.'

'Ach,' she says, pleased.

He smiles.

'How old are you?'

'I am forty-four.'

'And when did you start believing in fate?'

'I don't know,' he says.

He is enjoying talking to her – there is something fresh and straightforward about her – so he tries to think of something else to say, something which is true. He says, 'When I woke up one morning and realised it was too late to change anything. I mean, the big things.'

'I don't think it's ever too late to change things,' she says.

He just smiles. And he thinks: That's the thing about fate, the way you only understand what your fate is when it's too late to do anything about it. That's why it is your fate – it's too late to do anything about it.

'So it's something that only exists in hindsight?'

'I suppose so.'

'So it doesn't really exist?'

'Does that follow? I don't know,' he says. 'I'm not a philosopher.'

'Are you happy?' she asks, putting ketchup on the last slice of her pizza.

'Yes, I think so. It depends what you mean. I don't have everything I want.'

'Is that your definition of happiness?'

'What's yours?' And then, while she thinks about it, he says, 'I don't have a definition of happiness. What's the point?'

'You must know whether you're happy or not.'

'I'm not unhappy,' he says, and then wonders whether even that is true.

'That's not the same thing,' she says.

'And you?' he asks. 'Are you? Happy.'

'No,' she says, without hesitation. 'I mean, my life isn't where I want it to be.'

He wonders whether to ask her where she wants her life to be, whatever that means. Then he decides, after taking a sip of water, to leave it at that.

They talk about skiing.

After lunch they walk together to Les Chalets du Midi Apartments. Autumnal pink is starting to appear in the neat beech hedges that line the clean streets of the village. 'Now I've got to do my thing,' he says.

'Now *that* I am looking forward to seeing.'

He laughs.

That he only met her yesterday seems strange suddenly.

*

The valley brims with heat. Not a cloud in the sky.

After he has shown them the flats, they all sit down on the terrace of a place in the main square, the Bar Samoëns. This is him 'doing his thing'.

There are plastic tables and chairs outside, and he supervises the waitress as she puts two tables together for their largeish party. Then he takes everyone's order.

Paulette, he finds, is sitting next to him. He smiles at her. 'Alright?' he says.

She nods.

Then he is doing his thing again.

'Now that tree,' he says, deploying with some authority a factoid he has only just learned himself, 'is one of the oldest trees in France. Nearly, I think, seven hundred years old.'

Heads turn.

Its trunk is two metres wide, obese. Up among the big mossy boughs the leaves have, in places, already turned orange.

'What sort of tree is it?' someone asks.

'A lime, I think?' James turns to Paulette.

'Yes, it's a lime,' she says. 'It was planted by a famous Duke of Savoy.'

'A Duke of Savoy,' James echoes. 'This whole village is so full of history,' he says. 'I love it here.'

Someone has left the table and is inspecting a plaque at the tree's foot.

'1438,' this pedant, a shortish middle-aged man, shouts over to them, pointing at the plaque. He is very sensibly dressed in waterproof fabrics that make a lot of noise when he moves, and walking shoes with spongy laces. 'So actually less than six hundred years old then,' he points out, taking his seat again, next to his equally sensible wife.

'A mere sapling,' James declares, to some laughter from the others.

The drinks arrive.

'Still,' the man says, 'I can't believe that makes it one of the oldest trees in France. Less than six hundred years old?'

James decides to ignore him. He helps the waitress distribute the drinks.

'There's this olive tree,' the pedant is telling the others, 'it's like two *thousand* years old . . .'

Pensioners, the pedant and his wife. Might even be thinking of moving down here full-time, James understands. Selling their little flat in Stoke Newington, swapping it for the penthouse of Les Chalets du Midi Apartments. They speak French the way Air Miles speaks it – James heard Mrs Pedant asking for the loo – not so much with an English accent as *in English*. They speak French *in English*. Like Air Miles, the old-school way.

James passes Pedant his straw-pale Alpine lager.

'*Merci*,' Pedant says. '*Monsieur*.'

'Where else have you been looking?' James asks him.

'Oh, all over the place, really,' the man says, with a moustache of foam. 'We're just sort of driving around. You know.'

Arnaud (London-based Frenchman, there with his partner Marcus) asks, 'What can you tell us about the skiing?'

'It's fabulous,' James says.

'You have skied here?' Arnaud asks him.

There is a minuscule hiatus. Then James says, 'I haven't personally, no. Paulette's the expert there. She can tell you all about it. I mean,' he says, 'I'm not going to sit here and pretend it's Verbier or anything. It's properly serious, though. I mean, with the whole, er, Massif. There's something like two hundred and fifty kilometres of pistes. One pass for the lot. And up at Flaine, it goes up to what – two eight, two nine?'

Paulette says, 'Two thousand five hundred. More or less.'

'Okay,' James murmurs.

She says, 'No, there's always snow there. It's wonderful, the skiing here.'

She talks about it for a while.

James watches her, her eyebrows jumping about above her sunglasses as she tries to be enthusiastic. She's a bit stilted, to be honest. She's doing an anecdote now – something about skiing – and not doing it very well. It happened over lunch too. Somehow it touched him, the way she killed those anecdotes. Tells them too slowly, or something. She's just not very funny. Not in this sort of setting.

She's losing these people now. The nice ones are kind of willing her on, with fixed smiles. Some of the others are starting to look away. So she's hurrying it, which is just making it worse.

She's starting to laugh at it herself, even though no one else is.

Shit, now she's missed something out, something important, and has to go back and explain.

James looks up into the branches of the old lime, sun-filled leaves.

She has arrived, finally, at the end of the anecdote. It just ends.

Then people notice, and there are some polite sniggers.

And Mrs Pedant, in her seat again, wants milk for her tea.

While Paulette leaps up to see to that – in thanking her James laid a hand for a moment on her arm – he talks some more to the others about how lovely the area is, doing his thing, in lilac shirt and sunglasses, handsome, at ease.

Seemingly at ease.

He pays for the drinks. Then he takes them to the cheese shop, and talks them through the immense selection. One or two timid purchases – avoiding the most odorous examples – are made.

Outside, he says, 'We'll be around later, if anyone wants to get some supper. I know some of you are staying locally, and there are some fabulous places in the village we'd be happy to show you. Why don't we meet in the place on the main square at sevenish, if anyone wants to do that? Okay?'

There is a sense, as always, of acting.

And then, when the performance is finished and the audience has wandered away through the twisting streets of the village, this tinge of euphoria, this punchy energy.

They are standing in front of the *fromagerie.*

James says, 'Drink?'

'I think that went well, don't you?' he asks her, when they are sitting on the terrace of the Bar Samoëns again.

'Very.'

'I think there's at least one sale in there, with that lot,' he says.

She asks who he thinks it might be.

'Well, Arnaud and Marcus,' he says. 'I think they may well take the plunge. Thanks for saving me on the skiing, by the way.'

'You're very welcome,' Paulette says.

James shakes his head, with a sort of mock exasperation that makes her laugh. 'Fuck. That was so embarrassing, when he asked me whether I'd skied here myself.'

'What about the Knottbars?' she asks. The Knottbars – Mr and Mrs Pedant.

'Them?' James makes a face. 'No. Don't think so. I'm not sure how serious they are. Not very, would be my guess.'

They spend a while taking the piss out of them, the Knottbars – James at one point scampering over to the ancient lime tree, as Mr Knottbar did, and shoving his finger at the plaque.

Walking back to the table where Paulette is laughing, her index finger held in a sort of hook shape over her mouth, he decides he must be slightly drunk, to have done that. Sweating lightly with the exertion, he sits and looks at his watch. 'Another one?' he suggests.

She nods, and he signals to the waitress.

Seven o'clock. No one turns up. They wait until twenty past, sitting in the twilight. Then James says, 'Well . . . Looks like there aren't any takers for supper. Do you want to get something? Or do you have to head off?'

They end up in a restaurant in one of the narrow streets that wander away from the main square, narrow between tall stone houses.

It is only after the meal, after all that Savoyard wine and a sample of the local aquavit, that it occurs to him: 'You're not going to *drive*, are you?' he asks, as they leave.

'No,' she says. 'Of course not.'

'So what are you going to do?'

They are standing in the dark street. She says, 'I don't know.'

Leaving the question open, they start to walk towards his hotel. She is wearing his jacket over her dress – the temperature has dropped precipitously since they sat down to a meal that had turned extremely flirty.

For instance, the way he touched, at her invitation, the scar on her lip. (A spill from a moped had put it there, she told him, when she was fourteen.) The scar had started, at some point while they sat on the terrace of the Bar Samoëns, to mildly fixate him. It had distracted him throughout the early part of the meal.

He touched it lightly with his fingertip, and wondered out loud what it might be like to kiss it. And though she didn't say, 'Why don't you try?' he had had the feeling that she might have done if she'd had the nerve.

Instead she just looked at him, and he noticed how huge and earnest her hazel eyes were, and suggested they have a *digestif*.

That all took place in French. After the first half-litre of Mondeuse he had insisted on switching to French. And then he had had to explain why he spoke French so well – about how his father had lived in France when he was at school, and how he had spent all the school holidays there, in Paris or in the South. And she had asked him – with a sort of shining-eyed seriousness – whether he had had any homosexual experiences at boarding school in England, and he had said that no, he hadn't. The idea that that was widespread was, he told her, a myth. And then she had volunteered a pretty vivid story about an experience of her own, once, with another woman, while he felt his mouth drying out and poured them some more wine.

What she hadn't asked him was whether he was married or anything like that, and he had also avoided the subject.

She, it turned out, was a single mother. Her son's father lived in Norway.

And so, after a second aquavit and a shared dessert, they found themselves outside under the stars.

Which they looked up at for a minute, standing there in the street, looking up between the dark eaves of the houses at the sky.

It did occur to him, since she was the one who had started it, that this was in fact practically an invitation to kiss her. (She was waiting there, with her face tilted upwards, shivering slightly.) And he did, with the wine and aquavit singing in his veins, sort of want to kiss her.

For a moment he felt that he was about to. And then he felt he wasn't.

He looked at the dark street. The village was very quiet. She was still searching the sky.

He said, 'You're not going to *drive*, are you?'

He saw, as soon as he had said it, that the question would sound suggestive – that it would sound as if he actively wanted her to spend the night in the village.

She lowered her face to look at him tipsily, straight at him. 'No, of course not.'

'So what are you going to do?'

'I don't know,' she said.

'You don't know?'

She shook her head.

Another moment: the wine and aquavit singing in his veins.

Without saying anything else, they started to walk towards his hotel.

So what are you going to do?

The question was one for him as well. It seemed pretty obvious, anyway, what she had in mind.

In the oppressive light of the lobby, though, the idea seemed silly. Somehow unpalatable. There was a short pause as they stood there.

'I suppose we'd better get you a room,' he heard himself say.

To which, after a moment's hesitation, she just nodded.

And then he was at the desk, making the arrangements.

And now he is in his own room, sitting on the bed.

He pulls off his socks.

He is tired, that's true.

Still.

Might've been nice.

There is a melancholy sense, as he takes off his socks, of opportunity lost.

He wasn't willing to make any effort to make it happen. It was the prospect of *effort*, more than anything, of even a minimal amount of effort, that had made the whole idea seem unappealing as they stood in the lobby.

His friend Freddy would have put in the necessary effort. Obviously Freddy would have. Freddy, the last time they met, had told James proudly about how he had been playing the piano in a jazz quintet in Wales and after the show two members of the audience, a man and a woman, had asked him to join them for a drink. She was alright looking, Freddy said, so he had joined them, and they had had several drinks, and some lines of speed, and then they invited him to their place, where it was soon pretty obvious what they had in mind. Freddy was to fuck her while the husband watched, wanking. Thanks to the speed it went on for ever, Freddy said. It was daylight when he left.

The story was a bit pathetic actually, James thinks, screwing up his used socks.

Freddy was forty-five years old.

Eking out an existence playing the piano at weddings, in wine bars. Sleeping on people's sofas.

'Don't you worry?' James would say to him.

'About what?'

'About your life.'

'What about it?'

James took a moment to frame a more precise question. Then he said, 'Whatever. Nothing.'

Freddy was not as happy, not as entirely satisfied with his situation, as he made out. It wasn't so much that he worried about being the cricket in the fable, exposed to the oncoming winter. (Though he was.) It was simpler than that. He wanted to be looked up to. He wanted status. When he was twenty-five, lurid sexual exploits did it for him – they won him that status among his envious peers. Now, not so much. They still felt flickers of envy on occasion, sure. They no longer wanted to *be* him though. He had no money, and the women he pulled these days were not, for the most part, very appealing.

James is staring at his own face in the mirror as he moves the whirring, whirling head of the Braun electric about inside his mouth.

His face has a dead-eyed flaccidity. A flushed indifference. He is looking at it as if it isn't his own. He feels a definite distance between himself and the face in the mirror. The neon light – a bright lozenge on the wall – isn't kind to it. He is drunk, slightly. Maybe more than slightly. That wasn't supposed to happen. He silences the toothbrush, holds its head under the tap for a moment. Should've been here, thinking about what he plans to say to Noyer in the morning, not messing about with his PA.

It's not a joke.

Life is not a fucking joke.

3

Cédric Noyer is a few years younger than James. There is something fogeyish about him though, something which finds visual expression in an incipient jowliness, a softening jawline, a dewlap of self-indulgence threatening his razor-scraped throat. He is wearing a Barbour. He is smoking a cigarette. Parked near him, where he stands in front of Les Chalets du Midi Apartments, is a mud-streaked Mitsubishi Pajero.

He is the owner, James knows, of much land in the area. His father was a farmer – and still is, in a way. He still keeps a small herd, and the family income is swollen with agricultural subsidies. The land is the main thing now, though. The fields in and around Samoëns and Morillon; and, from Cédric's mother's side, further up the valley in Sixt.

These apartments are the first development Cédric has undertaken himself. For many years, since the eighties, the family has been selling fields to developers – a hectare here, two hectares there – for prices that went steadily higher and higher. (The latest parcel, with planning permission, fetched well over a million euros.) It was Cédric, support-ed by his sister Marie-France, who pushed the idea of developing the land themselves – moving up the 'value chain', as he put it. He had learned the phrase at the École Supérieure de Commerce in Lyon. 'I don't just want to sell milk,' he had said to his father, trying to put his ambition in terms the old man would understand. 'I want to make cheese, lots of cheese.'

He steps forward to shake James's hand and offer him a brief super-
cilious smile – he treats him like a sort of servant, someone with a
measure of technical expertise, like a plumber or a mechanic.

He is very proud of his apartments, James sees that immediately.

So he is tactful, as they inspect them together, the show flat first.

Paulette is with them. A quiet presence this morning. She left the
hotel very early in the morning, and drove home to Cluses. When she
showed up again at nine she looked extremely tired.

'Very nice,' James says to Cédric, of the kitchen in the show flat. His
tone is flat and polite, not enthusiastic. Cédric, wandering through the
apartment in his Barbour and mustard-coloured corduroy trousers,
does not seem to notice this.

They stand on the balcony, admiring the view.

'*Magnifique*,' James says, more fulsomely. They are speaking French.

The air has an autumnal feel this morning. The early mist has lifted.
The sun is warmer now. Now. Do it now. Say something.

'Do you have any other development plans?' James asks, still staring
at the dramatic mountain that hangs over the village.

'Of course,' Cédric says in a manner which suggests he is not minded
to discuss the subject. The sun has raised a sweat on his smooth forehead. He lights an American cigarette.

'I know you've been a bit unhappy with the service,' James says.

Cédric shrugs, still getting his fill of the view. 'If you sell the flats, it's
okay,' he says.

'Oh, we'll sell them,' James assures him. 'We'll sell them. There won't
be a problem there.'

'Then okay.'

'No, why I mention it is,' James says, 'we've been focused mainly on
the more traditional areas. I mean as a firm. Which is why we might
not have been able to give you the time and attention you're entitled

269

to. Now we're planning to start something more focused on some of the newer areas.' There is a short pause. Then he says, 'I'm planning to start something.'

There it is.

He's said it.

It's out there.

I'm planning to start something.

Is Cédric even listening?

James says, 'I think there's huge potential in some of the newer areas. I'm sure you agree.'

'Of course.' Cédric says this without looking at him.

'So I want to focus on this area,' James says. 'Make something happen here. I think together we can make something happen here.'

He is smiling.

'I'd like to talk to you,' he says, 'about what other plans you have. Maybe get involved at an earlier stage. For instance, these flats,' he tells him, 'are fine. They're very nice. I have to say, though, I think we can go upmarket with any future developments you have in mind. This is a stunning valley. It has a traditional feel unlike anywhere else I know in the French Alps. I mean the heritage aspect. Plus the ski infrastructure is improving all the time. There's more money to be made from high-end stuff. We could do luxury here. Do you see what I'm saying?'

He felt mortal, this morning, waking with a headache from the wine and aquavit, his lanky frame patched with sorenesses. A sort of weak milky light slipped through the curtains. Hardly enough to see his watch by.

Time is slipping away.

He is not young now.

I am not young, he had thought, sitting there in the hotel with his hands in his lap, staring at the floor. *When did that happen?*

He has started lately, the last year or two, to have the depressing feeling that he is able to see all the way to the end of his life – that he already knows everything that is going to happen, that it is all now entirely predictable. That was what he meant when he talked to Paulette about fate.

And how many more opportunities, after this one, will there be to escape that?

Not many.

Maybe none.

If indeed this *is* an opportunity. It seems it might not be, after all.

Cédric is showing no interest in his proposal. Squinting in the sunlight, lifting the cigarette to his small mouth, he seems more interested in the light traffic passing, leaving the village on the road to Morillon, than in what James is telling him. Which is now that it will be necessary to invest more up front in the future to maximise the potential of the property. 'There *is* more risk,' he says. 'If you want to offload some of that risk, we can find other investors to come in alongside you.'

Cédric grunts, unenamoured with the idea.

'Anyway,' James says, trying not to feel discouraged, 'let's talk about what plans you have, and take it from there.' He hands Cédric a business card, one of the new ones he's had made. 'I want you to call me,' he says.

When they have finished looking over the apartments, he stands Cédric a coffee in a promisingly chichi little place in the village. Watches him eat a pastry – a *tarte aux fraises* – breaking it up with the side of a fork.

Paulette is still there, with an empty espresso cup, emailing.

Cédric *has* now shown some interest in James's pitch – has offered anyway to drive him around the valley and show him some of the sites he has in mind for development.

And James is starting to think, while Cédric scrapes the *crème anglaise* from his plate with the side of the fork, about where he can find some money – a few million, let's say – to put into French Alpine property. He has some numbers. People Air Miles knows. It is, indeed, all about who you know. That much is true. Matching money with opportunity, taking a percentage. Taking something for yourself.

For about an hour, they drive through the valley. Cédric seems to own about half of it, keeps pointing to fields and saying they're his.

They stop at one of them. It is on a slope just above the old village, up where the houses thin out and the pasture starts. Cédric says his family have owned this land for eighty years – it was where the herd went when it first emerged from its winter quarters, until the snow melted higher up. *Le pré du printemps*, he says its name is. He seems to think it's his most promising plot for development.

'What are you planning then?' James asks him.

'Something like the other,' Cédric says, meaning the Chalets du Midi Apartments.

No, no. Forget that.

Small- to medium-sized chalets, James thinks. Eight maybe, nicely spaced. And apartments, in the middle somewhere. Maybe ten apartments. Parking underneath. Leisure facilities. Everything high spec. Plenty of slate, zinc.

He does some preliminary sums, standing there up to his knees in the tired summer grass.

Cédric is smoking.

'What about planning regulations?' James asks him. 'Do you know anyone who can help us with that?'

It turns out Cédric's aunt is the deputy mayor. His extended family is all over the local administration like ivy.

'This is an excellent site,' James says. He is looking down at the slate roofs of the village: disordered, monochrome, bright. It is eerily still now, the village, in the early afternoon. End of the season. Autumn dead here, nothing happening. Eagles turning over the shadow-filled deeps of the valley all day.

And far away, the other side, smothered in forest, in shade.

In silence.

4

Sunday morning. They are walking up Tranmere Road, past terraced houses, the windows of the front rooms sticking out like smug little paunches. Muscular black Audis, BMW estates, VW Touaregs are parked outside. The spaces that separate the houses from the pavement are marked off by low walls, sometimes a bit of thinning hedge. There is usually a metal gate, less than waist high. Then tiles to narrow front doors. It is fashionable, James notices, to have, in the pane of glass over the door, the house number as islands of dark transparency in a milky frosting.

His own house has something similar. Not quite as posh – the numbers just stencilled onto the glass, not picked out as negative space in the frosting. It was already there when they moved in. Miranda was pregnant at the time. The house was a mess. Ancient gas fire in the front room. Overgrown garden. A crust of dust on all the surfaces inside. Someone's parent had lived there, then died, and it was being sold. The price was well over half a million. It was shocking, how little you got for all that money – and all the way out here, in this windy low-lying part of London about which he knew nothing, with its prisons, and its playing fields.

Its empty expanse of sky.

They had taken the house in hand. Miranda had. Spaces opened up, painted pale colours. The garden paved, turfed, filled with daffodils. Halogen lights embedded everywhere, flooding on at the touch of a switch. Everything quite small, admittedly. The living room – the street hidden behind linen blinds – only two paces from end to end. The table in the kitchen unable to accommodate more than four. The nursery so tiny the window hardly fitted in the wall.

And outside, the daffodils shivered, the clouds massed and dispersed in the sky.

And that was five years ago.

Time passes.

'Tommy,' James shouts, as his son gets too far ahead of him. 'Tom.'

They are at the end of Tranmere Road, where it meets Magdalen Road, and the primary school is, and further on Wandsworth cemetery, strung out along the railway line towards Clapham.

Tom waits for him, and James takes his hand to cross the road.

They arrive at the station, as James does every weekday morning. The names of places in Surrey scrolling across the information screen are as familiar to him as his dreams. They are part of him now, those names: New Malden, Surbiton, Esher . . .

He arrived home on Friday night to find the kids asleep and his wife watching television, some panel show. Every few seconds: laughter. He joined her on the sofa, leaving his things in the narrow hall. He took off his shoes.

Later, her shapes under the sheets.

On Saturday, though, he was short-tempered.

Last week, in high winds, a substantial piece of chimney fell off the house – stove in someone's new Nissan Qashqai which was parked in front. An insurance nightmare. Miranda had been on the phone all week to the insurers, without much to show for it. Just to sort out the chimney, even that seemed problematic. He spent most of Saturday in the low bed under the sloping roof, peering at small print on a tablet screen, furious at having to spend his time on it. Tom sulking, damaging things. Alice wailing somewhere downstairs.

The train passes through sunlight. Passes allotments. Ivied walls. For a moment, some sort of waterway, shiny like mercury under dark trees. Masses of tracks run parallel as they draw near Wimbledon.

He is holding Tom's hand when they step off the train onto the platform. People everywhere. District line trains waiting in the intermittent brightness as clouds swim overhead.

Miranda's parents are coming for lunch today, driving in from Newbury. Miranda is in the kitchen, preparing food. Some sort of Italian lamb dish, James thinks.

Tom says, 'Why are trees so high?'

They are on the bus, the number 93, as it makes its way from Wimbledon station to the Common, up Wimbledon Hill Road.

James considers the question.

It is his part, this morning, to take himself and Tom off somewhere to be out of the way while Miranda makes lunch, and Alice hangs in that harness thing which is supposed to keep her out of trouble.

He says, 'I suppose they're trying to get as near to the sun as possible.'

'Why?'

Fond smiles from some of the people near them on the bus, which is not full. They are on the upper deck, near the front.

'Well,' James explains, 'the sunlight makes them grow. They need it to grow.'

Tom is looking with interest at the plane trees that line the road, loom leafy over the wide pavements. London Sunday, the hum of the place only slightly subdued. People walking down there, purposefully. James sees a man and a woman walking up the hill, the same way the bus is travelling – tall woman with dark mass of hair, long arms expressing something.

'They need it to grow,' Tom repeats, a stray moment of sunlight finding the leaves he is looking at.

'That's right,' James tells him, pleased.

Handsome red-brick houses here.

And new developments of flats.

Noyer. Never far from his thoughts.

Then Wimbledon 'village'. The High Street with its posh little shops – people energetically shopping – and what was once a village green. War memorial.

Miranda's parents will be on their way. They are fairly tweedy, Miranda's parents. Members at Newbury Racecourse. The four of them went once. Hennessy Day. Fuck, that seems a long time ago. It seems like something from another life, that afternoon.

Time passes.

*

The air sits thick and damp on the flat land of the common. There are people around – it is still summer, just, and the weekend. Ferns and bracken crackle as children rampage through their tired green fronds. Trees hang leafy limbs over dry bridleways. The showers that passed overnight just dampened the dust, and since dawn the sun has dried it. Falling through holes in the cloud cover, the sun is hot. It shines blinding white on the ponds.

James follows his son further out into the quiet of the common, away from the places where people are playing football, and dogs are sprinting after sticks.

He has been thinking, since Friday, whenever he has had time, about Noyer and the plot of land he showed him. He needs to come up with a plan himself, something he can present to Noyer, something obviously superior to his own idea of just plonking down a jumbo version of Les Chalets du Midi, full of shitty furniture. Eight chalets, was what James was thinking, and ten apartments.

They have left the rutted bridleway, its long brown puddles, and are pushing into the wood. Mature trees. Ferns everywhere, starting to turn on top, some of them. Keeping up with his son, wading through the damp ferns, leaves him short-winded. 'Tom,' he calls out. 'Tom! Oi. Wait for me.'

Eight chalets, ten apartments.

Five million to do it all? More? Utilities need sorting. Access. Just a track now. Yes, more, probably.

Noyer won't have that kind of money. Maybe one or two million he can put in.

So need say four or five million from somewhere. Leave Noyer with about – plus the land – about forty per cent. Will he be happy with that? With nearly half the profit? Double his money, pretty much. Should be happy: not doubling his money on Chalets du Midi, that's for sure.

He has lost sight of Tom. 'Tom!' he shouts.

He will have to, on Monday, tomorrow, start thinking seriously about who he might go to for money. He is already thinking about it. He has some old names. Starting points. Tristan Elphinstone, for one. (Number still work? Will soon see.) He pocketed some cards, that evening at the Gherkin with Air Miles. Time to find those. The thing is, he should leave Esher first, if he goes to Air Miles's people, probably. Shouldn't he? Something dishonest, otherwise.

Or worse – to be sued by Air Miles would not be fun.

Leave Esher.

That would be a major step.

So many overheads these days, that's the thing. Mortgage. School fees. Laima's salary – the Lithuanian nanny.

He has not even told Miranda about Noyer yet. The Esher job is something she likes. It is quite well paid. It seems secure. She thinks he likes it too – all those jaunts out to the mountains. Once or twice, in the early days, she went with him. Skiing weekends. Pre-kids, of course. He started there at almost the same time they got together, that summer.

Leave Esher. The thought frightens him. Firm things up with Noyer first. Send him a plan – see what he says.

And suddenly the whole thing seems totally speculative, insubstantial. Talk.

Lost Tom again.

Panting slightly, James stands on the trunk of a fallen tree, the huge trunk half-submerged in the ferns. He sees Tom in the midst of them, inspecting something. He is aware of neglecting his son, of not even talking to him much, too preoccupied with his own stuff. His own plans.

This is his life, these things that are happening.

'Tommy,' he says.

The boy's face looks pale, looking up at him from the sea of green ferns.

He has the clear blue eyes of his mother, not his father's more troubled blue.

The day is windless.

It's not a joke.

Life is not a joke.

7

1

Pearl Dundee, Murray's mother, died, finally, on Sunday afternoon. The funeral was the following Friday.

Murray himself was late. Heads turned in the pews when he opened the cumbersome door of the crematorium chapel. It was bleak and pale in the chapel. Outside it had started to rain again. The minister, who had been speaking, had been saying something about 'a long, full life', waited for Murray to find a place.

Afterwards, while they stand outside, he explains to his sister Beckie that his flight from London was delayed.

'Well, I told you,' she says, impatient with him, 'you'd've done better to come up last night.'

They are both dressed as if for the office, in dark suits. Murray in a murky tie. He offers her a cigarette and she takes one, and then they accept the condolences of some old lady – a friend of their mother's, he thinks she must be, who Beckie seems to know. Mauve-hatted, the old lady tells him, as he lights his cigarette, that his mother was 'a wonderful woman'.

'Aye, thanks,' he says, and sees his brother, Alec, emerging into the last day of September, the falling leaves, the shining wet tarmac. He has not spoken to Alec yet.

He has not spoken to Alec for years.

It seems he doesn't own a suit, Alec – over his white polyester shirt, his black polyester tie, he is wearing a dark blue Puffa jacket. He's almost un-recognisable, he's lost that much hair since Murray last set eyes on him.

'How's young Alec?' he says to Beckie. He says it with a smile, trying to be nice. 'He's put on a pound or two, anyway.'

'Why don't you ask him?' she suggests.

Murray is still smiling, sort of, as she moves away, to talk to someone else.

Alec is talking to someone else as well, is filling the doorway of the chapel in his Puffa jacket so that the last few people left inside are having to wait. No one seems to want to ask him to move, to step aside to let them leave. It's his mother's funeral, that's probably why.

Smoking hard, Murray turns to the road. The taxis are arriving, to take them to Beckie's house for the drinks.

He shares a taxi with some old people.

One of them, an old man with smelly breath, old man breath, seems to know him.

'So how are you, Murray?' he asks, tightly holding the moulded plastic handle of an aluminium walking stick.

'I'm okay, fine,' Murray tells him. 'Well, you know,' he adds, 'it's a sad day and all.'

'It is,' the old man agrees. 'Pearl,' he says, 'was a lovely creature.'

Murray moves his black leather shoes, and his eyes shift nervously to the sliding streets, the grey faces of the houses. Motherwell. It has been a long time since he was up here. Motherwell? No, actually. She passed away. The old man asks him something.

'No, I don't live in the UK now,' he says.

'Croatia,' he says, in answer to another question from the old man.

'Yugoslavia, it used to be part of,' he says, in answer to another.

In his sister's small house, even with all the people there, he is unable to avoid an encounter with Alec.

He is in the kitchen, tearing open another lager, when Alec is suddenly there – he's helping out, seeing to it that everyone has a drink, passing round the peanuts. 'Hello, Murray,' he says.

'Alec. Hello . . .'

'You still voting Tory?' Alec wants to know. His face has an upsetting fullness, a middle-aged quality. The shiny pink forehead is huge.

'Tory?' Murray says, and slurps from his lager. 'Nah, those fuckers are too left wing for me now.'

Alec smiles extremely thinly. 'How are ya anyway?' he asks, without much interest.

'I'm okay,' Murray says. 'I'm well.' Then, for want of anything else to say – 'You still with the union?'

'I am. What about you?'

'This and that,' Murray offers. 'I'm not based in this country any more.'

'No, I heard.'

'Not for a few years.'

'Some sort of tax exile, are ya?'

Murray smiles, liking the sound of that – liking the sneer in Alec's voice when he says 'tax exile'. He has another slurp of lager. 'Something like that,' he tells him.

He spends the night in Beckie's spare room. It was her son's. He's left home now, is in Australia or somewhere. (What was his name again?)

'Why don't we try and stay in touch?' Beckie suggests the next morning, early, as they drink tea in the kitchen and he waits for his taxi to the airport.

'Definitely,' he says, trying not to look at her. When he does, he thinks – *Fuck, she looks haggard.*

'You're sure you don't want any breakfast?' she asks.

'No.' *Less than two years older than me, and look at her. She looks like an old lady.*

She says, 'You look tired.'

'Do I?'

'I suppose you didn't sleep well,' she says, 'in Ewen's room.'

Ewen – that's it. 'I slept okay,' Murray says, thinking greyly of the hours he endured during the night, turning and turning under the Spider-Man duvet in his Y-fronts and vest. The heating turned up too high. The sound of the rain on the window, like someone muttering unpleasant truths. And the photo. In a frame in the upstairs hall. Himself, Murray, at about ten years of age, with Max, the Alsatian they'd had then, that he'd loved so much. Seeing that photo last night, of himself and the dog, had upset him somehow.

'I slept okay,' he says again.

'Lucky you,' Beckie says. 'I didn't.'

Milky tea. Too milky. The dregs, not even tepid, disgusting him.

'I couldn't stop thinking,' she says.

Murray puts down the mug, and tries to swallow what is in his mouth. He is in his suit again, tie in his pocket.

Beckie is in her dressing gown.

'I just couldn't stop thinking,' she says.

Yesterday, when everyone had left, she told him about their mother's last days. She hadn't shed a tear then, telling him the hospital stories – the meetings with doctors, the small-hours vigils, the hopeless dawns. She told him about them in the dry voice she probably uses in her office at the town hall. And he had listened without emotion, without feeling anything.

Now it seems she might break down.

Her mouth wobbles.

Murray, instinctively, looks away.

He looks at the window, straight out through that window with mould in its corners, to the dull morning.

And aye, Beckie is in tears now. Holding a dishcloth over her face.

Where the fuck, Murray thinks, looking at the fake Rolex that hangs too loosely on his sallow wrist, *is that fucking taxi*?

*

Twenty-four hours later, on Sunday morning, he is on a train to Stansted airport, and he feels very much worse.

Rainey was involved. Once they had worked together in telephone sales, him and Paul Rainey – they had spent years together on sales floors, under the strip lighting. Working the phones. The Pig worked with them for much of that time, and he was with them on Saturday night as well. They started in the Penderel's Oak in the middle of the afternoon. Ended up at the Pig's flat in Whitechapel about twelve hours later. Murray had slept for an hour or two on the floor of the Pig's sitting room, on the sofa cushions, in his suit. Then it was up at six – with an implausible pain in his skull – to make the lonely walk to Liverpool Street, and the train to Stansted.

Fucking obese, Rainey was now. It had been a shock to see him. He and the Pig still worked at Park Lane Publications, the office just off Kingsway. Lunchtime in the Penderel's. Everything the same.

And when they asked Murray what the fuck *he* was doing, he said, 'I'm just taking it easy. Enjoying life.'

'Where you doing that then?' the Pig said.

'Croatian Riviera,' Murray answered. 'I'm semi-retired,' he told them.

'*Semi*-retired? What's that mean?'

'Means no one'll give him a job,' Rainey quipped, adding an empty to the many on the table and turning his head towards the bar.

Murray tried to smile. 'I've had no end of offers,' he said quietly, as if out of modesty.

'Bollocks,' Rainey said.

And Murray felt that his old friend had still not forgiven him for the events involving Eddy Jaw, the things that had happened some years back.

They had worked together again since then, of course. When Murray was sacked by Jaw he had found his way, inevitably, to the taupe glass door of Park Lane Publications, had found Paul Rainey working there again – at the same desk even, as if nothing had happened, lifting the same white handset to his sweating head.

Murray had been sacked from that job too. He seemed to have lost his touch, whatever touch he might once have had. It was then that he had decided to explore other options. In a way, the Pig was his inspiration. The Pig, notoriously, had once spent two years in Thailand, 'enjoying life', living off the money he had saved. Though Murray hadn't saved any money, he did have a small house in Cheam – a sixties bungalow in a place called Tudor Close. He had acquired it in the glory days, around 1990. Twenty years later, the mortgage was negligible. So a tenant was installed and Murray set off to look for somewhere where he would be able to live on that small income.

The Croatian Riviera.

His flight to Zagreb is at ten thirty in the morning.

He is sitting in the departures lounge, with a headache. Outside, planes move silently. Sunlight torments him. He feels sick.

He had not told Rainey and the Pig why he was in the UK, about the funeral. He had not mentioned that at all, or even thought of it himself, as they went from pub to pub, moving east from Holborn.

Now, staring out at the planes through the shell of his hangover, he is surprised by a memory, a memory of a hand on his forehead, feeling for his temperature perhaps.

Sunlight throws shadows on the terminal floor.

Ma, says a small, frightened voice in his head, his own voice.

Ma, where are you now?

And finally, sitting there in the departures lounge, staring at the planes moving in the weak October sunlight, he finds the tears in his eyes.

2

Actually, the 'Croatian Riviera', the Adriatic seashore, even its least fashionable stretches, had turned out to be too expensive for Murray. He had ended up some way inland, over the hills and far away, in a town on a fairly arid plain, surrounded by dusty vineyards and fields of sunflowers and maize. The Turks had once been defeated there, in fifteen-something, and a monument in the main square memorialised the event. It was the last thing of any importance to happen in the town. In one of the streets leading off the square, there was a youth hostel, the Umorni Putnik, and it was there that Murray had lodged for a while when he arrived.

More than a year ago now.

The first person he had met, on the stairs, that first day, was Hans-Pieter, a Dutchman, and a long-term inmate of the hostel.

Hans-Pieter, Murray had immediately thought, was obviously a total fucking loser.

He was also, these days, his only friend.

The day after Murray's return from the UK, the two of them are passing the afternoon at a pub called Džoker. They are sitting outside, where there are a few tables under umbrellas advertising a local marque of mineral water – though already October, it is very hot. Murray is wearing white shorts that fall to just below his knees, overhanging his violet-veined and hairless lower legs which in turn taper down to dark office socks and large white trainers. Sweat oozes out of his manly face.

'It'sh hot,' Hans-Pieter says.

It's the kind of thing Hans-Pieter will say – the kind of fascinating conversational gambit he comes out with.

Murray just grunts.

Hans-Pieter is probably about ten years younger than Murray – somewhere in his mid-forties. He is unusually tall, obviously shy.

'I suppose,' he says, taking a quick, almost furtive, sip of his lager, 'it'sh global warming.'

Murray, sweating, scoffs. 'What the fuck you talking about?'

'Global warming,' Hans-Pieter says.

'What – you believe in that?'

Hans-Pieter looks worried, as if he might have made some elementary mistake. Then he says, 'You don't believe it?'

'Do I fuck.' With the hem of his white T-shirt Murray towels his face of freely flowing sweat. 'Don't tell me you believe in that?' he says, resettling his glasses on his nose.

'Well.' Hans-Pieter looks down at his flip-flops. 'I don't know. It'sh October,' he points out.

People are eating ice creams. Pigeons are wetting their wings in the fountain.

Murray is still staring at him. 'And?'

'Well.' Hans-Pieter sounds doubtful. 'Is this normal? This . . . this weather . . . ?'

'There is no evidence,' Murray tells him, 'for global warming.'

'Well, but I thought . . .'

'There's no fucking evidence.' Murray takes off his glasses to towel his face again. The front of his T-shirt is sodden.

Hans-Pieter's pale eyelashes flutter humbly. 'I thought there was,' he says, 'some evidence.'

Murray laughs again. 'You've been had.'

Shyly Hans-Pieter says, 'What about the Shtern report?'

Murray makes an exasperated sound.

'It says if there's no action taken on emissions . . .'

'For fuck's sake!' Murray shouts at him. 'There's other reports, there's reports that say just the opposite.'

'Aren't they paid for by dee oil companies?'

Murray sighs. He has heard this shit before, and he won't have it. The fact is, Murray feels a profound sympathy for 'the oil companies'. He feels, somehow, that he and 'the oil companies' are on the same side. That is, they are the successful ones, the winners of this world, and therefore envied no doubt by losers like Hans-Pieter – Hans-Pieter, who still lives in a youth hostel, while Murray, like some fucking oil company, occupies a well-appointed flat in one of the most elegant Habsburg-era streets of the town. It is his understanding, in fact, that Hans-Pieter is on the Dutch equivalent of the dole, which stretches a lot further here than it does in Amsterdam or wherever he's from.

'Do you not understand,' he says, taking a more indulgent tone with his slow-witted friend, 'that the whole thing's a plot *against* the oil companies? A left-wing plot. Against the market economy. Against individual freedom.'

'You think that?' Hans-Pieter says.

'I know that, pal. They lost the Cold War,' Murray explains. 'This is their next move. It's fucking obvious when you think about it.'

A large drop of sweat falls from the end of his nose.

Hans-Pieter says nothing. He turns his head to the hot square. He has a little earring in his left ear.

'Anudder one?' he asks, noticing Murray's empty glass.

'Go on then,' Murray growls.

Surprisingly, after that one, only their second, Hans-Pieter makes his excuses and leaves Murray there on his own, to have another half-litre of Pan, the local industrial lager, and survey the square in unexpected solitude.

That Hans-Pieter has something else to do is a surprise. The underlying premise of their friendship is that neither of them *ever* has anything else to do. No one else to see. There *is* no one else. That's why they are friends. Take that away, and it's not obvious what would be left.

Actually, it's not quite true that there is no one else. There's Damjan. An acquaintance of Hans-Pieter, a native. Damjan has a job though – he works at a tyre-fitting shop next to the train tracks. He has a family. He has, in other words, what passes for an ordinary life.

Murray meets him later in the bar of the Umorni Putnik.

Murray is disappointed, arriving there, that Maria isn't around. Inasmuch as Murray has a purpose in his life now, that purpose involves Maria, who serves drinks in the youth hostel. She is not, he feels, out of his league. For one thing, she is not very attractive. She is young and friendly, and her English is excellent – she even understands Murray when he speaks. He has had his eye on her for some time, since last winter. All year he has been planning to make his move.

He was particularly hoping to find her there this evening. He feels down. Outside, it is already dark. The evenings are shortening now. The nights, as they say, are drawing in.

He sees Damjan arrive.

'Damjan, mate,' Murray says, standing eagerly to shake the tyre-fitter's hand.

Damjan is short, muscular, untalkative – the sort of man that Murray instinctively defers to.

Damjan, while still shaking Murray's hand, looks around. 'Hans-Pieter?' he asks.

'Not here,' Murray tells him. 'I dunno where the fuck he is. Lemme get you a drink.'

'So,' Murray says, when they are sitting down. 'What you been up to then?'

'What you been up to?' Murray asks again when Damjan says nothing. 'What you been doing?'

Damjan, perhaps still not understanding, shrugs, shakes his head.

'You're okay, though?' Murray asks.

'Okay, yes.'

This is in fact the first time they have had a drink together without Hans-Pieter being there. It turns out to be surprisingly hard work.

They end up talking about tyres.

'So what about Pirelli?' Murray finds himself asking. 'How do they compare? With Firestone, say.'

Increasingly, there are long silences, during which they separately survey the room, trying to find a woman worth looking at.

Then Murray asks another question about tyres, which Damjan dutifully answers.

They have been talking about tyres for almost an hour.

'I had Mitchell-in on the Merc,' Murray says, after a long pause. 'Top quality.'

Damjan just nods, drinks.

'D'you think we're going to see Hans-Pieter tonight?' Murray asks.

Damjan shrugs.

'You don't know where he is?'

Damjan, lifting his drink, shakes his head.

Which, it turns out later, is a sort of lie. He knows more or less where Hans-Pieter is. Hans-Pieter is at Maria's flat, naked, watching an episode of *Game of Thrones* dubbed into Croatian on Maria's squat little TV.

3

In the morning, autumn has arrived. The temperature has fallen twenty degrees overnight. Surveying it from his window, in pants and vest, Murray is triumphant. He looks forward to shoving this turbulent autumn day, full of wet leaves, in Hans-Pieter's face and saying, 'So what about this then? You fancy an ice cream now, ya fucking parasite?' He starts to smile, until an eruption of coughing knobbles him and he turns from the window trying to force out the word *Fuck* as he doubles over and the veins in his temples swell and throb.

'FUCK!'

'Fuck.'

Silence settles on the flat, like dust. He found it, the flat, with Hans-Pieter's help, about a month after arriving in the town. His landlord is a middle-aged man whose mother lived here until she died, and most of her stuff is still in place – vast dark wooden furniture looms in the two rooms. Down at floor level Murray lurks among the old lady's pictures and knick-knacks, her pedal-operated sewing machine, her damp bedding. He had wanted it fully furnished. He uses her old steel knives and forks, her stained plates. There are even, on the walls, some framed photos of people in old-fashioned clothes, strangers with grave sepia faces.

The flat is still full of warm, stale air. The flapping grey scene outside its two grand windows seems disconnected from the tepid silence of the interior. It seems weird, histrionic. Rain comes at the windowpanes like handfuls of pebbles. Murray lights a cigarette. He smokes a local brand now – to that extent he has gone native. He sits in the hot shaft of the bathroom, surrounded by rust-furred piping, discoloured tile-work, a light bulb burning high overhead.

Afterwards, he dresses, and wrestles an umbrella the short distance to the Umorni Putnik.

Hans-Pieter is there, having breakfast at a table in the shadowy bar. A coffee, a buttered bread roll. He seems to be staring at a point about two feet in front of his eyes. *Fucking space cadet*, Murray thinks.

Without acknowledging his friend, he addresses himself to the bar, where Ester is on duty. Ester – she *is* out of his league.

She's pals with Maria, though, so it's probably worth keeping in with her: Murray smiles.

He feels the insufficiency of that smile himself, sees its insufficiency for a moment in the deep murky shadows of the mirror behind her. (The price list is written directly onto the mirror – his face peers out from among the numbers.)

'Yes?' Ester says.

'Cappuccino,' Murray's face says, in English.

While she works the machine, he looks at a local newspaper. The words mean nothing to him, his eyes drop from picture to picture. Pictures of local politicians – mean-looking men with terrible haircuts trying to smile, as he has just tried to, and with, for the most part, a similar lack of plausibility.

When he has his cappuccino, he joins Hans-Pieter. 'Morning,' Murray says, mutters, taking a seat opposite his friend.

Hans-Pieter, his mouth full, just nods.

He seems to be force-feeding himself a bread roll.

Murray regards him with distaste for a few moments. 'Where were you last night then?' he asks finally.

Hans-Pieter is swallowing the bread in his mouth. He tries to speak prematurely and the words are indistinct.

Murray squints at him irritably. 'What was that?'

'Ammarias,' Hans-Pieter says, swallowing.

'What?'

Hans-Pieter swallows properly. 'Maria's. At Maria's flat.'

'What d'you mean?'

Hans-Pieter is unable to hold Murray's stare. 'You know – Maria?'

'Maria,' Murray says, struggling, it seems, to understand who they are talking about, 'who works *here*?'

'Yes.'

You were at her *flat*?'

'Yes.'

'Why?' Murray asks, sincerely puzzled.

'Well.' Hans-Pieter laughs shyly. 'You know . . .'

'No, I don't know.'

'We've . . . We've got something going,' Hans-Pieter says.

Murray, for a moment, looks totally nonplussed. 'What – *you*?'

Hans-Pieter nods.

'You and Maria?'

Hans-Pieter looks down. 'Well, yes,' he admits. He seems embarrassed. And it might be that he misunderstands Murray's perspective. Maria is twenty years younger than Hans-Pieter, more or less. She is overweight and unattractive. Things that are, potentially, sources of embarrassment.

'How did that happen?' Murray says. He has turned quite pale.

Last Friday night, Hans-Pieter tells him, he was there in the Umorni Putnik until it shut, as he usually is, and it was pissing down outside, and she didn't have an umbrella – she was waiting for it to stop, so he suggested she come up to his room and wait there, have a smoke, and she did, and they ended up spending the night together. Since then, he tells Murray, he has twice spent the night at her flat.

'That's it,' Hans-Pieter says.

He starts on his second bread roll.

For some time Murray says nothing.

The little trees in the street outside shake and sway.

At the shadow-draped bar, Ester is talking to someone on her phone, laughing.

And I was at Beckie's place, Murray thinks, trying to sleep. The Spider-Man duvet. And they were. At that same moment. Last Friday.

He is staring at Hans-Pieter with an expression of shocked loathing. 'What the fuck does she see in you?' he says.

What does she see in Hans-Pieter? The question keeps Murray awake that night. He sits there, in the tall mausoleum-like spaces of his flat, smoking in the darkness. What seems obvious to him is that if he had only made his own intentions plainer, sooner, he and not Hans-Pieter would have her. That thought torments him for a while. Not that he even particularly wants to have her in any physical sense. There was something limply sentimental, something vague, something almost like pity, about his feelings for Maria. And what she sees in Hans-Pieter is obvious enough – Hans-Pieter is just a lesser version of himself, a poor woman's Murray. A foreigner from somewhere further west, with at least *some* money. Hans-Pieter even has a car – an old rust-perforated 1.2 litre Volkswagen Polo, leaking oil in a side street. In the context of the Umorni Putnik, that makes him a more or less plausible sugar daddy.

He's welcome to her, Murray decides.

He's welcome to the fat tart.

And the good thing is, this will give him more time to focus on his business interests. Which is what he *should* be doing anyway, not messing about with floozies. His business interests. Airport transfers. Minibus to

Zagreb airport. Blago has the drivers lined up. He has the advertising lined up. The website is ready to go. He just needs the minibuses. He has enough for one, he says, but he needs four to make the business viable. So he offered Murray the opportunity to invest. They talked about it in Džoker, and then over lunch. Put in the money for the minibuses, get a fifty per cent stake, was Blago's proposal. And sitting in an HSBC in Kingston upon Thames last Wednesday, Murray had finalised the loan, against the house in Cheam, and transferred the money to the account of Slavonski Zračne Luke d.o.o., the details of which – IBAN number and so forth – Blago had provided for him. Blago has shown him the minibuses he intends to buy – ex-police vehicles he found online, for sale in Osijek. Said he'd be going down there to get them just as soon as the money arrives. Murray said he wanted to come with him, to see the vehicles for himself. 'I know a thing or two about that,' he had told Blago. He had insisted on having a veto, if he didn't think they were up to scratch.

He has tried Blago's phone once or twice since he got back from the UK, to find out if the money has arrived.

No answer. That was typical Blago.

*

The most pressing issue, he finds, is the Hans-Pieter-shaped hole in his own days, which he now mostly drifts through alone. They used to meet every morning in the Umorni Putnik. These days, most of the time, Hans-Pieter isn't there. Murray drinks his cappuccino, while pretending to look at the paper. He stays there for more than an hour, sometimes.

Occasionally Hans-Pieter does show up. One morning, when he does, Murrays says to him, 'What you up to later then?' Which is what he always used to say – and the answer would always be words to the effect of 'not much', and they would agree to meet at Džoker 'later', meaning some time fairly soon after lunch.

298

Today, however, Hans-Pieter just shrugs.

When Murray suggests a drink in Džoker 'later', Hans-Pieter is initially evasive, and then says something about a film he's planning to see.

'Oh?' Murray says. 'What you seeing?'

Iron Man 3, Hans-Pieter tells him.

There is a silence. Then Murray says, 'Mind if I come along?'

Another silence. Hans-Pieter says, not particularly warmly, 'If you want.'

'If it's okay with you,' Murray says.

Hans-Pieter looks down at his Adidas trainers. 'It's okay.'

'Where shou' we meet then?' Murray asks.

'Here?' Hans-Pieter suggests, without enthusiasm.

So they meet there, in the middle of the afternoon, Hans-Pieter and Maria arriving together.

Maria does not seem pleased to see him – to see Murray, waiting there in his slacks. He tries to be friendly. She isn't having it. She hardly says a word on the bus out to the edge of town, where there is a tatty shopping mall with a few screens embedded in it.

It is then, strap-hanging, that Murray starts to wonder whether this was really such a good idea. The others seem to be deliberately not looking at him. When his and Maria's eyes meet, he tries to smile at her. She looks away immediately and he asks her about the film. 'So what we going to see then?' he says. 'Is it any good?' She pretends not to hear him.

Most of the other people in the ticket queue are kids – lads with faceted glass earrings and sagging waistbands and shrieking ladesses in tiny skirts or tracksuits, slurping sugary drinks and throwing popcorn at each other. Among these high-spirited youngsters, with Hans-Pieter and Maria sometimes snogging next to him, Murray sits for two hours, watching the noisy action film. It is dubbed in Croatian and he understands fuck-all.

Afterwards, while Maria is in the ladies, Hans-Pieter tells him they're going back to her place, and asks Murray what he's going to do.

'I dunno,' Murray says, just standing there in the foyer.

There is a short silence and Murray has the appalling feeling that Hans-Pieter is pitying him – that fucking *Hans-Pieter* is feeling sorry for *him*.

Well, fuck that.

'Don't you worry,' he says. 'I've got things to do. You give her one from me, okay?' And with an unpleasant smile, he nods towards Maria, who is approaching them.

He spends the next few hours in Džoker, drinking Pan lager and thinking, If the likes of Hans-Pieter can sort himself out with a woman, then *I* sure as fuck can.

Matteus nods.

Without meaning to, Murray had said it aloud. Matteus, tall and austere, possessor of a monastic vibe, is taking glasses out of the dishwasher and putting them on a shelf under the bar.

It is not even eight o'clock, and Murray is already quite drunk.

In Oaza later, he happens on Damjan.

They are sitting at a table together in the kebab shop and Murray is saying, 'If the likes of Hans-Pieter can sort himself out with a woman, then *I* sure as fuck can.' Inelegantly, he is eating a kebab.

Damjan says, 'Sure.' He and his friend have already finished, were about to leave when Murray arrived. They talk in Croatian, the two of them – a muttered wry exchange of words. Murray, shoving the last wet mess of the kebab into his mouth, wonders what they are talking about.

'What you gonna do now?' he asks, wiping his lips with a paper napkin.

Damjan's friend, it turns out, speaks perfect English. He sounds like an American.

'We're gonna go party,' he says, grinning. 'You wanna come?'

'Fuck, yeah,' Murray says. 'Good man. Let's go.'

As they leave, one of the twins says something to Damjan.

The kebab shop is owned by Albanian twins, identical, of vaguely thuggish appearance. Shaved, spherical heads. Fleshy noses. Strong necks and heavy eyebrows. Murray can never tell them apart. At first he didn't realise there were two of them; then one day he saw them together. They usually sit out on the terrace in front, under the awning where a water-feature tinkles, puffing at a hookah and drinking tea. Other, more desperate-looking men – often with moustaches – hang out with them there, and any number of women, young and old. A souped-up white Honda Accord EX 2.2 litre diesel is frequently parked in front of the shop, which Murray assumes must be owned by one of them.

And he envies the way one of them nods at Damjan as they leave, and offers him a few words of farewell. He wishes the twins would acknowledge *him* like that. He has been eating their kebabs for over a year, and he has always felt that he and they share something, something that sets them apart from the other people in this place, a superiority of some sort. And yet they never speak to him, as one of them just spoke to Damjan, or acknowledge him in any way.

On the spur of the moment Murray decides that he will be the first to speak. The twin who spoke to Damjan is standing there, near the door, slouching against the jamb, and poking about in his mouth with a toothpick.

'Al*right*,' Murray says to him, forcefully he hopes, as he passes him on the way out.

And the twin just looks slightly surprised – in his collarless shirt, his tan leather jacket – and watches Murray leave.

And how the fuck did that happen?

Safely in his mausoleum, hugging the toilet, Murray weeps. Drops tears onto the filthy floor.

How did that happen?

He has never been so intimate with the root of this toilet, with the rusty bolts that hold it to the old linoleum.

He sits up, after a while, and dries his eyes.

He inspects, in the mirror, his fat lip.

This mirror always gives the impression of fog. His face looms out of it, damaged. He stares at himself with contempt.

There was a woman. Aye, there was a woman. There were lots of women. With Damjan and his friend he had trawled through the nightspots of the town – two or three of them, there were. Nightspots. Full of students, kids. No success there, though he had tried, God knows. He had tried in the noise of the new music to have it off with a few of them. Kids with dyed hair. And Murray leering over them, trying to make himself understood. Shouting about the S-Class he had once owned. Shouting, 'You been to London?' Shouting, 'I'll show you round, okay?' He had offered her a job, that one. And she was about to give him her number, he thinks, when her friends pulled her away. (Later, seen her being sick in the car park. Was it her?) Damjan's friend disappeared. So just him and Damjan went on to the all-night place. 'I know one place,' Damjan said, speaking more fluently than usual. 'I know one place is open all night.' Taxi. Yes, taxi. And then tumble out into the raw air again. Damjan paying. 'You got any smokes?' Murray asking him. And then the place. The woman, perched up there on her stool. Not a kid, this one. Or maybe he was perched on the stool and she was there, suddenly, talking to him. And he was telling her about the S-Class he had once owned. Asking her, 'You been to London?' She was, what? Forty? Fifty? And no oil painting. Even then, in the state he was in, he knew that. She kept touching him. Hand on his leg. (And where was Damjan?) Hand on his leg. And he said to her, straight out, 'You wanna come back to mine?'

And she just nodded, and moved her hand up his leg.

'Okay then,' he said.

'A minute,' she said, squeezing his leg. 'Wait.'

'Okay then,' he said. And waited, feeling pleased with himself. And then starting to worry about whether he'd be able to do it, the state he was in. And he looked for her and saw her talking to two men near the toilets. And something about the way she was talking to them made him understand. He just wanted out of it then. He slid off the stool, trying to keep his footing, and started to move towards the door. And then she was holding his arm. Holding it hard. 'Okay?' she said, 'we go?' 'Look, I'm tired,' he told her, trying to pull his arm free, 'I'll see you another time.' 'Don't say that,' she said, her hand on his trousers, feeling for something. 'I'm fucking tired,' he snapped, shoving her away. Outside, the cold night air. Haloed street lamps. He started to walk quickly, not knowing where he was. And yes, those were footsteps following him, and as soon as he started to jog, hands seizing him. Threw him against the side of a parked van. The two men. Faceless in the shadows. His voice emerging as an effeminate squawk: 'What d'you want?' There were various issues. He had, they seemed to be telling him, entered into an agreement. So he owed them money. And he had hit her, they said. They wanted more money for that. 'I did not hit her'. Everything he had on him, seemed to be what they wanted. 'I never hit her . . .' He took a punch to the face. Then, from a position on the pavement, handed over his wallet, and they emptied it of kuna and threw it on top of him.

And then he was alone, lying on a wet pavement, wondering if he was in fact dreaming. *Please, let me be dreaming*

His mouth seemed to be the wrong shape. Near his eyes, something . . . What *was* that?

Hubcap.
    Fuck.
    Hubcap of a . . .
    Toyota Yaris?
    Dizzy when he stood up.
    And sick. Suddenly he felt very sick.

*

Two days later, when his mouth has deflated, he emerges and finds Hans-Pieter in the Umorni Putnik.

'I heard about your night out,' Hans-Pieter says.

'Yeah, that. It was quite a night.'

'I heard it,' Hans-Pieter says.

It is some time in the afternoon. Maria is working, is there.

'Oh, yeah?' Murray wants to know, smiling worriedly. 'What'd you hear?'

'Damjan said it was a good night.'

Murray's smile turns less worried. He says, 'A fucking massive night, actually.'

'You've been recovering,' Hans-Pieter asks, 'since then?'

'That's right. In the recovery position. If you know what I mean.' Murray himself isn't sure what he means. He tastes his lager, the first that has passed his lips since then.

Yesterday he experienced a sort of dark afternoon of the soul. Some hours of terrible negativity. A sense, essentially, that he had wasted his entire life, and now it was over. The sun was shining outside.

As it is now, igniting the yellow of the leaves that still cling to the little trees in front of the hostel.

He sees them through the dusty window.

'How about you?' he asks Hans-Pieter. 'You okay?'

'I'm okay,' Hans-Pieter says.

Murray sees one of the leaves detach and drop.

Hans-Pieter says, 'Damjan says you were sort of on the pull, the other night.'

'What – *I* was?'

'That's what he said.'

Murray does something with his mouth, something uneasy. 'Don't know about that.'

'Well,' Hans-Pieter says, 'I know a very nice lady, you might be interested in.'

'Who's that then?' Murray asks snootily.

'A very nice lady,' Hans-Pieter says again. Then he whispers, 'Maria's mudder.'

In a savage whisper Murray says, 'Maria's *mother*?'

'Yes.'

'No fucking *way*.'

'Why not?'

'Fuck off,' Murray scoffs.

'Why not? She's quite young . . .'

'What's that mean?'

'Forty-eight, I tink. And she's in nice shape,' Hans-Pieter tell him.

'You've seen her, have you?'

'Sure.'

Maria, having no one to serve, has ventured out in search of empties. She stops at Hans-Pieter's shoulders, puts her hands on them. Her substantial hip is smack in Murray's line of sight.

'I was just telling Murray,' Hans-Pieter says to her, half-turning his head, 'about your mother.'

'Yeah?' she smiles. She seems to have forgiven Murray for the way he tagged along to *Iron Man 3* with them the other day. It occurs to him, in fact, that the way he tagged along that day might actually have *suggested* to her the idea of fixing him up with her obviously lonely and desperate mother.

'Just take her out for a drink,' Hans-Pieter . . . what? Suggests? Orders? Murray is still wondering what to make of this development – fucking *Hans-Pieter* telling him what to do – when Maria says, 'She's really pretty. And much thinner than me.'

'We won't hold dat against her,' Hans-Pieter says, almost suavely.

'She's always telling me I should lose weight.'

'Don't listen to her.'

'It's true – I should.'

'Absolutely not,' Hans-Pieter tells her. And then says to Murray, 'So will you do it? Take her for a drink?'

It's awkward, saying something like, 'Not on your life, no fucking *way*,' with Maria standing there, still smiling at him, a piece of pink-dyed hair falling over her eye.

'You got a picture?' he asks her after a few moments. 'I mean, on your phone or something?'

'Maybe,' she says. 'Yeah, here.'

Leaning forward over Hans-Pieter's shoulder, she passes Murray her phone.

He looks.

A woman holding a cat. Not very easy to make out. Thinner than Maria, yes. Okay? Maybe.

'What about your father?' he asks, handing back the phone without saying anything about the photo, and smirking. 'He won't mind?'

'He lives in Austria,' she says. 'And they're divorced. Obviously.'

'Obviously,' Murray says. It had been a joke. He had assumed that her father wasn't still on the scene. 'Okay,' he says. 'I'll give it a go.'

'Do you want her number then?' Maria asks.

'She speaks English, does she?'

'Of course.'

'Or why don't you call her?' he suggests, suddenly nervous. 'Set it up.'

Leaning on his shoulder, she looks at Hans-Pieter, wanting his opinion, perhaps even his permission.

'Sure,' Hans-Pieter says. 'Set it up.'

Without warning, another leaf detaches itself from one of the trees outside and drops down to the pavement.

On his way home, a few hours later, Murray stops at Oaza to pick up a kebab. The plastic sign – palm tree, smiling camel – is illuminated in the gloom. One of the Albanian twins is standing around near the entrance, keeping an eye on things. He does not acknowledge Murray, and Murray, after a moment's hesitation, says nothing to him either. Having ordered in English, he just waits there for his kebab, eyeing the slices of baklava as if wondering whether to have one. He wishes more than ever that the twins would offer him some sign, some little sign, that they looked on him as an equal – as an equal, no more than that. Damjan had been honoured with a nod, a few words, had been thereby elevated in Murray's estimation. He thinks more highly of Damjan now. The baklavas shine, sodden with honey. Yes, Damjan seems in some way superior to him now.

Seemingly unaware of Murray's presence the twin exchanges a few words, in some language Murray does not know, with the kebabist, who is shoving tongfuls of shredded salad into a pitta. He spoons on the sauces and hands Murray his supper, tightly wrapped in tinfoil, warm to the touch.

'Thanks,' Murray says.

The man just nods.

And then, as he leaves, Murray does it. He looks the twin straight in the eye. He says, in a loud firm voice, 'See ya, then, pal.'

And then he is outside, in the night air.

The twin had said nothing to him. Nothing.

Maybe he was just surprised.

That night Murray has a dream. He is lying on his bed. Outside, rain is falling – falling heavily and steadily. The window is open. He is lying on his bed, listening to the rain. It is like rain he might have listened to somewhere else, long ago. The room is strangely empty. There is nothing in it except the bed on which he is lying with his head at the wrong end, where his feet should be. He lies there listening to the rain and from the darkness of the bathroom, a large dog emerges – an Alsatian. Panting quietly, the dog lies down on the floor next to the bed. As it lies down it knocks over a glass that is there – the sound of the glass falling and then rolling a little way across the floor. With a tiny whimper the dog yawns, and then starts to pant again. The rain is still falling. Without otherwise moving, Murray has stretched out his hand and is stroking the dog's neck, the deep fur. The dog pants quietly. The rain falls and falls, making a puddle on the floor next to the open window.

On Sunday afternoon he takes Maria's mother out for a drink.

He was relieved, when they met outside the Irish pub, not to fancy her at all. Not at all. She was a tallish middle-aged woman, ungainly in a pair of jeans, her short hair dyed a deep purple like the outside of an aubergine.

When they shook hands, her hand felt frozen and knobbly in his.

The Irish pub was just about the poshest place in town, where the top people from the town hall went, and the senior members of the local mafia. A Guinness in there was almost as expensive as it would be in London. The interior was like a transients' pub near a large British mainline station. Very tired and heavily soiled. To that extent, it was authentic. The table service was not.

They sat in a padded booth facing each other and Murray asked the waiter for a half-litre of stout. Maria's mother had a white wine.

Not fancying her at all, Murray was less nervous than he had feared he might be. Her English was excellent, and soon he was telling her about London and telesales and, less forthcomingly, about Scotland. She seemed interested in Scotland, kept asking him questions about it. He didn't much want to talk about that. As darkness fell outside, he was telling her about the Mercedes S-Class he had once had, and the top-of-the-range Michelin tyres he had put on it. 'Top *top* quality,' he told her.

She nodded. She was drinking her second glass of wine.

He was on his third stout. 'Makes a big difference, the tyres,' he told her, encircling the stout with his hands.

'I know,' she said.

'Huge difference.'

She was a schoolteacher, an English teacher. And maybe, he thought, he did fancy her slightly after all.

She'd seemed as interested in the S-Class as any woman ever had, he'd say that for her. She'd wanted him to explain what an S-Class *was*, for a start. So he'd walked her through the entire Mercedes range, from the 1.8 litre A-Class through the C- and E-Classes, the various engine options available for those, all the way up to the S 500 L.

It took about half an hour.

Then he said, 'What sort of car do *you* drive?'

Some Suzuki, she said.

He said he didn't know much about Suzukis.

'Never mind.'

'Happy with it?' he asked.

She nodded, smiled. 'It's fine.'

'What . . . What size engine's it got?'

She seemed to find something funny about the question. She laughed anyway. 'I don't know. I'm so happy about Maria and Hans-Pieter,' she said. 'He's such a nice man.'

'Oh, yeah,' Murray agreed vaguely, looking out of the window for a moment. He didn't want to talk about Hans-Pieter, that was for sure.

'I wish Maria would lose some weight,' her mother said earnestly. 'Don't you think she should lose some weight?'

'Definitely.'

'Will you mention it to her? She doesn't listen to me.'

'Me?' Murray said, not knowing quite what to make of this. 'Sure. I'll have a word wi' her. D'you want another drink?'

'I'm okay. Thank you.'

Starting on his fourth stout he decided that he definitely *did* fancy her, quite a lot.

He was telling her about his business – the airport transfer thing. He had finally managed to get hold of Blago – 'my local partner' was how he described him to Maria's mother – and Blago had told him that the money had arrived safely. They would drive down to Osijek next week, was the idea, to have a look at the ex-police minibuses. Make a decision on that. It was moving forward. He told her it had the potential to turn into something 'fairly major'. Looking her intently in the eye, he said, 'The transport sector's woefully underdeveloped in this part of Croatia.'

She agreed.

It was then that he tried to take her hand. She quickly withdrew it, but with a little smile that was open to misinterpretation.

So he went to the gents and promised himself to have another try later. He zipped himself up and washed his hands. 'Death,' he said to his preened, sickly image in the mirror, 'or victory.'

*

The Wednesday of the following week.

Maria is working, so Hans-Pieter and Murray are having lunch together. They walk to the Chinese place, Zlatna Rijeka. It's in a melancholy little square, cobbled, and full of drifting leaves.

Inside, they confront the buffet.

Hans-Pieter chooses a heap of beansprouts and carrot slices bright with MSG.

Murray starts with a plate of dark shreds of meat, also very shiny.

They sit in the window and watch the world go by. There is an old bookshop opposite. Some bicycles chained to a metal frame.

It's obvious what Hans-Pieter, shovelling beansprouts into his wide mouth, will want to talk about.

He must already know what happened. He must have heard from Maria. Still, he says, 'How'd it go on Sunday?'

Murray concentrates on his glossy meat mixed with pieces of onion and green pepper. 'You tell me,' he murmurs.

'Well,' Hans-Pieter admits, pursuing the last slippery beansprouts on his plate with the tines of a cheap fork, 'not too good, I heard.'

'I don't know what happened,' Murray protests quietly. 'I don't know how that happened,' he says again.

Hans-Pieter watches him for a moment. 'The police?'

Murray seems very low.

'Maria still not talking to me?' he asks, his eyes down.

Hans-Pieter says, 'She wants an explanation. From you. About what happened. She doesn't understand.'

'About what happened?'

'Yah.'

'When we left the pub,' Murray says, 'I took her hands. She let me do that.'

Hans-Pieter nods and swigs from his Sprite.

'She *let* me do that,' Murray says again.

'Yah.'

'So I thought, *Okay*. You know . . .'

Hans-Pieter indicates that he does.

'So I was holding her hands . . .'

Her hands were icy, knobbly. He was in a fog of Guinness at the time. She *was* smiling. He sees it now, that fearful rictus.

'. . . and I tried to kiss her,' Murray says. He meets Hans-Pieter's pale, blonde-lashed eyes. 'And then. And then. She sorta *scRReeemed.*'

'She screamed?'

'Aye.'

'Why did she scream?' Hans-Pieter asks. He seems to put the question to his Sprite – he is not looking at Murray, anyway.

'I was just trying to kiss her,' Murray says.

'And then what happened?'

'Then some fucker was holding me down, someone else was phoning the police.'

'And what was she doing?'

'What was she doing? I don't know.'

'So then the police arrived,' Hans-Pieter prompts.

'Aye,' Murray says. 'They arrived. And I suppose I musta given one of 'm a shove or something.'

'Why did you do that?'

'I don't know . . . The way they were treating me . . .'

'I understand,' Hans-Pieter says.

'So then they took me to the station. With the fucking siren going and everything.'

Hans-Pieter just nods sympathetically.

'And I spent the night,' Murray says, 'in a fucking cell.'

'They let you go in the morning.' Hans-Pieter obviously knows the story already.

'They said Mrs Jevtovic didn't want to make a case against me. And I thought, *Who the fuck is Mrs Jevtovic?*'

'That's Maria's mudder.'

'Yeah, I know. I just wasn't thinking straight that morning.'

That morning. Not nice. One of the very lowest points. Emerging into the daylight . . .

'I just tried to kiss her,' he says, almost tearfully. 'I didn't do anything.'

'Okay.'

'What does *she* say I did?'

'I'm not sure,' Hans-Pieter says, evasively.

'I don't know what to do,' Murray tells him.

Hans-Pieter says nothing. He has finished his lunch.

Murray picks up his fork and sets about finishing his own, those strings of meat in dark, sticky sauce.

His teeth encounter something. 'What the fuck,' he says. He spits the object, small and hard as a shotgun pellet, into a paper napkin.

'What the fuck is that?'

Hans-Pieter peers down at the wet napkin, the tiny object.

Murray is eating again.

After examining it for a while, Hans-Pieter says, 'Shit, you know what I think it is?'

'What?'

'I think . . . I mean, I'm not sure . . . I think it's one of those microchips.'

'What microchips?' Murray says, with his mouth full.

'They use to identify animals.'

'Animals?'

'Yeah, like dogs,' Hans-Pieter says.

Murray, after a moment, spits out what is in his mouth.

'What are you saying?' he pants, distraught. 'Are you saying I'm eating a fucking *dog*?'

'I don't know,' Hans-Pieter says.

'Am I eating a dog?' Murray shouts at him. 'Is that what you're saying?'

'I don't know . . .'

'Am I eating a fucking dog?'

'I don't know,' Hans-Pieter says, shocked and embarrassed by the shouting, and by the tears that are so unexpectedly now welling out of Murray's eyes, that are starting on their way down his strong, flushed face.

Preposterously he tries to hide it, his face, with a scrap of paper napkin.

'I don't believe it, I don't believe it,' he mumbles.

Hans-Pieter looks helplessly at the Chinese woman overseeing the buffet.

With his face in his hands, Murray is sobbing openly now. He says something it's hard to make out through the sobs, the wet fingers, the fraying paper napkin.

The Chinese woman has made eye contact with Hans-Pieter. She wants him to do something, to stop his friend upsetting her other patrons.

So Hans-Pieter puts a timid hand on Murray's shoulder and suggests, in a low voice, that they leave.

4

Knocking. Knocking.
   And voices.
      Murray?

                                            Murray?

   Then silence, again.
   Shame.

5

They meet at Džoker. Hans-Pieter and Damjan are already there. A few weeks have passed. Murray has not been seen much in that time, though Maria has sort of forgiven him – will let him sit quietly in the Umorni Putnik, even if she is still not speaking to him. He has not seen much of Hans-Pieter either. Hans-Pieter has been painting Maria's flat, painting out the fluorescent orange with something less oppressive, less like living inside a migraine.

Murray fetches a Pan from Matteus, and joins Hans-Pieter and Damjan at the table near entrance, under the mirror.

'*Živjeli!*' It is the only Croatian word he knows.

He takes off his scarf. A cold front is moving across the flat land, laying down frosts in the morning, frosts that quickly melt to leave everything shining wet. 'So,' he says, sitting.

'So,' Hans-Pieter echoes, his face stippled with paint.

Damjan says nothing. There is a TV showing a Champions League match, with the sound off, and he is watching it.

'We've not seen much of you, Murray,' Hans-Pieter says.

'No,' Murray says. 'I've been staying in.'

'Okay.'

'End of the month,' Murray says. 'You know.'

End of the month, money tight. Hans-Pieter knows. He nods. He says, 'How are you?'

The question seems loaded. Murray looks at him suspiciously. 'Okay. I suppose.'

'You've not been out much?'

'No. I *said*. I've been staying in.'

'Okay.' Hans-Pieter seems tense about something. He says, 'I told Damjan about your situation.'

'My situation? What situation?'

'Your . . . Your life situation.'

'What's that mean?' Murray looks at Damjan, who is watching the football. 'What's this about?'

'Damjan thinks,' Hans-Pieter says. He stops.

'What's he think?'

'He thinks that maybe . . . Maybe . . .'

'Maybe what?'

'Maybe you are cursed,' Hans-Pieter says.

Murray emits a strangled laugh. 'What?'

Hans-Pieter appeals to Damjan, who is still staring at the TV, Real Madrid against someone. 'Don't you think that?'

'Maybe. I don't know. Maybe,' Damjan says, still following the match.

'You had a similar problem, I think,' Hans-Pieter says to him.

'Yes.'

'What the fuck are you talking about?' Murray asks.

Hans-Pieter has some sympathy for this point of view. 'It sounds weird.'

'I was victim,' Damjan says, 'for five years. Victim of curse.'

The fact that it is Damjan saying this – *Damjan*, the tyre-fitter, a man even now unable to tear his eyes away from the football – prevents Murray from dismissing the whole thing out of hand as total fucking shite, as he undoubtedly would if it were Hans-Pieter alone putting the idea to him.

Still, he says, 'This isn't some kind of wind-up?'

Damjan turns to Hans-Pieter, who doesn't know what a 'wind-up' is either.

'You're not taking the piss?' Murray says. 'This isn't a *joke*?'

'It's not a joke,' Hans-Pieter says.

Solemnly, Damjan explains. 'I tell you, for five years I am victim. Okay. Everything is fuck up for me. Then I go to see lady. Powerful lady.'

Murray has a question. 'What fuckin' lady?'

'Here, in the town.'

'She is quite famous here, I think,' Hans-Pieter puts in.

'I hear about her,' Damjan says. 'I go. I see her. I pay to her five hundred kuna. And she help me. She take away this thing.'

'Ah, bollocks,' Murray scoffs. 'Five hundred kuna?'

Damjan seems unwilling to joke about this, or treat it lightly in any way. He seems to find Murray's attitude disrespectful. 'Is not expensive,' he says, 'to take away this curse.'

'It's not so much,' Hans-Pieter agrees. 'Fifty euro?'

'Who was it cursed you, then?' Murray wants to know. 'Who cursed me?'

Damjan just shrugs. The question doesn't seem to interest him. 'I don't know. Impossible to know.'

Real Madrid score a spectacular goal.

'You really believe this?' Murray asks him.

'I believe it, yes. I believe it.'

Damjan has noticed that something has happened in the football and is watching it again.

'Smoke?' Hans-Pieter suggests.

He and Murray stand outside, under the wet awning. The square is dark and dripping. The fountains are switched off. Pigeons huddle on the facades, high up, over unlit windows. There's one other smoker there, a small furtive man with a trim beard who spends even more time in Džoker than Murray does. They exchange nods.

'This is bullshit, isn't it?' Murray says.

Hans-Pieter's hands are in the pockets of his enormous jeans – they seem to be made of various different shades of denim, stitched together haphazardly. The cigarette hangs wagging from his lip. He shrugs. 'I don't know,' he says. 'Damjan doesn't think so, I suppose.'

Weird that, that *Damjan*, of all people, takes shite like this seriously. Turn out he does fucking yoga next. Murray says, 'I mean, honestly . . .'

'Maybe it's worth a try,' Hans-Pieter says.

'It's just shit, isn't it?'

'It's only five hundred kuna.'

'*Only* five hundred kuna! Fuck's sake.'

'Maybe she can help you . . .'

'Do I look like I need help?' Murray asks.

Hans-Pieter says nothing.

'Fucking mumbo jumbo. Does she even speak English, this woman?'

*

Sunday. The last, dark Sunday of October. Even the rain has stopped. There is nowhere to hide on a day like this. Streets. Murray walks down them. Days and days he has spent in the flat, among the daguerreotypes, the old lady's decrepit stuff – dresses still hanging damp in that huge wardrobe, funereal woodwork, moths moving on ancient fabric, eating at the velvet padding of mildewed hangers. The desolate atmosphere of musty, discolouring lace.

A few people, here and there, in the streets. Sounds, at least, of life. He will stay out until it is dark, he says to himself, just walking – though he has started to feel an unfamiliar, frightening stiffness in his joints this autumn, more and more as the weather gets wetter. In the mornings his hands hurt. His knees needle with pain on the stone steps of the house, in the vast silent stairwell. He has to stop, halfway up. Lean on the wall, working incandescent lungs.

A few people, here and there. The air is heavy with moisture. The trees are black with it. Leaves plaster the twisting streets near the main square. Unlit windows.

He feels totally desolate. It is something he notices, at a particular moment – that he feels totally desolate.

He is looking down at the wet leaves at his feet.

It is almost dark.

He takes out his phone and stands there for a minute. Then he does something he has never done. He phones Hans-Pieter.

'Hello?' he says. 'Is that you?'

His voice sounds quiet there, under the empty trees.

'It's me – Murray. What you doing? Fancy a drink?' He says, 'Nowish? Okay. Okay. See you there.'

He puts his phone away.

Hans-Pieter said he was with 'some people'. Who these people are, Murray has no idea. However, that Hans-Pieter now seems to have some sort of social life, as well as a woman, only deepens his sense of desolation.

They turn out to be Dutch pensioners, loads of them. They live permanently in the area, have taken over one of the villages a few kilometres outside town, and they appear to have adopted Hans-Pieter. They have just finished a lunch which went on all afternoon and when Murray joins them everyone is fairly tipsy, the wine-flushed Netherlanders shouting and laughing in their own language. Hans-Pieter is fully involved in this jolly scene. Stuck at the end of the long table, wedged in where there isn't really space, more or less ignored even by Hans-Pieter, Murray does not feel very welcome.

There seems to be no possibility of the party ending soon – another mammoth drinks order has just been fulfilled by the waitress – so he leans over to Hans-Pieter, at whose elbow he is lurking, and says, 'Look, I'm off, okay?'

Hans-Pieter has just shot a *slivovica*, the plum stuff they make here. His eyes are watering. His face is all mottled and hot. He does not try to persuade his friend to stay. He just says, 'You sure?'

'Yeah, I'm fucking sure,' Murray tells him.

He has been sitting there for an hour without speaking to anybody.

'Anyway,' he says, 'I've got to go to Osijek tomorrow.'

'Osijek? Why?'

'To look at these minibuses,' Murray says. 'You know.' He has spent a lot of time, the last few months, telling Hans-Pieter about this investment, about how the transport sector in this part of Croatia is underdeveloped, about the opportunities thus presented for a man like himself. 'With Blago,' he says.

Hans-Pieter seems surprised. 'With Blago?'

'Aye, with Blago.' Murray notices Hans-Pieter's expression – something odd about it. 'Why? What is it?'

'Nothing,' Hans-Pieter says. A song has started up among the drunken Dutchlings, a noisy singalong. 'It's just I thought Blago went to Germany,' Hans-Pieter says.

'What you talking about?'

'Someone told me . . . I think Blago's in Germany or something. A job there,' Hans-Pieter says.

'You don't know what you're talking about,' Murray tells him. 'We're going to Osijek tomorrow. We've got minibuses to look at.'

'Okay,' Hans-Pieter says, turning back to his table of drunk, elderly friends. 'I just heard he was in Germany.'

'Who *told* you that?' Murray almost has to shout over the loud, tuneless singing.

'Someone told me. I don't know. They said he's got a job there. He's not coming back. They said. I don't know.'

Hans-Pieter is being encouraged to take part in the singing, which he now does, in a shy mumbly way.

Standing out in the raw night, Murray tries the number. Not even voicemail – a woman's voice telling him something in Croatian. He tries the number again. Same thing. Same message. Number doesn't exist. Something like that.

6

She does not speak English. Her daughter is there to translate. There is something wrong with her, the daughter. She needs help walking. Her voice is slurred. She looks weird. It's hard to say how old she is. Maybe twenty.

Her mother – Vletka, Murray has been told her name is – instructs him to sit.

'Please, sit down,' the daughter says, with a sweet smile. She has a very sweet smile. Among strands of lank black hair, her ham-pink scalp is visible.

Murray, nervously, sits on a green velvet sofa.

There is something dead about the light in the room. It all arrives at one end, where curtains of yellowing lace half-hide a balcony hung with clothes-lines.

At the other end, facing the window, this velvet sofa, in which Murray now feels trapped, his feet hardly touching the brown carpet, stuff looming all around him. The place is low-ceilinged, oppressively so. Along one wall, there is a large sideboard. He catches sight of himself in a convex mirror, looking hideous. Vletka is lighting candles. The daughter smiles at him from where she is sitting at a small table placed against the wall opposite the sideboard. Next to her head, in tapestry, a tearful Jesus. Porcelain dogs clutter a shelf.

Vletka, lighting candles, says something snappishly.

The daughter translates, smiling: 'Do you want some tea?'

'I'm okay,' Murray blurts, uneasily feeling the soft velvet with his hand.

The place wasn't easy to find. It's in a part of the town he doesn't know, a twenty-minute taxi to a whole nother world of weather-stained estates, solemn cuboid structures separated by parked cars and dreary parks, hard paths under sad trees, deserted playgrounds, an electricity substation garlanded with barbed wire. Each of the buildings has a name – some Croatian hero. Murray was looking for Faust Vrančić House, number eleven.

He punched one-one into the entryphone and waited while crackly electric pulses sounded. Then a voice. *'Da?'*

'It's Murray,' Murray said. 'I'm here to see, uh, Vletka?'

The fizzing voice said, *'Tko je to?'*

'Murray,' Murray said again, louder. 'I've come to see Vletka. Murray.'

A more high-pitched electric noise, insistent, and something happening in the door, a heavy metal door with safety-glass panels. Murray fought it open.

A pungent stairwell.

He was shitting himself.

She sits down on the sofa, Vletka. She's in a dressing gown. A solid, surly woman, she seems to Murray. Like someone who sells you a train ticket to Zagreb, frowning at you through the perforated glass as you try to explain what it is you want, while the queue lengthens. Short hair. Little buds of gold in her earlobes. Breath that smells of cigarette smoke, bacteria.

She says something to Murray in a sharp, imperative voice.

'She says you should relax,' is the translation.

Murray's mouth: strange munching movements. A fixed, terrified smile. She has taken one of his hands now.

He has this weird fear that she's going to ask him to strip.

She doesn't. She is staring into his eyes, though, which is almost worse. Her own eyes are greyish-brown. Her eyelashes are short and unfeminine. She has no eyebrows.

When Murray looks away, she snaps something at him.

'Please, you should look into her eyes,' the daughter tells him, more softly.

Murray does so.

Those *fucking* eyes. The stress of the stare is like some terrible sound that just won't stop, a squealing scraping of metal . . .

She's still holding his hand, all damp in hers.

The stare softens perceptibly. She says something. Her voice sounds dry and detached.

'She says you are in a very bad situation,' the daughter says.

Murray, still holding the stare though it's making his head hurt now, says, 'Yeah?'

The room is hot. He is sweating. It's not just the heat. It's the sense that some sort of invasive procedure is taking place.

The daughter translates a brusque instruction: 'Shut your eyes, please.'

He does.

Her mother's hand is now on his face. The whole situation is so odd that this seems okay, sort of.

'Is this about some curse?' Murray asks, feeling safer with his eyes shut.

The daughter translates. Vletka answers.

'She doesn't know what it is,' the daughter tells Murray. 'Just that you are in –' the same phrase – 'a very bad situation.'

'What does she mean by that?' Murray says, his eyes still shut. Vletka's hand has taken hold of his skull, the front of his skull, and is squeezing it quite hard.

The daughter translates.

The mother answers, sounding exasperated now, squeezing Murray's skull still harder.

'She says it is like a poison,' the daughter finally says, after some follow-up questions in Croatian, while Murray waited, the strong points of Vletka's hard fingers starting to hurt his head.

'Poison? What's that mean?' he wants to know.

Vletka loudly shushes him.

An instruction arrives via her daughter's polite voice: 'Please, do not speak.'

The fingers are starting to properly hurt. It's as though some metal instrument is being tightened on his head.

Suddenly, it stops.

He opens his eyes, tentatively, just in time to see the slap flying at him.

He feels the numb shock of it in his face. Then the heat arrives, intense, a moment later.

'What the fuck was that for?' he shouts, his hand at his stinging face.

Vletka is speaking at him angrily in her own language. Her hand is on his forehead now, applying pressure, or holding his head in place.

Then she slaps him again.

'*Stop* doing that!' Murray yells, trying to stand up. She snatches his arm, while he is still off balance, and pulls him back down onto the sofa.

'Sh, sh, sh,' she says, as if to a small child, stroking his face.

'Stop doing that,' Murray says again.

'Sh, sh.'

'*Zatvorite oči*,' Vletka says.

'Please, shut your eyes,' her daughter instructs him.

'Is she going to hit me again?'

'Please,' the younger woman says softly, 'shut your eyes.'

Vletka is still stroking his face in a way Murray finds he quite likes. He shuts his eyes. She is all soft-voiced now, and holding his hand. Singing something, holding his hand, stroking it. The singing stops. He is aware of her weight moving, leaving the sofa. He opens his eyes to find her on her feet, extinguishing candles.

'Are we done then?' he asks.

The daughter translates for him.

Vletka shakes her head. She says something and indicates the table where her daughter is sitting.

'Please, sit down here.'

'What happens now?' Murray says.

Vletka just tells him to sit at the table again. So he does, sitting opposite her daughter. And then Vletka joins them too, having taken something out of a drawer. A pack of cards.

She sits at the table, taking the seat facing the wall, the histrionic Jesus tapestry. On her left, her daughter's oversized, smiling head. On the other side, Murray, asking if he can smoke.

He can.

He lights up while Vletka shuffles the cards.

And in fact she is smoking too, letting a cheap cigarette hang whorishly from her lip – the mid-afternoon dressing gown is part of the effect as well – as she skilfully shuffles the old pack. The air in the room, already somehow grey and dim, is soon harsh and blue with smoke.

She puts the pack face down on the tabletop. Then, with a single practised movement, spreads it into a perfectly symmetrical fan.

The instruction arrives, as always, via the daughter: 'Please, take one.'

Murray looks furtively at Vletka. She is looking the other way, drawing tiredly on her fag, waiting for him to take his card. His hand ventures out into the middle of the table. It hovers for a moment over the fan and then his index finger lands on a card and tugs it free of the others. As if she is in a hurry, Vletka snatches it up and looks at it. '*Prošlosti*,' she says, placing it face up on the table.

'The past,' the daughter tells him.

The card shows a man, seated, facing out, hugging a large coin. He also has a coin on his head – as well as something that looks like a simple crown – and his feet seem to hold two further coins in place on the floor. His posture is hunched, tense, defensive. He is staring straight out of the card and his expression is grim. There is something about him that suggests exhaustion. Blood-saturated eyes, strangers to sleep. Behind him, some distance away, is a city.

'Please,' the daughter translates, smiling at Murray across the table, showing him her large yellow teeth, 'take another one.'

Murray does.

When he has pulled it free of the fan, Vletka turns it over and says, '*Prisutna*.'

'The present.'

A tower against a black sky. A huge zigzag of lightning has just struck the top of the tower, violently dislodging the crown that was there. Flames leap out of the broken summit. Two figures tumble down through the dark air, as if the force of the explosion has thrown them out of their tower, which seemed so secure. Their faces are open with terror. One of them is wearing a crown.

The daughter tells Murray to take another card.

He presses his cigarette into the notch of the ashtray and does so.

Vletka adds it to the other two and says, '*Budućnost*.'

'The future.'

Murray, having reclaimed his cigarette, is staring at the three cards.

The guy hugging his coins.

The shattered tower.

The greybeard with his lamp.

The final card shows an elongated figure in a monkish habit. Hooded. White-bearded. Holding in one hand a lit lamp, in the other a long staff. His head is bowed and his eyes might be closed, even though he is holding the lamp up as if to illuminate something. He seems to be standing in a frozen or snowy wasteland. There is, anyway, nothing there.

Vletka studies the cards for a minute, finishing her cigarette. Then she stubs it out with a few gentle, thoughtful movements. She seems bored, actually. She says, indicating the first card, *'Ovo je tvoja prošlost.'*

'This is your past,' the daughter says to Murray, who has taken a position with his hands knitted on the table in front of him, his shoulders slumped. He feels tired. 'Yeah?' he says.

Still indicating the first card, Vletka starts saying words. It sounds like a list. Her daughter translates, her words overlapping with her mother's. 'Materialism,' she says, 'acquiring material possessions, only interested in wealth, power, status, winning your share, and keeping what you have, ownership, jealousy, wanting to impose your will, denying weaknesses.' She is smiling at Murray. She is always smiling, despite the fact that most of her hair has already fallen out, and her voice sounds slurred and stupid, and she needs help to walk even a few steps. She says, 'This is your past.'

'If you say so,' Murray says, with some sarcasm. His mouth makes those strange munching movements. His eyes flit fearfully between the two women.

With her finger on the lightning-struck tower, the shattered phallus spilling fire, the plummeting victims, Vletka is now telling Murray about his present.

'This is your present,' the daughter says. 'Upheaval, turbulence, plans destroyed, disorder, pride humbled, humiliation, violence even . . .'

His eyes narrowing, Murray unknits his fingers to find his cigarettes. The daughter says in her silly voice, 'The destruction of a way of living. The impact of things over which you have no control. The final end of a . . . a part of your life. This is your present.'

With the lighter that is there on the table – a souvenir lighter from a Macedonian health spa or place of pilgrimage or something – Murray lights his cigarette.

Vletka's finger moves to the final card.

'This is your future,' her daughter says.

And Vletka says sternly, '*Ne – to može biti vaša budućnost.*'

'This *might* be your future.'

'*Moguća budućnost.*'

'A possible future.'

'*Moguće,*' Vletka emphasises.

'It is possible.'

Vletka starts on the final list, and her daughter says, still with a stupid smile on her face, 'Solitude, introspection, stillness, quiet, seclusion, withdrawing from the world, silence, submission, meditation . . .'

Fuckin' wonderful, Murray thinks.

'That it then?' he asks.

'That's it,' the daughter says, still smiling at him.

He is putting his jacket on. The daughter, leaning on Vletka and on a walking stick, has lurched out of the room in her old woman's knitted shawl. It's like one of her legs is six inches shorter than the other, Murray thinks, pretending not to notice, finishing his cigarette at the table on his own.

The cards are still there.

He ignores them.

Still, the stuff she said about his present wasn't so wrong.

Fuck though, she *knew* he was in a bad way – people only show up here when they're in a bad way.

And his past?

The smouldering end of the cigarette crackles, the cheap tobacco, as he inhales strongly.

Ah, bollocks.

That was everybody's past, what she said. We all think we're special – we're all the fucking same.

That's how they operate, people like her.

Five hundred kuna. Fuck's sake.

He is putting on his jacket, looking forward to leaving, when the women are there again. The daughter is holding a plate of sticky-looking cakes.

Murray is just shrugging his shoulders into his jacket – a sensible thing with a hood, elasticated wrists, lots of pockets.

'You would like a cake?' she says, smiling as always.

He looks, for a moment, at the things on the plate – lumps, each with a layer of sugary frosting. They are misshapen, sad-looking.

'A cake? Uh . . . Yeah, okay. Thanks.'

He takes one. They are watching him as, after a pause, he lifts it to his mouth. In his other hand the cigarette is still going. He puts the cake into his mouth. The first thing is: it hurts his teeth. A lot. It's shocking, how much it hurts. Sharp lines of pain lance down into his jaw, up into his skull. He forces himself not to wince, his miserable teeth working on the stuff. It has a weird texture – it seems to melt away in his mouth, melt into something sandy, muddy almost. It tastes of sugar, and something else, something foul. They are still watching him. The daughter still smiling, her upper lip downy, her lower lip glistening. He tries to smile back as he swallows, his Adam's apple forcing the thing down. 'Nice,' he says. 'Thank you.'

She lifts the plate up towards him, offering him another.

'No. Thank you,' he says. 'No.'

Ushered through the dark, narrow hall – past hanging coats and hats, and a mirror that tells him nothing – he finds himself in the stairwell again.

The door of the flat closes and he starts down the stairs, spurning the besmirched lift. The cement stairs are darkly shiny, polished by decades of footfall so that they look wet even though they aren't. At each landing there is an island of light from the window, and a line of communal pot plants – rubbery leaves, dead leaves, crusty soil. At the bottom, metal postboxes with little nameplates. A metal thing set in the floor for scraping the mud off your shoes. Some notices on the wall, a slew of junk mail. The heavy door with its two panes of safety glass, the lower one spider-webbed with damage.

He stops there.

For some time he stands there, in the dim daylight.

A strand of cobweb waves in the air over a radiator. He is looking at it, waving in the rising heat of the radiator. Everything is perfectly still, except for that strand of cobweb, waving.

He stands there, watching it.

He is still standing there, watching the cobweb, weirdly absorbed in the way it moves.

Then he shoves through the heavy front door, makes it screech on its hinges.

He shoves through it, out into the world again.

7

Two and a half hours it takes, to drive to the sea. First the flat land, then the limestone hills, then mountains. Sparse vegetation. The motorway, which starts at Zagreb, is empty. It is a Wednesday morning in early November, that might be why. And now Hans-Pieter has switched on the windscreen wipers – a slow, intermittent setting. They sweep, and stop. They sweep, and stop. Each time with a little squeak. Drizzle obscures the distances of flat farmland in the early part of the drive. The wipers sweep, and stop. Deserted villages, strung out along the road. Dark fields of stubble or ploughed soil. The landscape undulates slightly, is the most that can be said for it.

Next to Hans-Pieter in the front is Maria.

From where he is sitting, Murray can see her chewing at her gum, staring without interest at the dull landscape.

He is actively pleased, at this point, that she is Hans-Pieter's lookout, not his own. She isn't his problem. He turns the other way. They are just passing through one of those villages, fucking awful place. One-storey houses line the road, in little fenced plots of land. There is some sort of pub, he sees – a sign with a Pan logo, a sign saying *Pizza*. That's it. That's the village. That's the life you have here. Murray watches it taper to nothing. More dead fields.

There's this point when you think, Why pretend? What's the point? Who're you trying to fool?

Who *are* you trying to fool? Yourself?

So what *is* the point?

There is no point.

What difference does it make anyway?

We're all headed to the same place.

They are talking in the front, Hans-Pieter and Maria. Talking in low voices so that he can't hear, over the noise of the engine and the wheels and the wind, what they are saying exactly. It surprised him, this invitation. Last night, he was in Džoker, talking to Matteus about football, when Hans-Pieter turned up in his duffel coat, ordered a white wine. He put in his two cents about the football – a stupid opinion, Murray thought. Then Hans-Pieter said, 'We're thinking of taking a trip to the seaside tomorrow. You want to come?'

They were perched up on tall stools, facing the shelves of spirits, and the postcards that people had sent over the years, and that Matteus had pinned up. Not that many of them, less than ten.

Murray said, 'Isn't the weather a bit shite for that?'

Hans-Pieter had a quick, timid sip of wine. 'Should be okay tomorrow,' he said. 'They say.'

Murray shrugged. 'Okay then. If Maria doesn't mind.'

'It was her idea,' Hans-Pieter told him.

It was her idea.

What was that about?

Part of Murray allowed himself to think that this meant it was him she fancied, and had done all along.

That just wasn't true, though, was it?

What this was actually about was that she felt sorry for him. That she and Hans-Pieter, when they talked about him at all, talked about how fucking pitiable he was.

Word was out about Blago, what had happened with that. Blago did indeed seem to have gone to Germany. Murray's money seemed to have gone with him. The man *and* the money had vanished, anyway. Hans-Pieter's advice was to tell the police, tell them everything. Murray was too embarrassed to do that. And anyway the police already knew him, from that time after the Irish pub. He just didn't want to see them again, simple as that.

The rain is intensifying.

Hans-Pieter ups the tempo of the wipers.

So much for the weather forecast.

Maria turns to Hans-Pieter to make a similar point. She has a fat whitehead near her mouth. A stud in her nose. He's welcome to her, Murray thinks.

Once they hit the motorway it takes an hour and a half. Murray nods off. Wakes to stark limestone hills. Then the sea, greyly glittering. They park in a municipal lot – plenty of space, today – and find a place for lunch. A mixed grill for Murray, with that sweetish red-pepper sauce they do here. A glass of the local plonk. A squall passing outside. Maria is being friendly. She does most of the talking. Hans-Pieter hardly says anything. He picks at his grilled fish, prising flesh from bone, and rarely lifts his eyes from it. The lazy silence of a man in settled circumstances, letting his other half entertain the guest. Intervenes to correct her sometimes, that's all. She has rings on most of her fingers. Blue eyeshadow. She's encouraging Murray to go to the police – they're still talking about that. It's what they've been talking about for a week. He hasn't even told them the true amount Blago took from him. He doesn't want to talk about it. He wants to forget all that. She's just trying to be nice, though. Shouldn't be impatient with her.

'What's the point?' he says. 'They'll not find him.'

She is adamant. 'How do you *know*?'

She just likes the drama of it, he thinks. At least it's something –
something has happened at least.

'You can't let him get away with it!' she insists.

'I shouldn't have trusted him,' Murray tells her, feeling the wine a bit.
'I was an idiot. End of.'

It's raining outside again.

Murray and Maria have flaming sambucas.

I was an idiot. End of. Put that on my fucking tombstone, Murray
thinks as they leave and head for the sea – down some steps, through
some drizzly streets. He has dropped back now. Hans-Pieter and Maria
are hand in hand, up ahead of him. Jack Sprat would eat no fat . . .
That's what they look like, those two – Jack Sprat and the wife.

No, he's okay, Hans-Pieter, the shy Dutchman in his duffel coat.

She's okay as well, waddling along next to him.

They're my only friends, anyway.

I was an idiot. End of.

There aren't really beaches here. There are walkways along the shore,
winding paved paths, overleaned by spry old pines. Dry patches of pav-
ing stones under the pines. On one side as they walk, former villas of
Austro-Hungarian notables, now hotels. On the other side, steep steps
or even ladders down to strips of shingle, or empty terraces, or little
marinas. The sloshing sea. Slapping at green-matted walls. At squeaking jetties.

He is kissing her. Hans-Pieter is kissing Maria, leaning down to her,
snogging in the shelter of his upturned collar.

They are about twenty yards ahead of him. They seem to have forgotten he is there. Murray stops, to save himself embarrassment, and
turns to the sea.

Hooded, he takes up a position of heroic reflection, hands resting
on the top bar of the metal railing that follows the edge of the walkway,

eyes seeping water and fixed on the distant island, far out over the windy inlet, no more than a dark horizontal smudge.

And, nearer, in the middle distance, some sort of yacht. More of a fucking ship, actually. How many decks does that thing *have*? Four, five? Must be a hundred yards long, at least. It moves on the waves, you can see, if you keep your eyes on it.

And look at that! Look at the way the sunlight falls down between the clouds! White the sea underneath it. Sudden islands of blinding white. The yacht turns black, waves blink around it. Sudden islands of blinding white. And in Murray, watching, an unfamiliar euphoria. Sudden islands of blinding white. Then melt away. Dull sea.

Damp wind in his face.

He turns his head in the hood of his jacket, sees the lovers still necking further up the walkway, in the shelter of a wind-mangled pine.

Fuck it.

His eyes find the superyacht again.

And fuck that as well.

Aye, fuck the lot of it.

8

1

Yesterday. In the afternoon, he left the house in Lowndes Square, the huge house still holding the shock of what had happened. Chelsea, seen through the window of the Maybach. Sloane Street, its familiar shops – Hermès, Ermenegildo Zegna. Cheyne Walk. Traffic heavy-ish at four. Dark November day. Low tide, the Thames, dull mud-flats. That park, on the other side, the south side. Then small streets, and the heliport. The windy platform over the water. The loud, leather-trimmed pod of the Sikorsky. They were about to fly upriver, over the western districts of London. As the helicopter turned over the water, wavelets fleeing from the downdraught, he looked back at it, at London, the place that for some years had been his home. Then it was dropping away, to something merely schematic, a monochrome expanse spread out in the light of the late-autumn afternoon. He would never see it again.

The decision had been made standing at a window in Lowndes Square, staring out. The decision to jump into the sea. To drown himself. It had seemed like some sort of solution.

Farnborough airport.

A two-hour flight to Venice.

From Venice airport, a hired limousine.

Venice itself hidden in darkness and drizzle. It was there, some-where, on the other side of the water, an eroding monument to lost wealth, to lost power.

The harsh, tall light of the docks. The hum of the pump as the yacht took on fuel. The smell of the fuel. Someone holding an umbrella.

And Enzo, the first officer, waiting for him at the end of a strip of drizzle-wet carpet: 'Welcome aboard, sir.'

Enzo told him that they would be all set in half an hour, wanted to know where they were headed.

A pause.

He had not thought about it. It made no difference.

'Uh,' he said. 'Corfu.'

Enzo nodded, smiled.

And Mark, the head steward: 'Will sir be dining this evening?'

'Just a snack,' he said to him. 'Thank you.'

It arrived, later, with a half-bottle of Barbaresco. He did not touch the food. He had a glass of the Barbaresco.

It was from his own estate, a property he had acquired some years ago. An impulsive thing. He has only been there once. He finds it hard to picture the place. They had flown over it in the helicopter, he and the previous owner, a Piedmontese or Savoyard aristocrat, a young-ish man, pointing things out to him, shouting over the shriek of the machine . . .

Silence.

He was lying on the bed, waiting for the yacht to start moving.

He did not mean to fall asleep. He meant to jump into the sea. He meant to drown himself. And yet, for the first time in many days, he simply fell asleep.

2

In the morning, the yacht is at anchor, a kilometre or two from the Croatian shore. Enzo has phoned to say there is a storm out in the Adriatic. He has apologised for the delay, and said they will be on the move again at some point in the afternoon, when the storm out at sea has passed.

Nearer the shore, where the yacht is anchored, it is a windy, unpleasant day. Sometimes rain.

He turns down Mark's suggestion, in the middle of the morning, to take the launch and visit the little seaside town that they can see.

Instead, he picks at his lunch in the small private dining room – a single table, able to seat only eight – on the middle deck.

He feels like an imposter in the world of the living, still in the same clothes he fell asleep in, still carrying the stale, days-old scent of Cartier Pasha.

When he woke up this morning, grey light was gathering at the windows. Lifting his head, he looked at it, puzzled. Then he understood. One more day.

It would have to be done at night. No one would notice then, and try to save him. No one would notice – just, in the morning, his quarters empty, and all around the inscrutable sea. The long, dissolving wake.

He is a man in his sixties, with a heavy paunch. A hard handsome face. He has lost much of his hair. He is wearing a shirt with an exaggeratedly large collar, black silk. White leather shoes.

The sea is blue like flint and cold and unforgiving. Squally rain speckles the tall windows of the private dining room, and across the restless grey water, the Croatian town huddles on the coast. Stony hills loom above it, collide with clouds.

He puts down his fork and summons Mark. When he appears, he asks him for a cigar, and Mark addresses himself to the humidor.

Mark presents him with the cigar and asks whether he would like a digestif. A shake of the head.

'Will that be all then, sir?' Mark asks. Mark is from Sunderland.

'Yes. Thank you.'

With the laden tray, Mark leaves.

Some minutes later the cigar is still unlit.

He lets himself out onto the terrace and stands there, looking down at the surface of the sea, which moves with smooth, heavy movements.

Smooth, heavy movements.

Heavy shapes finding the light and losing it as they move.

Heavy, more than anything.

Heavy.

And he wonders, half-hypnotised by the heavy shapes finding and losing the light: *How much does the sea weigh?* And then, his logical mind working on the question: *What is the volume of the sea?* And then: *What is its average depth? What is its surface area?* Those two facts, he thinks, must be easy to find out – and then you would have the answer, since the volume of water is effectively the same thing as the weight.

He steps inside, out of the wind, and summons Mark.

When the steward appears, he says, 'Mark, I want you to find out two things for me.'

'Yes, sir.'

'What is the average depth of the sea.'

'Yes, sir,' Mark says.

346

'And what is the surface area.'

'Of the sea, sir?'

'Yes.'

'Anything else, sir?'

'No.'

'I'll find out for you, sir.'

'Thank you, Mark.'

Alone, he waits impatiently for the numbers, and sitting at the dining-room table, finally he lights the cigar.

A few minutes later there is a little tap on the door.

'Yes.'

'I have that information for you, sir,' Mark says.

'Yes?'

'The average depth is three thousand, six hundred and eighty-two metres,' Mark says.

'So deep . . . ?' he murmurs, writing it down. 'Okay . . .'

'And the surface area is three hundred and sixty-one million square kilometres.'

'You're sure?'

Mark hesitates. He googled the questions. His employer, though, only vaguely knows what Google is and probably thinks that Mark has spent the last few minutes phoning marine experts at the world's leading universities – people who would be happy to be interrupted in order to help him with his important work.

'I did double-check, sir,' Mark says doubtfully.

'Okay. For now this is okay.'

'Do you need anything else, sir?'

'Not now. Thank you.'

'Yes, sir.'

Mark withdraws.

Excitedly, he is already doing the sums – on paper, as he was taught in a Soviet technical school, long ago.

The surface area is in square kilometres, so the first step is to convert that to square metres, one square kilometre being . . . being one *million* square metres . . .

And then multiply *that* by the average depth . . .

There are a lot of zeroes to write.

Which is the volume . . .

Which is the same as the weight in metric tonnes.

1,329,202,000,000,000,000 tonnes.

One point three million *trillion* tonnes.

Success!

The weight of the sea.

He throws down the pen, and tugs smoke triumphantly from the cigar. Shoves it out through his nostrils.

Then other questions start to trouble him.

The sea is salt water – does *that* affect the weight?

And what about the pressure? Does the pressure in the depths of the sea make a difference? Does a cubic metre of water, under the enormous pressure of the depths, weigh *more* than one metric tonne, perhaps?

More questions, then, for Mark, who is sent to look into them while his employer waits, finishing his cigar, hunched over his own reflection in the varnished tabletop.

Mark takes longer this time.

Nearly half an hour has passed when the little knock sounds.

And he finds, listening to Mark talking at some length about factors affecting the weight of salt water, that he has entirely lost interest in the subject.

The question of the effects of pressure on the mass of water is particularly long-winded, and he stops listening totally. He just sits there, studying the stub of his cigar. Mark's soft Geordie voice keeps talking for a while. Then it, too, stops.

There is a long silence.

'Sir?' Mark says.

He seems to snap out of a trance. 'Yes?'

'Will that be all, sir?'

'Yes. Thank you.'

'Thank *you*, sir.'

*

It is late afternoon. The twin Pielstick diesel engines have started, and the hundred-and-forty-metre-long yacht is on the move again. Light still lies on the open sea. Hard late light on individual dark waves. The distant shore slides very slowly past. It is dissolving in the early twilight, is indistinct now except for the lights that appear, the tiny silent lights of towns.

Enzo, in his smart white uniform, personally delivers the weather outlook – 'smooth sailing' – and says that they will arrive at Kérkira in the morning, at about ten o'clock. Will sir wish to dock there? Should he arrange facilities to do so?

'No.'

And where will we be heading, from Corfu?

'I don't know.'

Enzo nods tolerantly. He waits for a moment – sometimes his employer, if he is on his own, as now, invites his Maltese first officer to join him for a drink at this hour. They drink whisky and talk about ships, about the sea. He asks Enzo, sometimes, about his former life as the master of an oil tanker, or lectures him on politics, economics, the state of the world. Not today. He is not in a talkative mood.

He tells Mark he will have his dinner in his quarters.

Mark asks him what he would like to eat.

He just shrugs and says the chef should make him something, whatever he wants.

What arrives on the tray, an hour later, is, Mark explains, a lobster soufflé, a *filet mignon* with grilled winter vegetables, and a miniature *tarte tatin*. There is a half-bottle of champagne, and another of Château Trotanoy 2001.

He has eaten hardly anything for twenty-four hours and he is hungry now – a sort of dull emptiness inside him. He eats the soufflé, and the steak and vegetables. He does not eat the *tarte tatin*. He drinks some of the Trotanoy, none of the champagne.

It is dark outside now, totally dark. Only the lights of the ship lie weakly on the water.

Into that dark water.

Into those frigid depths.

And, actually, how does one jump from a vessel this size? He is standing on the terrace outside his quarters, the owner's quarters, near the top of the yacht – it faces the stern, and the wind is not strong – looking down at another terrace, much larger, where the swimming pool is. After that there is a still-larger terrace – he is only able to see a small part of it from where he is standing – where there is space for eighty people to eat at tables and afterwards to dance.

There is someone down there on the lower terrace, where the parties once took place, on the part of it that he can see, walking up and down, and smoking a cigarette. A small figure in the dark. He does not know who it is. There are dozens of people on the yacht. He does not know them all, would not know them by sight. There is Enzo and his team. There arc the kitchen staff. There is Mark and his assistant stewards. There are the specialist technicians who look after the swimming pool and other leisure facilities, the power systems, the midget submarine. There are always various minor figures mopping the decks. And there are Pierre and Madis, the ex-soldiers, with their weapons. Perhaps it is Pierre down there, smoking. Yes, it is probably Pierre, standing down there and watching the wake spread out on the surface of the sea.

In the darkness, and from up on his terrace near the top of the yacht, it is only half-visible, the wake.

Floating like phosphorescence on the darkness.

Teasingly, half-visible.

From where he is, there is a drop of at least twenty-five metres to the surface of the sea. He would not drown – he would die on impact, possibly with one of the lower decks. Which is not what he had in mind.

He has not fully thought through the practicalities of this.

And with every minute that passes it seems less likely that he will actually do it.

He imagines, with a shiver of horror, himself in the dark wet water.

He will not actually do it.

The feeling that his nerve has failed fills him with despair.

And now what?

If he is to live, what now?

He finds that he is shivering, and steps inside.

What now?

The question is simplified by the fact that he is, suddenly, extremely tired.

He shuts the terrace door.

'Lights off,' he says in a soft dry voice, and the lights go off.

3

The next morning Lars joins him.

Aleksandr stands there, in the warm morning sunlight, watching the stony coast of Corfu, and from the harbour mouth the motor launch skimming over the sea towards where *Europa* lies at anchor. The launch is *Europa*'s own, and deploys from a hatch on the waterline in the yacht's side. As it nears the yacht, it slows abruptly.

From the terrace outside his quarters where he is standing in his dressing gown, he loses sight of it.

It is down there somewhere at the waterline, moving into a position parallel to the opening hatch. The launch, like some space vehicle, has small engines that allow it to move slowly sideways. They will be engaged and it will enter the hatch. When it is in position, the seawater in the hatch will drain away and the launch will settle on a steel frame. A lift travels directly from the dock in the hatch to the upper areas of the yacht.

Some years ago, he had watched a demonstration of this manoeuvre at Lürssen's shipyard on the Kiel Canal.

He was visiting the shipyard with a view to placing an order for a yacht – *Europa*, which was then undergoing final sea trials, had been made for someone else.

'I like it,' Aleksandr said, watching the demonstration. 'I want it.'

'We can make you one just like it,' the smiling Lürssen's man said, standing next to him. They were both wearing high-visibility vests, helmets.

'How long will that take?'

'Two or three years,' the Lürssen's man said, proudly watching the end of the demonstration.

'I don't want to wait that long. I want this one.'

The Lürssen's man's orange moustache twitched as he laughed.

'You don't understand,' Aleksandr said. 'You think I'm joking. I'm not joking. I want this one.'

The man tried to explain that this yacht was someone else's, had been made for someone else . . .

'How much is he paying for it?'

The man looked doubtful for a moment. Then he said, 'Two hundred million euro. More or less.'

'Offer him two fifty,' Aleksandr said. 'Phone him now and offer him two fifty. I want an answer today.'

Hearing the whine of the hatch shutting on the waterline, he pads unhurriedly inside, into the vast oval of the owner's quarters.

When he meets Lars, twenty minutes later on the pool deck, he is dressed and doused in Cartier Pasha.

It is pleasantly warm on the sheltered pool deck, in the November sunshine.

Lars stands when he sees Aleksandr coming towards him.

'Good morning,' he says.

Aleksandr says nothing, just pats the lawyer's shoulder and sits down at the table.

Lars also sits. He is wearing linen trousers, a blue T-shirt, leather sandals. He was semi-holidaying at his villa on Corfu when Aleksandr phoned last night to say he was in the area, and asked for a meeting. He has not finished eating the omelette he was served.

'Finish it,' Aleksandr tells him.

Lars presses on with the omelette.

'How are you?' Aleksandr asks.

'I'm okay,' Lars says tactfully. 'You?'

'Not so good,' Aleksandr admits.

Lars wipes his mouth with a stiff linen napkin.

'The case in London?' Lars asks.

Aleksandr shrugs, looks depressed.

The major legal action on which he embarked a year ago has just failed. He had sued a fellow Russian and former protégé in a London court. He maintained that this man, Adam Spassky, had swindled him, many years earlier, out of an enormous amount of money. He was suing him for that money, a ten-figure sum. The judgment, issued only last week, was emphatically in favour of Spassky. Not only that, it had explicitly questioned Aleksandr's own integrity. 'It's not just that we lost it,' he says. 'It's what the judge said. That . . . whore.'

Lars nods. He says, 'Yes, that was harsh.'

'And totally untrue!'

'Of course.'

'How much do you think he paid her?'

'Stranger things have happened,' Lars says, privately doubtful that an English judge would be so easily for sale.

'How much, do you think?'

Lars shrugs, unwilling to speculate.

And Aleksandr says, excitedly, 'I was thinking – we should investigate her, find the money. Eh? It would destroy her. And then the whole thing would have to be heard again. And this time we would win, maybe. What do you think?'

'It's up to you,' Lars says.

'You think we should do that?'

Pressed, Lars says, 'I'm not sure it would help.'

'He paid her, fuck!' Aleksandr shouts.

'It's possible.'

'Did you hear what she said?'

'Yes . . .'

'She said I was a liar, fantasist . . .'

'She didn't use the word "liar".'

'Oh, she didn't use the word! Fuck. She might as well have.'

'The language *was* strong,' Lars admits.

'Until now,' Aleksandr says, 'I always believed in English justice.'

'It's not perfect,' Lars says philosophically. 'Nothing is.'

'It's rotten.'

'I wouldn't go so far . . .'

'It's fucking rotten . . .'

'There's not much we can do about it now,' Lars says. He advised against the whole thing in the first place – it was, he had thought, obviously doomed. He had wanted no part of it. He does not mention that now. He says, 'We have to look forward.'

Aleksandr almost laughs. 'What is there to look forward to?'

Lars smiles, slightly sadly. He has finished the omelette and puts down his fork. 'Life?' he suggests. He is wearing very expensive sunglasses with tortoiseshell frames.

'Life,' Aleksandr murmurs, looking at the sea.

There is a longish silence.

'Where do I stand?' he asks sombrely. 'Tell me.'

This is the purpose of the meeting – to take stock, now that the legal action has definitively failed. And Lars, the steward of his fortune, the lawyer who hid the assets in a labyrinth stretching from Andorra to the Dutch Antilles, says, after a few moments, 'The picture is not very positive.'

That, Aleksandr already knows.

His principal asset, Rusferrex, once the world's second-largest producer of iron ore, is worth nothing now. Fatally over-leveraged, it was sunk by the steep fall in the metal's price, the end of the super-cycle, which Aleksandr had failed to foresee. Lars, and many others, had advised him against embarking on an ambitious, debt-fuelled expansion programme – anyone keeping half an eye on China could see the danger of that. Aleksandr wouldn't listen. It never occurred to him that he might be wrong.

His other mining assets went down with Rusferrex in a net of interconnected accounts.

The Ukrainian airline he owns is in liquidation.

('The timing,' as Lars put it, 'was sub-optimal.')

(Aleksandr's less equivocal verdict: 'It was a fucking stupid idea.')

They talk for a while about the Moscow-based bank, whether that has any life left in it. No, seems to be the answer.

Then Lars says, 'You do still have a number of significant assets, that I know of.'

'Tell me.'

Lars takes a little scrap of paper from the pocket of his linen trousers. There seems to be some sort of list scrawled on it. He says, 'The house in Surrey. The house in London. The Dassault Falcon. The villa in Saint Barthélemy. The Barbaresco estate and vineyards. And this yacht. All of these assets are held by offshore trusts and can be liquidated without tax liability,' Lars adds. 'Plus you have a minority stake in a Belarusian mobile-phone operator with subsidiaries in Moldova and Montenegro, worth perhaps twenty million sterling.'

Aleksandr says, 'Oh, yes, that.'

'Those shares are held by a trust in Gibraltar,' Lars says.

'Why do we have that?' Aleksandr asks.

'When you took over the lignite miner,' Lars says.

'Oh, yes.'

'You were going to spin it off.'

'Yes.'

'So those are your outstanding assets,' Lars says. 'Total value, about two hundred and seventy-five million sterling. I would estimate.'

A steward – not Mark – wheels a trolley over to them and pours coffee from a silver pot.

Lars thanks him.

They wait until the steward has withdrawn. Then Lars says, taking another scrap of paper from his pocket, 'Now, the liabilities.'

Aleksandr releases several pellets of sweetener into his coffee. 'Hit me,' he says.

'Legal fees – at least a hundred million and still increasing,' Lars says.

This includes, though Lars does not spell it out, the two million pounds Aleksandr owes Lars's own legal practice, itself an opaque trust domiciled in Liechtenstein.

Lars says, 'Plus additional liabilities arising from ongoing litigation – another hundred million. That's just an estimate,' he tells him. 'So let's say two hundred million. Maybe a bit more. Which leaves you with.' Lars, finally, takes off his sunglasses. The understated tan sharpens the blue of his eyes. He is in his mid-forties: he looks younger. He says, 'Fifty to a hundred million?'

Aleksandr, still wearing his own sunglasses, looks away and says, in a hard neutral voice, 'There's something you don't know.'

'What's that?'

The wind is up. Whitecaps are appearing on the vivid blue water. Just perceptibly, the immense yacht moves in the steepening swell.

Aleksandr says, 'Ksenia is leaving me.'

Lars looks surprised, says nothing.

'Yes,' Aleksandr says.

She had sat next to him every day at the trial. Those long hours of lawyers' voices. Of shuffling feet, and shuffling papers. She had sat next to him, sometimes looking worried and engaged, sometimes stifling a yawn in the middle of the afternoon as the lawyers whispered to each other up near the judge. For more than a month, that had lasted.

And then, on Thursday morning, the judgment.

And it wasn't just that he had lost – that financially his wipeout was now final, an immovable fact, and all the implications of that.

It was what she had said, the judge.

'The language was strong,' even Lars had admitted.

And then while she was speaking, Adam Spassky's smile – the way he had smiled, nearly imperceptibly and with that usual strange look of vacancy in his heatless blue eyes. Seeing that smile – that's when Aleksandr understood that this was actually happening, that it was not in fact a nightmare. That it was his life.

Facing the media scrum on the steps outside he had been in a state of shock. Not sure where he was. Still seeing that smile. Minders hurried him to the Maybach, Ksenia hanging on his arm.

Then the house in Lowndes Square. Shadowy hotel-like spaces. Impersonal work of interior designers. And it was then, in the shocked hush of the house, that she told him.

'I've waited long enough,' she said. 'I didn't want to do it during the trial,' she said. 'The trial's over now.'

She said, 'It's no use, Aleksandr.'

He was shouting at her.

'You say that,' she said. 'When was the last time you actually noticed me? When was the last time you thought about what I might want? What do you want me for? You're not even interested in sex any more . . .'

That's when he threw the Japanese vase.

When he threw the Japanese vase, she froze up.

She said, 'I'm taking the twins to St Barts for two weeks.'

And that afternoon, when the twins got home from their expensive English school, everything was packed, the huge pile of luggage in the hall, and they went to the airport, she and the twins, and her PA, and her personal trainer, and the two English nannies, and all the earpiece-wearing security men – from the window he watched the four-vehicle motorcade move away.

He was too shocked to try to stop her.

His throat was sore from shouting. His eyes were pink.

He was standing at the window, staring out.

'What does she want?' Lars asks.

He says, 'The London house. The villa in St Barts. Money.'

'How much money?'

'I don't know. Her lawyers are talking to mine.'

'You're not married?' Lars says delicately.

'No,' Aleksandr says, sounding tired. 'So what? We've been together fifteen years. We have the twins.'

'How old are they now?'

'Ten.'

There is a silence.

'You have children?' Aleksandr asks.

'Yes,' Lars says, surprised.

It is the first time, in all their years of association, that Aleksandr has asked him about his family, has shown any interest in his life.

'Yes,' he says again. And then, trying to be friendly, 'They are a little older than yours. Fifteen and twelve.'

'Oh, I have older children,' Aleksandr says. 'I have been married twice, and divorced twice. The first divorce was okay, not too expensive. The second . . .' He sighs heavily. 'What am I going to do, Lars?'

Lars takes the question to be a practical one. He says, 'To meet legal fees and other liabilities you will need to sell some assets. I advise you to settle all pending litigation now. The prospect of winning,' he says, 'has been materially diminished by last week's judgment.' He waits to see what Aleksandr will say.

Nothing. Staring at the sea, he seems to be thinking about something else.

'To do that,' Lars goes on, 'to pay all outstanding fees and settle everything, you will need, as I said, about two hundred million sterling.'

He lets that sink in.

'With luck,' he says optimistically, 'this yacht might fetch that on its own.'

'No,' Aleksandr says, evidently listening after all. 'I don't think so.'

'A hundred and fifty?' Lars suggests.

'Maybe.'

'So we need another fifty million,' Lars says thoughtfully. 'I think you must sell the Falcon,' he says. 'The overheads, I imagine, are very high.'

In fact, Lars does not need to imagine how high the overheads are: he established, some years ago, a trust in the Isle of Man to own and manage the jet and it eats several million pounds a year.

'So, the jet?'

'Okay,' Aleksandr says, absent-mindedly.

'I hope we will get twenty million,' Lars says. 'The market is pretty strong for that sort of aircraft these days.'

'Okay.'

'So we need another thirty million.'

Aleksandr says nothing.

'The London house and the house in St Barts will go to Ksenia?' Lars asks.

'She wants them.'

'And will she get them?'

'I suppose so.'

'And money?'

'She will want money,' Aleksandr says.

'You don't know how much?'

'No.'

'Not more than ten million, I would say,' Lars says. 'She shouldn't have more than ten million.'

Aleksandr, in his black silk shirt, just shrugs.

'If you sell the house in Surrey,' Lars says, 'and the Barbaresco estate, you will be able to meet your outstanding liabilities and pay her ten million.'

Wind moves over the terrace, which someone is now mopping – an African woman in a white *Europa*-logoed polo shirt and tracksuit trousers, the uniform of the vessel's menials, mopping the deck some distance from them.

The wind disturbs the surface of the sea, making it scintillate in places.

Aleksandr says, 'And what does that leave me with?'

'It leaves you,' Lars says, looking at one of his scraps of paper, 'with that stake in the Belarusian telco.'

'Only that?'

'Yes. It's worth about twenty million sterling,' Lars points out.

'Twenty million?' Aleksandr says vaguely.

'Yes. And it pays a decent dividend. About five per cent. A million pounds a year, more or less. It is possible, I think,' Lars jokes, 'to live off that.'

A pause.

Then he says, no longer joking, 'With appropriate tax arrangements.'

Lars himself, indeed, manages to live off not very much more than that, with appropriate tax arrangements.

Aleksandr does not laugh at Lars's joke. He does not seem to have been listening. When he finally looks at him it's as if he has forgotten what they were talking about. 'You will stay for lunch, Lars?' he asks.

They eat on the small terrace outside the private dining room – a table set for two. Mark and the young Vietnamese trainee steward wait on them. Aleksandr says he wants sushi. Sushi, unfortunately, is not available. Obviously disappointed, Alexander yells at Mark for a while, while Lars looks the other way. He looks at the sea – a wonderful dark blue, with here and there a foaming wave. In the end, they have grilled salmon with a fennel salad and new potatoes, and a bottle of very nice Pouilly-Fuissé, and Aleksandr tells Lars, forgetting that he already knows the story, about the time when he was in Ulaanbaatar and decided, at some point during the day, that he wanted sushi for his supper.

'Now *then*,' he says to Lars, 'at that time, it was actually not possible to get a decent sushi in Ulaanbaatar. Maybe it's different now, I don't know.'

Trying to look amused, Lars nods.

'So I said to Alain,' Aleksandr says – Alain being a man whose job it was to make sure that Aleksandr always had whatever he wanted, wherever he was – 'I said to Alain, "I want sushi tonight. Proper sushi, okay? Not some local shit, okay?"'

Lars tries to increase the intensity to his smile a notch or two – from wryly expectant, say, to definitely amused.

'So you know what Alain does?' Aleksandr asks him, as Mark, standing at his shoulder, pours more Pouilly-Fuissé.

Still smiling – and though he does in fact know what Alain does – Lars shakes his head, and pats his mouth with his napkin. He murmurs a word of thanks to Mark.

'He phones Ubon in London,' Aleksandr says. 'You know that restaurant?'

'Yes,' says Lars.

'He phones them and he orders something like . . . something like a thousand quid's worth of sushi,' Aleksandr says, 'to take away.'

Lars's eyebrows jump up politely.

'Then he arranges for someone to take the sushi to Farnborough, and has it flown, by private jet,' Aleksandr emphasises, 'to Ulaanbaatar.' He says, 'It gets there about eight o'clock, local time, just when I want to eat. So Alain is very pleased with himself. And I say to him, "This is excellent sushi, Alain. Where did you get it?" And he tells me from Ubon in London. And I say to him, "London? Are you out of your mind? It would have been quicker to get it from Japan!"'

Lars manages a quiet laugh.

Aleksandr tells him, quite seriously, 'That was in the newspapers.'

'Oh?'

'The most expensive takeaway in history, they said it was.'

Quietly, Lars laughs again.

'They said it was fifty thousand pounds. I don't know. I don't know if that's true.'

At that time – not so much any more – Aleksandr kept everything the newspapers printed about him in a large scrapbook. For a while there was quite a lot of material – he was known as the 'Emperor of Iron' and his lifestyle and wealth were a matter of fascination to them. It was someone's job, full-time – an attractive young woman, just out of Oxford – to manage the scrapbook.

'I should have put some money into commercial property in Ulaanbaatar,' Aleksandr says wistfully. 'I thought about it.'

'It would have been a successful investment,' Lars says, sipping wine. He does not mention that he himself owns a small amount of stock in an investment trust, managed by an acquaintance of his, specialising in Mongolian property – one of the best-performing assets in the world, the last few years.

Enzo joins them.

Aleksandr had asked to see him. He says, 'We're going to Monaco, Enzo. I've offered Lars a lift home.'

The offer had been made earlier in the meal.

It is what Lars had hoped for.

It is why he has his suitcases with him.

Though it does mean, for most of the afternoon and evening, listening to Aleksandr talk. Aleksandr does not seem to be able to stop talking now.

Over dinner, he talks about Russian history, a subject he is obsessed with. He seems tired, as he explains how Russia ended the twentieth century exactly where it was at the start – a somewhat shambolic authoritarian state lagging behind Western Europe and America in terms of economic and social development, its natural wealth held by a small number of families, with a stunted middle class, and most of the population living in sullen fatalistic poverty. The whole Communist experiment, with all its hope and suffering, had passed like a storm, he says, and left things exactly as they were.

Lars nods at that appraisal.

On the other side of the table, Aleksandr is slouched in a fog of cigar smoke. He is talking about his own attempt in the 1990s to transform Russia, as he tells it, into a liberal free-market democracy, about how that failed.

They are inside, in the small dining room where the smoke hangs heavily in the air.

On the table is a large plate of chocolates. They have an artisanal misshapenness, a dusting of pure cocoa powder. Lars has already eaten two. He says, wondering whether to have another now, or wait until Mark arrives with the coffee, 'It was a missed opportunity.'

'It was a historical tragedy,' Aleksandr tells him.

Historical – his favourite word.

Lars knows that Aleksandr thinks of himself as a historical figure. He likes to talk about the sweep of history as one who knows it at first hand. He had once asked him, 'How do you think history will see me?'

Lars had not known what to say. After a moment's hesitation, he had fallen back on a hackneyed quip: 'It depends who writes the history.'

It was then – in Davos, a few years ago – that Aleksandr had told him about his plan to write a monumental multi-volume account of his own life and times.

He has not, as far as Lars knows, started it yet.

He is talking about his uncle now. Lars has heard about this man before. The KGB officer – a man who sent people to their deaths in the purges of the thirties and forties. And yet – Lars knows the story – someone whom Aleksandr admires.

'When I was a kid I thought he was just an old fart,' Aleksandr says. 'Old-fashioned – you know.'

'Yes,' Lars says, trying to seem interested.

'He wore an old-fashioned hat,' Aleksandr says.

'Yes?'

'He had a shit haircut. That's what I thought about him. Later I understood he had iron in his soul. He was strong. When the wind changed, in the fifties, he was in a tough position.'

'I'm sure . . .'

'I mean, Stalin,' Aleksandr says, as Mark arrives with the coffee, 'was his hero. He worshipped him. Sincerely.'

'There were some who did.'

'And then Khrushchev makes that speech.'

'Yes, the so-called Secret Speech,' Lars says.

'And so everyone was supposed to say they're sorry, and how they never liked Stalin anyway. Well, he wouldn't say it. Even though he knew he might be killed. He wouldn't say it. It was like the end of *Don Giovanni*,' Aleksandr says, 'when he won't say he's sorry, even with hell opening in front of him. He won't be a hypocrite. You know.'

Lars just nods.

'My father, he said sorry,' Aleksandr tells him.

'Yes?'

'Oh, yes.'

Having served the coffee, Mark has slipped out.

'My father said sorry. My uncle – his name was Aleksandr, like me – he wouldn't say sorry. In his own mind he had done nothing wrong. It was his enemies who were wrong, he thought. He thought history was on his side. It wasn't. In the end, he took his own life,' Aleksandr says. 'He killed himself.'

'I'm sorry to hear it.'

Aleksandr shrugs exhaustedly. 'He was old, then. He had nothing left to live for,' he says. 'He had devoted his whole life to the cause of Communism. It was his whole life. He had nothing else.'

Lars nods thoughtfully.

'What did he have left to live for?' Aleksandr asks him, insisting on the point.

'Nothing, I suppose,' Lars says.

Aleksandr nods and presses out the soggy end of his cigar. 'Nothing,' he says. 'It was over. That was it.'

*

In the morning, Capri passes off the starboard side. Naples under a layer of smog. Lars, from his little terrace, wearing a fluffy *Europa*-logoed towelling robe, watches them pass. The air is mild, fresh. He did not sleep well. Too much fine wine and pre-war Armagnac last night. And then, when he was back in his cabin, he had found among the hundreds of films available on the entertainment system, Tarkovsky's *Nostalghia*. He had started to watch it. It was strange to see Erland Josephson, whose voice, speaking Swedish, was so familiar to him, dubbed into Italian. He had fallen asleep less than halfway through.

There is a knock at the door.

It is Mark.

He says that Aleksandr has invited Lars to join him for breakfast.

Which is exactly what Lars was hoping would not happen.

'Thank you,' he says. 'Tell him I'll be along in a while.'

When he presents himself, half an hour later, Enzo is there informing Aleksandr that he expects to dock in Monte Carlo at about midnight.

Lars sits down. He is wearing a sweater and his hair is still damp from the shower.

'I had a phone call this morning,' Aleksandr says, when Enzo has left, 'from my solicitor in London.' Aleksandr does not sound pleased.

Lars, eating scrambled egg, looks up quickly.

Aleksandr says, 'They've heard from Ksenia's lawyers, with her demands.'

'Yes?' Lars says, still eating hungrily. 'What are they?'

'The two houses . . .'

'London and Saint Barthélemy?'

'Yes.'

'And . . . ?'

'And twenty-five million,' Aleksandr says.

'Sterling?'

'Yes.'

'That's impossible,' Lars says, forking egg into his mouth. 'You'll fight it?'

Aleksandr nods. He is drinking some sort of effervescent liquid – probably he too has a hangover. He looks, anyway, as though he did not sleep well. Actually, he looks as though he did not sleep at all.

'It's just an opening shot,' Lars says. 'They want to get more than ten, so they ask for twenty-five. They'll settle for fifteen. And even that's too much. Fight it,' he advises. 'Don't go above ten.'

'I will fight it,' Aleksandr says.

Lars accepts some tea from the steward with the pot.

'Don't go above ten,' he says again. The tea is extraordinary, the finest he has ever tasted – it is like some new thing; not tea at all, something finer, subtler, more intense. He says, 'Is she aware of your . . .' He is not sure how to put it. 'Impaired position?'

For a moment Aleksandr says nothing. He is still staring at the sea, at the waves pursuing each other towards the grey horizon. He says, 'I don't know.'

'So perhaps she doesn't understand,' Lars says, trying to be helpful, 'that in asking for twenty-five she is in fact asking for . . .'

Everything you have, he was going to say.

'You will have more money than me, Lars,' Aleksandr says desolately, 'at the end of this.'

Again unsure what to say – it may well be true – Lars just has another taste of his tea, and then says, after a few seconds, 'We need to discuss the disposal of assets. As we agreed yesterday. The details.'

He looks at Aleksandr, worried that he may have upset him again.

Aleksandr seems okay.

He is eating grapes now – slowly and methodically tearing them from their stems and transferring them to his mouth.

Lars takes out one of his scraps of paper.

For the next hour they talk about the disposal of assets – the sale of the Dassault Falcon, and the Barbaresco estate, and the house in Surrey, and the super-yacht. For most of these assets, Lars has possible buyers in mind.

Aleksandr, eating grapes, is matter-of-fact. He seems more interested in the long green grapes than in the subject under discussion.

Lars expresses the hope that he will end up with some millions in cash, when everything is settled, as well as the shares in the Belarusian mobile-phone operator.

'This isn't the first time,' Aleksandr says, 'that I've been wiped out, you know, Lars.'

'Ninety-eight, the Russian default?' Lars ventures, still making notes.

'Exactly.'

Lars is still writing. He says, 'Yes, that must have been quite something.'

'It was, sure,' Aleksandr says.

Lars murmurs, his thoughts elsewhere, 'Total mess, wasn't it.'

'Sure.'

In fact Aleksandr now thinks of that time with something like love. In his memory, it is one of the most vivid periods of his life, along with the period earlier in the decade when the Soviet Union just suddenly vanished, and he was in his early forties and already a fairly senior official in the Ministry of International Trade. All international trade had been handled by the ministry. The individual enterprises that might wish to trade internationally – most importantly in the natural-resources sector – just had no idea how to do so on their own, and had no access to trade finance. He saw the opportunity. Still, what happened next exceeded anything he might have imagined. For a while nothing seemed impossible. He set up his own bank, InTradeBank, to provide trade finance, and soon it was accumulating stakes in industrial enterprises – especially after the loans-for-shares scheme that financed the second election of Boris Yeltsin and transferred gargantuan portions of formerly state-owned industry into the ownership of a few men. Some ended up with oil, some with nickel, or aluminium, or Aeroflot. He ended up with iron. The Emperor of Iron. In just a few years he went from modestly pampered Soviet official to world's number-one iron-ore magnate.

The default of '98 didn't actually wipe him out. It had the potential to; and though InTradeBank went under in a storm of litigation, he managed to save the Empire of Iron by secreting the shares in an offshore labyrinth – this was when Lars started to play his part – in trusts with mysterious names in the Cayman Islands, and other distant, tranquil places.

Aleksandr is sitting at the table staring, it seems, at something far away, over the horizon. Lars is still writing things down.

The panic of '98. When he thought he might lose everything, and somehow managed to preserve it. His fiftieth birthday happened that summer, in the middle of the meltdown. 'Fuck it,' he said. 'I want a party.' Blenheim Palace hired for the occasion. A party for a thousand people. His hero, Rupert Murdoch, there. Helicopters on the lawn. In his prime, then. New woman on his arm: Ksenia. Fireworks. Those were the days.

Those were the days, my friend.

'Those were the days, Lars,' he murmurs.

Lars looks up. 'When?' he asks.

'Then.'

4

And then it sinks, from light into darkness. Up there it was all sunlight, all sun-filled, squint-inducing blue. Then darkening. Deepening. Ever deeper, and ever darker. And then, suddenly, the wet November morning. The sodden land, still lurking in semi-darkness. It is the morning rush hour in south-east England, under a lid of weeping cloud. Headlights hurry along motorways. Houses huddle in dull towns. They are near now, as the jet descends. Drops of water smear across the window, through which he sees a sewage-treatment plant, wind-flattened grass, whizzing tarmac . . .

Last night they docked at Monte Carlo just after midnight.

The jet was already at Nice airport, having flown in from Venice the previous day.

Early this morning it took off for London. Lars, humiliatingly, had to lend him ten thousand euros for the fuel. The pilot had phoned and said, embarrassed, that Total were wanting payment up front.

Smoothly, the plane is taxiing. The English morning is very real now. It is right there, on the other side of the window's oval, where the rain is steadily falling.

The small terminal building shines in the twilight.

He was not supposed to see this place again.

The plane stops with a slight jerk.

Ten minutes later he is in the Maybach, on his way into London, slumming it on the packed tarmac with everyone else – visibility is too poor, he was told, to use the helicopter. So it takes an hour of rain-lashed traffic-jamming to reach the Mayfair office, where the solicitor is waiting for him.

Aleksandr is late. He apologises and they sit down. The offices – *Iset Holdings*, it says on the polished plate next to the front door – are in an eighteenth-century town house near Park Lane. The room they are in is on the first floor – high ceiling, heavy hardwood doors, some contemporary office clutter too.

The solicitor, a Mr Heath, starts to set out Ksenia's demands, as transmitted to him by her legal team. The London house, the St Barts villa . . .

'I know,' Aleksandr says, 'you already said.'

Mr Heath looks up from the papers. 'Yes,' he says. 'So you know what Ms Viktorovna is asking for.'

'The London house, the villa, and twenty-five million.'

'Yes,' Mr Heath says. 'And also the use of your plane, precise terms to be worked out between the parties.'

'The plane is being sold,' Aleksandr tells him. Though it is a dark day – the taxis passing in the street have their headlights on – the light from the tall windows troubles his tired eyes.

'Ah,' Mr Heath says. 'Alright. I'll communicate that to the other party.' He writes something down and has a sip of the coffee they have been served. 'We also feel,' he says, 'that, in addition to the two very valuable houses, the twenty-five-million cash component is excessive.'

'Yes?' Aleksandr says, not seeming very interested.

'We would advise you to contest that,' Mr Heath says.

'Contest it?'

'We think it highly unlikely that a court would award Ms Viktorovna such a large sum, in addition to the houses.'

Aleksandr says nothing.

Mr Heath says, 'Of course, you may prefer to offer her the sum she wants, plus only one of the houses.'

'You think I should contest it?' Aleksandr asks, as if he hasn't heard the last thing Mr Heath said.

'Yes, we do.'

'It would mean going to court?'

'Not necessarily. I would say probably not, if Ms Viktorovna is being properly advised. But possibly, yes.'

Aleksandr, again, says nothing. He is not looking at the middle-aged solicitor. He seems to be looking at the green exit sign over one of the doors. Enormous dark pouches hang under his eyes. His face seems somehow to have fallen in. He has lost quite a lot of weight, Mr Heath thinks, since they last met, only a few weeks ago. He seems much older.

'I don't think you would have anything to *fear*,' Mr Heath says, 'if this should come to court.'

There is another long silence.

Then Aleksandr says, in a soft tired voice, and still not looking at the solicitor, 'Let her have what she wants. Everything.'

Mr Heath looks puzzled. 'Everything?' he says.

'Yes.'

'With respect, that isn't what we advise . . .'

'I know.'

Mr Heath tries again. 'Her solicitors are being aggressive,' he says. 'I very much doubt they expect to get what they're asking for. It's a negotiation.'

'I understand.'

'Perhaps you'd like to take some time to think about it,' Mr Heath suggests. 'There's no hurry.'

'I don't need time,' Aleksandr says. 'Let her have what she wants.'

Mr Heath seems at a loss. 'You're sure?'

'Yes.'

There is another long pause. 'Well, alright,' the solicitor says, looking almost sadly at his papers. 'If that's what you want. I must stress – it is *not* what we advise.'

'I understand,' Aleksandr says.

When Mr Heath has gone, he sits alone at the long table, until his secretary finds him there some time later and tells him that, in case he has forgotten, he is having lunch with Lord Satter. They have a table, she says, at Le Gavroche.

He looks at her with a strange, empty expression.

He had forgotten.

He is not supposed to be here.

He is not supposed to be having lunch.

Nevertheless, at twelve thirty, he walks the short distance, followed by Pierre and Madis, to Le Gavroche.

Adrian Satter is already there, sitting in an armchair in the waiting area upstairs. He is about Aleksandr's age. His half-silvered hair rises in silky corrugations from the rich pink glow of his forehead.

'Shurik,' he says, in a single movement slipping his glasses into the pocket of his immense-lapelled suit and standing up. He takes Aleksandr's hand and pats his shoulder. 'Good to see you.'

'Hello, Adrian,' Aleksandr says.

Pierre and Madis loiter outside, where men are hanging Christmas decorations from street lamps.

Aleksandr and Lord Satter study menus.

'The soufflé Suissesse, I think, for me,' Adrian Satter says. 'And then the turbot.' An early intimate of Tony Blair, and elevated by him to the peerage, he was now part of the establishment furniture. He was one of many such figures to be wooed by Aleksandr when he arrived in London, around the turn of the millennium. Aleksandr had wanted very much to be part of the

British establishment, or at least to be publicly accepted by it – or, if even that was not possible, to be seen by it as an equal of *some* sort.

'I'll have the same,' he says to the maître d', and they are ushered down the quiet, dark-carpeted stairs to their table.

'Awful,' Adrian says indignantly.

They are talking about last week's harsh judgment in the High Court.

'I've never heard anything like it. It made me ashamed to be British.'

'I'm finished, Adrian,' Aleksandr says.

'Nonsense. You mustn't talk like that, Shurik.' Adrian is looking at the wine list. 'You've taken a knock,' he says, smiling at Aleksandr. 'You'll be back on your feet in no time.'

Aleksandr says, 'It's not just that.'

'You're one of the great men of our time, Shurik.'

'I thought that, once.'

'Well, think it now.'

'I would like to.'

'Look at what you've achieved.'

Assuming that the meal will be, as usual, on his friend, Adrian tells the sommelier to bring them a Lafon Perrières 2005.

Satisfied, he removes his glasses.

Looking very sad, Aleksandr says, 'I'm sixty-five years old, and I don't know what to do any more. I just don't know what to do. I feel like everything is finished for me.'

'Tell me,' Adrian says, after a short pause, pocketing his glasses, 'have you got a hobby?'

'A hobby?'

'Yes. You know.'

'No,' Aleksandr says. He has never had a hobby – in his *Who's Who* entry, he had listed his 'interests' as 'wealth' and 'power'.

'I suggest you take up a hobby,' Adrian says. 'Take an interest in your garden,' he suggests. 'Did you know,' he asks, twinkling, 'that in his declining years Josef Stalin was more interested in producing the perfect mimosa than in fomenting global revolution?'

'No, I didn't know that,' Aleksandr says.

'He spent most of his time in his garden down on the Black Sea, pottering about among his mimosas, and pretty much left Beria to run the empire.'

'I didn't know that.'

'It's perfectly natural,' Adrian says. 'You have to step back. I'm having to slow down a bit myself,' he admits, as the starters arrive.

'Somehow . . .' Aleksandr looks miserable. 'I've lost the *meaning* of life. Do you understand?'

Adrian smiles. He says, 'Who needs meaning when you have soufflé Suissesse?'

Aleksandr tries to smile too.

He wonders, as he tries to smile, whether Adrian knows that he has been wiped out financially. That the Empire of Iron is no more. Adrian, now tucking into his soufflé, has shown no sign of knowing. Though he wouldn't, would he? Aleksandr picks up his fork. That was the thing with the English – it was impossible to know what was happening in their heads, what was hidden under their mild, ironic manner. Did they know themselves?

He tries to eat some soufflé. Then he puts his fork down next to the heavy, expensive plate and waits for Adrian to finish.

'Something wrong with it?' Adrian asks, still feeding himself.

'No, it's very good. I'm just not hungry.'

'Oh?'

Again, Aleksandr tries to smile.

'Are you alright, mate?' Adrian asks. 'You look very pale.'

'I'm tired.'

'Yes, you seem a bit tired. What have you been up to? Tell me.'

Unable to think of anything else, Aleksandr says, 'Ksenia's leaving me.'

Adrian looks pained. 'Oh, I am sorry,' he says.

The turbot in chive-and-butter sauce arrives. Someone tops Adrian up with Lafon Perrières.

Aleksandr just looks at the dead fish on his plate while Adrian, with silver knife and fork, starts expertly to prise his apart.

5

Ampleton House, on the outskirts of Ottershaw in Surrey, is not visible from the road. Only a high wall, and the tops of the tall trees in the famous arboretum, nearly leafless now, are visible. Darkness is falling when they arrive. The long, turning driveway takes them to the expanse of gravel in front of the mansion – Sir Edwin Lutyens, 1913 – where the Maybach and the Range Rover pull up. 'Here we are, sir,' Doug says through the intercom, as if his employer might be asleep.

Aleksandr is not asleep. He is just sitting in the silent, padded interior of the Maybach, wishing that he never had to leave it. For a moment he even wonders whether to ask Doug to take him back to London.

'Here we are, sir,' Doug says again. His voice sounds tired. He has been on duty since early in the morning, waiting at Farnborough for the Falcon to arrive.

Normally, someone would have emerged from the house by now, with an umbrella, and opened the door for him, and held the umbrella over him as he walked over the wet gravel to the house and into the double-height hall.

The staff, however, are all on leave, or in the London house.

So it is Madis who opens the door of the Maybach for him, and lets him into the house, and, having dealt with the alarm, turns on the lights in the hall.

He asks him whether he needs anything.

'No,' Aleksandr answers.

'I'll be in the flat,' Madis says, 'if you need anything.'

Madis lives in a flat with a separate entrance, at the side of the house, in what was once the stable yard.

'Okay. Thank you, Madis,' Aleksandr says.

Alone, he unwinds his scarf and sits down in the hall.

He shuts his eyes, tries to stop thinking.

Wherever his thoughts wander they find something that hurts.

Like the face of Adam Spassky – the way he smiled as the judge delivered her verdict.

His thoughts move from the unendurable humiliation of that moment to the practical fact of his poverty. And then to the humiliation again. And then the poverty. There seems to be nothing else – only those two things.

And he would be able to stomach the loss of his money, he thinks, if it weren't for the humiliation. And he would be able to take the humiliation, just, if he still had his money – though of course the loss of the money is *part* of it. The sheer idiocy of losing so much money. His other humiliations, however, would not be so total if he still had the money – the money itself would be a sort of answer to them, as it was always an answer to everything in the past.

He is still just sitting there in the hall, holding his scarf in his hands.

Madis opens the door. He seems surprised to see Aleksandr standing there, in the damp darkness.

'Madis.' Aleksandr is trying to smile. 'I hope I'm not disturbing you.'

'No,' Madis says.

'I was wondering.' The situation is definitely more awkward than Aleksandr thought it would be. 'Would you like to have a drink with me?'

Madis is wearing a T-shirt, tracksuit trousers, has no shoes on, only white sports socks on his feet. There is the sound of a television from somewhere in the flat. He says, 'I . . . I don't drink.'

'Oh, of course,' Aleksandr says. 'I forgot. Okay.'

Madis, perhaps out of embarrassment, says nothing.

'Well,' Aleksandr says. His shoulders are hunched against the frigid darkness – the temperature has dropped and over his silk shirt he is wearing only a thin black sweater. 'Goodnight, then.'

'Goodnight, boss,' Madis says.

He is just shutting the door of the flat when Aleksandr, who has turned to leave, says, 'Oh, Madis.'

The door is half-open. Madis is looking out at him.

'You don't have anything to eat, do you?' Aleksandr asks, with a small laugh. 'It's just that . . . In the kitchen . . . There doesn't seem to be . . .'

Madis hesitates for a moment. Then he says, 'Sure.'

'I'm sorry,' Aleksandr laughs. 'It's embarrassing.'

'No, sure,' Madis says. 'No problem.' And then he says, 'I'm just eating now, in fact. Do you want to join me?'

'Well, I don't want to disturb you . . .'

'No, don't worry about it,' Madis says.

'Okay then. It's very kind of you.'

Madis opens the door and steps aside to let Aleksandr in.

It is the first time he has seen the inside of Madis's flat. Madis leads him into a living room with a small dining table and a sofa and a TV which is switched on and showing the early-evening news, and some pictures on the walls. A framed print of Titian's *Allegory of Prudence*.

'Lamb rogan josh,' Madis says. 'That okay?'

'Fine. Of course.'

And then Madis says, as if something has just occurred to him, 'It's a supermarket one.'

'Fine.'

He leaves Aleksandr standing there, and in the small kitchen puts another Tesco's Finest lamb rogan josh into the microwave.

Madis, Aleksandr knows, lives there with his wife Liz. He is Estonian, originally. He emigrated to the United States as a teenager, and served in the army there, in some sort of special forces unit. He was in Iraq.

He must be about forty. Not very tall. Stocky.

He speaks English with a strange accent.

'It'll take a few minutes,' he says, emerging from the kitchen.

'Where's Liz?' Aleksandr asks.

'She's out,' Madis says. 'Sit down.'

It sounds almost like an instruction.

'Thank you,' Aleksandr says, and sits.

Madis turns off the TV.

Which was perhaps a mistake. There is just silence now – just the hum of the microwave from the kitchen.

Aleksandr sits at the table, and looks at his hands.

There is something strange about the way he is sitting there, looking at his hands, not speaking.

He looks up, and finds Madis watching him. Madis is standing near the kitchen door, waiting for the microwave to finish. 'It'll be done in a minute,' he says.

'What's the best way to die?' Aleksandr asks him. His eyes are shining, as though with tears.

'The best way to die?' Madis says, surprised.

'Yes.'

'The best way . . . The best way is to die happy.'

'No, I didn't mean . . .'

The microwave pings.

381

Madis, in the kitchen, peels back the heat-darkened plastic foil of the packaging and spoons the food onto two plain white plates. He takes the plates to the table and puts them on the straw place mats, then returns to the kitchen for the knives and forks.

'Thank you,' Aleksandr says.

They start to eat in silence.

Aleksandr does not seem to want to eat after all – he just pushes the food around the plate.

Eventually he stops, and sits there, while Madis, embarrassed, finishes his own meal.

'I'm sorry,' Aleksandr says. He indicates the half-eaten meal on his plate.

'No problem.'

'I'm sorry,' he says again. When he stands, Madis stands too, and walks with him to the door.

'Goodnight, Madis,' Aleksandr says on the threshold.

'Goodnight, boss,' Madis says. 'If you need anything . . . I'm here, okay.'

'Yes. Thank you. Goodbye.'

Without undressing, he falls asleep at some point, and wakes in the darkness later – is wide awake and knows he will not be able to sleep again.

Waking itself is a terrible experience. Everything still there, just as it was, there in the darkness.

Except for a second after he wakes there is nothing. An empty second. A sort of peace, for a second. And then it is over, and everything is there again.

He lies there in the darkness.

He is thinking of the last time he saw his father, in that hospital in Sverdlovsk, the *nomenklatura* hospital. The hospital seemed luxurious then. His father was proud to be treated there. He had told his son, when he visited him, who else was there – some well-known general – and it was almost as if he was happy to have had the heart attack just so that he could share a hospital with such a high-status individual.

And his son had enjoyed the sense of privilege too, sitting in his father's private room. He had tried to impress his father by translating the German text on a packet of medicine. He was at university in East Germany then, and spoke German perfectly, and his father, who spoke not a word of anything except Russian, *was* impressed, and he enjoyed impressing him. And that was the last time he saw his father, since the operation went wrong somehow and he was in a coma for a few weeks, and then he died.

There was someone else in the room, he thinks, when he was translating the German on the medicine packet. Someone else was there. Who was it?

Strangely, he imagines Stalin, unshaven, silver stubble on his chin, doddering among plants with a pair of secateurs . . .

It is light in Surrey.

Light outside. Yellow leaves.

One more day.

He is still just lying there.

He feels numb.

And also tired. Just so tired. So tired of everything.

It was his uncle, he thinks, who was in the room while he was translating the German on the medicine packet.

His uncle, Aleksandr. Aleksandr, like him.

And ten years later he took his own life.

He had nothing left to live for. He had devoted his whole life to something, and it had failed.

What else did he have left to live for?

Nothing.

It was over.

That was it.

9

Time will say nothing but I told you so,
Time only knows the price we have to pay;
If I could tell you I would let you know.

1

The next morning he needs to do the shopping. There is nothing in the house. He drives, as soon as it is fully light, at about eight, to the Lidl in Argenta. From the house, near Molinella, the main road points straight towards it. Dead straight, and lined in places with windy poplars. This is flat land. The horizon dominates here.

Argenta: a suburban fragment in the middle of the plain. He waits at a traffic light and passes through the centre, and then along the canal, its surface giving back the winter sunlight. The car park is empty this early on a weekday morning. He parks near the entrance and wheels a trolley into the bright warmth of the interior.

He knows where to find what he needs. When he was last in Italy, earlier in the year, he started shopping here. He pushes the trolley past the piled-up stuff, sometimes taking things, or stopping to look at what there is. He needs to put his glasses on to study the label on a packet of tea. Then he takes them off and nudges the trolley on to the next thing. He is evidently in no hurry. He takes a moment to remove his overcoat and fold it over the edge of the still nearly empty trolley.

He selects his fruit with care. He tears off one of the small plastic bags and then, after failing for a few moments to separate it open, starts to fill it with tangerines.

He turns his attention to the apples.

He selects, with inquisitively squeezing fingers, an avocado.

One lemon.

He takes his list out of the pocket of his trousers to make sure he has not forgotten anything in this part of the shop. Apparently satisfied, he pushes on, towards the drinks, where he spends some time comparing the prices of the various lagers they have, still packed on pallets. The prices of things hang on signs – loud yellow signs, with the price printed in a font that looks almost as though it has been handwritten with a marker pen. (He wonders, for a moment, whether the signs are, in fact, handwritten. No – too uniform.) He puts a six-pack of Bergkönig lager into his trolley and moves on. He ignores the wine. He would never buy wine here.

Non-foods is next, and he spends some time fussing with sponges and washing-up liquid.

The stuff in his trolley, the small quantities of everything – he has just taken a shrink-wrapped pack of two sausages from a fridge – suggest a man who is living alone.

And indeed he is here on his own.

He arrived last night at Bologna airport – the late Ryanair flight from Stansted. The taxi through the wintry darkness to the house. The house was cold. Entropic forces were gnawing at it. There were mouse droppings on the floor. Signs of damp, again, in the wall at the foot of the stairs. Still in his coat he sat down on the small sofa in the hall. He felt weak and frozen. His breath hung in the air in front of his mouth as he sat there, with the key still in his hand. He had to start the heating – to struggle with the oil-fired furnace. He had a small glass of grappa. He managed to start the heating.

It is nearly ten when he transfers his shopping from the trolley to his old VW Passat estate, and then wheels the noisily empty trolley back to the mass of others near the entrance. He asks himself whether there is anything else he needs to pick up in Argenta. Nothing much springs to mind, and he wonders, starting the car, whether to stop somewhere for a coffee. The Piazza Garibaldi. There are a few places there where it might be a pleasure to sit in the cold sunlight with a cappuccino and a newspaper for half an hour. He is undecided as he drives back along the canal. What decides it is the lack of parking space in the small piazza. He feels a faint pang of disappointment. It is not worth trying to find somewhere else to park, though, and soon he is out of Argenta again, among fields that stretch to the luminous winter horizon.

*

He thinks about death quite a lot now. It is hard not to think about it. Obviously, he doesn't have that much time left. Ten years? In ten years he will be eighty-three. More than that? Well, probably not. So about ten years. Seen in one way, that is frighteningly little. It is terrible, how little it seems, sometimes. Waking at five a.m. on a December morning, for instance, in the large damp bedroom of the house near Argenta, the turquoise walls still hidden in darkness. The quiet ticking of the clock on the table next to the bed. It is terrible how little it seems. And since the operation two months ago he has understood that even ten years might be optimistic. He has had, since the operation, this strange permanent awareness of his heart and what it is doing, and this fear that it will suddenly stop doing it. He lies there, unpleasantly aware of its working, and of the fact that one day it *will* stop. He feels no more prepared to face death, though, than he ever has.

It is starting to get light in the large turquoise bedroom.

He has been lying there, awake, for two hours, thinking.

It still seems incredible to him that he is actually going to die. That this is just going to stop. This. Him. It still seems like something that

389

happens to other people – and of course friends and acquaintances are already falling. People he has known for decades. A fair few are dead already. He has attended their funerals. The numbers are starting to thin out. And still he finds it hard to understand – to properly *understand* – that he will die as well. That this experience is finite. That one day it will end. That ten years from now, quite probably, he just won't be here.

There is something very strange about trying to imagine the world without him. The strangeness, he thinks, still lying there, is to do with the fact that the only world he knows is the one he perceives himself – and *that* world *will* die with him. That world – that subjective experience of the world – which for him *is* the world – will not in fact outlast him. It is the ending of that stream of perception that seems so strange. So unimaginable. He is staring at the enormous walnut wardrobe that stands on the far wall of the room, and he is aware, in an unusual way, of that stream of perception, of perceiving things. Of the pleasure of perceiving things. Of seeing the light from the window pass through slits in the heavy drapes and in dust-filled shafts find the surface of the wardrobe, the deep, time-darkened varnish.

Of hearing footsteps on the gravel outside.

The footsteps are Claudia's. Claudia, the Romanian daily. His wife, Joanna, must have phoned from England and told her he was there.

'*Buongiorno*, Claudia,' he says, appearing downstairs in his dressing gown and slippers.

He has lost weight, a lot of weight, since she last saw him in the early part of the summer. Then he looked over-inflated, with a high, unhealthy colour. He doesn't look *healthier* now, particularly. He seems shrunken, diminished. '*Buongiorno*, Signor Parson,' she says. She is preparing herself for work. They speak Italian to each other – Claudia knows no English. Her Italian isn't perfect either. It is worse than his. She arrived a few years ago, to join her son, who installs kitchens for IKEA in Bologna. 'I am sorry,' she says. 'I don't know you are here.'

'Did Joanna call you?' he asks.

'Signora Parson, yes. I am sorry,' she says again.

'There's nothing to be sorry about,' he tells her. 'Thank you for coming in. I'm sorry I didn't call you to let you know I was here.'

'Is okay,' she says.

'I'm not sure how long I'm going to be here,' he says. They are in the kitchen and he starts to make his coffee, spooning it into the machine. 'Just a week or two, I think.'

It is unusual for someone to be here at this time, first week of December. Christmas, sometimes, they are here. Not so much any more. In the old days, quite often. When Simon was little, and Joanna's mother was still alive. In the old days. No Claudia then. An Italian lady, they used to have. And she had had to stop working. Some medical issue. What was her name? They stayed in touch for a while. Did they visit her in hospital in Ferrara or somewhere? He might have a memory of that, or he might be mixing it up with something else. Anyway, he has no idea what's happened to her now. All these people you know in a lifetime. What happens to them all?

He is pouring some muesli into a huge mug, pouring skimmed milk over it. The skimmed milk still seems more like water than milk to him.

Claudia is asking what she should start with.

'Maybe upstairs?' he suggests, wanting to be left in peace in the kitchen for a while.

He sits at the table, eating muesli, hearing her heavy feet making the old steps squeak as she marches upstairs with her things.

How old is she? he wonders. Not young. Her son must be thirty. A handsome man. He has met him a few times – he picks her up, occasionally, in his IKEA van.

When he has finished his muesli, he settles in the wing chair in the sitting room – an old one, in need of restuffing – tapping at his iPad. It was a present from Cordelia, while he was in hospital after the heart op. He has always been a technophile, what is now known as an 'early adopter' – he was the first among his friends, in about 1979, to own a video, a VHS player. He learned how to use the iPad in a day or two.

He taps at it.

Tap.

Tap.

Emails. Not many. Not as many as there used to be. He has had to stop doing most of the things he used to do – his post-retirement portfolio of interests. Down to nothing now, nearly. There is an email from Cordelia, which always pleases him. She talks about this and that. Asks how he is feeling. She says that Simon – her son, his grandson – has had a poem published in some magazine. Just a university magazine probably, though she doesn't say so – she wants to make it sound as impressive as possible. Simon is in his first year at Oxford. She has attached the poem to the email and he looks at it while Claudia stomps about overhead, making the little glass pieces of the chandelier tinkle. (The chandelier was there when they bought the house – very valuable, they were assured.) The poem seems to be inspired by the famous miniature of Sultan Mehmet II in which he is shown smelling a flower.

The portrait shows this – his eyes fixed elsewhere,
Mehmet the Conqueror holds a rose
To the Turkic scimitar of his nose.
The engrossing necessities of money and war,
The wise politician's precautionary
Fratricides, the apt play of power –
All proper activities in his sphere,
And he excelled at them all. So why the flower?
A nod, perhaps, to something less worldly;
Not beauty, I think, whatever that is,
Not love, not 'nature',
Not Allah, by that or any other name –
Just a moment's immersion in the texture
Of existence, the eternal passing of time.

Not terrible, he thinks. Some nice phrases. *The engrossing necessities of money and war.* Yes, that was nice. (He still misses them, after nearly ten years, those engrossing necessities, waiting for him at the end of the Tube journey to Whitehall, still feels that without them he is not properly *living*.) Yes, it was a nice way of putting it. And then there was . . . Where was it? Yes –

Just a moment's immersion in the texture
Of existence

The words had made him think of the way he spent a minute or two, earlier that morning, staring at the wardrobe upstairs. The sense he had had then of losing himself in the act of perception. A moment's immersion in the texture of existence – the *texture* of it. Yes. Well done, Simon. He will write him an email, he thinks. He will praise the poem – not too much, just enough to encourage him, and with qualifications. Cordelia has a tendency to praise her son unqualifiedly, which isn't healthy. Simon is, it has to be said, just a little odd. He was there, in Argenta, that spring, with a friend. They were travelling around Europe and had stayed for a day or two. The friend – what was his name? – had been a lively fellow. Fun to have about the place. Simon, as usual, solemn and withdrawn. Less so towards the end. They had had some nice talks, the three of them, about serious subjects – literature, history, the state of Europe.

Claudia is at the door.

She wants to know if it's okay to start on the kitchen.

When she has left, he showers and dresses, and makes himself lunch. He sets a place at the table in the kitchen – the dining room seems too formal a setting in which to eat a two-egg omelette, alone. He wonders whether to have a glass of wine with his omelette and salad. In the end he has two, which means he will not be able to drive anywhere for a few hours. He had thought he might drive somewhere. To the Valli di Argenta, perhaps, and walk there for half an hour – he is supposed to walk a few miles a day, and today the weather is dry and mild.

The afternoon seems to stretch out interminably in front of him. He tidies up a few drawers that haven't been attended to for years – loses himself for a while in looking at old opera tickets and tourist maps and invoices for things he has long forgotten paying for. He sits at the piano and tries to play – it is terribly out of tune, and his fingers also soon start to hurt. They won't do what he tells them to do. He keeps making mistakes and stops in frustration. He still feels strangely depressed about the trip to Ravenna yesterday. He went to Ravenna yesterday – just on a whim, he had nothing else to do – and got into difficulties with the traffic. He got lost and flustered, and ended up driving the wrong way down a narrow one-way street. He didn't know what he had done until he met a van halfway down, its lights flashing irritably, and without space to do anything else, he had to reverse out the way he had arrived, looking over his shoulder, squinting with stress and an increasing sense of isolation. The street was straight; it shouldn't have been a problem. Somehow, though, he kept losing the line. He kept having to stop and start again. He was holding the wheel tightly as if it was something preventing him from drowning. The driver of the van was shouting inaudibly like someone in a silent film.

He thinks of the faces of the people on the pavement, witnessing the scene, laughing, pointing to show him his mistake, smiling at him. Not unsympathetically, some of them. In a way that just made it worse. It was obvious from their expressions that what they were seeing was something pitiful – an old man, out of his depth, making a mess of things.

That was what their faces said they were seeing.

And it was a shock.

That wasn't how he thought of himself at all.

Afterwards, when he had finally found somewhere to park, he walked the streets for a while, feeling absurdly shaken, and found himself, eventually, outside Sant' Apollinare Nuovo.

It was hardly warmer inside than it was outside.

There were a few people there, not many, milling about, looking at the mosaics, those echoes of Byzantium. He himself had seen them many times – the long frontal lines of white-toga'd figures, white on gold. He has never been a Christian. Of course he was brought up in the vaguely or vestigially Christian setting of England in the 1940s and '50s, but even in his earliest years he had not believed in God, in Jesus, or any of that. They had always been just words to him. Just stories, like other stories. That was not particularly unusual, he thought, for someone of his generation. He stood there, looking up at the impassive, pink-cheeked faces. In lines like a school photo. And then that extraordinary image, at the end, of the curtains opening, as if to show us something – only there's nothing there, just a flat gold space, a surprising area of plain golden tiles. A pigeon had got in and was fluttering about up there.

He stayed for a few more minutes and then went out and looked at the outside of the basilica. The campanile, standing against the grey sky. He knew the history, sort of. Theoderic the Ostrogoth etc. Murdered his predecessor with his own hands – invited him for dinner apparently and personally murdered him. They were fighting over Italy. The Western Empire was falling apart.

Something about the whole episode depresses him. He is still weighed down, the next day, by the sense of his own uselessness that had taken hold of him as he was driving, as he was struggling with the Ravenna traffic – and then the fuck-up in the one-way street. It depresses him. Depresses him out of all proportion, you would think, to what actually happened, embarrassing as that was.

Later, and unexpectedly, Joanna phones.

She asks whether Claudia has been in.

'Yes,' he says, 'she was here.'

'You managed to get the heating going?' Joanna asks.

This question irritates him – the suggestion that he might not have managed it. He lets a moment pass, his eyes finding the photos on the sideboard where the phone is: family photos, and photos of himself with John Major, with Tony Blair – the prime ministers he served. 'Yes,' he says.

'So the house is warm enough?'

'The house is fine.'

There is a pause. 'Well, I just thought I'd call and see how you are,' she says.

'I'm fine.'

'Okay. Now listen, Tony.' And she starts to tell him how she has to go to New York for a few days, to head office – she is a seniorish manager in a pharmaceutical firm – for some annual appraisal.

Dusk is falling in Argenta. He sees it through the tall windows of the sitting room. Darkness settling on the flat land. She is off to New York. And he is here, in Argenta, with its tractor showroom, its marsh museum.

'Well, have fun,' he says.

'I'll be back on Friday.'

That doesn't mean much to him. He isn't sure what day it is today.

There is a pause, a longer one. 'You *are* okay, Tony?' she asks, sounding slightly embarrassed, as if the question were intrusively personal.

'I told you. I'm absolutely fine.'

She says quickly, 'Did Cordelia send you Simon's poem?'

'Yes, she did.'

'And? What did you think?'

'It wasn't bad.'

Afterwards, he wishes he hadn't been so offish with her. It was nice of her to phone. Something about the way she spoke to him though. It was like the way those people had looked at him in the one-way street yesterday as he struggled to reverse in a straight line. That was something he had once been able to do – reverse in a straight line. He looks at his watch.

He waits a little longer and then has some more wine. A very fine Barbaresco, a present from someone years ago that he had been saving for a special occasion. He opened it at lunchtime, impulsively, and drank half of it alone, in the middle of an ordinary weekday, with an indifferent omelette. What was the point of waiting, anyway?

He drinks some more now with some cheese and prosciutto, a few olives, assembled on a plate. A football match on the TV. Some Serie B match between teams he has never even heard of playing out a nil–nil draw on a December afternoon. The stadium is evidently half-empty. Still, it dispels the silence. It passes the time.

He wonders whether to phone Cordelia. In the end he doesn't. He doesn't want to disturb her. He is depressed – he wouldn't be able to hide that from her, she would hear it in his voice – and he doesn't want to make her feel down too. He doesn't want her, in future, not to want him to phone. Which she won't if he's always whining at her, droning on about his problems, asking questions that obviously don't interest him, leaving long despondent silences on the line.

He pours himself some more of the Barbaresco. Actually, it's excellent. One of the finest reds produced in Italy. He is able to appreciate that; there seems to be a sort of hole, though, where his *pleasure* in it should be. It's a waste, he thinks, to drink it in this state.

He looks at his watch.

It's too early, surely, to turn in?

The house, now that the football is finished and he has turned off the TV, is oppressively silent.

He sits in the wing chair and tries to read. His thoughts keep wandering. He thinks of Alan. He has a half-brother, Alan. How old is Alan now? Eighty-five? Hardly able to walk. Hardly able to stand up – any sort of movement at all involves physical pain and mental anguish. Humiliation. He thinks of the last time he saw him. Alan's hair looked soft and effeminate – and snowy white, obviously, like the large soft trainers he always wears now. He had tried to smile when he saw Tony. He hadn't been able to stand up. He had just shivered in his chair, trying to smile, his jaw wagging as he struggled to speak, to say something. 'How are you, Tony?' he had finally managed, in a weird, slurred voice.

His skin looked as though it was dead already, as if the outer layers of him were dead already. His faded eyes peered out with fear, and a sort of hostility, from that dead face.

He is still sitting there with the book in his hands – Christopher Clark's *The Sleepwalkers: How Europe Went to War in 1914*.

You couldn't really talk to Alan any more, that was one of the saddest things.

He was fading away.

Fading away.

Do we all end up just fading away?

*

There are moments of serious fear, during the night. At one point, he is sure that something is going wrong with his heart. Then later, a nightmare of some sort.

A huge stick-insect-like thing with lazy eyes.

For a long time it is motionless, until he almost stops fearing it.

Then it starts to move.

Touches him.

He wakes with a yelp of horror, and takes hours to fall asleep again, once the fluttery panic of the nightmare has swum away, thinking about Alan, and about how little time he himself has left. He lies there in the dark, somehow horrified by his situation, as if it is something he has only just found out about. As if someone has just told him, for the first time, that he is seventy-three years old.

2

When he next wakes it is light in the room.

It is nearly eight.

He feels, dragging himself into a sitting position, exhausted and depressed.

Today he must *do* something.

He decides, staring defeatedly at some fresh mouse droppings on the antique tiles of the kitchen floor, to drive to Pomposa abbey. When he was sorting out one of the drawers yesterday he found some old entrance tickets to the abbey – they went there years ago, with Alan and his wife, he thinks, when they were staying once – and he decides that he would like to see it again. He doesn't remember much about it. A medieval monastery, near the sea, some way north of Ravenna.

Anyway, what it *is* isn't really the point. He has to do something, drive *somewhere*. Where exactly hardly matters.

It will take an hour or so to drive there, he thinks. He'll arrive at eleven, say, have a look at the abbey, whatever there is. Have lunch perhaps – he seems to remember there was a place to eat there – and then drive home. Stop in Argenta to pick up a few things. And then have tea and spend an hour or two on Clark's *Sleepwalkers*.

Freezing fog hangs outside the windows. The sea of freezing damp that spreads over this floodplain every winter. He has, these days, an intense physical aversion to the cold. The house's old heating is just about doing its job – it is faintly warm in the tall rooms – and he finds the thought of leaving that warmth distressing. And driving in this fog. That would be asking for trouble.

He takes the stairs, slowly, and in the bathroom starts to fill the tub with steaming water. He will have a hot bath and see how he feels after that. He takes his pills, a multicoloured meal of them. Then he struggles over the tall edge of the tub and submerges himself in the heat of the water. He lies there sleepily in the steam. Feels his joints ease and loosen.

Afterwards, while he is shaving, the sun shines in at the window. The fog is lifting.

He dresses warmly. Two jumpers. His heaviest socks.

The trees that line the edges of the property – serving as a windbreak – are nearly leafless. The bushes and shrubs of the garden look brown and dead though the grass is still green. He opens the garage. A dark blue VW Passat estate. British originally, it has Italian plates now.

The idea of driving still makes him nervous. He takes his seat at the steering wheel with an unwelcome sense that he is perhaps not up to this.

Now that the fog has lifted, everything seems unusually well defined. The leafless poplars standing along the road, which is whitish with cold, throw faint shadows across his path.

He is not particularly aware of driving slowly. People keep overtaking him, though – there is a permanent little queue of them.

He has already passed through Argenta, and turned at San Biagio onto the road that leads to the lagoon, the long straight road across flat farmland. There is nothing in particular to love about this landscape. They had wanted, originally, something in Tuscany. This was twenty-five years ago, when Cordelia left home. Something in Tuscany. It turned out, however, that Tuscany was more expensive than they had anticipated. So rather than settle for one of the disappointingly poky little houses they were shown in the Chianti they decided to widen their search to other areas, and as they moved further and further away from Florence, the houses they were shown started to look more and more like what they had in mind – a substantial elegant villa with an acre of mature, secluded garden. That was what they wanted, and in the end that was what they got. What they had not foreseen was that it would be *here*, all the way over on the other side of the peninsula, in an area in which, at the outset, they had had absolutely no interest. And such a desperately flat landscape. (When, in the 1970s, as deputy head of mission at the embassy in Rome, he had had to attend an event in San Marino – to follow an oompah band and people in operetta costumes up to the top of the rock – he had seen it from up there, the flat land stretching north, and shuddered.) The house itself had won them over. Its distinguished, almost aristocratic demeanour. Still, it had seemed eccentric, and when it was theirs they wondered whether they had made a mistake. Slowly they made their peace with the place, until they felt a kind of love for it. You learn to love what's there, not what's not there. How can you live, otherwise?

Sun falls on the fields on either side of the road, on sudden expanses of still water. Even though the heating is not on in the car, he starts to feel too warm in his coat and stops to take it off – at a sleepy petrol station, Tamoil, one of the unmanned self-service ones they have around here. Next to it is a dirt track leading off into empty fields, and irrigation ditches, half-frozen now. Silence, except for a passing vehicle sometimes.

The lagoon, when he arrives at it, shines like a sheet of metal. From there he picks up Strada Provinciale 58, which wanders, even quieter, through the wetlands of the Po delta. There is something pleasantly hypnotic about the driving. The interior of the Passat is nice and warm. There is no impatient queue behind him now – he has the landscape to himself, until he joins Strada Statale 309 – the main road along the sea – and pootles in the wake of a truck, not wanting the stress of try-ing to overtake. The truck wallows in the wind that hits them from the direction of the sea, the sea itself not visible, only indicated by the signs pointing off at frequent intervals to lido this and lido that. Lido delle Nazioni. Lido di Volano.

He nearly misses the turning. He sees the campanile, and suddenly un-derstanding what it is, immediately indicates and turns. The time it took to drive here passed so quickly. He doesn't feel that he should be there yet. And yet here he is.

Nothing is familiar. If he was here before – and he was – he has for-gotten everything. The little track-like road winding away from Strada Statale 309, first seeming to wander in the wrong direction, *away* from the tall campanile that sticks out above a stand of trees, and then turn-ing on itself and taking him, past a vista of fields stretching to the hori-zon, to a little lake, a few dumpsters next to a wall, some parking spaces on an apron of tarmac.

He puts the Passat in one of the spaces, most of which are empty. The frigid air shocks him when he opens the door. There is quite a strong smell of dog shit. A sign indicates, surprisingly, that thieves are a problem here. He looks around at the silent, empty scene. The only sound is the quiet shushing of traffic on Strada Statale 309. Thieves? Not now, surely. Anyway, there is nothing in his car for them to steal. He puts on his scarf and locks the Passat.

The campanile is a few hundred metres off. He sees it through the leafless trees. Starting to walk towards it, he is weighed down, somewhat, by a feeling that this is pointless, what he is doing. He feels tired and cold, and he is not actually very interested in seeing this place. That is obvious now that he is here, walking towards it over the frost-blanched tarmac, quickening his step to keep warm. And in fact there does not seem to be much to see. The setting is a sort of sparse park. He passes two modest-looking places to eat, set behind empty terraces on one side of the road that leads to the campanile. Only one of them seems to be open – there is a sign outside, anyway. And it occurs to him that the abbey itself may not be open, on a weekday morning at this time of year.

It is open, however.

What there is of it.

After he has looked it over, he walks back to the place with the sign outside. A very simple place – not where they ate with Alan and his wife when they were here years ago. There is a slot machine with flashing lights. Old posters on the walls. Dusty bottles of wine for sale on shelves. He sits down at a small table. A man puts a paper place mat in front of him, and hands him a laminated menu. The only other people eating there are a middle-aged couple speaking in low voices at another table. German, they seem to be. He quickly scans the menu. He is not very hungry. He wants something hot. He orders soup.

He only spent half an hour looking at the abbey – a series of low brick buildings, very plain, with small windows. A few modest pieces of carved white marble. Inside, it was mostly just empty rooms. There was a courtyard with a square of lawn and a well in the middle. It was all quite evocative. A memorial to a way of life that went on here for a thousand years, a way of seeing the world. One side of the courtyard was formed by the side wall of the abbey church. The whole interior of the church was painted with scenes and figures. He spent some time in there, looking with a historian's interest at the painted walls, the strange and often violent scenes depicted on them. A man on fire. Naked women. A sort of devil, with suffering people in his enormous oval mouth.

When he had had enough, he stepped out into the porch. The low winter sun shone into the deep porch. Set in its walls were some marble tablets, memorials for the important dead. In a tranquil and unhurried mood, he studied some of these. They were in Latin, obviously, a language he learned a lifetime ago. He is still able, sometimes, to make something of it, and in one of the inscriptions he found five words that made him stand there thoughtfully for a while. A single Latin sentence, on a piece of stone in memory of a man who had died hundreds of years ago.

The waiter puts the hot soup on the table in front of him, and some bread sticks individually wrapped in paper.

'*Grazie,*' he says.

'*Prego,*' the waiter says, as he walks away.

The Germans at the other table have unfolded a map of northeastern Italy. Poring over it, they talk to each other in quiet voices.

The waiter is talking to someone too, though nobody is visible. He speaks again, in a scolding tone. And then a little girl emerges from somewhere and walks over to one of the empty tables where she sits down. She must be . . . Seven years old? She sits at the table, looking out the window, her feet swinging well short of the floor.

Tony eats his soup – *minestra di fagioli*. Green leaves of cabbage float in it, huge creamy beans.

Unselfconsciously, and still staring at the window, at the empty stillness of the winter day, the little girl has started to sing something in a soft, lisping voice.

While he eats his soup, he tries to understand the words of the song. She is singing it for a second time now.

'*Gennaio nevicato,*' she sings, her lips hardly moving.

In January it snows.

'*Febbraio, mascherato.*'

February is masked.

'*Marzo, pazzerello.*'

March is mad, madness.

'*Aprile, ancor più bello.*'

April, even more lovely.

'*Maggio, frutti e fiori. Giugno, vado al mare.*'

May, fruits and flowers. June, off to the sea.

'*Luglio e Agosto, la scuola non conosco.*'

July and August, school is unknown . . . No school.

'*Settembre, la vendemmia. Ottobre, con la nebbia.*'

September, the, er . . . harvest. October, foggy.

'*Novembre, un golf in più. Dicembre con Gesù.*'

November, an extra jumper. December, Jesus.

Having finished the song, she wipes her nose with the back of her hand. She has auburn hair, pale skin. She sees that he is looking at her. Her eyes are greenish.

He smiles. 'That was a nice song,' he says to her, in Italian.

She says, 'I learned it at school.'

'Did you?'

'Yes.'

'Well . . .' He is not sure what to say. 'Well done,' he says.

She shrugs and starts to sing it again, evidently with nothing else to do, staring out the window.

'*Gennaio nevicato. Febbraio, mascherato . . .*'

The Germans are paying for their meal.

They leave and the waiter starts to tidy their table.

'*Un caffè,*' Tony says to him as the man passes with an armful of plates. He acknowledges the order with a single nod. His daughter – if she is his daughter – is still singing.

Novembre, un golf in più. Dicembre con Gesù.

406

And the Germans are unexpectedly there again. They hurry in, obviously agitated.

The waiter is at the espresso machine, whacking something.

'*Polizei!*' the German man almost shouts. '*Polizei!*'

The waiter doesn't stop what he is doing. He just turns his head, and the German says something in his own language which the waiter does not seem to understand.

The man tries English. 'Please, you must call the police,' he says.

'You must call the police,' echoes his wild-eyed wife.

In Italian, the waiter says, 'The police? Why?'

'You must call them,' the man says, still speaking English. 'Our car . . . Somebody has.' And he motions with his fist.

'Somebody has broken into your car?' the waiter says, sticking to Italian himself, and sounding wearily unsurprised.

'Yes, yes,' the man says in English, understanding. 'You must call the police.'

'Okay,' the waiter says, unexcitably. 'I'll call the police.'

First, though, he takes Tony his espresso – something Tony appreciates, though it evidently exasperates the Germans, particularly the woman, who turns to the door with an outraged sigh. The waiter returns unhurriedly to the bar and picks up the phone, which is attached to the wall next to a calendar with pictures of agricultural machinery.

It suddenly occurs to Tony that his own car might be in danger. He says to the Germans, who are waiting nervously, 'Do you mind my asking where you're parked?'

The man stares at him as if he hasn't understood. However, he then says, motioning, 'Over there, next to the small lake.'

'Oh,' Tony says. 'I'm parked there as well.'

The man just shrugs, as if he has more important things to worry about than where other people are parked, and turns to the waiter, who is still on the phone saying something about 'another one'.

When the waiter has finished, Tony is standing there with a ten-euro note in his hand.

Fearing the worst, he leaves and starts to walk towards the small lake and the parking spaces, the insistent smell of dog shit. That sign, warning of thieves – shouldn't have ignored it. The Passat is in view now and he quickens his pace. It looks okay. Yes, it is okay. In one of the other spaces an Opel estate with German plates has had a window smashed. Poor Germans. Probably on holiday, and now this to deal with. As he tries to find his way back to the main road, he passes the arriving police. Maybe he should have stayed and translated for them, the Germans – they didn't seem to know Italian, and they'll be lucky if the police speak English. Not much English spoken out here. Even the tourists in summer are mostly Italian. Well. They'll sort it out. He is already at the junction with Strada Statale 309. He needs to turn left – he needs both lanes to be clear. He sits there with the indicator ticking, traffic coming from both directions. The sun, already starting to sink, is in his eyes and he lowers the visor. Distant trees melt into the cold yellowish glow of the horizon. Still the traffic comes. His index fingers tap the black plastic of the steering wheel. This is silly now. He stifles a yawn. There is a truck coming from the left. Nothing, finally, from the other side. It is quite far off, the truck. Surely it is far enough for him to pull out across it. Not if he waits. So don't wait. Do it. Now.

3

Amemus eterna et non peritura.

Amemus – Let us love. *Eterna* – that which is eternal. *Et non peritura* – and not that which is transient.

Let us love what is eternal and not what is transient.

4

He is in an unfamiliar room. The light is dim. It seems to be evening, or very early morning. He is lying on a bed, looking up at the ceiling, high above him. There is something up there, some sort of light fitting. *Maggio, frutti e fiori. Giugno, vado al mare . . .* His head feels very heavy, foggy. *Ottobre, con la nebbia.* He does not know where he is. From somewhere on the other side of a door, he hears what seem to be footsteps, voices. The door has a panel of frosted glass in it, and figures slide across it sometimes, dark smudges, animating the facets of the panel for a moment. *Amemus eterna et non peritura.*

5

It is sunny in the room. Joanna is sitting there. 'Hello, Tony,' she says.

'Hello,' he says.

'You don't know where you are,' she suggests.

She looks tired, he thinks. He says, 'No. Where am I?'

'You're in hospital, in Ravenna.'

'Aren't you supposed to be in New York?' he asks.

'Yes, I am.'

She is sitting on a chair next to the bed.

'And I have to go in a couple of days,' she says.

'Okay.' He still feels woozy and it takes him a while to ask the obvious question: 'Why am I here?'

'You don't remember anything?'

He tries. Then he says, 'I was at Pomposa abbey. Wasn't I?'

'There was an accident. The Passat's a write-off,' she informs him.

'What accident?'

'They seem to think what happened,' she says, 'is you were pulling out of a minor road, and trying to turn left, and a truck was coming, and someone was overtaking it, and you didn't see them until it was too late.'

There is a longish silence.

'I don't remember any of that,' he says.

'Well, you ended up in a field, apparently. And if it wasn't for the airbags we wouldn't be talking now. You've got concussion, the doctor says.'

'Concussion?'

'Yes. I think they want to do a CAT scan tomorrow, just to make sure there's nothing else.'

He feels slightly nauseous. He lies back on the pillow – he has been half-sitting up to talk to her.

'The car's in my name,' she says. 'That's how they found me.'

He is staring at the light fitting on the ceiling. His eyes follow the wire across the ceiling to the wall over the door, and then along the top of the wall to a small hole in one of the other walls. He feels strange.

'I've brought you some things,' she says. 'Pyjamas and so on.'

'Okay. How are you?' he asks vaguely.

The question sounds odd. She hesitates. 'Fine,' she tells him. Then she says, maybe feeling that that wasn't enough, 'You know how it is, at this time of year.'

He struggles to remember what time of year it is.

Joanna seems distracted by something and turns her head, though in fact there is nothing there, only the pale impersonal space of the small hospital room.

There is, undoubtedly, an awkwardness to this. The way they have lived, for twenty years or more, makes it awkward. They have each looked after themselves, more or less, for all that time. They have not often had to ask the other for help – and when they did it was in a worldly tone, as negotiating equals, and in practical matters – loans, professional favours. Not like this.

Tony seems helpless and dopey in the bed, wearing a hospital smock with a number tattooed on the fabric near his shoulder.

'I flew out last night,' she says, turning to him again from the oddly low sink. 'Ryanair. From Stansted.'

He doesn't seem interested. 'Yes?'

'You know – the flight that gets in about midnight.'

He does know that flight. He arrived on it himself, only a few days ago. The taxi from Bologna airport to the house, half an hour through the wintry darkness. And the house, unused for months, the temperature of a fridge, the olive oil opaque and waxy. Mouse droppings on the floor. Signs of damp in the wall at the foot of the stairs. They had made him feel overwhelmed, somehow, those things. The mouse droppings, the spreading patch of damp. Still in his coat he had sat down on the small sofa in the hall, his breath hanging in the air in front of his mouth . . .

'Do you want me to stay?' Joanna's voice says.

She is standing now, at the window, looking out. He does not know what there is to see. When he says nothing, she says, 'The doctor did say at this stage you just need rest. You should try and sleep, he said.'

'Okay.'

'Do you want me to stay?' she asks again, moving the emphasis slightly to the word *stay* this time.

She sits, again, in the chair – a low chair of scruffy green fabric – waiting for him to answer.

'No, it's okay,' he says.

'You should try and sleep,' she advises.

'Yes.'

She takes his hand for a moment. That too feels awkward, holding his dry hand like that. She isn't sure why she took it. The physical intimacy of it feels excessive, anyway, now that she is holding it. She understands that she has no feel for what to do in this situation. They have lived merely as friends for so many years. She isn't sure what she owes him in a situation like this. There is no precedent for it. The heart op – *that* long hospital stay – was all organised and prearranged and in the familiar surroundings of West London. She didn't have to fly across Europe overnight at no notice to appear at his side, surprising him, as she did today. She didn't have to tell him where he was, and what had happened to him. He never seemed as *helpless* then as he does now. She had wondered, on the plane, whether she needed to do this, whether it was her place any more. If she didn't do it, though, who would? She is still holding his hand. She squeezes it – out of embarrassment more than anything else – and puts it down.

'I'll look in tomorrow morning,' she says.

'Okay.' He wonders what time of day it is now.

She puts her coat on. It seems to take for ever. Then she says again, 'I'll look in tomorrow.'

She has already opened the door, letting in noise from outside, when he says, 'Joanna.'

She stops in the doorway, very aware now of how much she wants to leave.

'Thank you.'

She doesn't know what to say. 'That's alright,' she says finally, and leaves.

An hour or two later – it is already dark outside, the light on the ceiling is on – a doctor arrives. He is very young. Not much more than thirty, by the look of it. A nice-looking man. He asks how Tony feels. 'Okay,' Tony says.

'Do you feel sick?'

'Sometimes. A little bit.'

'Headache?'

'Slightly. Not really.'

The doctor says they will do a CAT scan in the morning. If everything is okay – if there is no haemorrhaging inside his head – he might be able to go home tomorrow, or perhaps the next day. 'You have been very lucky,' he says, smiling.

*

In the morning he feels more or less normal. He has, which he didn't quite have before, a normal awareness of his surroundings. He is in hospital. He is very much aware of that now. Already this year he has spent many weeks in hospital. He has already spent more time in hospital this year, he thinks, than in his entire life up till now. And here he is again. He is sitting on the edge of the tall bed staring at the scuffed grey floor. And there's just going to be more and more of this, isn't there? Hospitals. Doctors. His only purpose in life now, it seems, is to stave off physical decay and death for as long as possible. His life, in terms of any sort of positive purpose, would seem to be over already. He feels very depressed. *Amemus eterna et non peritura.* The words pass through his mind from somewhere. Painfully, he eases himself off the bed and plants his pale feet on the floor. The sink is two light-headed steps away. Over it there is a mirror. His face is a shock. No one told him about that. 'Fucking hell,' he says, furious. He stands there for a few seconds, leaning on the sink until his head stops spinning. The tap is weird – a horizontal lever about six inches long. He fiddles with it until water starts to flow. Fills one of the plastic cups and lifts it to his split, disfigured lip.

He is still looking at himself in the mirror. At his monstrously enlarged face, his partially shaved head. At the overall patheticness of the figure he presents.

Those words again.

Amemus eterna et non peritura.

Pomposa.

Memories of the hour or so he spent there materialise in his mind. It is almost disconcerting, the way they are just suddenly there. Walking through the plain spaces of the abbey. The inscription in the porch: *Amemus eterna et non peritura.* And the thoughts he had while waiting for his soup, his *minestra di fagioli*, and staring through the window at the still, winter day outside, winter daylight on leafless trees.

So what is eternal?

Nothing, that's the problem. Nothing on earth. Not the earth itself. Not the sun. Not the stars in the night sky.

Everything has an end.

Everything.

We know that now.

6

Joanna drives him home in a car provided by the insurance company. She has already sorted all that out.

He had so looked forward to leaving the hospital. On the drive home, however, his spirits are low. He isn't sure, now, what he was looking forward to. It is snowing lightly, ineffectually. Small flakes that won't settle, that melt as soon as they touch anything.

They arrive at the house.

They stopped at the Lidl in Argenta first and they take the shopping in, Joanna doing the heavy lifting.

'That damp patch needs seeing to,' she says.

'Yes.'

'And you know that we have mice?'

'Yes.'

They sit down to have lunch together. It is strange, them being here together like this, in this house. It has been many years since it was just the two of them, here.

'I have to leave tomorrow,' Joanna says.

'Okay.'

'I spoke to Cordelia,' she tells him. 'She's going to come and stay with you for a while. A week, she said she might be able to manage.'

He tries not to show how pleased he is. 'That really isn't necessary.'

'I don't think you should be on your own.'

'I'll be fine.'

'She's already got her plane ticket, Tony.'

'Well, it's very kind of her.'

Joanna says, picking at potato salad, 'I'm sorry I can't stay longer myself.'

He sort of waves that away with his fork.

They eat, for a minute or two, in silence.

'It's a shame about the Passat,' he says, obviously perked up by the news about Cordelia.

'Oh, come on, it was ancient. It was time to junk it, anyway.'

'I liked it.'

'So did I,' Joanna says.

'Remember we used to drive down in it?'

'Of course.'

'That was fun.'

She says, pouring herself some more wine, and in a tone which is almost drily flirtatious, 'It had its moments.'

They used to drive down in the Passat – and before that in an old Volvo 740 – down through France, through the Mont Blanc tunnel and out through the Valle d'Aosta into Piedmont, the shimmer of Lombardy. He always particularly loved driving through the Valle d'Aosta – the drama of the valley, and the way that heightened the sense you had there of passing from northern to southern Europe.

How wonderful those long drives seem now. Thinking about them makes something ache in him.

Memories of fresh damp air.

He has a sip of wine. Notices that his hand is shaking.

Anyway, that all stopped when the Passat was domiciled in Argenta, about twelve years ago. It was already fairly old then.

Joanna is telling him something: 'Cordelia's going to help you find a new car, she says.'

'Is she?' he asks.

It seems there was a hint of scepticism in his voice – Joanna says, 'She does know about cars.'

'Yes, she does,' he agrees.

'She'll help you find something. In Ravenna, I suppose.'

'Or Ferrara,' he suggests.

'If you like. Have you finished?'

He nods, and she takes his plate, with hers, to the kitchen.

Outside, it has stopped snowing – it's just miserable. A frozen, damp day. Joanna spends some time on the phone. He doesn't know who she's talking to. She speaks to several people. It sounds like work, he thinks, eavesdropping from his wing chair with Clark's *Sleepwalkers* on his lap. He's not making much progress with it. He's just not that interested, is the main problem. Things just don't interest him as much as they used to.

She asks him, when she has finished on the phone, if he wants to watch a film.

'A film?' he says, slightly as if she's interrupting him, as if she's distracting him from something important. 'Alright.'

He notices the full glass of wine in her hand. She's drinking a lot of wine, he thinks. She's uneasy, with them here together like this. 'What film?' he asks.

'I don't know. We've got all these DVDs.' She is at the shelf, in her voluminous woollens, starting to look through them. '*Groundhog Day*?'

'We must have watched that,' he says unkindly, 'twenty times.'

'Okay. *On Golden Pond*?'

'No.'

'*The Bucket List*?'

He snorts.

'How about *Driving Miss Daisy*?'

'God, no.'

She makes some more suggestions, all of which he irritably dismisses.

'Why don't you choose, then?' she says, starting to lose patience. 'Come here and choose something yourself.'

'Joanna . . .' He is still sitting in the wing chair. He puts his hands together, the points of his fingers, as if about to offer her some wisdom.

Then he just sighs, and says, sounding put-upon, 'What else is there?'

'There are loads. *About Schmidt*?'

He sighs again.

'*About Schmidt*?' she half-shouts, turning from the shelf.

'No!'

'Do you actually want to watch a film?' she asks.

'Not really,' he says, with a sort of defiance.

'Why didn't you say so, then?'

'Where are you going?'

She is leaving the room. 'I have things to do.'

'What things?'

'Work. I'm supposed to be in New York.'

That infuriates him. 'I didn't ask you to come here,' he shouts after her.

Alone he puts his hand over his eyes – feels the tenderness of his damaged face, which he had forgotten about.

Then she is there again, standing in front of him.

'Look,' she starts, making an effort, 'I'm here because I thought you needed help . . .'

'I don't need your help,' he hears his own voice say.

There is a moment of ominous silence.

'Well, fuck you, then,' she says quietly.

He hears her walk up the stairs, the sound of her door shutting.

After a few minutes he stands up, stiffly, and follows her. He feels dizzy on the stairs, has to stop for a moment.

Softly, he knocks on her door. 'Joanna?'

Nothing.

'Joanna . . . I'm sorry.'

'I'm sorry,' he says again. 'I'm not myself today.'

He doesn't open the door – that's not allowed, hasn't been allowed for years.

'Please come downstairs,' he says to the painted wood, which was once white, probably. 'I'm going to make some tea,' he says. 'I'm sorry – I mean it.'

Downstairs, he makes the tea – in a warmed pot, the old-school way. People just don't do that any more, he thinks sadly.

When he enters the sitting room – when he shuffles in with the tray – he is surprised to find her already there. She is on one of the sofas, with her large unfeminine feet on the pouf, looking unsentimentally at her own hands. 'It's just so depressing,' she says.

'What is?'

He puts down the tray.

'I mean, I'm only here for two days, and something like this happens.'

'I'm sorry,' he says. 'It was my fault.'

'Yes, it was.'

He sits down in the wing chair, flops down into it, so that his legs swing up slightly. He sits there, panting.

'How are you feeling?' she asks.

He says, 'Okay. A bit dizzy. I'll be okay.'

'You shouldn't be doing anything,' she says. 'The doctor told me you shouldn't do anything for a few days. You should have let me deal with the tray.'

'I'll be okay.'

She stands up and pours the tea.

Then they watch *The Best Exotic Marigold Hotel*.

He starts wheezily snoring about halfway through.

7

One always imagines that there will be some sort of serenity at the end. Some sort of serenity. Not just an awful sordid mess of shit and pain and tears. Some sort of serenity. Whatever that might mean. And what that might actually mean becomes problematic up close. *Amemus eterna et non peritura.* That would seem to be sound advice, if serenity is what one is after. The same problem, though – what is *eterna*? What is eternal, in his world? Wherever he looks, from the loosening skin of his weak, old man's hands – which somehow don't seem to be *his*, since he does not think of himself as an old man – to the sun shedding white light on the flat landscape all around, wherever he looks, he sees only *peritura*. Only that which is transient.

Joanna has left. She had an earlyish plane and left just as the late dawn was lightening the sky over the poplars of Strada Provinciale 65, a field or two away. The taxi was outside, vapour spewing from its tailpipe. She had hauled her suitcase downstairs and in the entrance hall she had stopped for a moment and said to him, 'Cordelia will be here this afternoon.'

A minute later he was alone, in the kitchen, trying not to succumb to an unexpected flood of emotion, with trembling hands spooning coffee into the percolator.

How little we understand about life as it is actually happening. The moments fly past, like trackside pylons seen from a train window.

The present, perpetually slipping away.

Peritura.

He sits in the wing chair with his iPad.

Tap.

Tap. Tap.

Emails. No new emails, other than the spam and semi-spam that never stops.

He still hasn't written to Simon about his poem. He will do that now. First he has another look at it.

> *The portrait shows this – his eyes fixed elsewhere,*
> *Mehmet the Conqueror holds a rose*
> *To the Turkic scimitar of his nose.*
> *The engrossing necessities of money and war,*
> *The wise politician's precautionary*
> *Fratricides, the apt play of power –*
> *All proper activities in his sphere,*
> *And he excelled at them all. So why the flower?*
> *A nod, perhaps, to something less worldly;*
> *Not beauty, I think, whatever that is,*
> *Not love, not 'nature',*
> *Not Allah, by that or any other name –*
> *Just a moment's immersion in the texture*
> *Of existence, the eternal passing of time.*

That final phrase. It didn't make much of an impression on him last week.

He stands up and fondles the radiator, fondles its warmth with his stiff hands.

The passing of time. That is what is eternal, that is what has no end. And it shows itself only in the effect it has on everything else, so that everything else embodies, *in its own impermanence*, the one thing that never ends.

Which would seem to be an extraordinary paradox.

Claudia says, 'Good morning, Signor Parson.'

Startled, he turns. 'Oh, Claudia. Hello. How are you?'

'I'm okay, Signor Parson,' she says, not trying very hard to hide the fact that she is tired and fed up. She also has problems with her joints in this weather. They have talked about it.

'Where you like me to start?' she asks.

'The kitchen?' he suggests. 'Or upstairs? I don't mind.'

He is trying to hold onto the feeling he had, a moment ago, of everything as the embodiment of something endless and eternal, of the eternal passing of time. For a moment he had felt it. *Felt* it.

'Okay,' Claudia says. 'I start upstairs, okay?'

And that through its very impermanence.

Only something as paradoxical as that, he thinks, has any hope of . . . Of what?

He says, 'Fine. Thank you, Claudia.'

He is still standing at the window.

Of helping.

For a moment he had felt it, and it had helped.

*

Cordelia arrives at four o'clock, just as it is getting dark. She is forty-three now. It seems incredible. 'Hello, Dad,' she says, when she has dismissed the taxi. He is waiting in the doorway, waiting to help her with her suitcase, which she does not let him do. In the sitting room they drink wine. He wishes now that he'd saved the fine Barbaresco to share with her. He tells her about the accident, what he can remember, that he was at Pomposa abbey. He thanks her, again, for coming to stay.

When he thanks her she just smiles, and stands up and looks at the books on the shelves. She is tall like her mother. 'I'm reading Clark's *Sleepwalkers*,' he tells her, from the wing chair.

'Oh, yeah? Interesting?'

425

'Very,' he says.

'Tell me about it.'

He tries to explain, what he understands of it – how Europe stumbled into this near-death experience – and then says, when it's obvious he isn't making much sense, 'I haven't finished it, of course. I'm less than halfway through.'

'M-hm.'

With donnish interest, he asks, 'What are *you* reading?'

'*Bring Up the Bodies*,' she says. 'Finally.'

'She's good on the politics,' he tells her, like someone who would know.

'I'm enjoying it,' she says.

Then she starts to talk about something else: 'How was it with Mum?'

The question is just perceptibly loaded.

'Fine,' he says vaguely. And then, with more emphasis, 'It was very sweet of her to come. She was supposed to be in New York or something.'

'I know.'

Somehow too solemnly, he says, 'And thank *you*, Cordelia, as well. I know how much you've got on . . .'

'That's about the fourth time you've thanked me,' she says. She is smiling. 'You can stop now. I feel fully thanked.'

'Okay,' he laughs, as always hugely enjoying her manner.

He is somewhat in awe of her.

'So it was fine with Mum?' she asks, pressing on with that.

Joanna must have spoken to her, he thinks, phoned her from the airport and told her something.

'It was fine,' he says. And then again, trying not to sound so threatened, 'It was fine.'

There is a short silence.

To end it, he asks after Simon. Says he read the poem she sent.

'And?' she wants to know. 'What did you think?'

'I was impressed,' he says, and Cordelia looks pleased. That was his aim – to please her. He says, 'He and his friend were out here in the spring, of course.'

'Yes,' Cordelia says, 'I know.'

'What was his friend's name again?'

'Ferdinand.'

'That's it. A very entertaining young man.'

'Yes.' The proposition seems to make her uneasy, slightly. 'I suppose.'

'I liked him.' He is sort of staring off into the middle distance when he says that. 'We had some very nice talks,' he says, smiling at her.

'You and Ferdinand?'

'And Simon, of course.'

He asks, after a few moments, 'Is, er, *Ferdinand* up at Oxford too?' There is something strange and deliberate, she thinks, about the way he says the name. And, actually, about the way he keeps talking about Ferdinand.

'Yes, he is,' she says.

'Same college? As Simon.'

'No, I don't think so.'

'Simon's at St John's, isn't he?'

'That's right.'

'Well,' he says, a little wistfully. 'It was fun to have them here for a few days. What do you want to do for dinner?' he asks.

'I thought we might go out.'

'Now that's an idea. Where?'

'That place in Argenta?'

He knows the place she means – they have been going there for years. 'Sure. That'd be very nice. I'll phone them up. Reserve us a table.'

'Do you want me to do it?'

'No, I think I can manage,' he says.

The phone is on a sideboard. Next to it is a tatty little notebook full of handwritten numbers. He turns the pages until he finds what he is looking for. Then he picks up the phone and very slowly and deliberately punches the number into it. While he waits for them to answer, holding the phone to his ear, he inspects his slumped, jumpered image in the dark window.

*

Over the next few days, Cordelia takes things in hand. She gets a man in to look at the damp patch at the foot of the stairs. She finds and installs an ultrasonic device that is supposed to dissuade mice from establishing themselves in the house. She sets Claudia to work on specific tasks, which Claudia seems to appreciate. Within a few days the whole house seems more orderly and hygienic, more inhabited somehow.

Together they look on the Internet at second-hand cars for sale in the area. They find something that she seems to think would be suitable for him – a five-year-old Toyota RAV4, automatic. The next day they drive to Ferrara to have a look at it and she haggles the price down a thousand euros and they take it back to Argenta, she driving the insurance company's car and he driving his new Toyota. He finds it much easier to handle than the old Passat. And there is something about the way she makes it *all* seem so easy – on his own, he knows, he would have been terribly daunted by the task of sorting it all out. Somehow she makes it seem effortless. She makes the phone calls. She takes him through the Italian forms, telling him what to write and where to sign. She sorts out the insurance. Yes, he is slightly in awe of her. She has such vitality. She wins at Scrabble when they play, which they do once or twice on those winter evenings that start at four o'clock, when darkness falls outside, suddenly, taking you by surprise.

*

One afternoon Claudia's son shows up in his IKEA van, to take her home. He arrives early, while she is still working her way through a load of ironing, and waits in the van.

'There's an IKEA van at the end of the driveway,' Cordelia says, having seen it from an upstairs window. 'Have you ordered something?'

'No,' he tells her. 'That's Claudia's son. He works for them. He's waiting for her.'

'Shouldn't we ask him in?'

'We could. I suppose.'

From the window he watches her tap on the window of the van and say something to the Romanian, who then leaves the van, and follows her back to the house.

He hears her speaking to him in her fluent if English-accented Italian as she leads him into the kitchen.

After a while he joins them and says hello. He only stays for a minute, hovering awkwardly. Then he is back in the wing chair with *The Sleepwalkers*, though less able to absorb its ideas than ever.

When Claudia and her son have left, Cordelia finds him there, and they talk about them, the two Romanians. Very nice people, they decide.

'He's very good-looking,' Cordelia says.

Her father nods, apparently in agreement. And then says, hurriedly, as if it was not something he had ever thought about, 'Would you say so?'

'Yes, I would.'

'He's married, I think,' he says, oddly.

'Well, so am I,' Cordelia points out.

'No.' He seems flustered. And knowing that he seems flustered makes him more flustered. 'I just meant . . .'

'I said he was good-looking, that's all.'

'Okay.'

He tries to smile – knows he doesn't quite pull it off.

She is looking at him strangely, is how it feels. He says, 'Well, it was nice of you to ask him in.'

She doesn't seem to hear – she just keeps looking at him in that strange way.

He has hoisted *The Sleepwalkers* up in front of him – is staring without seeing it at a map of Europe in 1914.

She *knows*, he thinks.

What does she know, though? What is there to know? What does he know himself? That certain men ... What would the word be? Fascinate him? And that disturbed by this fascination – if that *is* the word – he is sometimes ... What? Ineffably embarrassed in their presence? That's it, though. That's all there is to know. Not even in his imagination has he ever ...

Finally he lets his eyes leave the page – the same page, the map of Europe in 1914 – and look for her.

She isn't there.

There is a sense that something has happened. That something has passed between them. He feels slightly sick, as he did when, about twenty years ago now, Joanna said to him that he was 'obviously queer'. It had seemed an extraordinary thing to say. With Joanna, the subject was never mentioned again, not even alluded to. That was, however, when they started to live more or less separately. He doesn't know if she has ever said anything to Cordelia about it.

He finds her in the kitchen.

She is holding a framed photo – her parents. The way they live – mostly apart – has always upset her.

'What's that?' he asks.

She doesn't answer.

And he thinks, standing at her shoulder, sharing her view of the photo of himself and Joanna – *She's thinking it's all a sham*. It's not all a sham, though. He wants to tell her that. He doesn't know what words to use.

He is trying to find a way of saying it when it occurs to him that perhaps Joanna *does* see it as a sham, their marriage, the forty-five years they've spent together, and sort of together. And of course Cordelia will see it from her mother's point of view, mostly. She will pity her mother, for having had to live for so long like that. With someone who is 'obviously queer'. The words still seem to have nothing to do with him. He wonders if Cordelia knows about Joanna's affairs. Probably she knows more than he does – he knows nothing specific. It's difficult to know what information passes between them, his wife and his daughter.

She is still looking at the photo. He's in morning dress, you can just make out. It's the day he got his knighthood, twenty-odd years ago.

'The day I landed the K,' he says.

It is so obviously not what she is thinking about, so obviously not the aspect of the image that is absorbing her, that to say it makes him sound much less sensitive than he actually is, much less perceptive. He knows that, and knows that it's the price he pays for steering things away from what he does not want to talk about, or for trying to steer them away.

She seems to have taken the hint, though. 'Yup,' she says, and puts the photo down. 'Is it too early for a glass of wine?'

He looks at his watch.

It's not even five.

She says that in London it's office-party season, the Christmas drinking season, liver-punishing time. Afternoons in the pub. All that.

'I vaguely remember,' he says.

'Do you still miss work?' she asks, obviously not very interested, but knowing that he doesn't mind talking about *that* so much.

'Not as much as I used to.'

He stoops thoughtfully to the wine rack.

'Not as much as I used to,' he says again.

He puts a bottle on the table.

'I've had to accept,' he says, matter-of-factly, 'that my life, in terms of potential, is over.'

It's as if he is trying to make up for not wanting to talk about what she wants to talk about – the forty-five years he has spent married to her mother, what was the story there – by talking with unusual frankness about something else.

That's what he thinks himself as he starts to open the bottle, first nicking the lead foil, and then unpeeling it. With a satisfying heaviness, it separates from the glass underneath. He says, 'I don't have much left to offer. In a practical sense.'

'You shouldn't say that.' She still seems distracted, her mind on something else.

'Oh, I've achieved everything I'm going to achieve.'

'Professionally, you mean?'

'Yes. Partly. I mean, I'm not down in the mouth about it,' he says. 'I'm very proud of what I've achieved.' Which is true. Even as he says it, though, he is aware of how weightless, how intangible, how even strangely fictitious, his achievements feel – even the ones he is proudest of, like his minor part in negotiating, over many years, the expansion of the European Union in 2004. Something, he is not sure what, seems to nullify them. He says, trying to maintain his philosophical tone, 'I'm very proud. It's just that that's it now.'

'Do you want a hand with that?' Cordelia asks. She means the wine he is struggling to open.

He hesitates for a moment. He seems to think about what to do. Then he says, 'Yes, okay, please,' and passes it to her.

'Now this wine,' he says, obviously keen to talk about happier matters, 'we got, your mother and I,' he slightly emphasises, as if to point out that they did sometimes have fun together, which indeed they did, 'some years ago, when we went down to Umbria, in the old Passat, may she rest in peace, and we got this wine in Perugia, I think. Anyway, it's one of the best, supposedly, that they make down there, and I think it's time it was drunk.'

'Hear, hear,' Cordelia says – though something is still missing from her voice.

He pours out two glasses, not too much in each, and slides one over to her.

'So,' he says. 'To . . . ?'

He waits a moment – long enough for her to smile, and shrug. The smile is wistful, sad, it withholds something, is unpersuaded.

He does not let it deflect him.

'To life?' he suggests.

She seems to weigh this up, then acquiesces. 'To life.'

*

The next morning they drive to Ravenna. He needs to have another scan at the hospital. They take the new Toyota. Cordelia drives.

As they drive towards the sea the farming country gives way gradually to something more garish – the tourist economy of the sandy coast. There are signs for theme parks. Hotels. Everything shut up for winter. Except that the prostitutes who line Strada Statale 309 in summer are still there, though fewer. Bosnian girls, quite a lot of them, he has been told.

'Poor things,' he says.

Cordelia nods, driving.

They near Ravenna and there are signs for the *Area Industriale*. For the merchant port. She handles it all unproblematically – the tricky, poorly signposted approach, the Ravenna traffic, the one-way system; he is almost embarrassingly impressed by the way she handles it.

'You're doing very well,' he says, as they stop at a traffic light somewhere in the city – she seems to know where they are, though he has no idea.

She laughs and says, 'Thanks,' and they set off again, with that sureness of purpose that so impresses him.

They decided, that morning, that they would have lunch in town, and then present themselves at the hospital for his appointment, which is at two o'clock.

They park in a public lot near the *Zona Monumentale*, and start to walk. They are looking for a hat for him. She wants to get him one for Christmas.

Via Cavour is hung with Christmas decorations, and the smart little shops shine in the darkness of the day. They stop at shops that seem promising and in the end he gets a soft brown Borsalino, which somehow fits his thin face. His face is thin now, and haggard-looking. The damage from the accident persists in nasty yellowish patches. Obviously pleased with the hat, he wears it as they look for somewhere to have lunch. They find a place on Via Maggiore that he thinks he once went to, years ago, and, if it was the same place, has positive memories of. Snow is starting to drift down in small flakes when they go in, into the sudden, stunning warmth, and ask for a table for two.

'This *is* the place,' he tells her, as, having shed their outdoor things, they sit down.

'Okay.'

'The food's excellent. Or was. Now, who knows.'

The decor definitely tends to kitsch.

There is no written menu. Just a jovial man who wanders up and tells them, as if they were old friends, what he has today.

When they have told him what they want, someone else – a small woman, with a face as hard as a dried pea – arrives with his quarter-litre of red wine, and Cordelia's green bottle of sparkling water.

All around them, office workers, it seems, are eating lunch.

Outside the snow is still falling.

He is trying to tell her about *Amemus eterna et non peritura*, about 'the eternal passing of time'. It is on his mind again. This morning he woke very depressed. He lay there for some time, not moving as the turquoise walls appeared. The hospital loomed, that was part of it. The CAT scan, and whatever news it had for him. He has been having headaches, the last few days. He has been as weirdly aware of what's happening in his head as he has been for months now with his heart. That sense of physical fragility frightened him during the night, and he tried to find again the feeling he had last week of everything imper-manent embodying, through the very fact of its impermanence, some-thing endless and eternal.

He is trying to explain that now to Cordelia.

'It's important,' he says, struggling to make sense, he can see that on her face, 'to feel part of something larger, something . . . something permanent.'

'Yeah,' she says patiently, pouring herself some more water.

She doesn't see the point of this, he thinks.

He's not sure he does either. It seems so elusive, even to him, when he tries to put it into words – or indeed when he doesn't.

'I'm not making much sense,' he apologises.

'No, it's interesting,' Cordelia says.

The pasta dish arrives – some sort of massive ravioli, in a heavy iron frying pan, still sizzling, which the hard-faced woman puts down with-out a word on a wooden place mat, and leaves there for them to serve themselves.

'*Grazie*,' he says, as she walks away.

He is still trying to formulate his thoughts, what he was saying to Cordelia, trying to say.

Hungrily, she has started on the ravioli.

'Is it okay?' he asks.

'Lovely,' she says.

And he is very moved, suddenly, by the sight of her.

Overwhelmed.

His eyes overflow.

She notices his moist-eyed stare and smiles at him, questioningly.

Feeling foolish, he shakes his head, declining to explain, and starts to eat. In a sense this love he feels just makes it more awful, not less, that this is all going to end. It is extraordinarily painful to think that there will be a day when he sees her for the last time.

Still nearly tearful, he stops eating for a moment and looks up.

There is a sense, he is sure, in which he is tricking himself into these feelings, about everything embodying something endless and eternal. Fear and sadness are obliging him to come up with something. Something to soften the nightmarish fact of ageing and dying. These ideas about the eternity of time. Within the eternity of time there is only a mystery – only a sense that there is something that we will never know or understand. An empty, unknowable space. Like, in Sant'Apollinare Nuovo, that mosaic of the curtains opening to show us nothing, only a patch of plain golden tiles.

Cordelia is talking about Simon. Normally she talks about him a lot. This week she has made an effort not to. He is aware of that. Now she is talking about him, though.

He listens, his fingers on the stem of his wine glass.

She is touching on the aspects of her son that strike other people as odd and admitting, unusually, that she worries about them sometimes.

He tries to soothe her. It's not exactly unheard of to be a bit strange at that age, he says, especially highly intelligent people, and Simon is undoubtedly one of those.

'I wouldn't worry,' he tells her, putting his hand over hers.

She nods.

It's what she wants to hear. Whether it is true or not, who knows. Only time will tell.

He pays and they leave, putting on their coats and scarves near the door. He puts on his new hat and looks at himself in the mirror: an old man.

With a definite effort he pulls open the door.

He lets Cordelia leave first, then follows her out.

The air is frigid, stings the skin of his face.

Via Maggiore is fading away in the dusk.